W9-BCC-321

Face Off

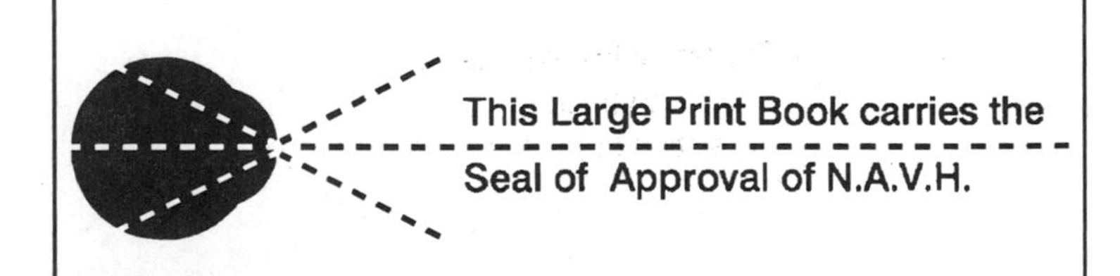

Face Off

Brenda Novak

WHEELER PUBLISHING
A part of Gale, a Cengage Company

Farmington Hills, Mich • San Francisco • New York • Waterville, Maine
Meriden, Conn • Mason, Ohio • Chicago

Wheeler Publishing, a part of Gale, a Cengage Company.

Wheeler Publishing Large Print Hardcover.
The text of this Large Print edition is unabridged.
Other aspects of the book may vary from the original edition.
Set in 16 pt. Plantin.

**LIBRARY OF CONGRESS CIP DATA ON FILE.
CATALOGUING IN PUBLICATION FOR THIS BOOK
IS AVAILABLE FROM THE LIBRARY OF CONGRESS**

ISBN-13: 978-1-4328-5907-7 (hardcover)

Published in 2018 by arrangement with Macmillan Publishing Group, LLC/St. Martin's Press

Printed in the United States of America
1 2 3 4 5 6 7 22 21 20 19 18

To Lee Ann Capehart, a member of my online book group and one of my most loyal readers. Thanks for the enthusiasm you have shown for my work over the years. It's been such a pleasure knowing you!

I believe the only way to reform people is to kill them.

— Carl Panzram, *American serial killer, rapist, arsonist*

Prologue

Anchorage, Alaska . . .

The cellar was almost ready. It'd taken months to put in the lighting, the plumbing, the Sheetrock and the flooring and to get it all soundproofed. Jasper Moore, aka Andy Smith, could've had it done in a matter of weeks had he hired a contractor, but he wasn't that foolish. No one could know about what he'd created. He'd bought the materials in small batches from three different stores, just to mix things up, and he'd done the work himself in the hours he was off from the prison.

He tested the restraints he'd ordered from a bondage site on the Web. He'd cemented the iron rings into the floor only yesterday and didn't think they were fully secure. He'd give the concrete another week to cure. Meanwhile, he'd finish ordering the rest of the torture devices that appealed to him. Shit like that was so much more accessible these days. God, he loved the Internet.

He stood at the foot of the stairs, giving what he'd created a final approving glance. Yep, he'd thought of everything. He'd even put a drain in the floor so he could wash blood and other bodily fluids down with a simple garden hose. Because he'd been married most of the past twenty years — he'd needed the income of a wife, since he didn't care to work himself — he'd never had a playground like this before. He'd always had to find an abandoned shack, trailer or barn where he could keep his victims and then worry that they might be discovered.

This was going to be *so* much better. He'd have constant access, complete privacy.

The excitement and awareness — the raw lust — he felt when he thought of Evelyn Talbot rose inside him, stronger and more powerful than ever.

He'd put in the time, done the work. He was almost ready to make his move.

Now that he had a place for her, a place no one knew existed, he'd be able to keep her indefinitely.

1

The weather was turning.

Sierra Yerbowitz stood at the window of the small, rustic cabin she'd rented with her brother and his two friends and felt her stomach muscles tighten as she watched a sea of dark clouds roll toward her. She'd always wanted to visit Alaska, had wondered what the last frontier was like. With climate change and population growth, she knew it wouldn't remain unspoiled forever. Because it was vastly different from Louisiana, where she and her family lived, it intrigued her. So when her brother offered to take her on the hunting trip he'd been planning for ages, she'd readily agreed.

She would've preferred visiting in the summer, when daylight lasted longer and bad weather wasn't much of an issue. But Leland and his friends Peter and Ted were each determined to bag a moose, and their permits specified that they could hunt only from September 15 to October 15. They'd hoped to come in September, but a conflict in schedules left them with no other option than to take the trip after October 8.

"Where are you?" she muttered, searching for any sign of the men driving through the trees beyond the snow that covered the ground immediately surrounding her. Surely Leland and his friends had spotted the clouds and were heading back. They'd taken the Ford Expedition they'd rented in Anchorage, along with a trailer carrying two ATVs, down a dirt road to a river. Sierra couldn't remember the name of the river because there were rivers everywhere in Alaska and she hadn't been paying attention when they were plotting their route. None of it pertained to her, since she wasn't interested in hunting. All she knew was that they planned to branch out from the SUV and go wherever the moose scat or tracks led them.

She hoped they hadn't wandered *too* far from their staging area. If so, it could take a long time to get back, and by then the storm would be upon them. . . .

She checked her watch. Noon. Her brother had said they'd return at four, which had sounded early when he'd mentioned it that morning. Now she feared it wouldn't be early enough.

"Come on, Leland." It would be like her brother to discount the weather, push his luck. He'd always been a risk taker and, after coming so far and going to so much expense, he wouldn't give up easily. They hadn't gotten a bull yet, and this was their last chance. First thing tomorrow, they had to leave for Juneau so they could see other parts of the state before going home.

Alaska could be unpredictable. She'd read that in all the literature. What if Leland and his friends got turned around and couldn't make their way back to the truck? What if they got separated trying?

If they didn't return, she couldn't even call for help. There was no cell service in this area, no phone service at all. And they'd taken the only vehicle, so she didn't have a car. Hilltop, the closest town — not that a few squat buildings and five hundred people constituted much of a town — wasn't far as the crow flew. But she'd have to use the roads, which made the trip significantly longer. She wouldn't be able to walk that distance even if it wasn't storming.

Determined not to let herself get too worked up, she moved away from the window. They'd been at the cabin for three days and were low on firewood. She needed to figure out how to get more from the shed behind the cabin, so she could be prepared, if necessary. But when Leland had gone out last night to do just that, he'd come back empty-handed. He'd said the combination they'd been given wouldn't open the lock, which hadn't been good news. The cabin had a generator for lights and hot water, but the wood-burning stove served as the only source of heat.

Still, they hadn't been too worried. They were leaving soon and had a few sticks they could use to get by. They'd thought they could make it. But a storm changed everything. They could get snowed in, be stranded for days. . . .

Sierra yanked on her heavy coat, shoved her feet into her boots and, when she left the cabin, closed the door behind her to preserve what heat there was before trudging across an icy bank of snow that rested in the shade of a thick stand of western hemlock and spruce trees. She hoped to get into that shed before the wind blowing at her back grew any stronger and the snow began to fall. Nervous as she was about being alone in this storm and having her brother and his friends out in the open, she'd feel a lot better if she at least had some firewood.

The lock was a simple padlock. She tried the combination provided by the rental company to no avail, proving Leland had been right.

Had the rental company accidentally transposed two digits?

She tried different options, stood there for twenty minutes, struggling to find the right combination.

Nothing worked.

"Damn it!" she cried, but wasn't willing to give up.

She supposed the combination could be written somewhere as a fail-safe. They'd already looked inside, but now she searched outside, too — on the shed itself, under the rocks nearby in case there was a note, on the tiny back porch of the cabin — hoping to discover it tacked up somewhere.

No luck.

Her ears were ringing from the cold by the time she went back in to warm up. Blowing on her hands, which felt like blocks of ice, she checked the front window. Still no sign of the men, and the sky was growing ever darker.

They were in for a big one. She could feel it in her bones. When they'd been gathering up all the gear they needed for the hunt, the locals in Anchorage had told them that winter was coming early this year and to be careful. They'd mentioned having their "termination dust," or the first snowstorm signaling the end of the summer working season, on the tenth of September, an entire month before it usually came. She hoped her brother was thinking about that right now and getting himself back to the truck . . .

"What should I do?" she asked herself. She got out all the food, water and candles they had left, in case the generator failed or they ran out of propane, and set it on the counter. There wasn't a lot, but they could stretch their supplies for a day or two.

Maybe the storm would blow over quickly.

Either way, they'd need more wood. So how would she get it?

She'd have to break the shed door.

She went back out to the shed, where she shoved, pulled and yanked, even rammed her shoulder into the panel, hoping to make the latch give way. But it was too sturdy; she didn't have the strength. She was walking around the small building, looking for any loose boards she might be able to pry away, when she remembered the ax hanging on the wall of the mudroom.

Although she'd been hoping to keep any damage to a minimum, she'd exhausted her other options. It wasn't *her* fault they hadn't been given the correct combination to the lock! That wood could be a matter of life and death; in her mind, she had every right to go after it.

Once she got the ax and returned, she swung it as hard as she could. The wind was nearly blowing her down, so it wasn't easy to wield such a heavy object, especially since she'd never used one before. The blade landed with a satisfying *thwack,* but the metal head bit so deep, she broke several fingernails trying to get it out, and she still couldn't manage.

For a moment she feared that would be the end of this idea. But after considerable effort, she managed to dislodge it. Then she swung again and again, until she'd completely destroyed the door.

If the storm didn't turn out to be a bad one and she was doing this for nothing, her brother wouldn't be happy if they got stuck paying for the damage. But she wasn't willing to take the chance of freezing to death when there was wood in this shed.

Once she formed a hole large enough to step through, she dropped the ax and went inside. The sunlight, already nearly obliterated by the roiling clouds outside, could scarcely penetrate the cracks between the slats. Even the big opening she'd made afforded almost no light. But she found wood. Plenty of it. Although she could barely make out the dimly lit pile, she could smell the sap.

"Thank God." Relief swept through her as she bent to pick up an armful. It wasn't until she stood and turned to go that she glanced anywhere else, but when she did she saw a shape that caused her to scream and drop the logs she'd gathered.

She wasn't alone. Unless her eyes deceived her, someone else was curled up in the corner — naked.

"Are you *sure* you want a baby?"

Now that the doctor had finished her pelvic exam, Evelyn Talbot sat up and straightened the lap covering she'd been given, along with the paper gown she was wearing. She and her boyfriend, Amarok, a nickname that meant "wolf" in the language of the native Inuit people around whom he'd grown up, had been sleeping together without birth control for the past eight months. Yet nothing had come of it. She was beginning to think nothing ever would. "I'm approaching forty, Dr. Fielding. If I'm going to have a child, it should happen soon, wouldn't you say?"

He peeled off his latex gloves. "I agree with you from a timing standpoint."

"But . . . I'm not physically capable? Is that what you're saying?" During the hour-long drive from Hilltop, where she both lived and worked, she'd worried about the news she might get today. She hadn't even told Amarok she'd made this appointment. If she couldn't have kids, she wanted a chance to absorb the blow before having that talk with him. He knew about her background, understood there was a possibility she might be sterile, of course. Since she'd been kidnapped and tortured — by her own boyfriend — when she was only sixteen, she hadn't had regular periods. But she and Amarok had been holding out hope that she might be able to conceive in spite of that. The doctors she'd seen before leaving Boston had indicated children were still a possibility.

"There's some scar tissue from . . . from before." He stepped on the pedal that opened the trash can and tossed his gloves inside. "It could cause problems."

She let her breath seep out. "You don't sound optimistic."

He rested a hand on the counter. "I wouldn't go *that* far, Dr. Talbot. You went through medical school before becoming a psychiatrist. You know human bodies are amazingly resilient, sometimes more resilient than human minds."

"You could make a case for that in certain situations," she agreed.

"Your body seems to have healed well."

Given his reticent manner, she felt a moment's confusion. "That's *good,* isn't it?"

"Perhaps. But may I speak frankly?"

"Of course."

"I admit I wouldn't have this conversation with just *any* patient. It might be going too far, even for someone I consider a colleague of sorts. But I respect who you are, what you've been through and what you've done as a result. So I'd advise you to think carefully about this. You study — interact with — psychopaths on a daily basis. From what I heard and saw of you on TV when you were lobbying for Hanover House to be built a few years ago, you're incredibly dedicated to your work."

"I am. There's no question about that." She had to be. Psychopathy was on the rise. Someone had to figure out why — and how to stop those who preyed on the innocent. After what she'd endured, she'd made it her life's work.

"You're still that committed?" he asked. "Even after so many close calls?"

She assumed he was talking primarily about what had happened with Lyman Bishop last winter, since that incident had been highly publicized in Alaska. "What happened with Bishop won't happen again. He had a brain hemorrhage while he was in the hospital trying to recover from . . . that night. These days he's in an institution. He can hardly speak."

"But you deal with hundreds of psychopaths, many of them extremely dangerous. Men who kill for pleasure. There could be another Lyman Bishop."

Or Jasper Moore could show up. Fielding didn't mention that, but she was always wondering when her former boyfriend might strike again.

"You're a bright, well-educated, attractive woman, and an authority figure, in a prison with an entirely male population —"

"A lot of people become infatuated with their doctor, preacher, teacher, et cetera," she broke in. "That's not unusual, even outside prison. Granted, with the men I study, it'd be more of a *fixation* than a true infatuation. But I'm well aware of the dynamic."

"I would guess that you are." He slid his glasses higher on the bridge of his nose. "What if you're carrying a baby the next time a sadist gets hold of you? Have you thought about that? You could be setting yourself up for some real heartbreak. And you wouldn't be the only one to suffer. Think about your family — and your partner."

She wanted to claim there was no chance of her being attacked again. The situation with Bishop had been unique. The institution was set up to protect the psychology team while they studied "the conscienceless," so it wasn't the convicts at Hanover House, the men behind bars, who worried her. It was Jasper Moore. He'd never been caught, was still out there somewhere, and she knew he'd like nothing more than to finish what he'd started when he'd killed three of her best friends, and tried to kill her, while they were in high school. The fact that he'd made another attempt to kidnap her two years ago told her he hadn't forgotten her. She hadn't seen his face that night. He'd been wearing a mask, so she had no idea how the years might've changed him, but he'd made no secret of who he was. He'd *wanted* her to know he was back.

She'd be dead now if she hadn't escaped almost immediately.

What if she'd been pregnant when *that* happened?

"I can't let fear stop me from living my life." She told herself that all the time. Told other victims they couldn't allow fear to paralyze them, either. But did that advice apply when an innocent child was involved?

Dr. Fielding drummed his fingers on the counter. "Then you're willing to accept the risks — and the consequences — if something goes wrong."

"Yes." She wasn't as certain as she made it sound, but she didn't want him to know that.

He seemed to accept her answer. "Well, then. I see nothing from a biological standpoint to indicate you *can't* get pregnant. Generally, we wait until a couple's been trying for twelve months before recommending any type of fertility treatment, but considering your background and your age, I think we're justified in starting sooner. Our first step would be to test Amarok, so we can get a clear picture of the entire situation."

After the terrible things Jasper had done, she *had* to be the one with infertility problems. But she understood why Amarok would need to be tested, as well. Although chances were small, he could have a low sperm count, low mobility or something else that contributed to the problem. He'd never been checked out, not for that. He'd told her he'd only been to a doctor twice in his entire life — and both instances were for broken bones.

Dr. Fielding didn't ask, but she could tell he was curious as to why she hadn't mentioned marrying Amarok if they might be having a child together. No one else could understand how truly complicated her situation was. She loved Amarok. There was no question about that. But at this point she wasn't committed to spending the rest of her life in Alaska. She had responsibilities back in Boston, where she was from, and she knew he'd never be happy anywhere else. He'd been born and raised in Hilltop, was a sixteenth-part Inuit, on his father's side. He was the town's only police presence, too, and he thrived on living in such a rugged part of the world. Alaska was in his blood. Dragging him down to the Lower 48 would be like caging a wild animal.

And yet her biological clock was ticking. She wouldn't leave Hilltop for another three or four years. By then, it'd be too late to have a baby, especially since she'd have to wait for another relationship to develop like the one she had with Amarok, which probably wouldn't happen. Other than Jasper, way back when, Amarok was the only man she'd ever truly loved. He was also the only man she'd ever been able to sleep with. After the violence she'd suffered at sixteen, she struggled with trust issues. If she *ever* wanted to be a mother, this could be her one chance. She didn't want to be childless without even considering her options. And if she did get pregnant? She'd simply *have* to stay in Alaska; that would make the decision for her.

"I'll speak to him about it," she said. But she wasn't sure how to bring up the subject. If she did, she knew Amarok would want to talk about marriage. He had every right to ask for a lifelong commitment instead of gambling with his heart.

2

Jasper was tempted to provide one of the inmates at Hanover House with a shiv. If someone were to get shanked, at least that would be intriguing, give him something enjoyable to watch. Those were the kinds of thoughts that went through his mind when he was bored, and he was always bored when Evelyn wasn't at the prison. He'd hated being a correctional officer in Florence, Arizona, had done whatever he could to relieve the drudgery, including aiding and abetting a few stabbings. But he wouldn't have been able to get on at Hanover House if not for the experience he'd gained at Florence, so he was glad he'd never been caught. Now he looked forward to going to work if he thought he might bump into his old girlfriend — or even catch a glimpse of her.

Unfortunately, that wasn't going to happen today. He'd heard someone say Evelyn wasn't coming in, which explained the desire he felt to create a diversion, something to cause a little excitement. But he couldn't draw too much attention to himself, especially negative attention. Ever since he'd moved to Anchorage eight months ago and started commuting to Hanover House in Hilltop, he'd worked hard to build the illusion that he was a dependable, nonthreatening, *normal* prison guard. Even Evelyn seemed to buy his act. Whenever he passed her in the halls, she had a smile for him. She believed he'd saved her life when Lyman Bishop attacked her last winter, so she *should* have a smile for him. But her complete trust wasn't easy to win. And her boyfriend, Sergeant Benjamin Murphy — or Amarok, as the locals called him — was ever watchful. Although Amarok didn't work at the prison, he visited Hanover House often to bring Evelyn lunch or pick her up if there was a storm.

It wouldn't be long now, though. And recapturing Evelyn would be all the sweeter for the patience and effort he'd invested in making certain that moment went down perfectly. Thanks to the plastic surgery he'd had twenty years ago, the dye he used to darken his hair and the passage of more than two decades, she didn't know what he looked like these days. He'd even grown a beard since coming to Hilltop. He had all that going for him but still had to be careful not to get overeager and ruin the perception of himself he'd so painstakingly created. If he screwed up, she might realize he was right under her nose.

"Hey, what are you doing standing there?"

Jasper clenched his jaw as Lieutenant Dickey approached. This wasn't anyone he wanted to see, not when he was leaning against the painted cinder-block wall outside the cafeteria, scraping the dirt from underneath his nails and wasting time until he could go home. "Nothing. Why?" he said, immediately straightening.

"Because last I checked, you were getting paid for being here."

"We just finished searching Cellblock B, and my shift is nearly over, sir. I go home at one." Waking up for work in the middle of the night wasn't easy, but Jasper liked getting off when he had so much of the day ahead of him. He wished all his shifts started and ended at the same time, but they varied.

"That's no excuse for loitering in the halls. If you're done with Cellblock B, search A."

Most of the COs hated doing searches. Trying to drag a belligerent inmate out of his cell could be dangerous. The men incarcerated here didn't have a lot to lose, which made them unpredictable. And the searches were mostly a waste of time. In Florence, a search turned up all kinds of stuff — handmade weapons, drugs, even cell phones. But the prisoners incarcerated at Hanover House didn't have many visitors. That just left the guards and other employees to smuggle in contraband, and in an institution containing only 350 beds the risk of getting caught was too great.

Irked by Dickey's imperial tone, Jasper felt his muscles tense, but if there was an aspect to his job he liked, it was rummaging through the inmates' meager possessions. Threatening the men, invading their privacy, humiliating them whenever possible . . . Jasper found it all quite enjoyable. He figured any good sadist would. "Who should I get to work with me?"

"The same guys who helped you search the other cellblock."

"No problem." As far as Jasper was concerned, the sooner they started the better. He didn't want to stay late. He had plans for after work. He had to go back to the cabin he'd been using so he could finish cleaning up.

"Then get your ass moving!" Dickey bellowed, even though Jasper was already on his way.

Jasper refused the temptation to throw him a dirty look. He hated taking direction from someone so obviously inferior to him. But most men were inferior to him, both mentally and physically — except, perhaps, Sergeant Amarok. It was because of Amarok that he'd had to kill his own parents. After all the help they'd given him over the years, that wasn't something he'd *wanted* to do. They were the ones who'd gotten him out of the country in the very beginning, after he'd killed Evelyn's three friends and tried to kill her. They'd also paid for all the plastic surgery he'd had back then, while he was in Europe. Without them, he would've been caught and prosecuted.

Yes, Amarok had made a brilliant move last winter. The Alaska State Trooper had forced Jasper to make a costly sacrifice. He was a worthy opponent, but this Lieutenant Dickey . . . he was just an asshole.

Ignore the bastard, Jasper told himself as he rounded up the other guards. Jasper had a reason for being at Hanover House, a reason to put up with Lieutenant Dickey and all the other pricks who enjoyed telling him what to do and when to do it.

He smiled as he pictured Evelyn. He

certainly wasn't working here for the money.

Amarok felt the tension that'd been knotting his muscles ease as soon as he saw a call from his home number come into the trooper post. "Where have you been?" he barked into the phone as soon as he picked up.

Evelyn hesitated. "What do you mean?"

"I tried calling you at work," he replied. "I was told you never came in this morning."

"How did you know I wasn't at home?" she asked sheepishly.

Since he'd left before she did this morning, at first he *hadn't.* That was why he'd gone back to check. "When I couldn't reach you, I drove to the house. I've been in a panic ever since, trying to find you. I've got everyone in town on the lookout — Shorty over at the Moosehead, Garrett at the Quick Stop, all the waitresses at The Dinky Diner, even Margaret Seaver at The Shady Lady, not that I could imagine you having any reason to go to the motel."

"You thought I might be having an affair?"

He heard the humor in her voice. "No. Considering your background, I realize that's unlikely. Although you did eventually allow *me* in your pants." They'd made love again this morning. That was why he'd called her. He couldn't stop thinking about her. "So I guess it's not *impossible* for a man to get past your defenses."

"No one else has ever managed it — not after Jasper."

She hadn't had much sexual experience when she and Amarok got together, but they'd come a long way from the days when he'd had to be careful not to make her feel pinned down, overpowered or threatened. Now that she knew she could trust him, now that he'd put in the time to build that trust, she wanted to touch him or feel him inside her almost every day. Amarok couldn't believe how lucky he was that the situation had changed. When he'd fallen in love with her, he'd decided he'd just have to cope with a difficult sex life, but the opposite was turning out to be true. "I was only being thorough, stopping by the motel," he said. "Why would you scare me like that?"

He heard her sigh.

"What's going on?" he pressed. "You can't simply disappear. You're not like other people. I can't assume everything's okay and go about my business, not when there's a chance you could be in trouble. Jasper could pop up at any time. He's done it before. And you've had other close calls since you moved here."

"I know," she said. "I just . . . I wasn't gone long. I thought I could get away for a few hours."

"Away where?"

"I went to Anchorage."

"With a storm coming in?"

"I felt I could beat it, and I did. It's ugly out there now, but I'm home safe."

"Don't tell me you went shopping."

"No, I went to see a doctor."

He gripped the phone tighter. "What kind of doctor?"

Another pause.

"Evelyn . . ."

"An ob/gyn," she said at length.

A burst of excitement brought him to his feet. "Are you pregnant?"

"No."

He tried to shrug off the disappointment, careful not to let even a hint of it enter his voice. "Then what?"

"I went to see if . . . if anything had changed with my . . . ability to have a child since I was last checked."

Obviously, she was trying to figure out why she hadn't gotten pregnant. They hadn't been doing anything to prevent it. He'd been wondering, too — and worrying that it wouldn't be possible to have a child with her. "And?"

"My doctor thinks fertility drugs will help. But he needs to check your sperm count before we do anything else."

"I'm willing. When?"

"I'll have to call him back and set up an appointment."

"Do it."

"Okay."

Silence fell as he tried to get a sense of what she was feeling. "Evelyn?"

"What?"

"Why didn't you tell me about the appointment?"

"I don't know," she said, "but I've got several things I need to take care of for work, so . . . can we talk about it later?"

"Of course. I'll see you tonight."

After she hung up, Amarok stared down at the phone. She loved him; he knew she did. But his mother had also loved his father, and yet she'd hated Alaska. She couldn't tolerate the dark, the cold, the isolation. She'd broken up the family, taken his twin brother and moved to Seattle when Amarok was only two and never looked back. Amarok hadn't even known he had a brother until his eighteenth birthday, when he received a call from his twin. They'd remained in contact ever since, but Amarok still refused to have any sort of relationship with his mother.

By falling in love with Evelyn, having a child with her, was he setting himself up for the same kind of heartbreak his father had experienced?

The weather was so bad that Jasper almost decided to put off returning to the cabin. After assisting with the search of Cellblock A, he wasn't in the best mood. Tex, one of the other COs, had seen him tearing up a picture of an inmate's grandmother and had the nerve to call him on it.

Jasper had claimed he hadn't meant to destroy the photograph, but that was a lame excuse. It couldn't have been torn to pieces by accident, and he could tell Tex thought the same thing. This was the first time since coming to Alaska that Jasper had done something for which he could be written up — a stupid mistake.

He scowled as he left Hilltop behind. What was the big deal, anyway? So he'd torn up a picture? The inmate's grandmother had died of a stroke while he was incarcerated. But if his grandmother was gone, she was gone. Why would the stupid idiot be trying to sketch her photograph, especially when he didn't have the talent to begin with?

There was no use being maudlin and sentimental over a photograph.

Hopefully Tex would let the incident go, forget about it.

"He'd better," Jasper mumbled as he strained to see the road through the rapid *slap-slap-slap* of his windshield wipers. The snow was coming down so thick, he couldn't drive very fast. More than once he considered turning back. But because the day had ended badly, he persevered, figured he might as well get this over with. Disposing of the body was always the worst part of any kill. He couldn't simply bury "Kat" like his victims in the Lower 48; the ground was frozen.

He could try to outwait the storm and come back in the next day or two. The problem there was that if another cold front hit right away and then another, he might not be able to reach the cabin until spring. And he couldn't leave it that long. If someone else beat him out there, for whatever reason, and found the body in the shed, it would spook everyone in Hilltop. Amarok would open an investigation and the locals would feel twitchy and frightened and doubt anyone they didn't know well.

That could screw with his ability to get to

Evelyn now that he was finally ready.

He shouldn't have nabbed Kat in the first place, since he hadn't been ready to take a victim to his house. But she'd been right there, walking down Spenard Road, the red-light district of Anchorage, which wasn't far from where he lived, such easy pickings he couldn't resist. And he'd known the hunting cabins in the mountains were rarely used after September. That constituted an Opportunity.

Besides, he'd been confident he could get away with whatever he wanted. Nothing he'd done had caught up with him yet. He'd been killing for more than twenty years, had fooled his parents whenever he needed to, two wives — both *ex*-wives these days — and various bosses.

Basically, he'd fooled everybody in one way or another, even Evelyn and Amarok last winter.

But he was now operating in a very different theater, and he should've taken that into account. Alaska offered him a lot of freedom and space, without a lot of police presence — outside of Anchorage. He'd kidnapped Kat a week ago and chosen to keep her in a cabin that wasn't far from Hilltop so he could get to her more easily before or after work. He had yet to deal with the full brunt of an Alaskan winter, however, and this year winter was starting early. He might've underestimated how difficult returning there might be.

He gave the truck more gas. He could make it. At least he'd already scoured the cabin. Once he arrived, all he had to do was put her body in the back of his four-wheel drive, under the tarp he'd picked up at the hardware store last night. After the weather cleared, he'd drive her an hour or more to the other side of Anchorage and dump her in some isolated wilderness area. With any luck, she wouldn't be discovered until spring.

Even if she *was* discovered sooner, she'd be so far away from Hilltop there'd be nothing to alert Amarok or anyone else in the town where he worked that they should take notice.

His tires slipped. He turned into the slide to avoid going over the side of the mountain and managed to regain control, but he was mad at himself for having to make this drive to begin with. He should've taken Kat's body when he left her there the day she died. It would've saved him this nightmare of a trip. But she'd been such a weakling, she'd died before he was ready, and he'd had to get to Hanover House for work right after.

The radio had fallen to static, so he turned it off. If he had one complaint about Alaska, it was the lack of radio reception. Everything else he considered a plus, especially for a man like him. The sparse population. The isolated areas. The long, dark months.

Evelyn . . .

He immediately cheered up when he thought of the woman he'd fantasized about for so many years. He'd set everything up perfectly, recovered beautifully from what could've been a disaster last winter with Bishop. No one was as brilliant as he was. He was a good driver, too. He'd get through this storm, and he'd get around the small mistake he'd made letting Tex see him tear up that picture.

By the time he reached the cabin, he felt much better. He was humming "Heathens" by Twenty-One Pilots as he navigated the final hairpin turn. But then he saw something that made the hair stand up on the back of his neck.

There was a light in the window.

3

Sierra was trembling. She hadn't found another person. She'd found a body — one with missing fingers, contusions, broken bones and ligatures.

Falling to her knees, she vomited everything she'd recently eaten. She couldn't stop retching, so it took a while to gather even the small amount of strength required to stand. Her legs felt like rubber. But once she got to her feet, she forced herself to peer closer. She was hoping there might be a chance of saving the woman. Unlikely as that was, considering the temperature outside and the condition of the body, she'd read about miracles when someone who was thought to be dead had survived.

No. There was no chance, she decided. This poor woman wasn't only dead, she was frozen solid. That was why Sierra could smell no stench, no odor of decomposition. And that was, undoubtedly, why the combination provided by the rental company hadn't worked. Whoever had killed this woman must've used the sheet of paper the rental company kept on the counter with the combination to take off the original lock, after which they put on another, one of their own. So late in the season, he or she probably hadn't expected the cabin to be rented but had taken that small precaution, just in case. The person who'd done this must also be the one who'd stacked extra wood on the back porch, which was how they'd gotten by until now.

"Oh God," Sierra murmured, and scrambled away, nearly tripping as she burst through the hole she'd chopped in the door. They shouldn't have come to Alaska, not in October, she told herself as she hurried back to the cabin and locked the door behind her. They'd been overeager, determined to squeeze in the trip, despite the early onset of winter. Now her brother and his friends were out in the wilderness in the worst storm she'd ever seen and she was alone in a cabin where a woman had recently been murdered, her corpse dumped in the shed, and Sierra couldn't run for help, couldn't call for help, either. She couldn't even leave or she might die of exposure — not that she'd go anywhere without her brother.

"What am I going to do?" she whispered aloud as she listened for the Ford Expedition the men had taken. Leland, Peter and Ted would be back soon. They needed shelter, wouldn't be able to stay out in this weather for long. When they arrived, she'd run out, get in the truck with them and insist they leave immediately. She didn't want to be here another second; she'd go crazy if they didn't come soon.

But one minute after another ticked away, and she didn't hear anything except the eerie rattle of the windows and the pounding of what sounded like torrential rain on the roof.

Calm down. Keep it together, Sierra. You have to be patient. There's nothing you can do except wait — and get warm.

She added a log to the stove and sat in front of it, staring at the glowing embers as she rocked back and forth, back and forth. She was trying to get over the shock, but it didn't matter how much heat the stove threw off; she remained cold as ice. Even when she finally recovered enough to pack — for her and all the people she was with — she couldn't seem to get warm. And every time she peered out the window, the storm looked worse.

She hoped the guys had at least made it

to the truck. Were they sheltering inside it, waiting for the onslaught to let up before trying to drive out?

If they didn't get going soon, they could end up trapped. She'd never seen so much wind and snow. What with the narrow dirt roads they had to travel to reach the backwoods, it could already be too late.

Maybe that was why they hadn't returned. They couldn't.

Leland and his friends had two ATVs with them. Even if the Expedition got stuck, they'd get out. They *had* to come back, because if they didn't . . .

She couldn't let herself think about what might happen if they didn't. She'd have to get help somehow. Their lives could depend on it. And she had to tell the authorities about the body in the shed. That woman did not die of natural causes. The ligatures and the injuries — *terrible* injuries — indicated murder. That meant there was a killer on the loose, and a brutal killer at that. What had been done to the woman wasn't what any normal person would do, even in a rage.

Just when Sierra thought her nerves couldn't take any more waiting, not with that battered, frozen body so close, she spotted a glimmer of light in the darkness.

What was that? Headlights? Could Leland, Peter and Ted finally be back?

Pulse racing, she pressed her palms to the glass and stared into the inky blackness.

What she'd seen was gone, just that fast. And she couldn't hear a motor. Had she imagined it? Could that glimmer have been a flash of lightning instead? The sun penetrating the storm clouds for a few seconds?

"Come on, come on." She stood, transfixed, for probably fifteen minutes, hoping and praying that her long vigil would be over at last. But she never did see any more light, couldn't see anything at all.

Why not? Leland and his friends should be tramping through the front door by now.

It wasn't until she heard the doorknob rattle at the back of the cabin that she realized she'd been right about someone being outside. Only a human could make that sound, not the wind. But Leland and the others wouldn't come through the back. There'd be no reason for them to do that.

So who was trying to get in?

"What are you doing?"

Evelyn tilted her head to the side as Amarok came up from behind and bent to kiss her neck. He'd been on the phone with Phil Robbins, a middle-aged local who assisted him in the capacity of Public Safety Officer during the summer. In the off-season, with most of the hunters and fishermen gone for the winter, Phil manned a plow and helped with snow removal, so Amarok had been trying to coordinate with him to make sure the streets were cleared well enough that everyone could get home from work. While Amarok talked in the kitchen, she'd picked up a psychology book and propped her feet up on the coffee table. Makita, Amarok's Alaskan malamute, sat nearby, hoping for more of the scratches she'd been giving him periodically, and Sigmund, her cat, played with the drapes of the big window that showed nothing but black outside. It wasn't like her to take a day off. Although she'd done quite a bit of work from home after she got back from her doctor's appointment, she'd never made it to the prison. She hadn't cared to fight the weather. And she was happy to stay in for the night now that Amarok was back. "Just flipping through a book I've been meaning to reread," she told him.

He turned her wrist to see the cover. "*Mask of Sanity*?"

"Yeah. It's an older title, but I like comparing what I've found through my own studies with what's been published in the past, and some of the pioneers in my field were right about a lot of things."

"Like this Hervey M. Cleckley? He was a pioneer?"

"Yes. Bob Hare — you've heard me talk about him, since he's the one who developed the psychopathy test we use, the PCL-R — based some of his findings on Cleckley's work."

He indicated the other book — Martha Stout's *The Sociopath Next Door* — waiting on the table next to her feet. "Looks like you're planning to be up late."

"Not really. I'm just skimming." She and the rest of the mental health team at Hanover House — which, besides her, consisted of five psychologists and one neurologist — kept a selection of the most popular titles on psychopathy in the conference room, where they met once a week to recap and plan. Evelyn wasn't sure why she'd decided to bring a couple of the books home with her last night. "To be honest, I'm almost becoming more interested in ambulatory psychopaths than —"

"Ambulatory?"

"Garden-variety psychopaths, the subclinical ones who purposely submarine a friend, lie without compunction, take advantage of others, that sort of thing. Not the kind who rape and kill."

He came around and nudged Makita to move a bit so that he could sit next to her. "I like where this is going. These other psychopaths have to be safer. But it's the criminal ones you're trying to stop. That's why you started Hanover House. So why the interest?"

"I find it surprising that there are so many people without a conscience, and that so many of the rest of us still believe everyone else is basically empathetic, like we are. That allows us to be blindsided when we run into either kind of psychopath, and we're bound to run into one eventually. Our society is facing a pandemic. The rate of incidence for anorexia is lower than that of psychopathy!"

"Which stands at four percent."

"According to our best estimates. Wow, you *do* listen when I talk about my work."

He grinned at her. "I was thinking it's a damn good thing not all those people are the kind of psychopaths who kill."

"Even the subclinical ones are harmful. They empty bank accounts. Break hearts. Lie, steal, cheat and use. They can make life difficult for anyone they come into contact with, and do it without a single regret." She put her feet down so she could lean forward. "Here's a shocking statistic. The rate of psychopathy is one hundred times greater than the incidence of colon cancer in the United States. We hear about colon cancer all the time, and yet the general populace knows very little about psychopaths, except for what they associate with 'serial killer,' and that isn't the whole picture."

"That's why, in addition to all the murderers you've had transferred to Hanover House, you've got a couple hundred psychopaths there who *haven't* killed anyone."

"Yes. Alan Harrington says —"

He raised a hand in the classic *stop* gesture. "Who's Alan Harrington?"

"He wrote a book called *Psychopaths.* I don't have it with me tonight, but I've read it. Although his views have been highly criticized, his claims are food for thought. He believes psychopaths are being produced by the 'evolutionary pressures of modern life.' "

Amarok shook his head. "I don't buy that."

He didn't buy a lot of things when it came to psychology, and he didn't hesitate to let her know it.

"There may be a whole bunch of these monsters out there, but humanity in general seems to be getting gentler and kinder," he said. "They used to hang people in public, for crying out loud — to the cheers of a large crowd that included children. They also dreamed up new ways to torture 'heretics' for their religious beliefs or lack thereof."

"In some places they still torture unbelievers," she said dryly.

"I'm talking systematic torture, which they carried out for five hundred years. During the Inquisition, they tried to police people's *thoughts.* Think of the progress we've made with the rights of women, minorities, even animals."

"Maybe most of the population is evolving, developing a more refined conscience, but some people are losing theirs entirely."

"You've experienced that." He toyed with a strand of her hair. "What I don't understand is why some psychopaths murder and maim and others don't. You've told me plenty of psychopaths are doctors, policemen, lawyers, businessmen and politicians. How is it that so many of them function normally?"

They'd talked about this before. But it remained a subject they rehashed occasionally, since there wasn't any "absolute" answer. "As far as we can determine, it's simply because everyone's different. People have different joys, different goals, different tastes, different inhibitors, different talents. The same holds true for psychopaths. One might delight in killing. The next might need to be top dog at his firm and will do anything, step on anyone, to get there. For the next one, sponging off the people around him makes him happy enough. That's why it's so hard to come to any kind of consensus on how to detect psychopaths, how to treat them — even how to define them. There are *so* many variables."

Amarok got up, went to the kitchen and uncorked some wine. "Would you like some?" he asked, holding up the bottle.

"Sure."

She watched as he poured two glasses and carried them to the couch.

"You've met some of the inmates at Hanover House," she said as he handed her one. "Lyman Bishop was very different from Anthony Garza, wouldn't you say?"

He took a drink of wine. "I would. And from what you've told me, Jasper is different still."

She couldn't help grimacing. "Jasper's the most frightening psychopath I've ever met."

"He's what's called a 'charismatic psychopath.' " He nudged her. "See? I *have* been listening."

She tapped the book she'd been reading.

"Cleckley uses words like 'likeable,' 'charming,' 'intelligent,' 'alert' and 'impressive' when he's describing some of the psychopaths he studied."

"I've heard *you* use some of those words."

"Yes. They fit Jasper to a T. He was the most popular boy in school, could charm anyone. I felt so lucky he chose me." A wave of resentment passed through her as she remembered the moment she'd found her three girlfriends, murdered, in the little shack she and Jasper had used when they wanted to be alone. He'd lured her friends there and killed them for telling her they'd caught him flirting with another girl — a terrible punishment for such a minor offense, especially because he probably *had* been flirting.

Amarok held her hand. He didn't even have to say anything. He was there for her, comforting her, helping her forget and move on. That had to be why she could talk about her past more easily these days. Still, she doubted even the scars she carried on the inside — not to mention the one on her neck — would ever entirely go away.

"I had no clue what he was really like until he dropped the mask," she said as the worst of her memories, the ones she generally tried to repress, darted across the stage of her mind. "Psychopaths are master manipulators."

"Look at you, talking about this with such objectivity."

She chuckled. "I'm healing in so many ways." She put her drink on the coffee table and took his face between her hands. "And a lot of it is because of you." She pressed her lips to his and knew that kiss could turn into much more. She heard him sigh in satisfaction, felt his arms go around her and draw her close.

Then the phone rang.

She broke away. "Phil?"

"I don't know. Ignore it," he said, and pulled her back for another kiss.

As soon as the ringing stopped, it started up again. Someone wanted to reach him — or her.

Reluctantly, he lifted his head. "Hold that thought," he said, and walked over, but once he answered, the way his forehead creased suggested it wasn't good news. "Right now? . . . What'd you say? . . . When? . . . All right, I'll be there in a sec."

"What is it?" she asked as he hung up.

"I have to go."

"Why?"

"There are some hunters at my trooper

post. One claims his sister has gone missing."

"Gone missing from where?"

"A cabin in the mountains. No idea which one. I don't have many details. All Phil could tell me is that he stopped to get something hot to drink before plowing Main Street again and ran into three guys as he came out. They were frantic, especially one called Leland. He said they were hunting when the storm hit, made it back to their SUV but got stuck in the snow. By the time they dug out the tires and finally reached where they were staying, his sister, who was supposed to be waiting for them, was nowhere to be found."

Evelyn sat up straight. "Where could she have gone?"

"That's what I have to find out," he said as he shrugged on his heavy coat.

Evelyn stood up and came around the couch to meet him at the door. "You don't think she went out looking for them and got lost. . . ."

"In a storm like this? I hope not. If she did, it could already be too late."

Amarok managed to convince two of the three hunters to get a room at The Shady Lady rather than risk the trek back to the cabin, but Leland Yerbowitz refused to be left behind. He was determined to help look for his sister, even though Amarok had tried to tell him to stay with his friends. Amarok preferred not to take a *cheechako* — someone who wasn't from Alaska and didn't know how to live there — out into this weather. He shouldn't be out in it himself. With night coming on and the storm getting worse, he was taking a risk. But he had to do what he could to find Leland's sister before the temperature dropped any further.

"What's your sister like?" he asked as they drove. He was trying to distract Leland from his worry, but he also wanted to learn if Sierra was knowledgeable about the outdoors, if she'd done much traveling or exploring or if she was the type who might wander off on her own because of some emotional problem.

Leland stared out at the torrent of snow that made it difficult to see through the windshield. "You know this road like the back of your hand, right?" he said instead of answering.

Amarok didn't generally have much reason to visit individual hunting cabins. He checked on them occasionally, if the owners requested it, but typically only during the summer. Most were empty throughout the colder months. “I’m somewhat familiar.”

“Somewhat” didn’t seem to offer the reassurance Leland was hoping for. He gripped his seat belt. “How are you going to keep from going over the side?”

Amarok had put chains on all four tires, even though he had four-wheel drive and a shovel on the front of his truck. “I’m taking it slow.”

From Leland’s expression, Amarok wasn’t taking it slow enough, but Sierra’s brother obviously felt the same pressure Amarok did to return to the cabin as quickly as possible, so he clamped his mouth shut and let Amarok drive.

“Can you tell me a little about your sister?” Amarok prompted, trying again.

“What about her?” he asked, his words clipped. “She’s twenty-eight and due to be married soon. We need to find her. I can’t . . . I can’t even imagine how I’ll feel if something’s happened to her. My mother, my father, our pregnant sister. What’ll I tell them? And her fiancé? I’ll feel responsible for this. I’m the one who wanted to go hunting. She just wanted to do the touristy stuff.”

“We’ll find her,” Amarok said.

“I can’t imagine where she is.”

“Why didn’t her fiancé join you?”

"Couldn't. He's a long-haul trucker and had a big delivery."

"I see. Is she familiar with Alaska?"

No response. It was easy to tell that Leland could only concentrate on finding her, didn't want to talk or do anything else until that happened.

"Leland?"

"Not at all," he replied. "This is our first visit, something we've been looking forward to for months."

That wasn't the answer Amarok had been hoping to hear. Not only was Sierra completely new to the area, she was also young and inexperienced enough that she might feel capable of more than she could accomplish in conditions like these. "Is she prone to wandering off on her own?"

"No. That's the thing. She has a good head on her shoulders. She's the one who was worried about coming to Alaska so late in the fall, but" — he shook his head as if he was too anxious to go into any great detail — "we had certain constraints we were working under with our hunting permits."

The tires struggled to grip the pavement. Ice was forming quickly, and it was so hard the chains could barely bite into it. At some point, the road would simply become impassable. But Amarok managed to keep the vehicle under control and rolling along. "How was she dressed when you saw her last?"

Leland, who'd felt the truck slip, pressed a hand to the door to steady himself. "She was in bed, asleep."

"She wasn't interested in going hunting with you?"

"Nope. She was happy to stay where she was. She warned us to be careful and mumbled good-bye before we left. That's it. What could've happened to her? Where could she have gone? There's nothing but wilderness for miles around that cabin."

"Maybe the storm frightened her. Maybe she thought you were in trouble and needed her."

"That's not it."

He sounded so certain. "What do you mean?" Amarok asked.

"Something else happened."

"How do you know?"

"Because of the ax and the woodshed."

This was the first Amarok had heard of any ax or any woodshed. "Would you mind explaining?"

"I don't know what to make of it. You'll see."

Amarok shot him a meaningful glance,

wondering why he hadn't mentioned this earlier. "We've got time to go over it now."

He sighed. "Someone used the ax to chop down the door to the woodshed."

"*Someone?* That had to be your sister, right? She was the only one there."

"She might've done it. The combination to the lock on the door wouldn't work, so we couldn't get any wood."

"Then it makes sense she'd force her way in."

"Except . . ."

"What?"

Worry lines creased his forehead. "The back door to the cabin was busted, too."

Amarok slowed even more as he navigated a particularly tricky turn. His headlights were almost no good; he couldn't see more than two feet in front of him. "Busted how? You mean it was also chopped down with the ax?"

"Not like the door to the woodshed, no. That was awkward, messy. The cabin door looked like it'd been pried open, probably with the ax, since the ax was lying on the back porch instead of hanging in the mud-room like before."

Again, his tires scraped and dug into the snowpack as Amarok pushed the truck to keep climbing. "Maybe she went out with the ax to get the wood and managed that, but when she returned to the cabin she realized she'd accidentally locked herself out."

"Could be." He acted like he *wanted* to believe that. "There was some fresh wood inside."

"There you go."

"But she packed all our stuff, had our bags waiting by the door. Why would she do that? For one thing, she knew we still had another night. For another, we're big boys. We can pack our own shit. We packed at home and in Anchorage, for crying out loud."

"Everything was by the door?"

"Every single thing any of us brought, even the cards and games we played at night. That makes me believe she didn't plan on going anywhere without us."

"Maybe she got scared for you, went out to find you."

"If she'd gone looking for us, she would've come out the front. There'd be no reason to go out the back and then have to walk around the cabin. Besides, she left the back door standing wide open. Why would anyone do that in the middle of a terrible storm?"

"Maybe she didn't. Maybe she didn't latch it tightly and the wind did the rest."

An expression of despair distorted Leland's angular features. "She didn't come after us, okay? She didn't even take her coat!"

Amarok felt a chill run down his spine. He'd gone into this assuming some *cheechako* had done something foolish and gotten herself in trouble. But he was beginning to wonder if he'd jumped to that conclusion prematurely. A woman alone in a remote cabin wouldn't simply wander away from warmth and safety, and she wouldn't go out searching for her brother without suiting up.

"Besides you and your sister, the two friends who came to town with you are all the people in your party?"

Leland nodded. "It was only the four of us."

"And you've had no problem with anyone since you arrived? No one could've followed you out to the cabin?"

"No. We've been there for three days without a moment's trouble. We haven't even seen another human being."

More determined to reach the cabin than ever, Amarok shifted into a lower gear as he headed up the steep grade of the final ascent. He had a bad feeling about this.

4

Leland Yerbowitz hadn't been exaggerating. His sister was gone, and there wasn't much to indicate what'd happened to her. The storm had obliterated all footprints and tire tracks. There was no way to tell how many vehicles had approached the cabin or how many people had gone inside, where they might've come from or which direction they might've traveled when they left. Although the floors were wet, especially near the front and back doors, the fact that Leland and his two friends had come in soaked would be enough to create those puddles, so that didn't prove much of anything, either.

Amarok found it interesting that she'd packed everyone and piled the luggage by the front door. It didn't look to him as though she was planning to stay another night. Why would she decide to go early? Was she hoping to beat the storm before they could get snowed in?

Possibly. . . .

Sierra's coat and boots were wet, so she'd been out in the elements. But she'd come in and cast her outerwear aside. She'd also stoked the fire. Leland insisted that he and his friends hadn't bothered with the stove when they returned to find her gone, and yet there were still a few glowing embers. That meant it couldn't have been more than three or four hours since she was here, depending on how much wood she'd used.

What had she done after she packed up? Why would she go back into the cold without protection?

She wouldn't. No one with any sense would. He had to find another answer.

He unzipped her suitcase. Some of her clothes were neatly packed. The rest had been tossed into the bag as though she'd been in a hurry to gather up what she'd recently used.

He checked her makeup case. He had no idea what she'd brought with her, of course, but he doubted anything was missing. He saw plenty of makeup, shampoo, hairspray, deodorant — that sort of thing. Although her toothbrush was no longer wet, there'd been plenty of time for it to dry. Her purse was still in the cabin, too, on the floor next to the luggage, and it didn't appear to have been disturbed.

Whatever this was, it wasn't a robbery.

Leland followed him from room to room and stood at the bottom of the ladder in the living room as Amarok climbed up to peer into the loft. Using his flashlight, he swept the room.

Nothing. Just a bed, with a blanket folded neatly at the foot of it, and a dresser.

"We didn't even go up there," Leland told him. "No one wanted to climb the ladder, so I slept on one of the bunk beds in Peter's room and Ted slept on the couch."

That gave Sierra her own room, which seemed polite but didn't mean anything. Amarok might've suspected that her own brother or one of his friends had harmed her and they were pretending she'd gone missing as a way to cover it up. After all, they were the last ones to see her. They were also the ones to discover she was missing. But Leland seemed genuinely distraught. Although he'd been quiet since they arrived, Amarok had seen him, several times, turning away to wipe tears from his eyes. The fact that he wasn't trying to put on a show lent him credibility.

"Are you sure you haven't seen anyone out and about in this area since you arrived?" Amarok asked.

Below, Leland cleared his throat. "No. I told you that in the truck. But maybe someone we met in Anchorage followed us out here."

If so, where would that person have hidden for the past three days? There wasn't another cabin within five miles. Or did he — or they — leave and come back?

Amarok climbed down the ladder. "Were there any vehicles behind you?"

"None that followed us for any length of time, and none once we got away from Hilltop. That would've been pretty obvious."

True, but Amarok had to eliminate the possibility. "Where did you go while you were in Anchorage?"

"Nowhere of any consequence. We wanted to see the touristy stuff — Denali and the glaciers — but the tours close down in mid-September. We missed all that. So we simply tried to experience Anchorage like the locals would for a day and a half while preparing for our hunt. Then we came here. We're supposed to move on to Juneau tomorrow morning."

Amarok didn't say it out loud, but he figured they wouldn't be finishing the trip. "If someone *had* followed you, my guess is they would've struck before now. Why wait for your last day?"

"Exactly. There's nowhere close by to watch what's going on here, so one day would seem as good as the next. It's not as if this was the first day she was alone."

"Your sister doesn't have any problems with drugs or alcohol?"

Leland seemed frustrated by his own emotions as he wiped the dampness from his cheeks again. "No. She doesn't drink more than an occasional beer or glass of wine. She's not a party girl, if that's what you're thinking. She's a *reader.* That's what she did while we were out; she read — and she was happy to do it."

"So she's not someone who would ever *purposely* harm herself?"

"Absolutely not! If you want to know what she's like, I can tell you. She's solid. Smart. Kind. She —" He choked up and had to stop talking.

This guy hadn't hurt his sister; he loved her.

Amarok touched Leland's arm. "I'm going to do everything I can to find her."

Still too overcome to speak, he nodded.

"How did she get along with your friends?" Amarok asked as he looked through closets and drawers and under all the beds. He didn't come across a single questionable thing.

Leland replied without hesitation. "Great. We've known Peter for most of our lives. He lived down the street when we were growing up. She met Ted just before we left Louisiana, but they were cool, too."

"There was no romantic interest between her and either friend?"

"None. Peter and Ted are both married, and she's engaged."

That didn't necessarily mean anything, but Leland seemed convinced. "And you were with them all day. There was never a time they were out of your sight?"

Leland grimaced. "I don't like the implication. They're my best friends. They'd never hurt her."

"Good to know," Amarok said. "But the question stands — *was* there ever a time they were out of your sight?"

Sierra's brother raked his fingers through his fine blond hair. "No. They were with me every minute. They couldn't have snuck back."

"Okay. Let's take a look at the back door — and the woodshed." There had to be *something* here that would tell a story, provide a clue. Amarok had been a police officer for ten years. Not long as most careers went. But he'd seen some crazy shit when it came to the outdoorsmen who visited from the Lower 48 — stupid, drunken antics where one guy or a couple of guys put themselves or others in danger. He'd never encountered a situation like this one, though. One so inexplicable . . .

Leland led him back through the cabin. Sierra's brother must've gained control of his grief and fear while Amarok studied the splintered wood where the door on to the back porch had been pried open. When he spoke, he sounded steady, less in danger of breaking down. "It would take some strength to force that door."

More strength than his sister possessed?

Amarok raised his voice, as Leland had done, in order to be heard over the bluster of the storm. "Can you show me where the ax was when you first noticed it?" Right now, it was leaning against the back of the house, visible in the dim glow of the porch light. But that wasn't where Leland claimed to have found it when he'd first mentioned it in the truck, which meant it'd been moved.

As that thought registered, Amarok bit back a curse. If this *was* a crime scene, having three hunters stomping through the house, touching, moving and dripping on everything, wasn't going to make his job any easier.

"There." Leland pointed at the rough wooden planks that served as the porch floor, about five feet away.

Amarok rubbed the beard growth on his chin. He hoped this wasn't what he feared. Two years ago, the owner of the Moosehead had stumbled upon a severed head behind his bar. That had launched Amarok's very first murder investigation. He didn't want to be in charge of another one. "Did the ax look as though it'd been dropped? Or was it placed there?" he yelled above the shriek of the wind.

"Dropped. Discarded in a hurry," Leland replied.

Pulling his flashlight from his utility belt, Amarok squatted to take a closer look. He couldn't see any blood or human tissue on the blade. *Thank God.* He hadn't noticed any blood inside the cabin, either, and he'd been looking for it. That gave him hope Sierra *hadn't* yet been the victim of foul play, but it also deepened the mystery. If someone had broken into the cabin with the intention of harming Leland's sister, where was the evidence that she'd been hurt? The blood spatter? The body?

Or had she been dragged off to another location?

That was possible except there were no

signs of a struggle. And how did the perpetrator know she was here alone and it was safe to strike? Why would he risk coming out in such a terrible storm when Leland, Peter and Ted could return at any moment? And what did he stand to gain by harming her?

Some killers *enjoyed* inflicting pain on others, killed for pleasure — like most of the psychopaths Evelyn studied. But Amarok was trying not to let his mind automatically shoot off in that direction. There were over three hundred psychopaths, many of them serial killers, at Hanover House, which wasn't far.

But they were all supposed to be locked up.

He needed to bag the ax, see if he could get any fingerprints off it, but he'd left his forensic kit in the truck so he could walk through the cabin first, discover what he could from a macro perspective.

Unfortunately, he'd discovered much less than he'd hoped. "Did your sister have any known enemies?"

Leland blew on his hands. He wore no gloves. Wasn't wearing a hat, either. He didn't seem concerned about the cold; he was too worried about his missing sister to let the weather distract him.

Amarok wore the hat that went with his uniform in the colder months, the one he could Velcro at the chin to keep his face warm, but that didn't help his hands. Since he knew he'd be entering what could be a crime scene, he'd put on a pair of latex gloves instead of his heavier GORETEX ones, and boot covers.

"No enemies," Leland replied. "Even if she did, they'd be back in Louisiana. This is the farthest she's ever been from where she was born. I can't believe anyone would follow us to Alaska to snatch her. It would make more sense to stay in Louisiana and follow her home from work one night. She lives alone."

It was a long shot, but if the killer thought murdering her in Alaska would make the crime easier to get away with he or she could've hopped on a plane. If someone had kidnapped her, it might be someone with whom she'd shared the details of her trip.

Louisiana to Alaska would be a long way to come, but Amarok had heard of crazier things, and he had to start his investigation *somewhere.* Hilltop was the closest town, but he knew all the locals and knew them well. None of them would seriously harm a young woman. Besides hunting and fishing infractions, which were a big part of his job in the summer months, he typically dealt with bar fights, petty theft and domestic disturbances. Anything worse had always been tied to outsiders.

Or Hanover House . . .

He hated to jump to conclusions. He'd made that mistake before. But had one of the dangerous criminals Evelyn studied somehow escaped?

He didn't have anything else to explain how or why Sierra had vanished.

Bracing against the wind, he used his flashlight to survey the area directly off the porch. No visible tracks. No clothing or blood. Nothing that seemed out of place. But, of course, just about anything could be buried in the snow, including a body.

Amarok frowned as he watched the blizzard continue to pummel the cabin and the mountain rising behind it. They had to go. If they didn't leave soon, they'd be stuck here. But he had to check the woodshed, in case there was something inside to indicate what had happened.

"Point me in the direction of the woodshed." Amarok couldn't see it; the darkness was too complete, and the beam of his flashlight couldn't penetrate the snow beyond a few feet.

Leland didn't point. He started to lead

the way.

Amarok caught hold of his arm. "I've got it. You need to go back in before you freeze," he said, but Leland refused to listen. Pulling away, he lifted his other arm to block the onslaught of the storm and continued to wade through the knee-deep drifts.

When Amarok's flashlight landed on the five-by-eight-foot structure not far from the back porch, he pushed Leland out of the way. Whoever had broken into the shed hadn't known how to use an ax, not efficiently, but *had* managed to get inside. That, in addition to what he'd seen so far, made him think it was Sierra. She came out, broke into the shed and carried more wood inside.

"That look like vomit to you?" he asked as Leland squeezed into the small space with him so they'd have some shelter and be able to hear each other.

Leland stared at the puddle Amarok had found. "Yeah. Smells like it, too."

"She was sick out here. Was she ill before you left?"

"If she was, she didn't say anything."

Amarok wasn't sure what to make of that, so he turned his attention elsewhere. "You told me the rental company didn't give you the correct combination to the padlock?"

"They didn't. If she broke in here, it was because she had to. There was no way to keep the stove going without more wood. When we left, I thought she had enough to get by, but that was before it started to storm."

Amarok stepped back through the hole in the door, then lifted the lock, which still hung on the latch. "What was the combination the rental company provided?" he yelled. "Do you have it?"

"I can get it."

The cabin gave off a faint glimmer in the dark, so Leland didn't need a flashlight to trudge back to it. He hurried off and returned a few minutes later with a crumpled sheet of paper.

Sheltering the paper and holding the flashlight so they could both see what they were doing, Leland read the digits while Amarok tried the lock — which opened easily.

Leland's jaw dropped at the sight. "How'd you do that? I tried at least ten times. Peter came out and tried, too. Didn't work for either of us."

So why did it work for him? Amarok refastened the lock and used the combination again — with the same result.

"This is nuts!" Leland cried. "Totally crazy!"

Amarok needed to bag the lock, too. "Are you *sure* you did it right?"

"Positive. It's a standard combination lock, for Christ's sake! Must not have worked for Sierra, either. Why else would she hack down the door?"

She could've been hiding in the shed for her own safety, and *he* could've been the one to use the ax. Maybe that was why she'd thrown up. She'd been terrified.

Apparently, Leland could tell what Amarok was thinking because he raised his hands. "I know how this looks, but I didn't do anything to my sister. I swear it! I *love* her!" He gestured at the damage to the door. "And I can swing an ax a hell of a lot better than whoever caused this damage."

Amarok couldn't help believing him. Leland had seemed sincere from the start. Besides, he had two buddies who confirmed that Sierra had been fine when they'd left this morning and that the three of them had never been separated during the time they were out hunting.

Leland looked white as a ghost in the glow of the flashlight. Amarok worried that Sierra's brother might be dealing with shock on top of the extreme weather. "Go get in the truck," he said. "I have to take some pictures and bag the ax and the lock. Then we're out of here." He also planned to take a sample of that vomit, just in case it was needed for DNA testing.

"What do you mean?" Leland cried. "We can't leave without Sierra!"

Amarok hated to say it, but there was nothing more they could do right now. Not until the storm blew over. "We have no choice."

"Yes, we do!" Leland tried to block him. "We have to keep looking. She could need help!"

This *cheechako* didn't understand. Alaska wasn't Louisiana. If they didn't get their asses off this mountain, and fast, they could wind up in serious trouble themselves.

Amarok grabbed hold of Leland's coat and jerked him hard. "If you want to survive so you can find your sister, you'll do *exactly* as I say. Do you understand?"

Tears filled the other man's eyes as the reality of their situation pierced through the panic — and he nodded.

She'd lost phone service *again.* Born and raised in Boston, where her parents and sister still lived, Evelyn was used to being able to communicate easily, move around easily and interact with a wide range of people. She hated feeling cut off, whether it was because of the size of the town, the distance to the closest urban hub, the weather or all three. She wasn't ready for another hard winter. Going without cell service was difficult enough. She hadn't owned a smartphone since she'd moved to Hilltop two years ago, and she missed the conveniences it provided. But a big storm often knocked out even regular phone service, which was the case tonight.

"Why couldn't the government have decided to build Hanover House in Texas instead of Alaska?" she muttered. That was one of the other states the site committee had considered. In West Texas, which had been suggested, the worst things she would've had to deal with were a few hot summers. Or some dust and wind and bigger than normal bugs.

But then she never would've met Amarok. . . .

She bit her lip as that thought crossed her mind. Maybe there'd come a day when she'd wish she *hadn't* met him. As much as she loved him, grateful as she was for the fact that he'd rebuilt her trust in love and intimacy, sometimes she was overwhelmed by a sort of . . . claustrophobic restlessness.

Then she worried that she couldn't remain in Alaska, couldn't be completely satisfied here. And if she *wasn't* going to stay, she and Amarok were racing toward a brick wall. In those moments, she knew she was crazy to be thinking about having a baby with him.

But when she was feeling lucky to have found him, when she was in his arms enjoying his incredible strength and tenderness, she wondered why *any* woman wouldn't want to have a child with Amarok. Even if it meant living in a frozen wilderness for the rest of her life.

Absently, she petted Sigmund, who was curled up in her lap while Makita lay at the edge of the room, as far from the heat of the fire as he could get. Makita accompanied Amarok a good 80 percent of the time, hated to be away from his master. At every noise — a tree branch scraping against the house, an icicle cracking and falling from the eaves, the whistle of the wind as it whipped the snow — he'd lift his head and stare at the door with his ears cocked. As if he expected Amarok to realize he'd been left behind and come back for him.

"Are you going to sulk *all* night?" Evelyn asked.

When Makita realized she was talking to

him, he barked in response, and she laughed. "He'll be back," she told him, but her smile lasted only as long as it took to say the words. She was trying to convince herself *and* the dog that Amarok would soon be joining them. She knew that going out in a storm like this was dangerous, or he *would've* taken Makita. The fact that he'd left his dog behind made Evelyn worry about him even more.

To keep from obsessing about his safety, she returned her attention to the papers strewn across the kitchen table. It used to be that while she was at work Amarok spent a great deal of his time searching for Jasper. He'd kept his efforts secret to protect her from all the ups and downs that went with such a long and painstaking investigation. Since Jasper had never been apprehended, she'd been disappointed so many times.

But last winter, Amarok had caught a break. While researching every murder in the United States that carried Jasper's particular signature, he came across an investigation into the deaths of five women in Peoria, Arizona — all of whom had been disposed of at a remote location in the desert, all of whom had been tortured before being murdered and all of whom had looked a great deal like Evelyn. Feeling that he was finally on to something, he told her what he was doing and started digging openly. He went so far as to confront Jasper's mother at her home in San Diego. Although Jasper's parents had never been cooperative, Amarok managed to get Maureen Moore to admit that she knew more about her son's whereabouts than she'd ever revealed. She'd pulled back after letting that slip, but Amarok had believed, if given another opportunity, he could get more out of her. He'd planned to follow up — until Jasper eliminated that possibility by killing both his mother *and* father and then setting their house on fire.

That had been a terrible setback just when Evelyn's hope was the highest it'd been in years. That Jasper could murder the two people who'd risked so much to help him proved how narcissistic he was. It also proved he'd stop at nothing to evade capture. So here they were, eight months later. He was always one step ahead of them, but Evelyn knew Amarok wasn't giving up and neither was she. If she ever wanted to feel safe, *truly* safe, they had to find him and get him off the streets before he made another attempt to kidnap or kill her, as he had shortly before she moved to Alaska.

Fortunately, the Peoria investigation was

ongoing. By testing Jasper's parents' DNA against the genetic material found under one of the victims' nails, the police were able to confirm that Jasper was indeed the one who'd murdered the five women outside of Phoenix. The police then used Jasper's DNA to connect him to another case in Arizona, one in which he'd attempted to kidnap a woman who managed to fling herself out of his van while he was driving away.

News of the match between his parents' DNA, the Peoria murders, which gave them Jasper's DNA, and the attempted abduction in Casa Grande an hour south, had come only this week. Due to a backlog at the lab, the samples from Stanley and Maureen Moore had taken eight months to be processed. But at least now they knew for certain that Jasper was in Arizona when those crimes occurred and might still be living there. What they'd learned also confirmed something else, something that had troubled Evelyn all along — he hadn't quit killing, just as she'd always said he wouldn't. He enjoyed it too much. Lust killers didn't stop; they kept going until someone or something else intervened.

"We're going to get you," she murmured, but she'd been saying that for over twenty years. It was difficult not to feel discouraged, especially after learning of Maureen's and Stanley's fate last February. Maureen had indicated to Amarok that Jasper was a "family man" these days, implying that he was no longer a danger to society. That was what had tipped Amarok off, telling him she knew more than she'd said earlier. Jasper's parents had wanted to believe that what he'd done in his youth had been caused by drugs. That he'd gotten past that terrible incident and grown into an upstanding citizen. But Evelyn knew Jasper would never be anything other than what he was — an anger-excitation sexual murderer. Torture and killing brought him sexual satisfaction. She could only hope his being married meant he was tied to the area, so she and Amarok, and the police who were investigating in Peoria and Casa Grande, could narrow the search and eventually find him.

Even pinpointing one particular county or counties didn't make the job easy, however. The metropolitan Phoenix area was huge. Where, specifically, should they look? She believed Jasper worked in Casa Grande, since the murders in Peoria were older and the Casa Grande attack happened around the time he murdered his parents, but there were no guarantees.

With a sigh, she put down her summary of the police interviews with the people who lived closest to the abandoned farm where those five Peoria victims had been found and checked her watch. Amarok should've been back by now. He'd been gone for hours, and it was getting late.

Unable to sit any longer, she nudged Sigmund out of her lap and got up to pace. Makita whined as if he shared her concern over Amarok's prolonged absence — the storm was only getting worse — so she went over to give him a pat. "He's smart, and he's tough," she told the dog. "He's lived here his whole life. He knows how to deal with the weather."

That was all true, but something as simple as breaking down or getting stuck could cause a person to freeze to death, and he'd push beyond what was safe if it meant finding that missing woman.

Evelyn's hand went to her stomach as she stood — a symbolic gesture, she supposed, since they'd been hoping for a baby. It was at times like this that she hated Alaska.

But it was also at times like this that she felt she couldn't live without Amarok.

5

Rigid with fury, Jasper could barely move. As if he hadn't had a bad enough day, now he couldn't go home. He had two bodies in the back of his truck he needed to get rid of, and yet he had to stay over in Hilltop. He didn't like that, didn't like being so close to Amarok, not when a quick glance under the tarp in the bed of his new F-250 would so easily expose him. Amarok was totally committed to hunting him down. The trooper made Jasper far more wary than the detectives working his case in Boston, where he'd first killed, or Peoria, where they'd found the remains of five of his victims, or San Diego, where he'd murdered his parents. He could outsmart all of those investigators. They didn't communicate, didn't coordinate. They put in their nine to five and went home feeling safe and happy, no worse off for not getting the job done.

Amarok, however . . . That bastard was

different, more of a challenge. Jasper had to be careful of Evelyn's lover; he certainly didn't relish the idea of driving around town in possession of two dead women, especially when the one he'd just killed had been screaming for someone called Leland before he choked her. If "Leland" ever returned to the cabin, he'd no doubt report the woman missing — if he could get off the mountain. Jasper was hoping Leland was snowed in and wouldn't be able to sound the alarm until the cargo in the back of the F-250 had been dumped in a safe place. But Jasper couldn't dump the bodies right away. They'd closed the road to Anchorage. He'd gotten partway there and had to turn around. It wasn't as if he could take an alternate route, either, not in the middle of a blizzard. Only 30 percent of Alaska's public roads were paved. That equated to less than five thousand miles, which hadn't sounded all that minimal when he'd been reading about the state before moving here. After he'd arrived, however, he'd realized just how vast Alaska really was.

Fortunately, the proprietor at The Shady Lady, a diminutive Eskimo named Margaret Seaver according to a placard at her elbow, told him she had an opening. Since it was the only motel in town and it was small —

twelve tiny cabins strung loosely together — he hadn't been confident he could even get a room. A large number of the other COs commuted, like he did. If they'd stopped for a drink at the Moosehead or lingered at the prison before heading home, as they sometimes did, they could also be stuck for the night.

Margaret ran his Visa card while he stood across the counter from her in the front office. "Can you believe this weather?" she said as they waited for credit approval.

Still filled with rage at the woman who'd discovered what he didn't want found in the woodshed, he took several deep breaths as a way to absorb the impact of his intense emotions and make it easier to modulate his voice. He needed to come across as pleasant, not particularly upset. He didn't want to say or do anything that would make Margaret remark on her encounter with him to someone else. He needed to hunker down until they opened the road, then get his ass home.

Problem was, that might not happen soon enough for him to drive home before he had to report back to work. Returning to Anchorage *and* disposing of two corpses would require several hours, and he couldn't arrive at the prison late. He'd get written up, and since he was probably already going to get written up for destroying an inmate's photograph of his grandmother, that would be twice in two days.

The way Margaret Seaver watched him suggested she was waiting for a response.

"It's bad out there, all right." He wasn't interested in engaging someone who mattered so little to him. She wouldn't even be a good candidate for a victim. She was too old, looked nothing like Evelyn. But he was good at playing his part. He'd learned how to act at a very young age; he'd known he was different almost from the start.

She printed out the slip for him to sign. "You work at the prison, huh?"

He was still wearing his uniform. He'd strangled the woman he'd found in the cabin, so he wasn't worried she'd spot any blood on him. His latest victim had urinated just before she died, but he'd expected that and taken steps to avoid getting anything on him. "Yeah. Been there since last February," he told Margaret. Actually, he'd stayed at this motel once before, two years ago, when he'd come to Alaska to check out Evelyn's pet project. Margaret didn't realize it, since her daughter or sister or someone else had been at the front desk when he checked in and out. Jasper had seen Margaret outside the motel once or twice, but only in passing. He spent quite a bit of his free time at the Moosehead. He was trying to become so familiar to the locals they wouldn't find his coming and going any more remarkable than if he were one of them. And he liked watching Evelyn. She hung out there with Amarok a few nights a week, since Amarok had to be on hand to keep the peace.

"Where do you live? Anchorage?" Margaret asked.

Jasper scribbled what passed for his signature these days on the credit slip. "Yeah."

"But you're not a native."

"No, I'm originally from Florida." He'd never lived in Florida, but he lied smoothly, easily. That was one of the tools of his trade, so he took it seriously. Everything he was, everything he did, depended on his ability to deceive.

"Florida, huh? The cold up here must be quite a shock to you."

"It is. Please tell me it isn't always this bad in October."

She frowned at the torrent coming down outside the window. "Not quite this early, no."

She returned his Visa card, which read: "Andy Smith" — he'd been Andy for a number of years, had used other aliases before that — and he put it back in his wallet. "My luck, I guess."

"Well, you're not totally unlucky. At least you got a room. This is my last one, so if you'd come in any later, you might not have had anywhere to go."

If not for the corpses in his truck, he could've returned to the prison. They had a small dorm for situations like this. But he couldn't go through the checkpoint with two murdered women in the back of his truck.

He maintained a smile as she handed over an old-fashioned key, rather than one of the card keys used by more modern places.

"Need any food or water?" she asked. "I stocked up when I heard we had a storm coming."

He hadn't eaten since lunch; he was hungry. Both The Dinky Diner and the Moosehead — the two most common places to grab a bite to eat in this postage-stamp-sized town — would both be closed, since no one was going out in such ugly weather. "How much you charging?" he asked.

"I'm not charging anything," she replied. "Just trying to be neighborly."

"Nice of you."

She winked at him. "We look out for each other here in Alaska."

He hoped they didn't look *too* closely, not at him. "That's what I like about this place."

She beamed at the compliment. "Well, I wouldn't want any of my patrons to go hungry, especially one of our brave COs from Hanover House."

She didn't care how brave he was or that he was a CO. She was responding to the way he looked, and he knew it. She was too old for him, wasn't actually *flirting,* but it was his handsome face — and his body, which he was careful to keep fit — that lent him credibility with women of all ages. He used his good looks as a lure, but if he wasn't careful they could get him in trouble, too. Women paid attention to him and what he was doing. He wasn't one of those nondescript killers who could come and go without anyone noticing; he was attractive enough to be memorable. That meant he had to be smarter than most other killers, more adept at fooling people.

"What do ya got?" he asked.

"A turkey or ham sandwich, some chips and a soda, or bottled water if you prefer. Cleaned out Quigley's Quick Stop down the way."

"I'll take whatever you have the most of."

She went in back and returned with a sack and a bottle of water. "Here you go."

"Appreciate it," he said, and gave her a grateful smile before bracing himself to go back out in the cold.

His room was at the far end, which suited him fine. He didn't want to be too close to anyone. He moved his truck in front of it and checked on what he'd put in the bed. Both bodies were still wrapped up together, under the tarp, which was quickly being buried by snow.

Leaning into the wind, he used one hand to block the snowflakes stinging his face and turned in a slow circle.

No one seemed to be showing any interest in him or his vehicle. Everyone was too worried about the weather.

He was going to be fine — as long as he could get out of town before someone raised the alarm about the woman who'd gone missing from that cabin.

Evelyn couldn't sleep. She'd tried, but not long after she climbed into bed the power went out, so she didn't have phone service *or* electricity. She lay in the dark, feeling the house slowly cool, with no radio or television to distract her — only the shriek of the wind.

Just last summer, Amarok had installed a backup generator. Although the storm wouldn't make it easy, she could take a flashlight, go outside and try to get it started; he'd shown her how.

She considered doing that. She desperately wanted the lights to come back on. But after what had happened in this very house last winter, she was too scared to abandon the meager safety of remaining behind locked doors. Although she'd been pretending the incident with Bishop hadn't affected her, it had set her back, made it more difficult to cope with all the fear she carried around. Ever since that attack, she couldn't abide total darkness, just as she hadn't been able to abide it for three or four years after that first incident with Jasper. As much as Amarok had helped her heal sexually, the recent trauma with Lyman Bishop had sent her reeling in other ways; it made her jump at every shadow, fear every noise, constantly glance over her shoulder. There were even times she felt as though she was being watched when she knew it couldn't be true.

Go turn on the generator. Getting the light to come back on in the hallway would be worth suiting up for the weather. But she couldn't make herself crawl out from under the covers, not even to go into the living room to put more wood on the fire. She felt paralyzed beneath the thick, heavy blankets, could hear her heart thumping in her ears as her imagination began to kick into overdrive — showing her a face at the window or making her hear the creak of footsteps in the hall.

Why are you allowing this? She'd been doing so well! She'd thought she could cope with everything she'd been through, *had* been coping. But she hadn't faced a night like this. Thinking about the woman who'd gone missing made her remember what it had been like when *she'd* gone missing herself — for three days.

Stop! If she didn't get hold of herself, she'd fall into a full-blown panic attack. She was cold and clammy and beginning to tremble. And the fear, rising to ever greater heights inside her, seemed to be squeezing off her windpipe. With Amarok gone, she didn't possess her usual coping skills.

She closed her eyes, opened them and closed them again. Total blackness either way. Just like the night Jasper had tied a bandana around her head so she couldn't see what he was going to do to her next. He liked how that frightened her, relished making her quake and beg as he led her to believe *this* was the moment he was going to kill her.

What he'd done instead had been demeaning, revolting, excruciating. Mercifully, her brain had blocked out the worst of it.

But certain sights, smells or sounds could trigger an emotional memory even if her brain refused to fill in all the blanks. In those moments, she felt sick.

"I won't let you win. You will *not* beat me," she told him through gritted teeth. She couldn't allow him to imprison her mind as he'd once imprisoned her body. Being Evelyn Talbot meant breaking out of that shack again and again and again — almost every day — but she had to do it, had no other choice.

Curling into a tight ball, she struggled to dig deep, find calm. She hadn't had an episode quite this bad in years, which only went to prove she probably needed counseling again. Recently, she'd been able to sense that she was slipping into the anxiety and fear that always hung on the fringes of her psyche. Her parents had warned her this would happen if she continued to study violent behavior and the men responsible for it, especially in such an up close and personal way. But because of Amarok and the happiness he brought her, she'd been able to move forward, hold herself together. The long days of spring and summer, which were filled with beauty and sunshine here in

Alaska, had helped, too — helped her ignore and even cloak the damage Bishop had caused.

But now summer was gone and so was Amarok, and she was alone in the cold darkness, without phone service and power in a place that felt vast and lonely. And she couldn't go to counseling, couldn't seek that kind of help. If her boss at the Federal Bureau of Prisons and the other mental health professionals on her team learned she was struggling, they could lose confidence in her. Perception was everything; she couldn't undermine her own credibility, or she could be stripped of everything she'd worked so hard to create. Then how would she solve the mysteries of the psychopathic mind and arm would-be victims with knowledge and power?

"Hang on. Amarok will be home. He'll be here soon. Just wait for Amarok."

As she struggled to regulate her breathing, various sensory impressions assailed her like arrows. The grittiness of the dirt floor in the shack where Jasper had kept her. The acrid scent of the fire Jasper had set after he'd slit her throat and left her for dead. The confusion and pain as she'd dragged her broken body through the woods. The blaring of the car horn when she'd finally stumbled into the road and was nearly hit by the man who'd eventually stopped to help her. The pavement scraping her heels as a masked man dragged her from her vehicle only two years ago. And Lyman Bishop's high, almost effeminate voice as he told her she'd asked for what he was about to do when he stood over her outside the front door of this very house.

Tears were streaming down her face when she heard the noise outside her bedroom window. *That* wasn't just the storm. She heard *purposeful* movement.

Makita agreed. Although Amarok's dog had followed her when she went to bed — he typically slept at their feet — he jumped up, raced to the front door and began to bark like crazy.

Someone was out there.

Who?

The face of Jasper and the many other psychopaths she'd dealt with over the years passed before her mind's eye. She was about to scream when the hum of the generator rose above the wind and the lights snapped on.

Amarok. He was home. He *had* to be home. Who else would take the time to turn on the generator? Or even know it was there?

Gasping for breath, she quickly wiped her

face, sat up and hugged her knees to her chest as she waited.

Sure enough, she heard the front door open and Amarok's voice as he quieted his dog.

He was home. He was safe. And so was she.

Falling back onto the pillows, she tried to gather her composure before he could realize how badly off she'd been, how close she'd come to *really* freaking out.

Fortunately, he was so preoccupied or tired he didn't seem to notice she was awake when he came in and quietly pulled off his boots.

She waited until he was completely undressed and crawling under the covers to speak to him. By then, she could talk without a wobble in her voice. "Did you find her?"

"No."

"What do you think happened?"

"I don't know. But let's not talk about that right now. Go back to sleep. We'll discuss it in the morning."

She didn't tell him she hadn't slept a wink so far. "But you're okay?"

"I'm fine."

He was concerned about the situation. She could tell. And he'd be concerned about her, too, if he knew she'd fallen into such a distressed state.

Which was why she wasn't going to tell him.

"But . . . what do you *think* happened to her?"

"I don't know," he said again, "but I'm not going to jump to any conclusions." He pulled her into his arms. "Come here. I need to feel you against me," he said, and she was only too happy to oblige.

The warmth of his body, the solid muscles that moved beneath his smooth skin as he anchored her back to his chest with one arm, quieted her mind and slowed her pulse. Sex was the last thing she should be thinking about. After the night he'd had she couldn't imagine he'd be interested, but she hoped he was, because she needed to feel him inside her.

She turned to kiss him, to test his response, and felt his hand slide into her hair as his tongue met hers. Maybe he needed to blot out the negative emotions he'd experienced, too — reassure himself of the love she offered — because he rolled her onto her back almost as soon as she reached down to make sure he had an erection.

It was quiet when Jasper woke up several

hours later. He wasn't sure what had disturbed him. The wind seemed to have died down, so it was quieter than before. But then he heard voices, raised in alarm, right outside his room.

"Leland, no! You *can't* go back up there."

"I have to! I should never have let him talk me into leaving. Sierra's there somewhere. She could need me!"

For a moment Jasper thought he had to be dreaming. He'd never met anyone called Leland. The only place he'd ever heard that name was on the lips of the woman he'd strangled earlier, at the cabin.

But, surely, this wasn't the man she'd been crying for — *was it?*

He supposed it *could* be. If Leland had returned to the cabin in time to get off the mountain, where else would he go? He'd be stranded in Hilltop, same as Jasper — who had the woman this man was so frantic to find in the bed of his truck only ten feet away.

The realization of what was happening sent a jolt of adrenaline through him, clearing the cobwebs and making him hyperalert. He climbed out of bed and went to the window, where he parted the drapes, but the glass was too foggy to be able to see clearly.

What time was it? It was still dark out, but that didn't mean anything. The length of days in Alaska swung so widely — from more than nineteen hours of daylight in mid-June to barely five during the winter solstice in December. It could be late morning and still look like it did now.

He hoped it wasn't *too* late. He'd set the radio alarm on the nightstand for four, but it was blinking zeroes. The power must've gone out after he fell asleep.

He checked his watch and relaxed; it was only three. If the road was open and he left now, he could dump the bodies and be back in time to reach the prison by one.

Good thing he'd let another CO pay him fifty bucks to trade shifts! Otherwise, he'd have to head back to Hanover House right now, since he most often worked the early shift.

He cracked open his door so he could see and hear what was going on. As the men continued to argue, a third guy came out of the room closest to Jasper's and tried to talk some sense into Leland, too. "You heard what Sergeant Murphy said. He's got this. He's gonna do everything he can to find your sister."

So *that* was Leland's connection to the woman he'd murdered. He was her brother.

At least she wasn't his wife. Jasper figured Leland should be grateful for that.

Leland tried to shove the others away. "By the time the sergeant goes back, it could be too late."

It was already too late. Leland was a fool. But Jasper didn't care if the guy risked life and limb returning to the cabin. He just wanted them *all* to clear out so he could leave. He preferred not to be seen in the same vicinity or have them observe him driving off at such an odd hour. Anyone could get snowed in, and since the motel was now full, he certainly wasn't alone. But he knew better than to do anything that might attract Amarok's attention. He couldn't account for the hours after he'd left the prison before he got snowed in, couldn't say he was at the Moosehead or the Quick Stop or even The Dinky Diner. This was a small enough place that there'd be people who could refute any claim he made, and those people would be easy enough to find.

Better to keep his head down a little longer.

He closed the door as the two men who were trying to talk Leland into staying started wresting his keys away from him, which caused Leland to break down crying.

When Jasper heard his deep wail, he *had* to peer out again. That emotion, that profound grief, was a curiosity to him. He'd never experienced anything similar, couldn't even begin to imagine what it was like.

But he never tired of studying it.

Terror was another interesting emotion.

6

Harold Childress. Evelyn sat at her desk at Hanover House and stared at the name of her former therapist on a greeting card he'd given her the last time she'd seen him, nearly six years ago. Forty years older than she was, he'd retired nine months before their last meeting, so she'd no longer been his patient. They'd gotten together for lunch, as friends.

She wished she could talk to him again. Although he'd never experienced anything remotely like the trauma she'd been through, he'd possessed a wise mind and an understanding heart. No one else could soothe her fears in quite the same way. No one else could shine such a bright light on the goal of normalcy or show her a clear path for reaching that target. His rational thinking made so much sense to her.

But she couldn't reach out to him, not anymore. He'd had a heart attack and died not long after that lunch date. And now Jasper's attempt to kidnap her two years ago, the corruption she'd battled when she first started Hanover House, the stalking behavior of the psychiatrist who'd helped her launch the facility, the recent murders of two more of her friends in Boston and Lyman Bishop's attempt at revenge — all of that had reopened old wounds.

She put the greeting card carefully back inside her drawer and gazed at the Starship *Enterprise* model on her desk. Brianne, her sister and only sibling, had given it to her at her going-away party before she'd left Boston. A small placard at the base read: "Going where no man or woman has gone before." Back then, Evelyn had thought she'd make such great strides, had been determined to break new ground in psychopathy, which was the reason for that analogy. Plus the fact that she was moving to the last great frontier. But now? She felt like the *Enterprise* after it'd passed through an asteroid field and sustained too many hits. Not only were her shields inoperable, she could no longer escape the gravity of the alien world, the one inhabited by the monsters she studied, the one that held her captive.

Perhaps all the people who'd second-guessed her in the beginning — her parents, so many of her colleagues, the opponents she'd faced when trying to establish Hanover House — were right. Perhaps she *couldn't* handle what she'd set out to do.

She thumbed through the contacts on her old-fashioned Rolodex, which she used since she didn't have a smartphone. She needed to find another Harold. Fast. But who could replace him? Although she worked with five psychologists, she couldn't go to any of them for help. She'd consider Stacy Wilheim, the only other woman on the team, except that she couldn't confess her weakness even to Stacy. Not when Stacy and all the rest of the mental health professionals she'd hired had dragged their families and pets, if they had them, to this frozen wilderness expecting their fearless leader to be like Captain Kirk — strong, resourceful, always successful in the end.

She supposed she might be able to find a therapist in Anchorage.

She keyed "psychologists, Anchorage" into the search engine on her computer and several names populated the screen. But as she scanned the addresses, they all felt too close to Hilltop. She'd been on the news so many times while lobbying for this facility. She could easily be recognized going in or out of one of their offices and couldn't risk being questioned.

She had to remain stoic, had to forge ahead despite the crippling fear, the nightmares, the pressures of her job and the dark and cold of this place.

And she would, she told herself. She was just experiencing a moment of uncertainty. She'd functioned quite well since moving to Hilltop, despite everything that'd happened. She wasn't sure why she was struggling now that it was all over, but at least this was Thursday. If she could get through today and tomorrow, she'd have a short break from work. "Dr. Talbot?"

Closing out of her browser, Evelyn glanced over to see her assistant, Penny Singh, who was less than five feet tall, standing in the doorway. "Yes?"

Penny looked confused. "You're late for your session with Bobby Knox."

Evelyn blinked as she checked the clock. Where had the past twenty minutes gone? She hadn't even eaten the lunch Amarok had packed for her. It was still sitting, untouched, at her elbow. "Oh, right. Of course. I'm on my way."

"There's something else."

Evelyn closed the file that lay open on her desk, since she needed to take it with her, and stood. "What's that?"

Penny winced as she pulled an envelope from behind her back. "You've received another letter from Dr. Fitzpatrick."

Evelyn cocked an eyebrow at her assistant. "You mean *Inmate* Fitzpatrick?"

"Yeah. Should I just . . . throw it out? I can't believe I ever pushed you to take his calls, can't believe I ever felt sorry for him. You've told me that psychopaths are charming, that I shouldn't fall for their act. But I didn't want to believe he was a psychopath. He was supposed to be one of the good guys."

Evelyn had wanted Tim Fitzpatrick out of her life almost since the day Hilltop had opened. Older by nearly two decades, he'd had quite an illustrious career by the time they joined forces, and since she was a relative newcomer, she'd needed the credibility his support provided. But after they came to live in Alaska, she'd begun to realize that he wanted much more than a professional relationship. And once she'd made it clear that she had no interest, he'd changed to the point that she almost couldn't tolerate him.

Still, she was having trouble believing the man she'd worked with was guilty of killing Mandy Walker and Charlotte Zimmerman

Pine, two women she'd been friends with in high school. She didn't like him and had a hard time forgiving him for what he'd done before quitting and returning to the Lower 48 a year and a half ago. But would he really murder two people in order to convince her Jasper was once again murdering friends she'd had more than twenty years ago?

She couldn't say for sure. Now that she and Amarok had Jasper's DNA, she planned to have it compared to the DNA found at the crime scene where Charlotte was killed. A match would rule Fitzpatrick out. So instead of telling Penny to throw away his letter, she took it, figuring she might as well let him know that much. "No, I'll have a look. Thank you."

After shoving the letter in her desk to read later, she skirted around her assistant and headed over to the double glass doors that separated their offices from the rest of the prison.

The phone rang as she was leaving, and Penny stopped her just before she could walk out. "Dr. Talbot?"

She turned. "Yes?"

"Janice is on line one."

Janice Holt, her boss at the Bureau of Prisons. Evelyn hesitated. She didn't want to be any later for her appointment with

Bobby Knox, but she'd been waiting for this call and Bobby wasn't going anywhere. "Let the COs who are with Mr. Knox know I'm running a few minutes late and will be down as soon as I can," she told Penny.

"Will do."

Evelyn returned to her office and closed the door behind her before picking up the phone. "Dr. Talbot."

"Evelyn, I'm sorry it's taken me so long to get back to you."

"No problem." She didn't sit down. She didn't plan to let this conversation take that long. Instead, she walked over to look out the window. Everything was covered with a thick blanket of snow, but the storm had, for the most part, cleared. Although it was still dark out, it was now just dark and wintry. "I hope you have good news."

"Actually, I do. You'll be getting your first female inmate on Monday."

The department had been planning to fill the new section with more men, but Evelyn had pushed to use the expansion for another purpose — to bring a few female psychopaths to Hanover House instead.

Fortunately, Janice had liked the idea from the beginning. She saw it the way Evelyn did — why shouldn't they study both sexes? Especially because, with the addition of the new section, it was now possible. "Wow. You did it! I can't believe it."

"You doubted me?" Janice teased.

"I shouldn't have. You're a force of nature."

"We faced our usual opponents — all the people who're afraid of change and want everything to be done the same old way. But I pointed out that what you're doing is making a difference. Beth Bishop is a prime example. If not for you, she'd still be living with her brother and Lyman would probably still be kidnapping women and performing ice-pick lobotomies on them. You're doing good work. I believe in you."

Evelyn gripped the handset a little tighter. Janice didn't know about the girl who'd gone missing from the cabin last night. She didn't know that just hearing about someone who couldn't be found, who could be lost or hurt in this lonely place, made Evelyn fear the worst. She couldn't help wondering if someone from Hanover House could be responsible for whatever had happened. She'd checked to make sure all inmates were present and accounted for when she'd arrived at the prison this morning, but that didn't mean this incident wasn't connected in some peripheral way. "Thank you," she said, and hoped to God

Janice's faith hadn't been misplaced.

After *that* compliment, Evelyn knew she couldn't get counseling. Any hint of instability would hamstring her boss when it came to lobbying for anything else she requested or needed up here.

She had to soldier on and pray the missing woman would soon be found safe, that whatever happened had nothing to do with the institution and that the psychological scars she bore wouldn't cause her to unravel and ruin everything she'd set in motion.

Most days Jasper craved a glimpse of Evelyn like an alcoholic craved booze. He thought of her constantly, peered around every corner, loitered near the mental health department if he could come up with an excuse to be there. So it was ironic that today, the one day he *didn't* want to bump into her and had stayed away from that side of the prison entirely, she happened to get on the same elevator.

She wasn't wearing a lab coat, like so many of the other doctors did, or a name tag. But everyone, both inside and outside the institution, knew who she was. He'd made her famous, made her *Important* with a capital *I*. The whole world was watching to see what the "brilliant and beautiful psychiatrist" would accomplish in her "fight against the conscienceless," but she'd accomplished all she was going to. He'd make sure of that — once he got out of the mess he'd created in the past week. He couldn't wait until she realized that she hadn't been able to escape him, after all.

She wore her silky dark hair in a ponytail and had a folder under her arm. The crease of concentration on her forehead suggested she was deep in thought. He could tell she wasn't paying any attention to her surroundings. Since she was all business today, he doubted she'd acknowledge him, and that bothered him. He hated the way she could so easily overlook him. He'd once been one of the most important people in her life.

And he would be again.

After the elevator doors glided shut, she looked over and did a double take. "Andy, I'm sorry. I was so preoccupied I didn't even recognize you."

She *still* didn't recognize him. Not really. But the cosmetic surgeon who'd reconstructed his face had been one of the best in the world. His own parents, who'd had the money to pay handsomely for the tremendous amount of work he'd had done, hadn't recognized him when he first returned to the States, and that was years ago, before he'd aged by two decades.

Besides, no one would ever dream he'd be bold enough to pursue employment at Hanover House. Certainly not Evelyn. Amarok, either. The uniform Jasper wore gave him instant credibility. And the fact that he'd been the man to step in and save Evelyn from Lyman Bishop last winter?

He was golden.

He managed not to smile at the fact that she was alone in an elevator with the man who'd once cut her throat and she didn't even know it. She had to want closure, had to want him caught more than anything else in the world. He *knew* she did. And yet . . . here he was.

So much for her ability to spot danger.

"No problem." He kept his hands locked behind his back and his eyes focused toward the front, as most people did in an elevator, but it wasn't easy to appear so unaffected. Just the sight of Evelyn, the way she dressed and the woman she'd become — so elegant and refined and intelligent — aroused him. Neither of his ex-wives could compare. None of his other victims could, either.

But he had to be careful not to let her sense his interest.

He was doing such a good job of maintaining a businesslike air, he expected that to be the end of the exchange, but she surprised him.

"How are you?"

"Fine," he muttered. Although he'd certainly been better. He'd had to stash the two bodies that were in his truck in a vacant field not far from the prison. The road to Anchorage hadn't opened in time for him to make it home and back; as far as he knew the road *still* wasn't open. He'd considered calling in sick so he could properly dispose of his cargo, but he'd worried that would actually be a greater risk. He didn't want to be even slightly conspicuous, so he'd forced himself to come in, and he was glad he did. Tex, the CO who'd seen him rip up that inmate's picture yesterday, had already ratted on him. He'd just had his ass chewed out by the warden. Missing work would only have given his superiors another reason to be upset with him.

The thought of Tex helped Jasper control his reaction to Evelyn. Tex was someone else he needed to get even with — and he would.

"I'm glad to hear it," she said.

He let himself glance over at her. He loved her eyes. They were the prettiest shade of hazel he'd ever seen. None of the other women he'd murdered in her place could match her beauty or her poise. None of them had her intelligence or strength of spirit, either. They'd been a diversion, nothing more. Soon he wouldn't have to worry about coming up with a good substitute.

"So you're adjusting to Alaska?" she asked. "You like it up here?"

The elevator dinged and the doors whooshed open. "I do. I love it here, don't you?"

"I like a lot of things about it," she said as they walked off. "Where did you live before you came here?"

Although he could still hear *her* Boston accent, he'd worked hard to eradicate his. The length of time he'd been gone helped. "I was born in Florida." That wasn't what she'd meant, but Amarok had figured out that he was responsible for the five women murdered in Peoria, and although hearing that a relatively new CO named Andy Smith was from the Phoenix area wouldn't necessarily set off any alarm bells, Jasper preferred not to draw the connection in the first place. His work experience was on his application. She'd see it if she ever looked over his employee file. But he assumed she'd have to go through the warden to gain access and was hoping she wouldn't be curious enough to go that far.

"I've never spent much time there," she said. "Is that where you worked before?"

He couldn't lie outright. If the truth ever came to her attention, that would be an even bigger red flag than telling her he'd just moved from Arizona. He had to answer. But as soon as he opened his mouth, a CO named Chad Peirano hurried up to them.

"Dr. Talbot. There you are! I was just coming to find you. Bobby Knox is pitching a fit that you're not there. He says if you have no respect for his time, he doesn't want to talk to you. Should we take him back to his cell?"

She shook her head. "No. I'm almost there now. I'll meet with him, see if I can't make the session useful in spite of his irritation."

Jasper was already moving away from her when she glanced back at him. "I won't hold you up any longer," he said, and waved as she started following Chad in the opposite direction.

Sierra Yerbowitz had an abusive fiancé. While Amarok wasn't exactly *excited* by the news, he was somewhat relieved. Maybe her disappearance wouldn't be so difficult to solve, after all. And maybe whatever had gone wrong at the cabin had nothing to do with Hanover House — or Hilltop, either. After the past couple of years, Amarok felt he deserved a break. Evelyn even more so. Ready answers, answers that gave her no reason to fear, would help. He hoped that if he could keep her world stable, and she didn't always have to deal with so much drama, she'd agree to marry him.

He was sure Leland would appreciate knowing what had happened, too, even if it wasn't the outcome anyone hoped for. And achieving a quick resolution was sounding more and more promising. Amarok had one of Sierra's coworkers on the phone — Loni Loose (an unfortunate last name for a woman, in his estimation) — who'd immediately pointed a finger at Sierra's fiancé, the long-distance trucker Leland had told him about. Loni said if *anything* had happened to Sierra, Allen Call was most likely to blame.

"Leland seems to think Call's a pretty stand-up guy." Amarok held the phone to his ear as he rocked back in his chair at the trooper post, relaxing for the first time since Leland and his buddies had hit town last night. He hadn't questioned Leland extensively about Sierra's relationship with her fiancé, but only because Leland had acted as though Allen would be devastated if anything had happened to her, just like the rest of her family and friends.

Loni seemed to have a different take on the relationship. "Of course he does. She can't tell Leland about all the shit Allen puts her through. Leland would try to stop her from marrying him if she did. Her whole family would step in."

"But she talked to *you* about Call's behavior."

"She talked to all of us here at the salon."

Amarok propped his feet up on his desk. "How bad did it get?"

"He's knocked her around a bit. I know that. One time I had to completely redo her nails because she'd broken three trying to shut him out of her bedroom."

"Did she ever show up at the salon with any nasty cuts, bruises, that sort of thing?"

"Nothing *too* bad. But he definitely had a temper."

He was hoping for more proof. . . . "Did she ever have to call the police? File charges against him?"

"I don't think so. But when they got into an argument a few weeks ago, he stopped the car at the side of the road and literally *pushed* her out onto the pavement. She scraped *both* her knees. We tried to convince her to break up with him, get him out of her life. She said she wasn't hurt that badly, that he'd apologized and would never do it again."

Amarok lowered his feet and sat up. Scraped knees were a far cry from murder, but maybe he had to dig a little deeper. "I don't mean to make light of those injuries, but do you know if he ever did anything worse?"

"I have no idea what she might've hidden from us. She was always complaining about his temper. She'd get so nervous if she thought he might be upset with her about something. We all hate him."

"I'm not saying this is the case, because I don't know yet, but if this comes down to the worst, would you say he's capable of murder, Ms. Loose? Could you see him traveling all the way to Alaska to *kill* her?"

After a slight hesitation, she said, "I hope not. We all love Sierra and we're praying she comes back safe. But he might know something. He didn't want her to take the trip, never wants her to go anywhere without him."

"Maybe she was fed up and trying to break things off." Amarok thought that would make it even more believable, but Loni quickly disabused him of that notion.

"No, she would've told us. She was still

planning the wedding."

Amarok refused to let his surge of optimism fade. "Was there anyone else in her life who might have reason to harm her?"

"Her ex-boyfriend still calls her. He's been trying to get her back. Maybe" — her voice broke — "maybe he decided he'd rather see her dead than married to another man."

Picking up the pen he'd used to jot down the number of the salon, Amarok rolled closer to his desk and waited, giving Loni a chance to bring her emotions under control. "How do you know he was trying to get her back?"

"She showed us his texts," Loni said with a sniff. "One said he'd love her till the day he died. We all thought it was pretty romantic, but . . . maybe it was obsessive and not romantic at all."

Amarok knew a little something about exes who were hard to get rid of. He seemed to run into Samantha Boyce, his ex-girlfriend, who'd moved back to town last winter, *everywhere.* To a point, that was to be expected. They lived in such a small town. But she'd also swing by the trooper post to bring him his favorite milk shake, to say "hi" or to relate some news about a member of her family he knew — her mother wasn't doing well but had asked about him; her brother was considering getting into law enforcement in Anchorage. She even approached him to dance with her whenever she could corner him at the Moosehead. "Do you know his name?" he asked Loni.

"Ward Something." She covered the phone, but he could hear her speaking to someone else. "Hey, do you know the name of Sierra's ex? The guy who texted her a few weeks ago about getting back with her?"

She sniffed again before coming back on the line. "Brothers," she said. "Ward Brothers."

"How did Sierra meet Ward?"

"I don't remember."

"How long was she with him?"

"I'm afraid I can't tell you that, either. I wish I could. I do know he's a telemarketer and he lives an hour away from Sierra's apartment. She told me she met up with him a week or so before she left and mentioned the trip to him."

"How long have they been broken up?"

"Three years. I know because that was when I started working here and Sierra had already met Allen by then."

"That gives me something to go on," Amarok said. "Thank you for your time."

"I don't mind helping. You're going to find

her, right?" She sounded worried, and he felt she had good reason to be. If he found anything at all, he was fairly certain it would be a body. Even that wasn't likely, given the abundance of wildlife in Alaska that could scatter the bones. But at least neither person of interest was from Hilltop or Hanover House. This time HH seemed to be in the clear.

"Yes. I'm going to find her," he replied, and prayed to God he could deliver on that promise.

7

When Evelyn met with the more dangerous inmates — those who'd committed violent crimes — she used a room where she was separated from her subject by plexiglass. It was a federal mandate that she take this precaution with any inmate who had a particular coding on his file. Although this policy had its critics, because some psychologists argued that no subject could be relied upon to speak freely under such "hostile" and "unnatural" conditions, she'd rather leave the men uncomfortable than risk her life. She never knew when one might try to throw feces at her, urinate on her or use a homemade blow dart to give her AIDS or hepatitis. Others couldn't be trusted not to attack her outright. It wasn't wise to take chances with certain inmates, even in the name of science.

Bobby Knox didn't require that much security, so she met him in one of the three small rooms that had no plexiglass, only a desk between them. He wasn't a killer; he was a con man. He'd bilked several hundred people out of millions by claiming he was going to build a boys ranch. He'd said that once the land was purchased and the school built, the state he was living in at the time would pay a certain amount for each child who attended, which was how his investors would receive their money back, with interest.

Some boys ranches were supported the way he'd described, so that part was plausible — except Bobby had no contract with the state and never planned to build anything. What he showed his investors was a forged document that, to the unsuspecting, looked pretty authentic.

Old ladies were particularly susceptible to his pitch. At forty-six, with light brown hair and dark brown eyes, he was fairly attractive and seemed trustworthy. They loved the idea of helping troubled teens while growing their retirement funds. But none of that ever happened. Bobby would string them along for three or four years with excuse after excuse as to why the building was delayed. Said he couldn't get this or that permit. That he needed more money, since one of his contractors had run off with a large sum. That he had to find a new site because toxic waste studies indicated the place he'd shown them wouldn't be suitable, after all. He said whatever he could to keep his investors patient or willing to write him another check. Then, when a vocal few began to get suspicious, he'd move on, only to run the same scam in a different state.

According to his file, he'd started running his scams about five years after dropping out of college with only a semester to go and stolen $5 million, mostly from people who were too old to continue earning, by the time law enforcement caught up with him.

"It says here that you were raised by your grandmother." Evelyn had met with Bobby once before but barely long enough to introduce herself and welcome him to Hanover House. He'd arrived a week ago, transferred from a federal correctional institution in California, which was where he'd run his last scam.

"Seriously?" he said. "Is that why I'm here? You want to go over everything in my file?"

"Do you have a problem with starting there?" she asked.

"No. Except I didn't need to come all the way to Alaska to confirm I was raised by my grandmother. We could've handled that over the phone."

She set her pen beside the pad of paper she'd been planning to use for notes. All she'd really intended to do was begin a conversation with him, and it appeared she'd done that. Today her goal was simply to gain some idea about the way he thought, so she could determine where he might fit best in her studies. "You don't believe you belong here?"

"You're kidding, right? I'm *nothing* like the crazy fuckers you've got locked up here. So why would *I* be of any interest to you?"

Because he was more like those "crazy fuckers" than he realized. What he'd left behind was a different kind of carnage, but he'd scored almost as high on the Hare Psychopathy Checklist as another inmate Evelyn worked with who was convicted of killing twenty-five prostitutes. That was what had attracted her interest. When Janice at the Bureau of Prisons brought his name to her attention and mentioned his outlandish score — 36 out of 40 — Evelyn had immediately requested he be transferred.

"How familiar are you with me and my work?" she asked instead of answering.

"I know you were attacked by an old boyfriend eons ago and won't let it go."

"Is that how you interpret my situation?"

"Pretty much."

He was being a smartass, purposely trying to upset her. But she merely smiled. "Then I think you've answered your own question."

His belly chain rattled as he jumped to his feet. "Don't give me that bullshit! I don't deserve this."

Evelyn clasped her hands in front of her. "What *do* you deserve, Mr. Knox?"

Seeming surprised by the question, he stepped closer to the desk between them. "Not twenty years! That's more than the typical rapist gets! And I shouldn't have to do my time in this godforsaken place."

"This is a brand-new, state-of-the-art facility where you don't have to deal with the overcrowding issues of so many other places."

"So? How many of my friends and family do you think will visit me here?"

She set the glasses she sometimes used to avoid eyestrain to one side. "How many visited you in California?" He was a user, someone who took advantage of other people. She couldn't imagine that evoked much loyalty among his friends, but perhaps his family was supportive. Or he had a girlfriend.

"I don't want to talk about it."

That meant he didn't get many visitors even when he was in California, but he was the one who'd brought it up. "Why don't we start with this, then. When's the last time you saw your parents?"

"I don't have any parents. You just asked me if my grandmother raised me, didn't you?"

"There could be a lot of reasons for that. It doesn't necessarily mean your mother was entirely out of the picture."

He dropped back in his seat. "Yeah, well, as it turns out, she wasn't. My mother lived with us."

"So why did your grandmother raise you?"

"That's not in my file? I'm surprised. They got everything else in there. My mother had Down syndrome, okay? Couldn't even take care of herself. Happy now?"

"What about your father?"

"Who knows where he is?" he said with an agitated shrug. "Or *who* he is. She was raped. My grandmother thought it was the weird, quiet dude who lived down the street. But the cops could never prove it."

Evelyn couldn't help feeling some empathy for him. As heinous as the actions of the men she studied were, they often had tragic stories themselves. "How old was she when this happened?" she asked gently.

"Sixteen."

"So . . . your mother was more like a sibling."

"Yes."

"Does she still live with your grandmother?"

"No. She died several years ago. In case you haven't heard, people with Down syndrome don't have a long life-span."

Evelyn ignored his condescending tone. She'd known that people with Down syndrome didn't live as long as most others, but their life-spans still varied. "Do you miss her?"

"No. It was a relief. She was an embarrassment to me."

"That's *brutally* honest . . ."

He grinned. "Not bad for a natural-born liar, huh?"

She picked up her pen again. "What do you call your grandmother?"

The smile slid from his face. "My grandmother's dead, too."

"Then what *did* you call her?"

"What does it matter?"

He'd defrauded people who were probably a great deal like his grandmother. Did he do it in spite of loving her? Or did he do it because he hated her? If he'd used her name, they probably weren't close. If he'd called her Grandma or used a nickname, chances were greater that they'd shared a real bond. The nature-versus-nurture battle still waged when it came to human behavior, so it was important to gain an accurate picture of what his early development had been like. "You're new here, and I'm trying to get to know you. Why? Is that question out-of-bounds?"

He hesitated but couldn't seem to figure out how answering her question would hurt him. "I called her Mom. What does that tell you? Nothing." He rolled his eyes. "You don't really care about me."

No, she cared about the innocent victims who constantly fell prey to people like him. She was working for *their* benefit, not his. But he saw the world only from his own perspective. That was the one thing that remained consistent, no matter which inmate she was studying — their absolute narcissism. "Is there something else you'd rather be doing than talking to me?"

"Maybe. I was watching TV."

She closed his file and stood. "Then I'll let you return to it." With enough time, he'd probably be eager to talk. At the very least, their sessions would give him an opportunity to get out of his cell. Most of the inmates were anxious to relieve the tedium. So she didn't feel the need to push him. She'd simply wait until he was ready.

He seemed taken aback that she'd give up so easily. "That's it?"

"That's it. We don't coerce anyone here, Mr. Knox. We try to keep things as pleasant as possible."

"Pleasant?" he echoed. "You call having my cell searched in the first week and some douchebag guard tearing up my grandmother's picture *pleasant*?"

She felt her eyebrows draw together. "What are you talking about? The correctional officers have no business destroying your personal property."

"Do *they* know that?"

"They most certainly do. Which guard are you talking about?"

"It's not like I know anyone here, but the tag on his uniform read: 'A. Smith.' "

"Andy." The CO she'd just seen in the elevator, the one who'd acted so quickly to save her life last winter. "Why'd he do that?" she asked. "Were you talking back, resisting the search, causing problems?"

"No! I was sketching a picture from that photograph. When he took it, I tried to get it back, but he tore it to bits. Just to spite me. Just to show me he could."

"Was anyone else there to see this?"

"Another guard. He didn't seem happy about it. I heard him mutter something that sounded like he was angry. But it was too late."

"Who was the second guard?"

"Guy in the next cell called him Tex, but that wasn't what was on his uniform. It was a long last name, one I couldn't even begin to pronounce."

"Tex Wojciechowski."

"Yeah. That must be it. I doubt there could be two guys named Tex in this place."

"And you're saying you did nothing to provoke Officer Smith . . ."

"*Nothing.* Ask Tex."

"I plan to." She pushed the button that would signal to the COs that it was time to escort Knox back to his cell. They came and got him, but she remained, sitting at that desk, staring off into space.

She'd never been able to decide why she didn't particularly like Officer Smith. He'd been friendly from the start, always eager to please. She'd never heard anyone else speak ill of him. And she owed him her life! Who could say what might've happened if he hadn't arrived at Amarok's house when he did?

Bishop would've completed the frontal

lobotomy he'd been about to start, so she wouldn't be sitting here today. She'd be like Beth, his sister. In an institution. Unable to care for herself. Or worse. She could be somewhere with Bishop, a constant but helpless victim. That was why she'd never allowed herself to mention her distrust of Andy Smith to Amarok or anyone else. She never allowed herself to think about it, either. She had nothing concrete on which to pin such negative emotions. She just knew he made her uncomfortable. But that seemed so unfair, so ungrateful.

She told herself that after all the good he'd done she should ignore the incident with Bobby Knox. Bobby was no saint, or he wouldn't be in here. But that photograph probably meant a great deal to him. Maybe his grandmother was the only person he'd ever cared about. Maybe she was the only one who'd ever cared about him. It was callous, even cruel, of Smith to destroy it. What would make him do that?

She needed to find out. So when she went back to her office, she asked Penny to summon Tex Wojciechowski. If the situation was really as Knox had presented it, Smith had to be warned that if he wanted to keep his job he'd better not act that way in her prison again.

■ ■ ■ ■

Amarok dreaded going over to the motel. Leland's friends had left him a message saying they'd finally given Leland a sleeping pill to get him to settle down after being up all night. But Amarok knew he'd be demanding answers again soon and didn't have a whole lot to tell him. Investigations took time, and Amarok was just getting started. But, thanks to Loni, he had a couple of hopeful leads, and he had to confront Sierra's brother at some point.

Besides, he had to get a list of people who'd stayed at The Shady Lady over the past several days. If Allen Call or Ward Brothers had come to town, maybe he'd find some trace of them.

As he entered the front office, he eyed the SUV sitting outside the motel room where Leland and his friends were staying.

Margaret was there, as usual. Her daughter had left for college in the Lower 48 in August, so Callista was no longer around to relieve her.

"Hey, Sergeant. Hell of a storm last night, huh?"

"It was a bad one, all right. At least it blew over quickly."

"Until the next one rolls in. Weather folks are saying it's going to be a rough winter."

"Winters here are always rough."

"I guess that's true." She lowered her voice, even though they were the only ones in the office. "What's going on with the men in Cabin Eight?"

Amarok lifted his eyebrows in question, but he could guess where Margaret was going.

"I saw you out in the lot with them, before they came in to book their room. They were really upset last night. I stopped by to make sure they had some food and water, and . . . Well, you don't often see a grown man cry."

Amarok hated to throw the whole town into a panic. They'd assume that Hanover House was once again to blame, and that wouldn't do Evelyn any favors. The murder of Sandy Ledstetter eight months ago had not been forgotten and wouldn't be for some time. There'd been other tragedies, but Sandy was the only one the community claimed as its own, and Evelyn had felt the strain on her relationships here ever since.

Amarok wanted Evelyn to be comfortable so she'd stay, but he had to talk to people, needed the extra eyes and ears. He couldn't keep the news that a young woman had gone missing to himself. Maybe someone had seen something and mention of the missing girl would bring that person forward. That was largely how police work progressed in Alaska — by informants.

"We've got a problem," he admitted.

"I gathered that much. Please tell me it's not another murder."

"I don't know. Leland, the man who was probably crying last night, can't find his sister. He left her at a cabin while he went hunting with his friends. When they returned, she was gone."

Margaret's eyes widened. "What could've happened to her?"

"Hard to say. With the storm, I couldn't really look for her."

"So what brings you *here*?"

He took a sheet of paper from his pocket. "Do you recognize either of these faces?"

She frowned as she studied the pictures he'd pulled off Facebook. "No."

"What about their names? Allen Call or Ward Brothers? Has anyone by either name checked in over the past week?"

"I don't think so, and I'm sure I'd remember. Until last night, business was slow. But just to be safe . . ." She quickly scanned her logbook, only to shake her head a few seconds later. "Nope. No one registered by either name."

Shit. "I knew it couldn't be that easy." He sighed. "Can you make me a copy of your logbook? I need to see everyone who's rented a room in the past two weeks."

"Of course. I'll do that right now. But who are the men you were asking about?"

"Romantic interests of the girl who's gone missing."

"You don't think . . . I mean, I hate to suggest it, but . . ."

"It wasn't her brother. He and his friends were together all day and their story's consistent."

"I wasn't going to say that. I was thinking about Hanover House. Have you checked to make sure all those psychos are still locked up?"

He scowled at her. "Don't even go there," he said, and left the office to walk down and knock on Leland's door.

Peter opened the door and blinked at the weak sunlight that somehow managed to pierce through the clouds. "I'm so glad to see you. Have you found her?"

"No. And I have to ask . . ."

"Is that the sergeant?" A shirtless Leland jumped out of bed and grabbed the door, inserting himself between Amarok and his friend. "What have you learned?"

Amarok felt terrible — for him *and* his

buddies. He hadn't been able to let Leland take any of the luggage, had insisted he leave the scene exactly as it was. Assuming they'd swung by Quigley's to pick up a toothbrush and a few other toiletries, they had only what they'd purchased and the clothes they'd been wearing to hunt. "I heard that her fiancé didn't treat her right," he said. "Did you know about that?"

Leland frowned as he raked a hand through his hair, which was sticking up all over the place — further evidence that he'd had a terrible night. "No. What do you mean? I like Allen. He's cool."

"Apparently, he wasn't always so cool to your sister."

He gaped at Amarok. *"Who told you that?"*

"The women who work with her at the salon."

"He might have a bit of a temper. He's no pushover. But Allen would never do *this.*"

"Are you sure?"

He opened his mouth as though he was about to confirm it; then he shook his head. "No. Right now, I'm not sure of anything. All I know is that she's gone and I have to get her back. I've promised my parents and everyone else back home that . . ." His words drifted off.

That it wasn't as dire here as it seemed.

Amarok could guess how the rest of the sentence was supposed to go. "I understand."

Leland peered up at the sky. "The storm seems to have cleared."

"For the time being."

"That's good enough for me. I'll get dressed and go back up to the cabin to look for her."

Amarok caught his arm before he could so much as take a step. "I'm afraid I have to ask you to stay away from the cabin. Maybe you were too upset to notice, but I put my own locks on it. You can't get in, and I've notified the rental company, who's contacting the owners. If there's anything of evidentiary value up there, I don't want it ruined."

"You're saying it's a crime scene. . . ."

Amarok cringed inside. *Damn it.* Here he was again. "Yeah. For the next few days at least."

"So what are we supposed to do?" He gestured at his friends. "Just sit on our asses and wait for you?"

"I'm afraid that's all you can do," he said.

8

"Can you believe it?" After speaking with Tex and confirming that Andy Smith had indeed torn up the picture of Bobby Knox's grandmother — for no particular reason that Tex could surmise — Evelyn had called Amarok and was lucky enough to catch him at his trooper post.

"Tex saw the whole thing?" Amarok asked. "Confirmed there was no inciting event?"

"Yes! Tex told me he was floored. He tried to stop Andy, but it was too late. And then, when Tex got mad about what Andy had done instead of being amused by it, Andy seemed irritated. Said something like, 'What's your problem? It's only a damn picture!' "

"Surely he had to understand it was more than a 'damn' picture to Bobby Knox."

"He didn't seem to care! That's what bothered Tex. He said he couldn't believe Andy could be such a jerk."

"Are you going to talk to Andy about it?"

"I can't decide. Tex turned him in, so Warden Ferris has been dealing with the situation. Maybe I should leave it there."

When Amarok didn't respond right away, she knew something had stolen his attention. "Amarok?"

"Sorry. Just saw something on my desk."

"Something about the investigation?"

"No, I guess Samantha came by while I was out."

"Again?" Samantha had been trying to get back with Amarok ever since she'd returned to town. And someone — Evelyn could only guess it was Samantha — had been leaving hateful notes on her car, telling her she wasn't wanted, to go home to Boston and never come back, that sort of thing. Evelyn had found two so far, one when she came out of the Moosehead and one when she came out of her and Amarok's house to go to work one day a couple of weeks ago.

"Apparently," Amarok said.

"What'd she leave you?"

"A note."

"And? What does it say?"

"Nothing much."

"Read it to me."

" 'Sad I missed you. Made your favorite

brownies. Wink. Will try to drop them off later.' "

She hadn't left them because he wasn't there; she wanted to see him. "What does she think she's doing?" Evelyn asked. "She knows you're with me!"

"I'm not interested in her, so it doesn't matter, anyway," he said. "Back to the CO who tore up that picture. If he's already been written up, that should probably be the end of it — unless he does something else."

Evelyn was reluctant to let Amarok change the subject so easily. Samantha's overtures were really starting to get on her nerves. But it wasn't as though he encouraged her. When they were all at the Moosehead together, he made it plain that he was with Evelyn. He never even gave Samantha a second look, so Evelyn couldn't fault him. It was just enraging that Samantha always tried to engage him. "Except Smith wasn't written up," she said. She figured they had enough going on without having an argument about Samantha. "I called Warden Ferris after I talked to Tex. He told me he would've taken stronger measures, made sure the incident was reported in Andy's file, but he didn't want to damage Andy's career if he'd simply acted in a stupid, thoughtless moment. If he'd let the stress of the job get to him, for instance. No one's had any other trouble with Andy, so it's not as if he has a track record of acting inappropriately. And Ferris said Andy felt terrible about the incident, that he apologized profusely, claimed he didn't know what had gotten into him and promised it would never happen again."

There was another slight pause before Amarok responded. "That doesn't satisfy you?"

It probably should, but it didn't, and she couldn't decide why. "Not entirely."

"You think he deserves some sort of punishment? Being reprimanded by the warden isn't enough?"

"I guess it would be if . . . I don't know, if I could *understand* his behavior. To me, what Andy did was just plain cruel, and that makes me angry. He should have more compassion!"

"For a killer, babe? Does Bobby have any compassion for Andy — or anyone else?"

"Bobby isn't a killer."

"He's in prison for a reason."

"He's a con man," she grudgingly admitted.

"Which means . . ."

Feeling defeated, she sank back into her

chair. "He swindled a lot of old ladies out of their life savings."

"And *that* isn't cruel?"

"It is. Especially when you consider that he was raised by his grandmother. But I expect more from my guards than I do from my inmates!"

"Then have a talk with Andy. Let him know."

She sat forward again. "Won't that seem petty after what he did for me last year? I would not be sitting here right now if not for him. Instead, I could be in the worst situation imaginable. I owe him a great deal."

"And you have to remember that a CO's job is hard. The inmates are often belligerent, will say or do anything to get under the skin of the people around them, especially those in charge. For all we know, Bobby muttered something that set Andy off, something Tex didn't hear."

"So I should let it go."

"Give him the benefit of the doubt this time, but keep an eye on him. If he does anything else that's less than admirable, you can feel justified in going harder on him in the future."

Pursing her lips, she rubbed the scar on her neck.

"I would've lost you, if not for him," Amarok added. "I can't forget that."

"Neither can I," she said. "That's why I feel so ungrateful, so disloyal, telling you I don't like him."

"You don't *like* him? You mean generally — outside of your reaction to this one incident?"

"Yes, generally. All the time. If I see him and can do it without being too obvious, I go the other way."

"That's sort of extreme, isn't it?"

"It might be, but he makes my skin crawl. Isn't that terrible?"

"I'd say it's . . . baffling. You don't have a reason?"

"None. Nothing I can explain, anyway."

"Why have you never mentioned this to me before?"

"Because it's far too negative a reaction to the guy who saved my life! And I haven't spent a great deal of time thinking about it."

"You don't run into him very often, do you? We see him at the Moosehead occasionally, but other than stopping to say hello, he's never bothered us."

She pressed her thumb and finger to the bridge of her nose. It'd been a rough twenty-four hours. Maybe she was just reacting to the difficulty of *her* job. "That's true. I don't know what's wrong with me. I won't say anything to Andy about Bobby Knox, since Ferris already has. But Andy had better not pull anything like that again."

"There's no one quite like you," he said.

She could hear the smile in his voice. "What do you mean?"

"No one else is so quick to do battle over any injustice."

"You hate that about me. It's the reason I can't walk away from Hanover House. I can't leave the fight to others."

"I don't hate *anything* about you, and I'm not sure I want you to leave Hanover House."

"You're the one who's always suggesting I go into private practice!"

"To keep you safe. But I'm afraid that if you go into private practice, you won't do it here in Alaska."

He was right; she'd always planned to go back to Boston. As much as she loved him, she wasn't sure she was willing to give up that dream. So she changed the subject. She hated knowing she couldn't commit to him and that Samantha Boyce was waiting in the wings. "What are you learning about Sierra Yerbowitz?"

"From what I hear, her fiancé isn't the

nicest guy in the world. I tried to call him and got his voicemail, so I haven't had a chance to form my own opinion yet. She also has an ex-boyfriend who's been pushing to get her back. I have a call in to him, too. I hope whoever's guilty is one of them."

"That would make our lives easier. Can you check with the airlines, get the manifests for any flights coming into Anchorage over the past week?"

"I'm working on that. I've already gone by The Shady Lady. Our friend Andy and a couple of other COs stayed over last night because they couldn't drive home with the road closed. The contractor putting the finishing touches on the new section at Hanover House and several of his men took the rest of the rooms. But there was no one who raised any red flags. There were no strangers."

"It's so puzzling. . . ."

"Everything seems normal at Hanover House?"

Although he asked the question casually, she tensed. "Yes. They count the inmates every morning and every evening, as you know. But I had them count twice today. There've been no problems here. This has nothing to do with us, Amarok."

"Good. Because if someone else from

Hilltop gets hurt, I'm afraid I'll have to put down a local uprising. Everyone will be calling for the closure of the prison. I doubt the government would listen to a mere five hundred people, but if they get enough press . . . who knows? In any case, that wouldn't be good for you or your work."

"I agree. The relationship between Hanover House and the community is already strained, and since I'm the figurehead here, that means my relationships are strained, too. Sandy's mother won't even speak to me."

"Try not to take it personally," he said. "She doesn't understand that Bishop's release was out of your hands, that you were the only one fighting to keep him behind bars."

She probably *did* know that. She just didn't care. Sandy's family, and others in the area, blamed Evelyn for Sandy's death — another reason Evelyn had been struggling. It was almost impossible to ignore that negative energy. The notes Samantha was leaving on her car — if, indeed, it was Samantha — didn't help. "Too bad I couldn't stop him from getting out."

"That's water under the bridge. Let's not dwell on it."

"I agree. We have plenty to worry about in

the present."

"I'll find out what happened to Sierra Yerbowitz. Don't worry."

"Thanks," she said, and meant it. The longer Sierra's disappearance went unsolved, the more difficult Evelyn's life would become.

Jasper's heart leapt into his throat. His headlights showed another set of tracks in the snow, very close to where he'd turned into the woods to stash the bodies this morning. What was going on? Why would anyone else have any reason to be out this way? It'd been desolate earlier! But there weren't many people moving about this morning, even in town. He'd been driving to work at the tail end of that big storm.

So . . . had someone been following him?

He didn't think so. He would've noticed. Although it was daylight at the time, it had still been overcast and gloomy. He would've seen headlights.

More likely someone had spotted his tracks *after* he'd left the bodies and followed them to see where they led. Perhaps a couple of kids after school, trying to relieve the boredom. But even something that innocuous could destroy him. He hadn't been able to stash Kat and the other woman very far off the road, couldn't risk getting stuck while he had two corpses in his possession. If he hadn't shown up for work and people started looking for him, they'd find his vehicle, even if he tried to leave the area on foot — and they'd discover what he'd done. But he'd been so careful to avoid that possibility he might've created a problem that would have essentially the same result.

"Son of a bitch." He checked his rearview mirror. No one seemed to be coming from either direction, so he slowed down and made the turn again. He hoped his day wasn't about to get worse. He was already fuming at the two dead women who were causing him so much trouble. And at Tex, who should've kept his mouth shut, not to mention the warden, who'd been such a hard-ass although Jasper hadn't done anything wrong. There was no law against tearing up a picture! He was also angry with Leland for making a fuss last night and keeping him awake, at Amarok for daring to stand up to him and at Evelyn for tempting him to move to Alaska in the first place. It was her fault he was here. She'd all but dared him to come after her with all those TV appearances. He wasn't about to let that challenge go unanswered.

But if someone had found the bodies, she

might have the last laugh. . . .

Should he leave the corpses where they were? Not take the chance of trying to recover them?

Amarok could be there, waiting for him. If that was the case, there'd be no way to escape suspicion. Unless he could get out of town right now and disappear, running into the sergeant out here might unravel everything. Then Amarok would look closer — might even try to get a sample of his DNA, which would reveal his true identity.

He stomped on the brake and stared as far into the distance as his headlights allowed. He saw nothing, only darkness. But that didn't mean anything. Was he being foolish to try to recover the bodies?

Perhaps, but he wanted them back. Which meant he was going to take the risk.

He pulled his handgun from its holster. *Fuck Amarok.* If the trooper was here, he'd shoot him on sight, claim one last victim, no matter what happened afterwards. At least he'd have the satisfaction of knowing he'd gotten Evelyn's man. From her perspective, losing Amarok was probably worse than dying herself, so there was that.

He rolled down his window so the glass wouldn't shatter all over him or provide evidence after the fact, and rolled very slowly forward, his prison-issue GLOCK in his right hand. He'd simply pull up and shoot.

Boom! Amarok wouldn't even know what hit him.

The snow crunched beneath his tires, crusty after the few brief hours of warmer weather. "Come on." Jasper felt his senses grow more alert, felt the old excitement rise in his blood. He'd wanted to kill Amarok since he'd found out Amarok existed. Was the long wait finally over?

The tracks went almost to the bodies before suddenly veering off to the left.

Jasper followed them. He needed to figure out if he still had company. But that seemed less and less likely. Whoever it was had driven past the bodies to a small, treeless depression — probably a frozen pond, although it was hard to tell, since he didn't know the area — and done a few donuts in the snow.

Jasper guessed it was kids, all right. A couple of hooligans, as his mother would've called them, out raising hell. He'd gotten himself all worked up for nothing.

He was feeling much better when he returned to the bodies, but his relief didn't last long. When he got out of the truck, he could see that they weren't undisturbed, as he'd thought a second earlier. Whoever had come in here had swung too wide on the way out and run over both corpses.

Jasper had left his headlights on. He could see the tire impression going right over the tarp. That alone probably wouldn't have been a big deal. The driver didn't seem to have noticed, or Amarok would be here. But the rear axle of that vehicle must've caught Kat's hair, which was spilling out the end of the tarp, and wound it around before yanking it off — because a huge chunk of her scalp was missing.

Evelyn had stayed late to compensate for the time she'd missed yesterday. She still wasn't caught up, had myriad tasks waiting for her — files to review and update, paperwork that required her approval, brain scans that needed to be analyzed and a summary report she owed Janice at the BOP, to name a few. But Amarok had called to check on her and said they might be getting more bad weather. He wanted her to head home before the full brunt of the storm could hit.

She was nearly finished packing up her briefcase when she remembered that letter from Tim Fitzpatrick. She was tempted to leave it in her drawer, to deal with it once Amarok found Sierra Yerbowitz and she wasn't looking at another catastrophe. But as of this last week they had Jasper's DNA, and if Fitzpatrick was innocent he might be relieved to know they could now test it against what'd been found at the site of Charlotte's murder. *If* the police would cooperate. Detective Dressler, the detective who'd worked that case, was so sure he had the right man, he wouldn't be eager to delve back into the evidence. Amarok had already called him, and he'd said he'd get back to them.

That was on Monday, and they still hadn't heard.

She sat down again and sliced open the envelope.

Evelyn, please. I've written to the Innocence Project. They're not interested in my case, but you could make someone take another look. Use your influence. Help me. I don't care what the evidence suggests — or how I behaved with you. I agree that doesn't make me look good, but I haven't killed anyone!

Tim

Evelyn checked the time. Boston was four hours ahead of Hilltop. It was too late to call anyone on the East Coast tonight. But perhaps, in the morning, she should reach Detective Dressler, try to push him a little.

Her phone rang.

She snatched up the handset. "Dr. Talbot."

"I thought you were leaving," Amarok said dryly.

She smiled. He knew her well, knew how easily she could get distracted. "I *am* leaving. What are you doing?"

"Still canvassing the town, flashing pictures of Sierra, asking if anyone's seen her."

"Any luck?"

"Samantha said she came into her store to buy ammo three days ago with her brother and his friends."

"She told you that when she dropped off the brownies?"

"I actually went over there."

That he'd gone to see his ex-girlfriend, even in the line of duty, bothered Evelyn. It wasn't just that Samantha made no secret of her desire to get Amarok back; it was also that Evelyn feared Samantha was a better fit for him.

Careful not to reveal her jealousy — she understood how tedious it would be to feel he was being harangued over the fact that an ex couldn't seem to move on — Evelyn kept her voice as normal as possible. "That's it?"

"So far."

He sounded tired. "Have you had anything to eat?" she asked.

"Not yet."

"Swing by the house in an hour. I'll have dinner ready."

"That's okay. I'll grab a bite later. I'm going to keep at it."

"Are you getting discouraged?"

"A little," he admitted.

"Why?"

There was a slight pause. Then he said, "I talked to Allen Call and Ward Brothers."

"And?"

"They both have airtight alibis."

9

Amarok sat at the kitchen table, listening to the latest storm moan and cry as he drank a cold beer and stared into the darkness of the living room. Since Bishop's attack last February, Evelyn had started leaving the hall light on when she went to bed, so there'd been no need for him to turn on any lights when he and Makita came in. He could see well enough.

After shaking off the snow and cold, Makita had gone to lie in the corner. He kept eyeing Amarok as if to say, *Aren't you going to bed? Isn't it time for us to go in with Evelyn?* The poor dog couldn't close his eyes for fear he'd miss his cue. But despite Amarok's exhaustion, he wasn't ready to call it a day. As he sat there, heavy coat and boots still on since he was too tired to remove them, he kept thinking he *had* to be missing something.

What could've happened to Sierra Yerbowitz?

He felt terrible for Leland, who'd had to break the news to his parents earlier. Leland had practically begged Amarok to give him some answers. But after spending the whole day trying to find something that might explain Sierra's disappearance, Amarok didn't know any more than he had before. No one had seen her since she and the men had eaten lunch and picked up a few things in town before they drove to the cabin. It was almost as if she'd disappeared into thin air.

Amarok unbuttoned his coat and took a long pull on his becr. Maybe when he returned to the cabin, he'd see some clue he'd missed. He hadn't been able to go out there today. The storm had dumped so much snow in the area, it would've been too hard to get through. And since no one else could get out there, either, he'd decided to see what he could learn in town first. That way he'd be armed with a little more information when he went back, which might make him view the scene differently.

He'd never dreamed he'd come up empty, especially after the hope he'd felt when he'd heard about Allen Call and Ward Brothers. . . .

"Aren't you coming to bed?"

Amarok glanced up to see Evelyn yawning as she wandered down the hall wearing one of his Alaska State Trooper T-shirts and nothing else. She was squinting at the light and her hair was mussed from sleeping, but he found her sexy as hell, the most beautiful woman he'd ever laid eyes on.

His chest tightened at the thought that she might pack up and leave one day. The more terrible things that happened here, the more likely that became. If any more of the locals grew hostile toward her, she wouldn't be able to tolerate living in Hilltop.

"I was just having a drink, unwinding a bit," he said.

"And trying to figure out what happened to Sierra Yerbowitz?"

He lifted his beer to signal that she'd guessed correctly.

She pulled out a chair and sat across from him. "Do you want to talk about it?"

"There isn't much to say. No one had anything against her. The only two people in her life who *might* have had some reason to harm her can prove they didn't."

She pushed her hair out of her face. "Then it has to be her brother. Or his friends."

Amarok shook his head. "It wasn't them.

Leland is completely torn up by her disappearance. And his friends were with him every minute. They all say the same thing, tell the exact same story."

"They could be colluding."

"No, I don't get that feeling at all."

"Then Sierra must've gone somewhere . . ."

"Where?" he asked. "She was at a remote cabin in a rugged environment she'd never been to before, in the middle of a terrible storm. She had no phone, no vehicle. They didn't see anyone else in the area the entire time they were there — even when they were out hunting. And they claim no one could've followed them."

"So someone took her. She wouldn't just wander off on her own."

"That's what Leland says, too, and he knows her best. But if that's the case, why didn't whoever it was strike sooner? They were at the cabin for three days without incident."

"Someone stumbled on the opportunity?"

"Way the hell out there?"

"How else can you explain it? You told me an ax was used to break in. That's forced entry."

"It could've been *her* using that ax. How do you know she didn't accidentally lock herself out and force her way back into the house?"

"I *don't* know that," she admitted. "I suppose it's possible. But what about the vomit in the shed?"

"What about it?" He finally shucked off his coat. "She could've been coming down with the flu."

"Or that vomit means something else."

"Like what?"

Evelyn flinched as if she didn't even want to think it, let alone say it. "Never mind. That would be a stretch."

"Say what's on your mind," he prodded. As beautiful as Evelyn was, he loved her as much for her intelligence, respected her opinion.

"I'd rather not risk sending your investigation in the wrong direction. But I'll say this. The shed is an odd place to be sick."

"Not necessarily. It's better than throwing up in the cabin."

"When you're sick, you're sick. You don't get to select the spot."

"Maybe it took a lot of effort to hack down the door and the timing just worked out that way."

She nibbled at her bottom lip, which — as tired and upset as he was — still made him want to pull her to him and kiss her, maybe carry her into the bedroom. Being with Evelyn provided a release from the frustration and worry. Making love to her convinced him that everything was going to be okay — until reality barged in again.

"Were there any signs that she wasn't feeling well in the cabin? Any blankets lying around, cold compresses, discarded tissues?"

"None."

"There wasn't even a bowl near the couch in case she needed to throw up?"

"Nothing like that. And not only did she pack her bags, she packed everyone else's. Left all the luggage by the door."

"She wouldn't feel like doing that if she had the flu or was feeling nauseous," she mused.

"She might've powered through."

Evelyn looked even more worried. "She obviously wanted to leave as soon as possible."

He'd been trying to keep an open mind, but he had to agree. "The question is why. Was she scared of the storm?"

"Could be. Or something else. I mean, a woman wouldn't pack up for her brother's friends, two grown men, otherwise."

Talking it out helped him solidify his own thoughts and opinions. "She must've had a compelling reason."

"You're going back to the cabin tomorrow, right?"

"If this new storm lets up."

She rubbed her arms as if she felt a chill. "Maybe you should take me with you."

She wasn't a forensic profiler, but he was willing to bet she knew as much, or more, about criminal behavior as anyone in the world. As far as he was concerned, having her there could only be an advantage. "Okay."

She came over and helped him pull off his boots. Then she pushed him back in the chair and undid his pants.

When she went down on him, he groaned and dropped his head back. "That's good," he said. "But aren't you too tired?"

She didn't respond. Her tongue moved over him, making him hard as a rock.

He got his second wind as he slid his fingers into her hair.

God, he loved her.

If only he knew she'd always be there. . . .

Somehow they got through the trickiest part of the drive, but that was because of Amarok's determination and his experience maneuvering a vehicle in bad conditions. There were several instances when Evelyn thought they'd be forced to turn back.

He probably *would've* given up in favor of visiting tomorrow or the next day, when the cabin was more accessible, but they were expecting the harsh weather to continue through the weekend.

"You're quiet today," he said. Only the wipers made any noise, working to shove aside the heavy flakes of snow bombarding the windshield. "You okay?"

"Fine." She adjusted the heat. "Just wondering why anyone would have reason to come out here this time of year."

"Leland and his friends have hunting permits good through the fifteenth. Anglers come here, too. Silver salmon run through November."

"From what I've seen, the number of hunters and fishermen goes down in September, along with the tourists," she said, but she hadn't been referring to people who'd have a legitimate reason to visit the cabin. She'd been trying to imagine what a dangerous person like a serial killer would have to be thinking in order to be interested in a place like the cabin. What would be the draw?

Privacy. They liked privacy. Thrived *on it.*

But finding prey came first and because most serial killers — 80 percent — were men and those men were often driven by a sexual motive as well as a deep lust for killing, women were far more likely to become victims. Still, it was hard to believe there was a predator targeting hunting cabins. The kind of killers who didn't leave a trace were careful to strike only when they felt confident of success. Evelyn doubted any of them would view a place where one was more likely to find men with guns than women as a promising location.

"We have fewer visitors once it starts to turn cold, but" — Amarok glanced over at her — "what are you saying?"

"I'm saying we're probably dealing with a crime of opportunity."

"A remote cabin provides an opportunity? Other than a handful of people, none of whom I can place in Alaska, I can't figure out how anyone even realized she was out here."

"Which is why I believe we're looking at someone who lives in the area, someone who came across her when she was alone and vulnerable."

His frown told her he didn't want to hear that the kidnapper or killer was local. But the fact that he didn't argue suggested he'd already come to the same conclusion. "*If* she was taken in the first place and didn't go out searching for her brother."

Evelyn loosened the chest restraint on her seat belt. "She would've worn her coat and boots if she went out searching for her brother."

The stubborn set to his jaw indicated that he didn't care to hear that, either. "Unless she was on drugs and wasn't thinking straight."

"You told me Leland said they weren't doing drugs. That they didn't have any."

"Doesn't make it true. I haven't searched their luggage yet. Didn't have time the other night, and I didn't want to remove or change anything before I could take a closer look at the scene as a whole."

"This must be a nightmare for Leland," she muttered as she imagined how confused and upset Sierra's brother had to be.

The growl of the engine deepened as Amarok shifted into Low. "Peter and Ted have to be hating life, too. Not only has a member of their party gone missing, but until I clear their luggage, they have almost nothing, other than the clothes on their backs. They paid a lot to experience Alaska — and got this."

"Even if drugs *are* at the root of it, that won't make things any easier on them," she mused.

"It'll make things a hell of a lot easier on us," he grumbled.

Such a simple, straightforward explanation was better than believing they had a murder on their hands. But the vomit in the woodshed bothered her and had from the first. It didn't seem consistent with someone getting high and wandering off. Recreational drugs typically didn't induce vomiting. And surely Leland would know, would've said something, if his sister had access to stronger opiates, like heroin or Demerol.

They probably had some alcohol at the cabin, however.

She decided to hope for that.

Once they'd parked and she climbed out, the snow went up to her knees. While wading through it, she wished for a few minutes of bright, warm sunlight. It was midday, after all. Even a glimmer would've felt nice. But the sky remained stubbornly overcast, and everything looked dark and shadowy despite the hour, making it difficult to spot the kind of small yet important details they needed to see.

She stopped before reaching the steps and tilted her head back to study the small A-frame cabin. "This is pretty rustic."

Amarok, who'd gone ahead of her to forge a path, was already at the porch, which was more of a deep overhang. "Guys who come here want to see what it's like to rough it," he said over his shoulder. "That's partly why so many choose to hunt or fish the interior, where they face harsher weather and fewer amenities. A lot of the cabins can't be reached without a bush plane."

Privacy. As she gazed at the cabin, that word popped into her head again. Provided a psychopath already had a victim, he'd like this remote location. *Jasper* would like this location.

She supposed it was natural that he'd come to mind at the first hint of trouble. After what she'd been through, she was predisposed to think the worst. She had to ask herself if he could be back. Somehow he'd learned his mother had been somewhat friendly to Amarok, so he'd killed both his parents, immediately cut off that avenue of information. But it had cost *him* something, too. Now he no longer had their help or their financial support, and no inheritance, either. They'd left everything to charity, since they couldn't name him, their only son, in their will.

He had to be angry, looking for revenge.

No doubt that was one of the reasons her panic attacks had returned. She knew it was just a matter of time before Jasper reappeared, and the longer it went the more anxious she became.

He was too smart to kidnap someone like Sierra, though — someone whose disappearance would be reported to Amarok.

Unless that was part of the game . . .

A tremor ran through her despite the warmth of her heavy coat, boots, scarf, gloves and earmuffs. Emotionally, she wasn't strong enough to face Jasper right now, wasn't where she'd been even a year ago. She needed to fix that, needed to get ready — and *stay* ready. But she'd been trying! She couldn't seem to recover on her own, and since she didn't feel she could get counseling, she wasn't sure what to do.

"What are you thinking?" Amarok had opened the door and was standing in the gap, waiting for her.

She chose not to say anything about Jasper, didn't want to bring up something so unrelated to what the facts currently suggested. "I'm thinking someone could be out to sabotage my efforts at Hanover House by making it look like we've got another problem. People will assume this is connected to me and what I'm doing in Alaska, since all the other problems have been, too."

"Who would go so far as to sabotage you?" he asked. "Fitzpatrick tried to discredit you, but that wasn't exactly sabotage. He was trying to take over at Hanover House."

"What about Sandy Ledstetter's father or brother?" Like Sandy's mother, both men glared daggers at her if she happened to see them at the Moosehead or elsewhere. She could feel the entire family's enmity. Again, the nasty notes someone had been leaving on her car came to mind, but Amarok wasn't aware of those. He didn't know how she was being treated, either. She was careful not to complain to him about smaller slights or snubs. She didn't want him feeling he had to stick up for her.

"I've known Davie and Junior my whole life, Evelyn. They'd never do anything like that. What makes more sense is that all the publicity surrounding Hanover House has drawn a previously unknown predator to the area."

She could easily imagine psychopaths being enticed by the challenge and notoriety of killing in the very shadow of the institution meant to arm the innocent against them. She and Amarok, at various points in the past, had discussed the possibility, which was probably why he mentioned it now. "You'd believe that over sabotage?"

He waved her off. "Even that's a stretch.

We haven't yet established that we *have* a predator, remember?"

She drew a deep breath. "Yeah, I remember."

A pile of luggage sat inside the door, just as Amarok had said. Evelyn watched as he checked the handles and tags, searching for fingerprints, which he attempted to lift with white powder, since the bags were black. "This is probably futile," he admitted.

"At least you're trying to get what you can."

When he was done collecting prints, he examined the bags with a magnifying glass, looking for specks of blood — and found none. Then he set his tools aside, opened each suitcase and went through them. Other than linens, now crumpled and balled up, which had to be brought in by each renter, since there was no washer and dryer in this remote place, he found what one would expect to find — clothing and other essentials. There was nothing unusual. No drugs. Not even a small bag of pot.

While he documented his efforts with notes and pictures, she donned a pair of latex gloves and went into the kitchen. There were some beers in the fridge and some empty cans in the wastebasket — a total of twelve. That equaled two six-packs.

"What did Leland tell you when you asked him if they'd been drinking?"

Amarok answered from the living room. "Said they each had a couple of beers."

Then Sierra might've had a couple, as well, but even more wouldn't have been excessive, given the amount of time they'd been here. There was certainly no evidence of heavy drinking.

"Find anything?" Amarok called.

"Not really. Unless there are more cans outside, they didn't bring much beer."

"They didn't put any trash outside."

"How do you know?"

"The rental company would've warned them not to."

"Oh. Of course. Because of the bears." Amarok handled their garbage, so she'd momentarily forgotten that refuse attracted some formidable animals here in Alaska. "Then we have twelve cans for four people over three days. That tells me it's highly unlikely Sierra was drunk, especially in the middle of the day, when the guys might come home and wonder what she'd done with all the beer."

He said nothing.

"And the lack of drugs and drug paraphernalia indicates she wasn't high," she added. "I wish I could suggest that she *did* tangle with a bear, except I can't imagine her going outside without her coat and boots."

"Maybe, instead of going to the trouble of suiting up again, she just ran out to grab a few more sticks of wood."

"And a bear got her?"

"Yes."

"I can't see it," she said. "Why wouldn't she take a few seconds to pull on her coat rather than let herself get soaked? And why would she run out in the cold to get more wood when she'd already carried in an armload, most of which is still by the stove?"

"I shouldn't have brought you," he replied. "You're a pain in the ass."

She chuckled because she knew he was just messing with her, and started to wander around the rest of the cabin, searching for anything that might be amiss. Besides the kitchen and living room, she saw two bedrooms, one bathroom and a small mudroom off the back, leading on to a porch that was quite a bit deeper than the one in front.

Sierra had taken the sheets off the beds so she could pack them, but she hadn't folded the blankets that would be left behind. She hadn't washed the dishes or picked up the plates littering the coffee table. She hadn't done *any* of the usual scrubbing, even though leaving the cabin as it was would cause her, Leland and the others to forfeit whatever they'd paid as a cleaning deposit.

What Evelyn saw confirmed what she'd thought before. Sierra had been anxious to leave — so anxious she'd shoved everything, including shampoo, soap and toothbrushes, into the suitcases, and she hadn't bothered to fold anything or empty the fridge and cupboards.

Sierra didn't seem to care whether they left the cabin fit for future renters. That seemed significant. So . . . why the hurry?

"Evelyn?"

When Amarok called her name, she poked her head into the hall from the back bedroom so he could hear her reply. "What?"

"Come on up here."

"Where's here?" She walked toward his voice. It sounded as though he'd discovered something important.

"The loft."

Evelyn had noticed the ladder in the living room. She'd planned to go up when she finished with the downstairs, but he'd beaten her to it. "What did you find?" she asked as she climbed up after him.

He lent her a hand so she could get off the ladder. Then he gestured to the small area around them, which had a ceiling so low he couldn't even stand upright. "You smell anything?"

She sniffed. "Bleach."

"That's what I smell, too." He shook his head. "I didn't come all the way into this room when I was here before. Still I don't know how I missed it."

"It's not *that* strong, but I can definitely smell it."

"Someone's been cleaning up."

True. But if Sierra didn't clean downstairs, she wouldn't go to the trouble up here. . . .

Evelyn curled her fingernails into her palms. "Why, in a room like this, would you ever need bleach? You wouldn't want to risk spilling it and ruining the rug. And there's only a bed and a dresser. I could understand smelling furniture polish, but . . . *bleach*?"

"Can you go see what cleaning chemicals are downstairs?" he asked.

"Sure." She scurried back down the ladder but couldn't find any bleach, only some dusting cloths, window cleaner, a powdered cleanser, dishwashing soap and a small vacuum.

When she came back, Amarok was wearing a dark scowl and he'd turned over the mattress.

"That's not a happy face," she said when he was too preoccupied with whatever was on his mind to help her up again.

He gestured to the mattress, where she saw a big, red stain. "Does that look like blood to you?"

10

"We have a murder on our hands." Amarok couldn't believe it. It'd been barely eight months since Hilltop's last murder. And the previous two were only a year before that. Three murders in eighteen months, after going years without a single homicide. He hated to admit it, even to himself — because he loved Evelyn — but he'd known all along that allowing her brainchild to be built so close to his hometown would not bode well for those in the area. That was the reason he'd been one of the few who'd tried to fight it.

"Evelyn?" He turned to see her reaction. "Isn't that what you make of this?"

Her eyes, round as saucers, never left the mattress, and she didn't respond.

"Are you okay?" he asked.

She didn't look okay; she looked drained, pale.

"Evelyn?"

When she startled, he realized she hadn't heard him before. "Yeah."

That was what she said, but that wasn't the impression he got. If he had his guess, she was struggling not to slide down the wall. "Are you sure?" he pressed, alarmed.

"No," she admitted, and as upset and angry as he was to be dealing with such a serious problem *again* — because of what *she'd* brought to the place he loved most in the world — he couldn't help pulling her into his arms. He supposed that was how he knew he loved *her. She* mattered more than anything else.

"Look at me," he said.

It took a moment to get her to focus on him, but she eventually lifted her gaze. "We're in the middle of a war, remember? That's what you always tell me. There's more than one battle in a war, and you don't necessarily win them all. I need you with me as we go forward. I need you to remain strong." He gripped her shoulders and gave her a little shake. "Together we can come through this like we have everything else. Right?"

Tears filled her eyes. "I'm not doing so well, Amarok."

Her words made his blood run cold. She'd never said anything like that before. "It's because you're working too hard," he told her. "You need a break. Maybe you should go home and see your family, spend a couple of weeks in Boston decompressing while I deal with this."

She stretched her neck to be able to see the blood on the mattress again. "No. I won't leave you with this."

She probably felt she had to stay and defend herself, defend what she'd built and what she was trying to do with it, but her overall welfare meant more than anything else. "I *want* you to go home," he said. "If I know you're safe, I'll have some peace of mind, and I can handle this."

"There's too much going on at Hanover House. Janice won't understand if I take off right now. I have my first female inmate arriving on Monday. And once Janice hears that we're very likely looking at another murder . . ."

She didn't finish.

"You don't want anyone to know you're struggling," he said.

"I *can't* let anyone know, Amarok."

He held her closer and rubbed her back. He hated what she'd been through, hated that he couldn't make everything better, no matter how hard he tried. If he could catch Jasper, perhaps things would be different.

Of course things would be different. Then she could heal without being thrust back into the nightmare that had started her down the path of researching the conscienceless. But knowing Jasper was out there, just waiting for his chance, meant she could never fully relax, never fully trust that the future would be everything they were hoping to build.

"Then we have to do something," he murmured.

"Like what?"

She needed more emotional support. A piece of home that she could hang on to like a security blanket. But he knew better than to invite her parents to town. Her mother struggled with depression and was constantly nagging Evelyn to come home. Evelyn always looked relieved, if not exhausted, when they hung up. So Amarok couldn't see how having her parents in town would help.

What about Brianne? Evelyn had mentioned, several times over the past few months, how much she missed her sister.

"You told me Brianne's been talking about coming to visit."

"So?"

"Let's make it happen. Have her come out, right away."

"In *this* weather?"

"Why not? We should be able to get her in and out. It's not like the whole state shuts down when it snows. We're used to this. Technically, it's not even winter yet."

"But . . ."

He tilted her chin up so he could look into her eyes. "But what?"

"What if this is Jasper?"

She thought Jasper was responsible for everything that went wrong, and he could understand why. "We were afraid the other murders we've dealt with over the past couple of years were Jasper, too. And they weren't. None of them. This one might not be him, either."

"What if it is?" she repeated stubbornly.

"Then having Brianne around will help keep you safe. I'd rather you weren't alone at the house while I'm out investigating. I'll be pulling a lot of late nights over the next few weeks or for however long it takes to figure out who's responsible for what happened here."

He thought she'd continue to argue. Having company meant she couldn't put in her usual long hours, and she was so driven. There never seemed to be a good time to interrupt her work. She definitely fit aspects of the "mad scientist" stereotype, and he often teased her about it. But she mumbled, "Okay," and pressed her cheek against his chest. Her agreement told him he had real reason to worry about her. Even *she* knew she needed someone.

"We'll call her as soon as we get home."

"She'll probably be too busy to just up and leave. She has her own work to worry about. And her own man."

"The wedding isn't until spring."

"That doesn't mean she won't be hesitant to leave Boston."

He and Brianne had only ever talked on the phone, hadn't actually met. But he felt confident she'd make the necessary arrangements — once he let her know Evelyn needed her, which he'd do secretly if he had to. "She'll come."

"Hey, handsome, why so glum?"

Jasper pulled his gaze away from his drink long enough to glance at the blonde sliding onto the stool next to him. Her name was Bambi, or maybe that was just her stage name. She danced here at the club, typically came on right before Vivian, the raven-haired beauty he liked to watch. Bambi had shown interest in him before, but he'd never found her particularly appealing. With bleached hair, tattoos covering both arms, a ring in her nose and fake boobs that bordered on caricature, she didn't look anything like Evelyn. But a sexual outlet was a sexual outlet. He'd only allowed himself to take one victim since moving to Alaska; he had to show some restraint if he hoped to achieve what he'd set out to achieve — so he had to relieve his powerful and constant lust somehow.

He offered her the smile that'd gained him so many conquests in the past. "Had a rough day."

Her bottom lip jutted out in an exaggerated pout. "Poor baby. What was so bad about it?"

Besides having to dispose of two dead girls? Nearly freezing his balls off in the process? Knowing some car was driving around with part of one victim's scalp on its axle, the discovery of which would intensify the investigation into Sierra's disappearance and focus it on Hilltop, when he'd be much safer if that connection was never made? "I won't bore you with the details," he said, and couldn't help chuckling at his own euphemism.

She seemed to take his levity as a hopeful sign. "Ooh, you're not only handsome, you're mysterious."

He laughed outright. "I've got more

secrets than you could ever imagine."

"I'm intrigued."

"Tell me something."

She tossed her hair back. "What's that?"

"Is your name really Bambi?" He was trying to picture the kind of parents who'd give their daughter a name like that.

"Of course it is," she said, but her coy smile suggested the opposite.

"Nice name," he said with a shrug.

"Why not?" She took a sip of his drink. "It's sexy and yet . . . innocent."

"There's nothing about you that's innocent," he said as he reclaimed his glass.

"Some guys think they want innocence, but experience is a hell of a lot more fun," she said with a laugh. "Anyway, I can play stupid if you like."

She *was* stupid. She just didn't know it. She proved that when she leaned so far into him the tassels on her pasties brushed his arm. "Want to take me home tonight?" she whispered.

He made no move to touch her, careful not to show too much interest. "Sorry. I don't pay for sex."

Immediately backing off, she scowled at him. "What are you, a cop?"

"No. I just refuse to pay for something I can get for free."

The smile slid from her face. "Then you might want to find a different place to hang out, sweetheart. The girls in here are professionals. We expect a little something for our time."

He caught her arm before she could slip off the stool and move on to someone else. "I'm not ungenerous."

She glared at the hand holding on to her. "What does that mean?"

"I have a dime bag of coke." He didn't have too much time to devote to getting what he wanted tonight. He had to be at work by four in the morning. But this would only take a couple of hours. Fortunately, he didn't need much sleep. He rarely slept more than five hours a night.

She lowered her voice. "You wanna get high?"

"No, *you* wanna get high."

Her eyes narrowed. "And you want something else."

He tugged on one of her tassels. "You don't have to play the innocent for me. I prefer a girl who doesn't mind a little kink."

She smacked his hand away. "What kind of kink?"

"Light bondage. A few toys."

She pursed her lips. It was a slow night, which meant she didn't have many options.

And he was a regular, familiar enough that she didn't seem concerned about what he'd just said. She was assuming he wouldn't go *too* far, and he wouldn't, but only because he couldn't upset or harm anyone he associated with. That would be the quickest way to get caught.

"Let's see if you have more than coke to promise me," she said, and grabbed his crotch.

He knew she couldn't really tell whether he was well-hung, not with his jeans in the way. She was trying to pretend *she* was in control. She seemed to think acting bold would turn him on, but it enraged him instead. The challenge in her eyes, playful though it was, reminded him that, despite all the penis extenders he'd tried over the years, he wasn't as impressive in that area as everyone seemed to expect from his general good looks and physique.

"Well?" If she made fun of him, he'd kill her. Which would be a mistake, but at that point it'd be worth it. He refused to allow anyone, especially a *woman,* to make him feel inferior.

Lucky for her, she didn't laugh. "Let's go have some fun," she said.

After they got back from the cabin, Evelyn

went straight to the prison. Not only was she behind she also needed to stay busy in order to take her mind off what had most likely happened at the cabin. She didn't even stop to have dinner after everyone else went home. She worked until she couldn't keep her eyes open any longer. Then she lay down in the conference room. Amarok had taken the evidence he'd collected to the lab in Anchorage, and she had no idea when he'd be back. If they closed the road, he might not get through until morning. She couldn't bear the thought of spending another night in their home alone, not after seeing the size of the bloodstain on that mattress and sensing that whatever new menace they were facing was close. She needed to feel secure in order to get the rest she so desperately needed and, inside the prison, with its tall fences, razor wire atop those tall fences and even taller lookouts, manned by armed guards watching the grounds, she felt safe. Maybe one of the many psychopaths housed within the walls would get her one day, but not Jasper. He was the only one she truly feared, and he couldn't get her here.

She was just nodding off when the phone began to ring.

That had to be Amarok, checking on her,

so she made herself get up to answer it. "Hello?"

"You're *still* at the prison?" he asked.

She steadied herself by leaning on the conference table. "Yeah. I've been trying to catch up on a few things."

"Sounds like I woke you."

"I was lying down, but I wasn't quite asleep."

"At the *office*?"

She tucked some hair, which had fallen from the tie holding the rest of it back, behind her ear. "The couch in the conference room isn't a bad place to sleep."

"So you're not going home."

"No. If you were there, I would, but . . ."

"That's probably for the best. After what happened last winter, and what's going on now, I'd rather have you at the prison."

"When will you be back?"

"It's going to take me a while. That's why I'm calling. When I couldn't reach you at home, I figured you'd be at work. I'm at my father's place, and I'd like to stay over so I can talk to a detective with the Anchorage PD who's supposed to be really good at solving homicides. I want to make sure I've covered all my bases at the crime scene, maybe even ask him to come out and double-check that I haven't missed anything."

As far as she was concerned, having another observer at the cabin — one with more experience than Amarok had in forensics — would be great. "Do it. And I'll stay here rather than fight the weather."

That was a lame excuse for sleeping over. She was fighting something much bigger than the weather, and he knew it. But he didn't call her on her bullshit. "Are you sure you'll be able to get enough rest there?"

She'd get a lot more than she would at home, listening to the storm rage and fearing that each scratch or bump was Jasper trying to break in. If it *was* Jasper who'd taken and/or killed Sierra, maybe that was why he'd done it — to draw Amarok away from *her.* That would be like him. He was the craftiest killer she'd ever met. He could look people in the face and make the most outlandish lie seem completely credible. "I should. Tomorrow's Saturday, so it'll be quiet around here. It's not as though the staff will be showing up bright and early."

"They won't be showing up at all, will they?"

"No, but some of the psychology team could come in to work on one of our studies or catch up on paperwork, like I'm doing."

"I wish I could pick you up and take you home with me."

He was worried about her. "I'm fine," she insisted. "You have to do your job."

After that, they talked about Brianne. Amarok had called her since Evelyn had rushed off to work, and she'd agreed to come. She was trying to get a plane ticket. Then they confirmed that Sigmund, the cat, had enough food. He did, because Evelyn had filled the automatic feeder just this morning. Amarok had left Makita at home so she'd have the dog with her tonight, but he'd sent Phil over to walk him and feed him at dinnertime, so Makita was set until morning, too. As the conversation was winding down, Amarok asked, "Have you called your doctor yet?"

The change in subject threw her, but she could tell he'd been waiting to ask this question through most of the other chitchat. "About what?"

"About that appointment for me to be tested."

She held her breath. He was talking about testing his fertility so they could have a child, but she wasn't going to make that appointment. Not now. She couldn't go through a pregnancy in her current condition, didn't think she could do it until Jasper was caught, and she was beginning to lose faith that would ever happen. "Amarok . . ."

He sighed when he heard the reluctance in her voice. "Don't answer. I already know what you're going to say," he said, and hung up.

Evelyn's chest constricted as she stared down at the phone. At first, she thought she couldn't move, couldn't breathe. But the next thing she knew, a blinding rage welled up from somewhere deep inside her, and she started bashing the handset into the base, breaking the phone. "Damn you, Jasper!" she screamed. "Damn your rotten, evil soul!"

She'd cut her hand by the time she sank, sobbing, to the floor.

Jasper was hungover when he drove up to the prison. The night with the stripper hadn't gone well. He'd managed to refrain from hurting her or losing his temper to the point that she'd remember it and tell others he was dangerous. But he had only so much restraint, and he'd used *all* of it. Just remembering how resistant she'd been to letting him do certain things made him angry. She'd snorted his coke, gotten what *she* wanted, but left him unsatisfied.

He should've forced her, should've taken her to his dungeon, tortured and killed her for her defiance. He'd recently dumped two bodies; he could always dump a third. But he'd been seen with her at the club, so he resisted that urge. He couldn't let anyone know about his dungeon, especially someone he planned to keep alive. That room was reserved for Evelyn.

As he stopped at the security checkpoint by the perimeter fence, he barely grunted at the guard who came out to check his ID and inspect his truck using a mirror to see the undercarriage. He was too busy wondering if it wouldn't be better to say he was sick and go back home. That raw hunger, the beast that rose up inside him and made him crave the darkest of things, was so close to the surface, so difficult to control. If he wasn't *extremely* careful, he'd do something to give himself away.

But then he saw Evelyn's SUV parked in her covered spot and stomped on the brake. What was she doing at the prison? She often came in on weekends or after hours, but this was four in the morning on a Saturday. He'd never seen her here at that time before.

The thought that she and Amarok might've had a fight, that she might've stayed over because of some discord between them, filled him with excitement. Suddenly he knew he wouldn't be able to make himself leave right away. He wanted to be where she was. The thought of her sleeping over, so unaware of the danger he posed and so accessible to him with no one else in that entire wing, made him hard.

He had to adjust himself before he could continue into the parking garage, where prison employees who weren't privileged enough to get a parking space close to the building had to leave their cars.

In a perfect world, he'd bring Evelyn to live with him while he continued to work at the prison and everyone else went out of their minds wondering what'd happened to their beloved champion of victims' rights. That was what he'd hoped for, what he'd planned. But since that woman staying at the cabin had discovered Kat's body and he'd had to kill her, he should change his plan.

Sometimes one had to take what one could get.

11

Evelyn was sleeping so deeply it took her a moment to realize someone was banging on the door.

She opened her eyes. She was still at the office. In the oblivion of sleep she'd lost track of that, of everything. But even though the lighting in the common area outside the conference room was dimmer than usual — thanks to the hour and the facility's attempt to conserve energy when the offices weren't in use — she could see well enough to determine where she was. She couldn't understand why anyone would be demanding entrance to this part of the building, though.

Was there an emergency?

Just in case, she struggled to regain full mental power quickly and sat up, blinking against the darkness immediately surrounding her.

Rap. Rap, rap, rap.

More knocking. As she left the conference room and started through the maze of cubicles that provided working spaces for the support staff, she checked the clock on the wall. It was only four thirty. She'd slept less than three hours. No wonder she felt as though she'd been run over by a bus — or, in this part of the world, maybe that cliché should be "run over by a snowplow."

Even before she could figure out who was trying to rouse her, she knew it was a CO. She could see the uniform through the glass, but not the face. The reflection of what light she did have hit at exactly the wrong place, and he was looking back behind him.

Then he turned — and smiled.

Evelyn's stomach dropped as she realized it was Andy Smith. She'd had an aversion to him *before* he'd torn up Bobby Knox's photograph of his grandmother. Since that incident, she liked him even less.

What could he possibly want, especially at this hour?

"What is it?" she called through the glass.

He raised a Styrofoam cup, probably filled with coffee, and a plate that held a donut. "I thought if you were working this late you might need a little fuel."

Did he have to wake her up *for that*? She

lifted a hand to indicate she wasn't interested in the food. "That's *very* nice of you, but no thanks."

"You don't want to take them for the morning?"

He was only trying to be nice. Maybe he felt bad about what he'd done to Bobby Knox and this was his way of compensating.

Regardless of her feelings about him, he'd saved her life. She should show him a little forgiveness and consideration.

With a sigh, she turned the lock.

Jasper hadn't felt so alive in years. His plan to get to Evelyn by working at the very institution she'd created was going to pan out, just not the way he'd initially envisioned. That came as a disappointment. He'd put so much work into his cellar. And Evelyn had cost him so much, he owed her more than a quick death.

But he'd already told his sergeant that he wasn't feeling well and had to go home, so it didn't have to be *too* quick. He'd have at least an hour to spend with her, during which no one would have any reason to come looking for him. He'd rape her with everything he could find before he killed her in the most brutal way possible. Then he'd leave her body in her office, walk right out of the prison and disappear.

Everyone would eventually realize he was responsible, of course. He wouldn't be able to work in the prison system ever again. But he didn't want to, anyway. That had always been nothing more than a means to an end. There was a woman out there somewhere who'd be willing to take care of him; he'd never been unable to find one. He'd shave his beard, let his hair go back to its natural color, assume a new identity, marry and use his new wife to provide for his needs. Meanwhile what he'd done here in Hilltop would have a chance to cool off. If anyone could start over from scratch, he could. He'd been on the run his whole life. And even though this form of revenge wouldn't be quite as satisfying as torturing Evelyn on a daily basis — practically under the nose of the man who professed to love her — he'd take pleasure in knowing he'd won the battle with her at last and Amarok would suffer and go on suffering for a long time.

When she accepted the plate and the coffee and began to thank him, however, the phone rang. As she hurried over to one of the reception desks to answer it, he followed her inside and paused to lock the door.

Since this section of the prison didn't

house inmates and it was the middle of the night when no one was expected to be working, the offices weren't well lit.

He considered that a positive.

"*Who* is it?" he heard her say. "Oh, Leland! Of course I know who you are. But . . . who gave you this number? . . . I'm sure Margaret thought she was helping, but I'm afraid I can't tell you anything. . . . You'll have to talk to Amarok. . . . No, you're wrong. He *is* working on it. If he hasn't contacted you tonight it's because he's been busy."

Jasper stood as close to Evelyn as he dared, at least while she had access to the outside world. He loved the smell of her, the rumpled look of her, too. He could see the scar on her neck he'd created when he was only seventeen, loved that he'd left a mark she had to see every time she looked into a mirror. Those days had brought him some of his best memories. He'd relished finally giving in to the fantasies he'd entertained from as young as he could remember.

He wished for a knife, for the ability to reopen that old wound. But he didn't have one. So he imagined wrapping the phone cable around her neck and cutting off her air instead. Watching her suffocate as the realization dawned that the man she'd been looking for since she was sixteen was standing right in front of her — that *he* was Jasper Moore and had been working with her for months — would be such a rush.

He flexed his hands and rose up on the balls of his feet in anticipation. But he forced himself to hold out a little longer. If he interrupted the conversation, Leland would very likely call back and, when he couldn't reach her, send someone over from the prison side to investigate. That wouldn't give him nearly long enough time to enjoy something he'd looked forward to for so many years.

As soon as she set the phone down, she was his. . . .

"Leland, these things take time."

Jasper smiled when she sent him an apologetic look and leaned against one of the cubicles.

"Listen to me," she went on. "He's in Anchorage with evidence collected at the cabin. . . . Yes, there was evidence. . . ."

Jasper's breath caught in his throat. What was she talking about? Before Leland and his party had arrived, he'd cleaned that cabin like he'd never cleaned anything before.

But why get worked up? Now that there'd been a change of plans, whatever evidence he might've left behind wouldn't matter.

"I can't tell you what it involves. . . . You'll need to talk to Amarok. . . . He doesn't have a cell phone. No one has a cell phone in Hilltop. We don't have coverage. . . . I'm sure you'll hear from him in the morning. . . . Trust me, he's doing all he can."

Irritated by the delay, Jasper was tempted to give her the windup sign. What more could she say to the sniveling brother of the woman he'd killed? The man was wasting his time and everyone else's. He wasn't getting his sister back. She was dead, her body dumped, permanently this time, in a wilderness area on the other side of Anchorage!

Evelyn tried to console Leland for another few minutes before politely telling him she had to go.

Jasper felt an electric spark as the conversation *finally* came to a close. The moment — *his* moment — was coming. But as soon as she hung up someone startled them by banging on the door.

Jasper turned to see that a CO was trying to get in.

"You locked it?" Evelyn asked, a puzzled expression on her face.

Jasper shrugged to indicate he hadn't meant to do anything wrong. "*You* had it locked, so I thought you wanted it like that."

She started to say that hadn't been necessary but stopped and simply shook her head. The CO was rapping on the door as though he couldn't wait even a second for a response.

Jasper ground his teeth as she went to see who it was. He couldn't believe this CO could be looking for *him,* so he wasn't worried. He had permission to leave the prison, could say he'd just come up to make sure the doc — as most of the COs affectionately called her — was okay before he went home.

"Dr. Talbot, I'm *so* glad you're here." It was "Easy" Hyde, who'd started at the prison only two months ago. They used nicknames at Hanover House so much — not for everyone but for their favorites, which was probably why Jasper didn't have one — that Jasper had no idea what the dude's real name was. But his corpulent face was flushed and sweaty — ridiculous as far as Jasper was concerned. Someone needed to kick his fat ass and make him lose weight.

"What's wrong?" Evelyn looked worried as she let in the obese guard. "Why are you so upset?"

Easy's gaze shifted from Evelyn to Jasper and back again, but he was too caught up in whatever he wanted to convey to express any surprise that "Andy" was with her. "I got off at four, but I hung out here for a while, hoping the storm would ease off. I didn't want to tackle driving home in a blizzard. But the moment the snow let up, I went out to get in my brand-new truck."

"Don't tell me someone crashed into it while it was parked in the garage," she said.

"No. Worse than that. When I came around the back of it, I saw something hanging from the axle underneath, you know? I don't know how the COs at the checkpoint missed it with their mirrors. They probably thought, like me, that it was a hank of long grass. But when I reached out to tear it away, I realized it was . . . It was . . ."

The big baby choked up. Jasper longed to punch him for being such a pussy, but he also felt his muscles go taut with expectation. He could guess what Easy was going to say.

Evelyn touched Easy's arm to soothe his distress. "*What* was it?"

Instead of answering, he opened the bag he carried to show her, and she immediately covered her mouth and turned away. "Please tell me that isn't what it looks like," she said.

"It is!" he cried. "It's a handful of human hair attached to part of a scalp!"

"Oh my God." Gripping the side of the cubicle closest to her, she put her head down as if trying to avoid passing out.

"Are you okay?" Jasper feigned concern to be able to touch her shoulder. He couldn't believe how wonderful it felt to put his hands on her after so long. Especially because he knew she wouldn't recoil, couldn't rebuff his kindness without being rude, and she was never rude.

She straightened slowly, but when she threw her shoulders back he knew she was tamping down her distress, taking charge. "I'm fine. Thanks again for the donut and coffee," she said, and started walking him out.

Knowing his opportunity had disappeared, he didn't try to resist.

"We'll call Amarok right away," she told Easy as she opened the door for Jasper. "Maybe he'll want Phil to take what you've found to him, so he can submit it with the other evidence on this case first thing in the morning."

"*What* case?" Jasper heard Easy ask as he stepped out of the office.

Apparently, not everyone had heard about the missing woman, even though, with Leland and the rest of his party staying in town, Hilltop had to be abuzz with the news.

Whatever Evelyn said in response was lost when the door swung shut, cutting Jasper off from the conversation.

He muttered a curse as he got on the elevator that would take him down to the first floor. He'd come *so* close. It made him more frustrated than ever to leave empty-handed, doubled the anger he'd felt after he'd had to let that stripper go. But with Amarok as busy as he was, Jasper would have other chances — probably plenty of them.

And it only took one.

"Say that again?" Amarok's voice was thick with sleep. Evelyn could tell he wasn't completely lucid, but he was lucid enough to speak quietly. No doubt he was trying not to wake his father and his father's wife.

After Andy Smith had left, Evelyn had beckoned Easy into her office. They couldn't use the phone in the conference room; she'd destroyed it. "It's me."

"I guessed that as soon as I heard the phone ring," Amarok said. "That's why my heart's in my throat. It's like . . . what . . . five in the morning? Are you okay?"

"I'm fine." She cringed when Easy, who was obviously eager to get rid of what he was holding, set the sack with the hair and scalp on her desk between them. "Sorry to drag you out of bed. You must be exhausted. But I'm with a CO who's discovered something you need to know about."

"What is it?"

"Human hair."

"You *did* say human hair?"

"Yes."

"I don't understand. . . ."

She shuddered as a vision of what the sack contained passed before her mind's eye. "It's attached to a pretty good chunk of scalp."

After a slight pause, Amarok spoke again, and she could tell he was now wide awake. "I see. More than you'd find if, say, that person was alive."

"Exactly."

"You believe it might belong to Sierra Yerbowitz."

"Don't *you*?"

He didn't answer the question; he didn't need to. "Where did this CO make his find?"

"I'll let him tell you. His name is Jordan Hyde, but we call him Easy, and he's right here. Let me put you on speaker so we can all hear."

She pressed the appropriate button, put down the handset and gestured for Easy to lean in. "Easy, have you ever met Sergeant

Murphy?"

"Not formally," he replied. "I've seen him at the Moosehead or around Hilltop when I was getting gas, that sort of thing. But I have a wife and family waiting for me in Anchorage when I get off work. I can't go to the bar as often as most of the other guys."

"So how did you come across such a gruesome thing?" Amarok asked.

Easy used his sleeve to wipe the sweat beading on his forehead. "I noticed something dragging from my rear axle. I can't tell you how it came to be there in the first place. I must've picked it up somewhere. That's all I can figure."

"Have you been anywhere unusual lately?"

"No. I've had to work the past five days, so that's about all I've done. And I've only owned my truck for a week. My wife and I bought it last Saturday."

"You haven't been out to any hunting cabins. . . ."

"No. None. I've gone from Anchorage to Hilltop, and Hilltop to Anchorage. Other than stopping at the grocery store and taking my older kid to school, if I'm available, that's it."

"How long would you guess that piece of scalp has been there?"

"I have no clue."

"You don't think someone *attached* it to your truck, do you?"

"You mean as a gruesome prank or something? No. I don't have friends like that. I don't even have enemies like that."

Before Amarok could lob another question at him, understanding dawned on Easy's face. "Oh, wait! You're asking if it's possible someone *wanted* me to find it — like that severed head I heard about behind the Moosehead a couple years back."

"Does that seem like a possibility to you?" Amarok asked.

"Not really. If I'd driven around with it much longer, it could easily have fallen off. Then I doubt anyone would ever have found it."

"So you picked it up somewhere — by accident."

A pained expression appeared on Easy's face. "No disrespect, Sergeant, but I certainly didn't pick it up on purpose."

"The question is . . . how'd it happen?"

Easy shook his head. "Like I said, I have no clue. No one would've had a chance to steal my truck from the parking garage or from my place. And with the weather as bad as it's been —" He stopped.

"What is it?" Evelyn could see his expression, knew he'd just thought of something.

"On my way to work yesterday, I saw a set of tire tracks leading off into a field. I was excited about my new truck, and I wanted to try it out in the snow, have a little fun without the wife around to worry and harp at me. So I followed those tracks and did a few donuts. The fact that someone had been there before me made me feel confident that I wouldn't get stuck, and I didn't. But I ran over something on my way out."

Amarok jumped in again. "You don't know what it was?"

"I assumed it was a large rock or maybe a log. Why would I think anything else?"

"You didn't get out to check?"

"No. It was an empty field. The ground was uneven to begin with, and I didn't want to be late for work."

"I see."

Easy stepped back, as if he'd done his duty and was ready to go. "Is that it? Because I'm completely creeped out and I'd like to go home to check on my wife and kids."

"Do you work tomorrow?"

"No, I'm off. Thank God."

"I'm afraid you're not going to like this," Amarok said. "And I can understand why. But if I get you a motel room, will you stay in town tonight so you can show me where you went off-roading yesterday?"

Easy scratched his neck. "Can't I show you now?"

"I'm in Anchorage."

"Then maybe I can point it out to Dr. Talbot before I go home. Or circle it on a map."

"I'm afraid not. This is important, Easy. I need to meet with you, have you go over everything you saw and show me where you found that scalp. We have a woman who's gone missing. I'd like to be able to tell her family what happened."

"Right," he said on a heavy sigh. "Of course. It's not far from the prison, so it shouldn't take long. Will you be back early?"

"Not sure yet. Head over to The Shady Lady. I'll let you know when we can meet as soon as possible."

"Okay," he said, but his tone of voice made it sound more like, *Shit.*

He'd already turned to go when Amarok said, "And Easy? There's one more thing."

The CO sent Evelyn a worried glance before asking, "What's that?"

"Don't mention what you found to anyone else. Until we know more, it'd be best to keep this between us."

"Andy Smith was here earlier. He heard what I said."

"That can't be helped now, and I'm sure

it'll be okay. I'll ask him to keep it to himself, too."

Easy shifted uncomfortably. "When I took this job, I knew I might see some stuff I'd rather not, but I assumed the worst would be a prison fight or . . . or a shanking. This is beyond belief. You don't think we have a *murderer* on the loose, do you?"

Evelyn didn't want a rumor like that to get started, especially when they couldn't say for sure. Not only would it throw the whole community into a panic, it'd put Hanover House in the news again, and she wasn't convinced the institution could survive more bad press. "Nothing's certain yet, Easy," she said. "For all we know, this woman wandered away from that rental cabin and froze to death."

"Did she have her own vehicle? Because I followed a set of tire tracks into that field — not footprints."

Sierra *hadn't* had a vehicle. So how would she have gotten that far? "There's a lot riding on this," Evelyn said. "Please use some discretion. We need to know what we're dealing with before we cause a panic."

He gestured at the sack. "I think that tells us enough, don't you?"

"It's possible the hair and scalp belong to Sierra, the missing woman, but we need to confirm it first."

"Waiting for confirmation could be dangerous, Doc. People should be warned. If I lived in Hilltop, I'd sure as hell want my wife and kids to know they should be extra careful, lock the doors, stay in a group, that sort of thing."

She cleared her throat. "Amarok will alert everyone if and when he feels it's necessary."

"If you say so," he muttered, and cast a final horrified glance at what he was leaving behind as he walked out.

Closing her eyes, Evelyn rested her head on the back of her chair.

"You still there?" Amarok asked.

"Yeah, I'm here."

"He has a point. You realize that."

She opened her eyes to stare at the sack on her desk. Was Jasper behind what was happening? If so, he'd destroy her yet. "I realize that."

"Can you give me Andy Smith's number? I'll ask him to keep what he heard quiet for now, but I'll have to make a public statement, revealing it, soon."

"I know."

"I'm sorry."

"I know that, too. Anyway, you're busy. I'll leave a voicemail for Andy Smith, asking him not to say anything. So don't worry about that."

"Okay. I'll call Phil and have him bring me what Hyde found."

"Do you want me to do that, too?"

"Have you gotten any sleep?"

She covered a yawn. What with Andy banging on the door and waking her, she hadn't gotten enough. She'd been seriously annoyed by the interruption. But since she would've been awakened, anyway — by Leland Yerbowitz's call and then Easy Hyde's appearance — it seemed childish to resent Smith. She felt like a jerk for disliking him so intensely. "Not much."

"Then no. Phil can do it."

She tested the coffee Smith had brought her, but it had gone cold. She picked at the donut instead. "With the blood on the mattress and this unidentified scalp . . ."

"Things don't look good," he filled in.

"It's Jasper," she said. "It has to be." She expected him to deny it, to tell her they didn't know that yet. She'd wanted to blame every problem they'd run into on Jasper, so she could see why he might argue. But he didn't. *Someone* had murdered Sierra. They hadn't recovered her body, but they were almost certain of that now. And they'd essentially picked a fight with Jasper last winter when Amarok had contacted his parents and managed to get a little information out of his mother. After all her research, Evelyn knew the kind of man Jasper was, how he'd likely respond. He certainly wouldn't let it go. "I've been waiting for him to come after me again."

"So have I," Amarok said.

Evelyn drew a deep breath. "Don't take this wrong. I feel terrible for Sierra and her family. I wish he hadn't harmed her. But he's been torturing and killing innocent victims for over twenty years. The bodies discovered near that burned-out barn in Peoria tell us that. So, as frightened as I am, I'm sort of relieved, too. If that makes sense."

"Relieved that it might all be over soon?"

"Yeah. One way or the other."

"Don't talk like it might not go *our* way. We'll get him."

She wished she could believe Amarok. But after twenty-two years spent chasing someone who seemed capable of slipping through the tightest net, she knew they could easily lose in the end.

12

"This is it?" Amarok glanced over at Easy Hyde as he pulled to the side of the road.

Easy nodded, but, unfortunately, there weren't any tire tracks they could follow today, so there was no way to be positive it was the *exact* spot. There'd been too much snowfall since Easy had come here before. But the skies were clear at the moment. Although it was still colder than normal for this time of year, Amarok felt he was catching a small break, and he was determined to make the most of the opportunity.

As they got out and stood at the edge of a large field surrounded on three sides by Sitka spruce, mountain hemlock and black cottonwood trees, Amarok was glad he'd left Makita at the trooper station. He loved having his dog with him, but Makita wasn't a trained police dog. Amarok didn't need him making tracks in the snow or doing anything else that might make his job harder. "Where were you when you hit that bump?"

Easy pointed. "Right about there, not far from that burned-out stump."

Amarok unloaded the snowmobile from the trailer he'd been towing and grabbed his snowshoes, a shovel and the avalanche probe he kept in his truck. "Get on," he told Hyde after he'd secured his equipment to their new mode of transportation.

Once he felt the other man climb on behind him, he gave the sled some gas and they jetted across the snow. The motor was so loud he didn't attempt to communicate again until he came to a stop at the place Easy had indicated from the road. "Here?" he asked as he let the engine idle.

Easy didn't seem completely convinced. He looked around, obviously trying to gauge where they were in relation to where he thought they should be. "I guess we could *start* here. I can't be positive it's the right place. I just rolled over something while I was driving. It happened fast, and I thought nothing of it, so there wasn't a lot to fix the location in my mind. But this should be close."

"Okay." If it *wasn't* close, Amarok could be out here for hours — until after dark. But he'd brought lights and he could only work with the information he had.

He killed the engine and they got off. After putting on his snowshoes, he deployed his avalanche probe to its full 240 centimeters. He had another probe that went to over 300, but while the snow was deep, it wasn't as deep as it was going to get in full winter.

He began poking the probe into the snow in a spiral pattern, making sure each new hole was no more than the width of an average-size body from the last.

Evelyn wasn't the only one who believed Jasper was back. Amarok had known he'd probably blame them for the fact that he'd felt the need to kill his own parents, which meant it was only a matter of time before Jasper tried to take retribution.

And maybe that time was now.

Just in case, Amarok had to be ready for him, had to outthink him *and* outwork him if he planned to keep Evelyn safe.

"We've got company," Easy said.

Amarok, breathing heavily from the physical exertion, looked up. Sure enough, there were several cars parked behind his truck and a handful of people stood at the edge of the field, gawking at them.

"Everyone's curious about what's going on," Easy added.

This road led to the prison, which meant

the COs, the kitchen help, the administrative staff, the warden and the mental health team came past here. So did the supply trucks. "No surprise there. I've been flashing Sierra's picture all over town."

"So most folks know a woman's gone missing?"

"By now they do."

"Then why are we keeping what I found a secret?"

Primarily because Amarok had been trying to buy some time so Evelyn wouldn't come under fire from the community again. But he didn't want to admit that. "They know someone's gone missing. They don't know she's *dead.*"

"Do *you*?"

"Not for sure. I'm still holding out hope," he said, but he was almost certain his hope would be in vain. And if he didn't find Sierra's killer *soon,* he could be searching for Evelyn's body next.

At four twenty, Evelyn was relieved when she saw a call coming in on line one. Penny wasn't at the prison to answer the phone. None of the support staff worked on Saturdays. Only a few of the mental health professionals ever appeared. Today there were two — Russell Jones, the youngest, at thirty, of the psychologists on her team, and James Ricardo, the only neurologist. She wouldn't have been at Hanover House herself today, except she had so much to do and she'd felt that working would make the time pass faster while Amarok was busy. She'd been waiting to hear from him all day.

She asked James, who'd stopped by to say hello, to give her a moment, and he shut the door as he walked to his own office. "Where are you?" she asked Amarok as soon as she was alone. Judging by the noise in the background, he wasn't at his trooper post.

"At the Moosehead, grabbing a bowl of chili," he replied. "I haven't had lunch, so I'm starving."

She'd been battling a headache since before noon, but good news should help. "Did you find anything in that field?"

"No."

The worry that had been plaguing her grew worse, made her feel like her stomach was churning with acid. "But her body *has* to be there. Where else would Easy get that hunk of human hair?"

"I have no idea, but I was in that field all day, probed the whole damn thing."

"Didn't Phil do part of it?"

"No, he didn't get back from the coroner

until I was well into it, and then he had to do something for his wife. Now I'm glad I didn't ask him to come out. I wouldn't have trusted the results if anyone else had helped. That's how positive I was she'd be out there."

Evelyn sank back into her chair. "So what now?"

"Easy must've picked up that . . . *biological matter* from somewhere else."

"Damn it!" She'd been going all day on almost no sleep, hadn't so much as managed to nap. Even after Easy left and she'd called Andy Smith, who'd already called her back to say he'd keep quiet, Phil had come to the prison to pick up the sack. Every time she tried to rest her eyes, she saw the shack where Jasper had murdered her friends and tortured her. He was here. *In Alaska.* He had to be. That was what everything that'd happened recently *had* to mean — and it left her with the creeping sensation that she'd be hearing from him herself soon. "What are we going to do?"

"We're going to keep looking."

"But we live in a vast wilderness! There are so many places to stash a body. And with all the snow . . ." She rubbed a hand over her face. Once again, Jasper would win. "You'll never find her."

"Yes, I will. Maybe it'll be in the spring, when the snow melts, but —"

"Did you say 'in the *spring*'?" she cried. If Jasper was here, she'd be dead by then.

"These things don't always move fast. Even if I don't find her body, there could be a piece of clothing or something the perpetrator dropped that we can't see right now."

A knock interrupted, and Russell Jones poked his head into her office. "Got a minute?"

She didn't. Neither was she in the mood to deal with him. He'd been Tim Fitzpatrick's protégé and had always sided with him against her. Even without the politics of the past and the frustration that had engendered, Russ was so negative it was difficult to like him. He was sloppy, too. Short and cannonball-round, he wore a shirt and chinos every day that looked as though he'd slept in them — and his appearance matched his general mood. She still wondered why he hadn't quit when Tim did so he could move back to the Lower 48. He did nothing but complain about Alaska.

Still, now that Fitzpatrick was gone, Russ was relatively harmless; that was the main reason she hadn't put any pressure on him to leave Hanover House. "I'm on the phone." She held up the handset as if to say, *Do I have to state the obvious?*

"I just need a second of your time," he said. "Please? I have to go, but before I do, I'd like to show you this." He came forward with a letter in his hand.

Evelyn managed to keep herself from snapping at him only because her conversation with Amarok was pretty much done. "I have to go," she said into the phone. "I'll see you tonight, okay?"

Amarok didn't seem eager to let their conversation end on such a sour note. "Don't be discouraged."

That was impossible. But he was trying so hard to keep her safe. She didn't want him to think she didn't appreciate his efforts. "I'm just tired."

"You need to get some sleep."

"So do you."

"I'm fine," he said, and from that she knew she probably wouldn't see him until very late. He'd drop off Makita so she wouldn't be alone once she got home, and he'd continue working — sifting through everything they'd ever learned about Jasper, trying to figure out if there was anything more he could do for Sierra. He felt the need to catch Jasper as much as Evelyn did and knew they could be running out of time.

She rolled her chair closer to her desk. "I'll see you later."

"When will you be home?" he asked before she could hang up.

"Soon." She'd rather not spend another night at the bungalow without him, but at least it wasn't storming. She'd be able to tell if someone was trying to break in, especially if Makita was there with her. And if the weather turned in a few hours, as it so often did in Alaska, she'd just have to cope. She refused to spend another sleepless night at the office.

"I'll stop by to see you," he said.

"Okay." When she put down the receiver, Russ shoved the letter he was holding in front of her.

She recognized the handwriting. "You've got to be kidding me."

He blinked at her. *"What?"*

"This is from Fitzpatrick."

"I know."

"You don't think he's writing me, too? You don't think I've already heard it all?"

After tossing the letter on her desk, he plopped into the seat across from her. "I feel so bad, Evelyn. He's *pleading* with us."

She shoved the letter back toward him. "A lot of convicted murderers never stop maintaining their innocence, Russ."

"Let's not forget everything Tim's accomplished. He's a renowned psychiatrist. That's why you enlisted his help to get this place approved and built. You were too fresh out of grad school to do it all on your own."

Tim might have been well respected at one time, but he'd definitely tarnished his reputation. "I understand that. I'm grateful to him for his help in bringing Hanover House into existence, but —"

"Before you go into all that, can I just tell you what I'm thinking?" Russ broke in.

She gestured for him to continue.

"Since it was Jasper who murdered three of your friends twenty years ago, it's far more likely that he also murdered Mandy Walker and Charlotte Zimmerman Pine last winter. The psychopath you've described to us all, in great detail, would love the idea of scaring you that way, of returning to the place where he committed his very first atrocities and taking two more lives — two more people you knew — as a little reminder."

Russ wasn't telling her anything new. She'd been over all of that in her own mind, thousands of times. But there were other considerations. "The murders in Boston stopped after Fitzpatrick was arrested. How do you explain that, Russ?"

"If it was Jasper and not Tim, how would *you* explain it? You'd say it was Jasper's way of laughing at the system, of hurting another innocent by letting Tim take the fall and of keeping you anxious and unsure at the same time, right?"

Right. But was that giving Jasper too much credit? Had she built him up too much, made him almost superhuman?

"You're forgetting how terribly Fitzpatrick let us all down in the end," she said. He became so obsessed with her, he'd started creeping around her house, watching her through the windows, even taking pictures of her in various stages of undress. He'd also undermined her authority whenever possible. He'd actually superimposed her face on pornographic pictures of women involved in sex acts, which he'd shown to the psychopaths he was studying, instead of using other pictures that were meant to determine how they reacted to certain stimuli. He should've lost his license and would have if she hadn't kept quiet for the sake of the institution. The only reason he hadn't been fired was because he quit.

Russ lifted a placating hand. "Adjusting to Alaska hasn't been easy for any of us. I understand he made some poor choices."

What he'd done went beyond "poor

choices," but Evelyn didn't care to dredge up the details, so she let the statement go.

"That doesn't make him a murderer," Russ finished.

"Have you looked beyond what he's been telling you — at the evidence?" she asked. "He was *following* Charlotte Zimmerman Pine. Calling her and hanging up. And the police found his shoe print at the scene of the crime *in her blood*!"

"He was following Charlotte because Mandy Walker had just been killed and he didn't want Charlotte to be next. He'd found a picture in your yearbook, one where you were painting a Homecoming sign with all your girlfriends, and he knew she was the only person in that picture, besides you, who was still alive. As far as he was concerned, that meant she had a bull's-eye on her forehead. So he was trying to keep her safe. He was calling to scare her enough to make her cautious, hoping she'd pressure the police to keep an eye out, too."

"What about the blood with his shoe impression on the bathroom floor?"

"Tim claims he was sitting in his van at the end of the block, watching the house where Charlotte was babysitting, when a vehicle came tearing past him. Something about the fact that it was obviously a rental car and it looked as though it'd come from around the block, where someone could've approached the house without his knowledge, made him go closer to check. That was when he saw the door standing ajar and went inside to find Charlotte lying in a pool of her own blood."

"The jury didn't buy that explanation, and I'm not convinced I should, either. That isn't the story he initially gave police."

"He admitted to following her *and* calling her. He also explained why he did both. So what if he didn't tell them he'd been inside the house? Would *you*? The police were already looking at him as a person of interest. He didn't want to become their primary suspect!"

"If he hadn't been trying to insert himself back into my life, he wouldn't have been anywhere near her!"

"He wasn't trying to insert himself back into your life. He was trying to be useful again, to recover from his previous mistakes and find meaningful work. Can't you have a *little* compassion for him?"

She couldn't help being offended. It was easy for Russ to forgive Fitzpatrick; Russ hadn't been victimized by him. "I do have some compassion for him. I just don't want to be blinded by it."

"The knife used to kill Charlotte has never been recovered. And there was no evidence tying him to Mandy's murder. None whatsoever."

"So?"

"So both those things speak in Tim's favor."

"That the knife was never found speaks in no one's favor."

"It says he didn't have the murder weapon in his house or car or anywhere the police searched. And whoever killed Mandy killed Charlotte. Not only was Charlotte murdered shortly after Mandy, they were both friends of yours, both in that same yearbook picture."

Evelyn couldn't argue that Charlotte's and Mandy's murders weren't connected. They had to be. But she had so much responsibility on her shoulders already. She didn't want to feel she had to take on the justice system in addition to everything else, especially for Tim. "Just because there's nothing to suggest Tim killed Mandy doesn't mean he didn't. He didn't have an alibi for either night."

"He lived alone. Rarely went out. Not having anyone to corroborate his whereabouts wouldn't be unusual for someone like that. Heck, I live pretty much the same way, so there'd be no one to vouch for me, either, if *I* was in trouble."

With a sigh at his persistence, she propped her chin on her fist. If not for Fitzpatrick's behavior with her and that shoe imprint, she would've been absolutely convinced it was more likely Jasper who'd killed Mandy and Charlotte than Fitzpatrick. Jasper had a history of killing people; Fitzpatrick didn't. And she could imagine someone in Tim's situation following Charlotte in an attempt to be involved in something he felt might resuscitate his career. At thc time, he'd been eager to reclaim his former prestige.

But he'd behaved so terribly when they worked together. How could she ever believe in him now?

"The justice system is supposed to determine his guilt or innocence, not me. And he's already had his day in court."

Russ took one of her tissues and tried to wipe away a stain on his shirt — part of his lunch, no doubt. "The system isn't perfect. You know that. If he *is* wrongly imprisoned, his jury won't be the first to get it wrong."

Did she have more responsibility in this situation than she was willing to take? "Okay, look," she said. "I'm not having the best day, and you're asking me to help someone I no longer admire. But I believe there's a chance Tim *might* be innocent. So I'll get in touch with an attorney friend of mine, see if he'll look into it."

Russ used both arms to shove himself to his feet. "You have a friend who might be able to help?"

"It's been a few years since we've talked, but yes. His name's Ashton Cooper, and he has an enviable record when it comes to winning difficult cases."

"How'd you meet him?"

"When I first started my practice, I was sometimes asked to give expert testimony for the prosecution. I came up against him in court several times, so I know how good he is."

"You became friends even though you were on opposite sides of every case?"

"Basically. He consulted with me on other cases I wasn't involved in when he had a psychology question and, over time, we developed a rapport." He'd even asked her to dinner once or twice — not that she'd ever accepted his invitations. He was loud, caustic, argumentative and intense. Not her type. But she liked how hard he tried, in his own gruff way, to make the world a better place. "He used to donate one day a week to pro bono cases, some that focused on trying to free inmates who might be innocent. Provided he still does that, I can ask him to take a look at Fitzpatrick's case."

Giving up on what'd turned out to be a futile attempt to remove the food stains on his shirt, Russ threw the tissue in her wastebasket. "Why didn't you mention this guy before?"

Because she'd been hesitant to ask Ashton for such a huge favor. What if Fitzpatrick was guilty? She didn't want him to waste his time trying to free someone who deserved to be in prison. "I didn't feel going to Ashton would change anything. But just this week, Amarok and I received confirmation that DNA recovered on some open cases in Arizona showed a familial relationship to that of Jasper's parents."

"Wait. . . . What are you saying? *You have Jasper's DNA profile?*"

She couldn't help smiling. With everything that'd happened recently, she hadn't taken the time to celebrate that small victory — and she should have. It could turn out to be a *big* victory. "We do."

"That's fabulous! Then . . . we just need to have it tested against all the DNA found at both crime scenes. If we can place Jasper at either one, it'll prove Tim is innocent."

"To *us*. We know the murders had to be connected, and if Jasper was at one or the other, *he* was the culprit for both. But where Fitzpatrick's concerned, that'll need to play out in the legal system."

"There's always *a lot* of red tape with that sort of thing. But if Jasper was there — the psychopath who killed three of your other friends — we should be able to free Tim, especially with a good attorney."

"I think so, too. But what if Jasper's DNA *doesn't* match? Does that mean it *was* Fitzpatrick who killed Mandy and Charlotte?"

"Not necessarily," Russ argued. "Jasper could've murdered both women without leaving his DNA."

"Exactly. Then we won't know any more than we know now, and Ashton will say there's nothing he can do. I'm wondering if we should wait and see if we have Jasper's DNA at the scene before we approach him. That's what I've been planning to do."

Russ shoved his hands in his pockets. "Let's not wait. Having Cooper involved should make the whole process go quicker. He'll know how to get hold of the evidence, get the DNA tested, file whatever papers are required to move the process along, et cetera."

"That's true," she agreed. "If we have to depend on Detective Dressler, who wholeheartedly believes he put the right man behind bars, we could run into some resistance and delays." The detective hadn't even called Amarok back! She'd tried to reach him Friday morning herself, before they'd visited the cabin, and he hadn't returned her call, either.

"Maybe Cooper will look at the evidence and all the testimony and believe in Tim enough to take on the case, anyway."

She gave Russ a doubtful look. "He won't be able to get past that shoe imprint in Charlotte's blood — unless he can offer up another plausible culprit."

"You can't say that for sure," Russ said. "Who knows what this might start? Can I tell Tim what's going on? That you're doing what you can?"

She locked her desk. "It might be smarter not to get his hopes up until —"

"He could use some good news right now. He's really depressed. He needs to feel he's got a fighting chance."

"Fine." She handed him back the letter he'd dropped on her desk. If Russ wanted to encourage Fitzpatrick, that was his choice. Even if Tim was innocent, even if she *was* going to try to help him, she didn't have any desire to remain in touch.

She listened to the soles of Russ's shoes squish as he left her office. She was eager to head home, but she had Ashton Cooper's cell phone number, so it wasn't as if she had to wait until Monday. Maybe Cooper *could* get the DNA tested right away. He'd certainly have a better chance than she would.

Setting her briefcase to one side, she took a moment to call him.

13

Amarok was having a second bowl of chili and a piece of corn bread at the Moosehead when Evelyn came in. He wasn't all that hungry anymore, but he had to visit The Shady Lady to give Leland another update, to let him know he was finished with the field and hadn't found anything, and he wasn't looking forward to it.

He stood as Makita trotted over to welcome Evelyn. "Hey, what's up?" Amarok hadn't expected to see her until he swung by the house.

She slid onto the stool next to his. "I noticed your truck outside, so I decided to stop in."

He checked his watch. "It's barely five. What are you doing off so early?"

"You know I don't have to work on Saturday. And I told you when we were on the phone that I'd be leaving soon."

"You put in so many hours, the day of the

week doesn't seem to matter to you," he said dryly. "And once you're engrossed in one of your studies, 'soon' could be four or five hours."

She rolled her eyes but smiled to let him know she understood he was teasing. "Since I met you, I've taken a lot more time off than I ever did before. Anyway, tonight when I said 'soon,' I meant it. I have a raging headache."

The concern he felt for her deepened. He had to determine what had happened to Sierra — and eliminate the threat of Jasper before Evelyn could unravel mentally or emotionally. She was already struggling. And yet he had this thing with Sierra, which may or may not be connected. "You need to eat, and you need sleep," he told her.

She rested a hand on his thigh. "So you keep telling me."

"It's true." He gave her a menu. "What would you like for dinner?"

She pushed the menu away without even looking at it. "A bowl of vegetable soup."

"That's all?"

"That's all. And I'm going to bed as soon as I get home."

"Good." He wished he could go with her, that they could curl up together and shut out the world. When it was just the two of them, nothing else seemed to matter. But he didn't have the luxury of relaxing. Once he'd figured out what was going on with Sierra, he could throw all his effort and energy back into hunting down Jasper. He couldn't wait to return to that. Although he'd been protective of Evelyn all along, he wanted to capture Jasper now more than ever. Jasper was keeping him from starting a family with the woman he loved, and Amarok took that personally.

He waved to get Shorty's attention and ordered the soup.

Evelyn asked Shorty how he was doing, but Amarok could tell that she was beginning to feel self-conscious around the locals again. "Shorty likes you, you know that," he murmured after the owner of the Moosehead had moved away.

"The news of Sierra Yerbowitz's disappearance has everyone thinking about Sandy," she said.

"That may be true, but Shorty doesn't blame *you* for what happened to her, and he won't blame you for whatever's happened to Sierra. Plenty of people here *wanted* Hanover House in the area. They were desperate for the jobs and prosperity it would bring."

"Not *everyone,*" she said with a pointed look.

He'd been opposed to the facility's close proximity to his hometown, and he'd been vocal about it. But the prison was here now. So was Evelyn, and he didn't want to lose her. "It's all going to work out," he insisted, and changed the subject. "I got a message from your sister."

"She called *you*?"

"I'm the one who called her, remember? You were too busy."

"I was procrastinating."

"Why? Don't you want her to come?"

"Of course I do. It's been over two years since I've seen her. But I don't want her to plead with me to go home."

Neither did Amarok. "She knows you're committed to what you've created, that you plan to stay for another three years." He hoped Evelyn was committed to him, too, and for a lot longer than that. "She won't try to talk you into returning to Boston. She misses you and would just like to spend some time with you."

"So she was able to get off work?"

"Yeah. Apparently, she has quite a few vacation days. She'll be here a full week."

"Won't she need those vacation days for her honeymoon?"

"I'm guessing she might have some bad news about that."

"Don't tell me they broke up!"

"She didn't say for sure, but I got that impression."

"My folks were really looking forward to the wedding and having some grandchildren in their future."

She knew he'd be happy to give them both, but he didn't say anything because she wouldn't even meet his eyes. "When will she arrive?"

"Tomorrow at three. You'll need to pick her up in Anchorage alone if I'm not available to go with you." He wished Brianne were coming tonight. He didn't like the idea of leaving Evelyn on her own, and yet he had to do his job.

"I wasn't expecting her to come so quickly," she said. "The airfare must've cost a fortune on such late notice."

"Don't worry about the airfare. I paid for it."

She frowned. "*You* shouldn't have to do that. *I'll* take care of it."

"I'm happy to do it. Having her with you at night will give me some peace of mind."

She'd grabbed a handful of peanuts from the bowl set out on the bar but hesitated before popping them in her mouth. "The fact that you're so worried is more proof that you believe Jasper's here."

"*Something's* going on. I'm not positive it's Jasper, but I don't have another answer at the moment." He took a long pull on his beer. "I'm hoping for the best but preparing for the worst."

She ate the nuts before quickly clearing a spot so Shorty could deliver her soup. "What are you going to tell Leland?" she asked once Shorty left to take another order.

"The truth."

"That his sister is likely dead?"

"That I don't know. Because I don't."

She frowned again. "I can't believe you didn't find her body in that field. Where else could Easy have come up with her hair?"

Amarok finished the last of his corn bread. "Who can say? He's only owned that vehicle for a week, and he insists he hasn't gone anywhere other than work."

"Maybe Sierra was there for a brief time, but someone moved her."

"It could also be that what we're assuming is part of Sierra's remains isn't."

"What do you mean?"

"The hair was so matted and muddy, I couldn't even tell what color it was. We have a missing woman, and we have part of a body. I assumed they had to go together."

"But . . ."

"When I finished probing that field and stopped by my post to drop off the snowmobile and call you, I got a message from the coroner's office."

"What'd they have to say?"

"They told me the hair is blond."

"And Sierra has long *brown* hair. . . ."

He pulled her photograph from his back pocket. "I need to confirm with Leland, but he never mentioned if she dyed it."

Evelyn took the picture so she could study it. "When was this taken?"

"While they were at the cabin. You don't recognize the background?"

"Now that you point it out, I do."

"Leland e-mailed it to me the night she went missing. He'd just taken it on his cell the day before."

"How'd he send it to you? There's no cell service here."

"He used the Internet at the hotel."

"So how do we account for the difference in hair color?"

He finished his beer. "We could be looking at *two* victims, right?"

Her eyes widened. "No. . . ."

"Do you have a better explanation?"

What little color she had left in her face drained away as she shook her head. "This just keeps getting worse and worse."

Brianne Talbot set the charging cord she'd purchased for her mother's phone on the counter. Anytime her parents needed *anything* that dealt with technology, they called on her. But she couldn't stick around to visit, as they were probably hoping. She had to be at the airport by six in the morning and still had to pack.

"I can't believe you're dropping everything and flying off to Alaska tomorrow," Lara, her mother, said. "Who'll run the hospital?" Grant, her father, sat in his recliner with the remote, watching sports highlights, but Brianne knew he was listening far more attentively than it appeared.

"The trip's a bit last-minute," she admitted. "But it's also the first vacation I've taken since I became administrator at Valley Regional. I deserve some time off."

Lara fussed about the kitchen, cleaning this and that. "So who'll take care of things while you're gone?" she asked again.

"I have a great staff. They can manage for a while." Brianne got out her keys and held them in her hand. She *really* had to go. "I don't want to miss the chance to see Evelyn. I miss her."

"We miss her, too, and yet she hasn't

come to see us since she left."

Brianne could hear the hurt in her mother's voice. "She has a lot of responsibilities in Hilltop, Mom. Hanover House is the first facility of its kind. It's difficult for her to get away." And from the beginning of her career, Lara and Grant had put so much pressure on her to quit her job and start a private practice dealing with damaged kids or something so she could back off from the dangerous men she studied. The constant barrage had to be overwhelming, which was why Brianne tried not to do the same thing. It wasn't easy. She believed as her parents did — that if Evelyn didn't stop what she was doing, she'd eventually wind up dead.

They'd been through so much angst and pain with her already; they couldn't take any more.

"But she expects you to leave *your* job at a moment's notice, to risk getting fired, so you can go up there?"

"That's a little dramatic, Mom. My job isn't at risk. Besides, Evelyn doesn't *expect* anything. She'd just like to see me." Although Brianne didn't let on, she needed to see Evelyn, too. She'd been so sure Jeff Creery was the man of her dreams, she'd finally let down her guard and fallen in love

— hadn't even been worried about birth control, since they were getting married. And now that he'd moved on, she was coping with the fact that she was pregnant. Since she'd received Amarok's call only a short time after learning that the wedding was off, that she wouldn't even be seeing Jeff anymore, she'd welcomed the chance to get away. Maybe Evelyn would be able to help her overcome the rejection that threatened to immobilize her. She wasn't about to confide in her parents. Not yet.

Lara wiped the counter for the second time since Brianne had been standing there. "Why doesn't she want to see *us*?"

Brianne wished she could pull her mother into her arms and simply hug her. But Lara had so much pride. She often pushed away the very thing she needed most. "She *does* want to see you. She's just busy. It was actually Amarok who called and invited me."

"The man she's living with."

Hearing the disapproval in Lara's voice, Brianne frowned. "You know who Amarok is. What are you trying to say — that you don't like him?"

"I've never even met him! She's never brought him home to introduce us!"

Maybe Evelyn wasn't ready. Brianne had made the mistake of bringing Jeff home, and her folks now cared about him. How was she going to tell them the wedding was off? That he would no longer be part of their lives and yet she was carrying his baby?

Suddenly unable to meet her mother's eyes, Brianne picked at her cuticles. "She's under a lot of pressure. She feels she can't leave Hanover House or something might go wrong."

"Because things go wrong even when she's there! She was almost killed again last winter, and she *still* won't quit. I don't know what else has to happen before she realizes that whatever she's hoping to achieve isn't worth her life."

Even more had happened in Hilltop than Grant and Lara knew — probably more than they all knew. Evelyn kept what she could from them. Lara was on anti-depressants and anti-anxiety drugs. Evelyn didn't want to make their mother's condition any worse. "Someone has to take a stand, do something to fight back."

"That's ridiculous!" Lara carefully folded the washrag over the edge of the sink. Obsessive as she was, everything had to be just so. "All the studies show that psychopaths can't be rehabilitated."

"Understanding how their minds work might help us find a way," Brianne said, but she wasn't sure why she was defending Evelyn. After all Evelyn had been through — after all the *family* had been through, starting with Evelyn's abduction twenty-two years ago — Brianne felt Evelyn *should* leave that battle to someone else. She wanted theirs to be a regular family, wanted to have her only sibling back in Boston, partly because she missed her but also because she was tired of being the one who had to look out for their parents. She hated that she sometimes resented the sacrifices she had to make so Evelyn could stay in Alaska. Although their father was steady and easygoing, Lara was *so* needy. Jasper and what he'd done to Evelyn had broken Lara; she was too sensitive to withstand the anger, the loss, the lack of justice and resolution, and the constant worry.

"She's been attacked so many times," Lara was saying. "One day they'll be sending her home in a box."

When Brianne's keys cut into her fingers, she realized she was squeezing them too tight. She'd been trying hard to support her parents *and* her sister, to let them all lead their own lives and choose their own paths. She filled in wherever and whenever she could. But Lara needed Evelyn at home. And with a baby coming, Brianne had to have a break from the pressure she felt from their parents. She couldn't continue to manage everything she'd managed in the past. "I'll talk to her," she said. "She's already done so much for the sake of psychology. Now that Hanover House is up and running and the critics have calmed down a bit . . . maybe that'll be enough for her."

Grant paused the TV. "If what happened last winter didn't convince her, nothing will."

Perhaps. And yet *something* had changed. Amarok had told her that a woman had gone missing from one of the hunting cabins in the area and Evelyn was struggling with the memories that evoked.

Brianne doubted he'd admit that or ask her to come to Alaska *right away* unless he was deeply concerned.

Maybe, considering all the recent developments, she'd be able to talk Evelyn into coming home.

Jasper tried to pretend he wasn't paying attention to Amarok or Evelyn, that he was only at the Moosehead to have a drink like everyone else. It was Saturday night and they hadn't received the snow they'd been expecting, so the bar was crowded. There were a lot of women — more than usual —

but no one interested him like Evelyn. It'd always been that way. Her presence acted like a high-powered magnet, drawing his gaze back to her again and again.

He watched her smooth some hair off Amarok's forehead before casually returning her hand to his thigh. Seeing them together, acting so familiar and demonstrative, bothered him. He hated Amarok, couldn't bear the thought of Evelyn spreading her legs for him.

Jasper took another sip of his whiskey. He'd been so patient. For almost two years he'd mapped out his revenge. He'd worked at Florence Prison in Arizona to establish the appropriate work history, managed to get hired at Hanover House and made the move to Alaska, where he'd painstakingly worked to create a particular image and become part of the community. But then Leland and his party had come to the area and rented the worst cabin possible, setting off the series of events that had caused all Jasper's plans to unravel. Watching everything go to hell agitated him so much he couldn't continue to deny himself.

He needed a release, couldn't wait any longer.

"Have you heard about that woman who's gone missing?"

Jasper glanced over at the man sitting next to him. Terrell Hillerman, a fellow Hanover House employee, was also at the bar. Terrell was still in uniform, which suggested he'd just finished his shift and stopped in on his way home.

Jasper hadn't come from the prison. He'd driven over from Anchorage, even though he didn't work today. He hadn't been able to make himself stay away. He was too interested in the investigation, too curious about what Amarok was finding. "What woman?" he asked, playing dumb.

"Don't know her name. Came here from Louisiana as part of a hunting party."

Jasper had thought he might see Leland at the bar or at least Leland's friends. There wasn't anything else to do in this town. But they weren't there. "Did she wander away from the group and freeze to death? Encounter a bear? What?" He took another careless drink, as if anything worse than a "natural" death weren't really a consideration.

"Hell if I know," Terrell replied. "On my way to work, I saw the sergeant using an avalanche probe to search an area not far off the road, though. I'm guessing he thinks she's dead."

Jasper felt a muscle twitch in his cheek.

Easy remembered where he'd picked up that piece of scalp?

That made Jasper feel as though he might have more to worry about than he cared to believe. The sergeant was only a step behind him. "Find anything?"

"Not that I know of."

Because Jasper had made it back and removed the bodies, taken them on the other side of Anchorage, the northwest side, as he'd originally planned. "Sucks for the hunters she was with. Must've ruined their whole trip."

The look he received from Terrell told him he'd missed a cue of some sort. That happened occasionally, since he didn't feel what most other people did. "Ruined their trip?" Terrell echoed. "One of the hunters was her *brother.* I can't believe he gives a damn about bagging a moose at this point. He just wants to find his sister alive and well."

Jasper almost said it'd be funny if the moose had bagged the sister instead of the brother bagging the moose, almost chuckled at the image that presented in his mind. But he knew better than to actually make the joke. If Terrell was offended by what he'd said already, he wouldn't think *that* was funny. "Of course. It's a bummer all the way around."

Fortunately, Terrell seemed to shrug off the gaffe. So many unique individuals lived on the final frontier that people seemed to be less critical overall.

"What'd the hunters do, go home?" Jasper wanted to keep Terrell talking, see if there was anything else he could learn.

"No. From what I've heard, they're still here, hoping for some word."

Would Amarok be able to give them that "word"? What did he have as far as evidence? Last night, Evelyn had mentioned he'd taken what he'd collected at the cabin to Anchorage to be evaluated. So he had *something.*

Must be the blood, Jasper decided. Hard though Jasper had scrubbed, he couldn't get it out of the mattress where he'd tied Kat to the bed. That was why he'd gone to the trouble of carrying the mattress up to the loft. He'd thought there'd be less chance of it being seen.

Apparently, his extra work had been wasted.

Was there anything else?

He looked over, once again, at Evelyn. He didn't have to worry about her or Amarok noticing *him.* They were too comfortable in their surroundings, too wrapped up in each other.

But Amarok wouldn't stay wrapped up in Evelyn for long. Because he was on a mission to bring Jasper down.

Jasper felt his muscles tense. His mistakes were regrettable. Word of Leland's sister was spreading, and with that piece of scalp now in Amarok's hands, it wouldn't be long before folks realized they were dealing with far more than a missing person. Everyone would soon be crying murder, which would send the whole area into a panic — exactly what he'd tried to avoid by killing Leland's sister in the first place.

Damn it. The people of Hilltop and everyone at the prison would be searching *everywhere* for their bogeyman.

But Jasper didn't look like a bogeyman, and they knew him. Sometimes the best place to hide was in plain sight.

"So what do you think happened?" he asked Terrell.

"The way the sergeant's acting? Must be another murder."

"No kidding! Why do you say that?"

"You know who Phil Robbins is, right?"

"Of course. He's the Public Safety Officer who helps clear the roads during winter, sort of acts like a deputy to the sergeant."

"That's him. Well, his wife — you know he got married just a few months ago — is a friend of my wife's sister, and *she* said he found a lot of blood on one of the mattresses at the cabin where that woman was staying."

Jasper feigned concern. "Wow. But what's the big mystery? It was probably one of the hunters who killed her."

"The investigation doesn't seem to be going in that direction."

Forcing himself to pause for a drink, so he wouldn't look too eager for the information Terrell was providing, Jasper embraced the hot burn of the whiskey as it rolled down his throat. "Why not?" he asked when he'd swallowed. "Do they have evidence to suggest it was someone else?"

Terrell lowered his voice. "Phil told his wife that the sergeant believes it's the bastard who slashed Evelyn's neck when she was only sixteen. That he's *here* now."

Jasper set his glass down so hard some of the liquor splashed out. Terrell rocked back, out of the way, but Jasper quickly covered for his reaction. "Whoops! That almost got away from me," he said as he dried his hand with a napkin from a stack Shorty kept on the bar. "Anyway, I hope what you said about the guy who nearly killed her — that he's here — isn't true. That dude's crazy."

"Not crazy. Twisted. A sicko. Like the

other psychopaths at Hanover House. You work there, too. You know what they're like. He's a sadist, a serial killer. No one'll be safe if he's come to town."

Jasper had always known he was different, but he didn't appreciate anyone talking about him in such derogatory terms. He'd rather be the hunter than the prey. "Even if that's the case, I'm not convinced we should get *too* worried."

Surprise registered on Terrell's face. "We shouldn't be worried? Who's he going to attack next?"

Jasper clicked his tongue to show skepticism. "This is such a small community. A stranger would stand out. We'd be able to spot him a mile away."

"Yeah, well, no one's spotted him so far, and yet we have a woman who's missing and very likely dead." Terrell threw a bill on the counter and got off his stool. "I'm just glad I live in Anchorage."

"Yeah. Me, too," Jasper said.

"See you at work."

Jasper nodded good-bye. Then he saw Evelyn get up to leave. She was taking Amarok's Alaskan malamute with her, which meant she was going home alone. No doubt the dog was supposed to protect her.

Jasper told himself to do nothing, to let

her go. He'd be much smarter to lie low and let the shitstorm he'd kicked up blow right past him.

But if he'd left something he didn't know about at the cabin, some piece of evidence that could be traced back to him, the storm wouldn't blow by.

This could be his only chance.

14

When Evelyn got home, she was surprised to find Phil's truck sitting in front of the house. What was he doing here? Surely he knew Amarok wasn't home.

She waited for Makita to jump out before she closed the door of her Toyota Land Cruiser. "Looks like we've got company, boy."

Amarok's dog followed her to the truck, but Phil wasn't in it. Evelyn turned around, thinking she must've missed seeing him waiting on the porch, but he wasn't there, either.

Since Makita had already set out to mark his territory, she whistled to call the dog from the telephone pole, which was about the only thing he could reach, thanks to all the snow, and went to let them both in.

The door was locked, as she would've expected, but Phil opened it from the other side before she could get out her key.

"Hey there," he said. "You're home, huh?"

Evelyn blinked at him. "Yeah, I'm home. What's going on?"

"Amarok didn't tell you?"

"No. . . ."

"He called me to say he isn't sure he'll make it back tonight. He's going out to that cabin, wants to throw on a pair of snowshoes and take a look around, see if it would be possible to walk to another cabin in the area."

"This late?"

Phil rubbed his beard growth, which was turning gray, and gave her his usual amiable smile. "It's dark eighteen hours a day this time of year. What difference does it make?"

She didn't like the idea of Amarok being out in the mountains alone, especially now that they were fairly certain they were looking at *two* murders. Two dead people suggested a different kind of killer, one far more dangerous than what might initially be expected from a missing person case. "He's had so little sleep. And he's already worked hard today." She didn't want him to encounter Jasper or anyone like Jasper when he was compromised in any way.

"Amarok can take care of himself," Phil said.

Against the elements, maybe. Against the

wild animals he'd lived with all his life and the occasional drunken and disorderly asshole. But he'd never come up against someone as callous and evil as the man who'd nearly killed her. Jasper would stop at nothing to gain the advantage and he wouldn't fight fair. She didn't care if Amarok was a big, strong man; a bullet or a knife, especially one coming at him unexpectedly, could kill him, just the same as anyone else.

"I'd rather he went out there tomorrow, after he's had some rest." Intending to call and see if she could convince him to wait, she started for the phone, but Phil stopped her.

"You won't be able to reach him. He'd just decided to go when he was leaving the Moosehead, which is why he only called me. He said he couldn't reach you."

"How'd you get in? Did he bring you the key?"

"No, he told me to let myself in with the key in his desk." He gestured at the counter, where he'd put the house key Amarok had given him.

She felt a little better knowing that having Phil watch over her for the night had come as an afterthought to Amarok, that he hadn't sat there all through dinner and simply not said anything. He was so worried when she left the bar, he'd called Phil to ask for this favor, which wasn't quite as high-handed as it might have seemed. If she hadn't gone to pick up a file she'd forgotten from Hanover House and then stopped at Quigley's to buy coffee and a few other staples, she might've had some input on the matter. But since it'd taken her an hour to get home, Phil was right. Amarok would be gone.

She set her purse on the counter and picked up Sigmund, who'd started rubbing against her legs. "I can't put you to the trouble, Phil, not when you have your own family to worry about."

"If Amarok thinks it's necessary for me to stay here, I'm willing."

"That's the thing. Amarok doesn't *know* if it's necessary. Neither do I."

"Better safe than sorry," he said.

Evelyn almost insisted he go home. She couldn't expect someone to look out for her like this. But her head was pounding and she was exhausted. With Phil in the house, she'd be able to sleep without fear, and having the opportunity to do that was too tempting to resist.

"It's *really* nice of you." She smiled to show her gratitude. "You have your gun, right? Just in case?"

He wasn't in uniform. He lifted his bulky sweater to show her his revolver. "Makita will let us know if anyone's out and about. And if we get company, I'll do the rest."

"That's comforting," she said. But even after she went to bed, she kept thinking that if Makita wasn't with Amarok, who'd let *him* know if he had company?

Jasper didn't slow down as he passed the sergeant's house. He didn't want to look like he was creeping around if anyone happened to notice him. He was just making an initial pass, anyway. Provided it all looked safe, he'd drive by again, a little slower, and decide if it was really wise to go to the door.

He checked his watch as he'd been doing every few minutes since he saw Evelyn leave the Moosehead. He'd given her ample time to drive home and get settled in. He'd thought it would be smart to wait a bit to make sure Amarok wouldn't be joining her after stopping by the trooper post.

Amarok's truck *wasn't* there, but Jasper saw some other vehicle parked out front.

As he came to a stop at the end of the street, he left his blinker flashing to indicate he was about to turn and paused to stare into his rearview mirror.

Whose vehicle was that? He recognized it

and yet . . .

"Phil Robbins," he said aloud. "Of course." Terrell Hillerman had just mentioned Phil to him at the bar, but the truck in front of Amarok's house wasn't the one with the plow. It was another vehicle, possibly his wife's, that Jasper had seen him drive occasionally.

What was he doing here?

Whatever it was, Jasper doubted he'd stay long.

"Get your ass moving," he grumbled, and scanned the area to see what else he might have to contend with. When he'd learned where Evelyn was living, he'd looked up Amarok's address on Google Earth probably a million times. He even had a map of it pinned up on the walls of his new dungeon. But he'd been down this street only twice — last winter when he saved Evelyn's life and now. Drawn to it though he was, he'd been militant about staying away. He had no reason to be over here and couldn't risk seeming too interested. He'd always told himself the time would come, and he hoped that time was now.

Jasper scoured the area for lights, vehicles, people, and saw nothing to be concerned about. Amarok didn't have any close neighbors, but Jasper viewed that as both a positive and a negative. He couldn't simply pull up in front of another house, turn off his truck and, while he waited, pretend he was visiting someone else. He'd be too conspicuous if he was seen.

The lack of people in the neighborhood gave Evelyn less chance of reaching help, however. It also meant he could fire a gun without bringing anyone running and any noise she made wouldn't matter. If he could only get Evelyn out of the house without being seen, his original plan might still work. He could keep an eye on the investigation, see if it drifted anywhere near him. If it did, he could kill her and leave Anchorage. And if it didn't, he could keep her indefinitely — or until he grew bored, if that was even possible with a victim he'd craved for so long.

"Come on . . . come on." He wanted to see Phil walk out, climb in his truck and drive away. He'd purchased a gun from a dope dealer in the same area where he'd picked up Kat — one that wasn't registered — but he couldn't shoot Phil and the dog and still be assured that Evelyn wouldn't escape in the process. He had to wait for Phil to leave; the dog would be enough to handle.

Grabbing the steering wheel in a death

grip, he drove back into town. He hesitated to return to the bar. He thought it would look strange that he'd left and then returned when he didn't live in the area. He could sit outside in the parking lot, though, make it seem as if, when he left earlier, he'd been too drunk to drive. But just sitting there doing nothing would be agony. He needed stimulation, satisfaction, the thrill he'd been denied for so long.

After passing the Moosehead, he went to Quigley's Quick Stop and perused the aisles, eventually buying a package of sunflower seeds and a six-pack of beer. He was too agitated to drink any more than the whiskey he'd had earlier. Too much alcohol would make him sloppy. He didn't particularly care for drugs or alcohol, anyway — hated being impaired or out of control. Although he sometimes used them as tools, like he had with the stupid stripper he'd picked up on Friday night, what he really enjoyed was torture.

He sat in the lot eating seeds and spitting the shells out the window for a while, then glanced at his watch again. He'd managed to whittle away twenty-five minutes. He figured that should be long enough to risk going back to the house. He was too cold to sit there any longer.

Once he pulled onto Main Street, he checked every business he passed to see if he could spot the sergeant's vehicle. Amarok wasn't at the Moosehead or The Shady Lady and, other than Quigley's, everything else was closed.

As he turned off the main drive, he hoped to find the sergeant's truck outside the trooper post, which was only a block away. That would mean Amarok was working late. Jasper would have to move fast, since Amarok could return home at any moment, but he didn't think it would take long to get Evelyn out of the house once the coast was clear. After all, she knew him as one of her COs. He'd saved her life last year. It didn't matter that saving her hadn't been his intention. She thought he'd intervened for her sake, so he'd use that in his favor. The moment she saw him through the peephole, she'd open up — especially if he told her he'd found Leland's sister's body. She'd have no reason to doubt or fear him, would completely understand why he might appear at her house so late, asking for Amarok. And when she let him in, he'd shoot the dog and drag her to his truck.

But Amarok wasn't at the trooper post. The lot was empty, the building dark.

Damn it! Did that mean the sergeant had

gone home?

"No!" Jasper groaned, and, calling Amarok every foul name he could think of, headed back to see.

The sergeant wasn't there, but Jasper felt no relief. Phil's truck was parked in the same spot as before and all the house lights were off.

This time, Jasper couldn't help slowing as he rolled by. It looked like Evelyn had gone to bed.

So what was Phil doing?

Maybe Phil *wasn't* there. Maybe he'd left his vehicle and gone somewhere with the sergeant.

That had to be it, Jasper thought. Amarok had left Evelyn with his dog, thinking Makita would keep her safe. Little did he know! Jasper would have Evelyn in his cellar trying out those new restraints within an hour or two.

He flipped the car around, intending to pull into her drive. But as he drew closer, he began to realize how recklessly he was behaving. He couldn't go to the door unless he knew for sure that Evelyn was alone. He'd have only one chance at this, couldn't allow his impatience to tempt him into making a mistake.

Speeding up instead of slowing down, he

turned the corner, suddenly eager to get as far away from Amarok's house as he could. This had been a shitty week, and today topped all the days before.

He'd get Evelyn soon, he told himself. Right now, he needed to head home and relax, wait patiently until the timing was right.

But he was too riled up to even think about going to bed. He had so much adrenaline rushing through him he felt he could wrestle a bear. So instead of driving toward Anchorage, he took Nektoralik Road to the cabin where he'd killed Kat and Leland's sister. He'd cleaned up after his first kill, but he'd been in such a rush when he'd strangled Sierra — not knowing when Leland and whoever was with him would return — that he might've left something behind.

He should've torched the cabin the day Kat died — left her body in the downstairs bedroom tied to that bed and burned the whole thing to the ground. He'd been trying not to put Amarok on high alert, but given the recent sequence of events, Amarok had been primed for trouble, anyway. There was no reason to risk leaving any evidence for him to discover.

He just hoped it wasn't too late. What with

the recent storms, there was a small chance Amarok hadn't been able to process the scene as thoroughly as he might've liked. Or he could've missed something that he'd find later.

Jasper punched the gas pedal as he sped out of town. Maybe he could rectify that error, he thought — if, in fact, he'd made one — and felt a certain amount of relief. At least he was keeping busy. At least he was doing something that would thwart Amarok's attempts to track him down. That brought him a degree of pleasure. It couldn't compensate for the disappointment he felt at not being able to get Evelyn tonight, but it was something. He needed to be satisfied with that until he had the opportunity to do more.

It would come. . . .

He kept a gas can in the back of his truck. In these parts, a lot of people did, so it wouldn't be considered unusual. With the changeable weather, one had to be prepared at all times.

He couldn't wait to see Amarok's reaction to having the cabin go up in flames and spent the entire drive relishing how frustrated, disappointed and angry the sergeant would be.

Once Jasper was close, he hid his vehicle

in the trees and traveled the last part on foot. He was still thinking about how furious Amarok was going to be about losing the crime scene when he saw the trooper's truck in the drive.

Amarok was breathing heavily by the time he reached the only other cabin within walking distance, but he couldn't really call it a cabin. It was more of a one-room shack with no running water or electricity.

Getting there hadn't taken long, but the hike was arduous, since it was farther up the mountain and there was no clear path between the two places. He was excited at first. He thought this would be the perfect place for a killer to lie in wait — close enough to watch what was going on but not close enough to be noticed.

His excitement dimmed, however, as soon as he forced open the warped front door, which wasn't even locked. There was no evidence of recent habitation. No pots or pans or utensils. No bedding. No food or traces of a recent fire. Dust covered everything, and it was thick and undisturbed.

Whoever had kidnapped and/or killed Sierra Yerbowitz hadn't been here, Amarok decided. No one had.

So now what? If the person he was searching for hadn't followed Leland's party, he — assuming it was a he — had to have *some* reason to be in the area. What had drawn him? *Why* was he here? If Amarok could figure that out, he might be able to create a list of potential suspects.

The beam of his flashlight flickered. The batteries were failing. Adjusting his assault rifle, which he'd slung over his back, he smacked the light, trying to keep it going as he started down the mountain. The thick canopy of branches overhead blocked out even the moon's rays, but he wasn't too worried he'd be stranded in the dark. If he could keep his flashlight working until he reached the halfway point, the light he'd left on in the other cabin would guide him from there. Then he'd get some new batteries out of his glove compartment and study the woodshed again. He'd found some interesting marks on the headboard and footboard of one of the beds downstairs. He'd categorized them as normal wear and tear, but after taking a closer look he'd decided those marks could've been made by a rope rubbing against the finish. The possibility that the perpetrator had used restraints, plus the blood on the mattress, made Amarok wonder if a lot more had happened at the cabin than he'd initially believed. That meant the vomit in the woodshed might mean more than he'd thought, too. He wanted to see if he'd missed evidence of someone being tied up or dumped there.

The flashlight held out longer than he'd expected. He was almost back when he heard the crack of gunfire, coming from the cabin or somewhere nearby. He froze, too shocked to move until another shot rang out. He had no idea where the first bullet had gone, but the second bullet must've hit a branch above his head, because pine needles showered his face. That was the moment he realized that someone was firing *at him.*

Dropping to the ground, he snapped off his flashlight so he wouldn't be such an easy target.

A third bullet struck a nearby tree trunk. He heard the shot and the corresponding *thwack.* Although his heart was racing and his adrenaline pumping, Amarok wondered if this was the man he'd been looking for since he'd met Evelyn.

It almost *had* to be Jasper, didn't it? Who else but their mortal enemy would appear at the cabin where a woman had recently been kidnapped and probably killed, see his trooper vehicle in the drive and come after *him*?

Or was that wishful thinking? Because if it was Jasper, Amarok was beyond excited that he might *finally* have the chance to confront him, to fight back, instead of feeling so damn helpless as Jasper terrorized the woman he loved and harmed other innocent people.

"Bring it on, you bastard!" he yelled as he pulled his rifle around so he could aim it. "But just remember — you're not in Boston anymore! If you fuck with me out here, you're going to lose!"

There was no response. "I've owned a gun since I was five," he went on. "If I catch *one* glimpse of you, you're dead." While crawling army-style through the snow to get behind a fallen log, he looked for any dimming of the light at the cabin, anything to suggest that someone had just walked in front of a window. Any clue at all that might help him place his attacker. He'd lived in Alaska his whole life; he was so used to the pervasive darkness during the winter months that he could almost sense movement, didn't need to actually see it. "No answer?" he shouted. "You must have *something* to say. I'm the one who's got what you want. Evelyn comes home to *me* every night. And you'll never get her back."

Still nothing.

If only he could provoke Jasper or whomever it was into responding. That would give him an auditory signal to go along with the shadows and changing light patterns he was hoping to read. The gunshots that'd been fired weren't enough. The sounds seemed to ricochet in his brain the way they'd echoed through the forest.

"If you think you scare me, if you think I haven't been looking forward to this opportunity, you're wrong!" he yelled. "Try and torture *me,* you son of a bitch! I'll take you out of here in a body bag or in handcuffs. Your choice. But to be honest, I prefer the body bag."

His opponent fired. Amarok had no idea how close that bullet came. He wasn't paying any attention to the bullets aimed at him. He was too hyper-focused on their source. Short of a verbal response, that was exactly what he'd been hoping Jasper would do, because this time he was ready. This time he was both watching *and* listening.

He saw a flash near the cabin, saw the subsequent change in light as Jasper or whoever it was shifted to the right.

"There you are," he whispered, and squeezed off a round.

15

He'd been hit! Jasper couldn't believe it. Amarok had shot him, even though he wasn't carrying a flashlight or anything else that would give his location away.

Jasper couldn't feel any pain. He supposed the adrenaline and the fear were compensating. He'd never come up against anyone as capable as Amarok. That made him hate the sergeant even more.

He shouldn't have started this fight. Had he hit Amarok with his first bullet, as he'd hoped when he opened fire, the situation would be different. But he'd missed, and now he needed to get out of there as fast as possible. Amarok could not only shoot better; he could also move around in the snow better. Jasper hadn't bothered to put on any snowshoes. That was why he'd had to stick so close to the cabin. If he had to take off running, it'd be like running through cement.

He fired again, randomly. Then he ducked. He knew he'd receive a hail of bullets in response, and he did. He could hear them hitting the wood behind him — right where he'd been standing before crouching down. Amarok was like an owl; he could see in the dark. But Jasper had only intended to distract him so he could get away from the cabin and its light. He needed to return to his truck before Amarok guessed he was planning to run instead of fight. If the trooper figured out it was safe to go into full pursuit, things might not end well.

After a brief pause, he heard Amarok fire off another bullet. He didn't know if that was a test shot, to see if he'd respond, or if Amarok was using it to cover his approach to the cabin. The sergeant could already be hustling down the mountain, but if Jasper couldn't see him clearly he couldn't hit him.

His left arm tingled where he'd been shot. He assumed there was blood dripping from his sleeve, but he couldn't feel it. He had no idea how badly off he might be; his hands were numb from the cold. He'd removed his gloves so he could fire his weapon and barely remembered to stuff them in his pockets before hurrying away.

A bullet whizzed past him. Amarok was adjusting his shot, somehow following his movements.

Shit! Jasper knew he'd made a gross miscalculation. He'd thought the element of surprise would be enough of an advantage, but he'd attacked Amarok in Amarok's element. The cold didn't seem to affect the sergeant; he was prepared for it. The dark didn't seem to hamper him, either.

Jasper didn't dare turn on the flashlight he'd brought so he could find his truck. He stumbled, hit rocks that gouged his shins and ran into tree branches that clawed at his clothes. At one point, he thought he heard footsteps behind him and his knees went so weak he almost fell.

It took a moment to realize Amarok wasn't close, that it was only his imagination.

He paused to catch his breath and *think.* He was fine; he needed to calm down.

After shoving his gun in the waist of his pants, he turned on his flashlight. He was getting disoriented, *had* to see.

Luckily, he wasn't lost; he was almost at his truck. If not for that, he suspected Amarok would be right — he'd be going with the trooper, either in handcuffs or in a body bag.

Jasper kept the flashlight up his sleeve so he could cover the beam with his hand. That way, it emitted hardly any light, and he turned it off as soon as he caught a glimpse of where he was going. He still had one major advantage. The sergeant wasn't like him. Amarok might suspect he'd just been in a gunfight with Jasper, the man who'd nearly killed Evelyn, but he wouldn't know for sure. And that doubt would make him hesitate. He had no real blood lust. Unless he was being shot at or directly threatened, he'd try to capture, not kill. By taking advantage of Amarok's humanity — the same as he did with everyone else — Jasper could escape.

Once he reached his truck, he climbed in, started the engine and tore off. He was risking his life traveling that narrow road so fast, but he couldn't let Amarok catch sight of the make and model of his vehicle or, especially, his license plate.

"Go, go, go," he chanted. He only needed a few seconds, because he already knew Amarok wouldn't be chasing him down.

Amarok spotted a dim light. It appeared and then disappeared. He also heard the engine of a vehicle. Whoever had tried to shoot him wasn't still stalking him; he was getting away.

Amarok had been descending the mountain cautiously. Now he whipped his rifle back around, hoping for an opportunity to shoot. If he couldn't hit the driver because of the distance and the darkness, he could possibly take out a tire or hit the vehicle somewhere that would provide proof later. He had to do *something.*

Problem was, he couldn't see the vehicle for all the trees. There was a brief flash of brake lights and he immediately fired, but he was pretty sure he hadn't hit anything. Those lights disappeared almost instantly.

With a curse, he moved as fast as he could in his snowshoes — so fast his lungs were burning by the time he reached his truck. He had to catch whoever it was, but he also had to remove the snowshoes that had made it so easy to walk in the deep snow.

He tossed them in the bed of his truck. But the moment he started the engine, shoved the transmission into Reverse and began to back up, he knew something was wrong.

"Son of a bitch!" he yelled, and smacked the steering wheel before getting out.

Sure enough, Jasper, or whoever it was, had slashed his tires. Since Jasper hadn't been near the truck while he was fleeing, he'd done it when he first arrived.

Amarok cursed again. He'd been in such

a hurry he hadn't even noticed, but all four tires were flat, and he had only one spare.

He studied the darkness surrounding him. If the shooter came back, he'd be a sitting duck. He'd be in real trouble if he went inside and fell asleep.

But he couldn't hang out in the forest forever, watching and waiting. He'd freeze to death.

The cabin was his best bet. He could barricade himself inside, where he'd have warmth and shelter and could keep his gun handy as he waited for daylight.

He was listening for the sound of a car as he started to trudge back.

That was when he smelled smoke.

The first thing Evelyn realized was that Amarok hadn't been to bed. According to the alarm clock it was nearly eight in the morning, and yet she hadn't heard him come in.

When she moved, Makita's collar jingled as he lifted his head. "You're worried, too, huh, boy?"

He stood, eager to go out, and she nudged Sigmund, who was curled up beside her, so she could climb out of bed and put on her robe. She hoped Amarok had at least called, that she'd been sleeping so deeply she just hadn't heard the phone. But when she reached the living room and woke Phil, who was snoring loudly on her couch, he said he hadn't heard anything, either. "He's probably over at the trooper post," he added. "There's a couch. Or he could be sleeping at his desk."

That did little to alleviate Evelyn's worry. Amarok had never slept at his trooper post before, certainly not since she'd moved in with him —

The phone rang. She jumped at the noise and then, relieved, hurried over to answer it. She thought for sure it would be Amarok.

"Evelyn?"

Not Amarok. Ashton Cooper. Evelyn easily recognized the attorney's deep, gruff voice. "Hi, Ashton."

"I hope it's not too early. If so, you can call me later."

He'd probably read the disappointment in her voice. It wasn't too early. She just wasn't in any frame of mind to think about Fitzpatrick. She was too concerned about Amarok. But she didn't want to put Ashton off when she'd called him first and said she hoped to hear from him soon.

Pushing her worry down deeper, she said, "No. It's fine. How nice of you to get back to me so fast."

"I'll admit I was surprised to hear from you. It's been a while. I've been following your progress, though, whenever something comes up in the news."

She glanced nervously at the clock over the sink. Eight ten, and the minutes were ticking away. "Then you know I've had a bumpy start with Hanover House."

"I hate to tell you this, but the road you've chosen will probably be bumpy all the way along. Nature of the beast."

She tightened her robe. "You've got a point there."

Phil, who'd slept in his clothes, waved to catch her attention. He'd rolled off the couch and put on his coat and hat. "I'm going to the trooper station to check on Amarok," he told her.

She covered the phone. "Thank you. Call me as soon as you get there."

"I will."

Trying not to panic before they had any reason to, she waved as he went out.

"So . . . you're taking pity on your fellow psychiatrist?" Ashton said once she'd returned to their conversation.

"Not exactly. There isn't much about Tim Fitzpatrick that makes me feel sympathy and even less I admire. He's arrogant, insufferable. But innocent is innocent, and if he isn't responsible for those murders, he doesn't deserve to spend his life in prison."

"What makes you think he might be falsely convicted? The evidence, at least what I heard of it on your voicemail, sounds solid to me."

"It is. Unless DNA found at either crime scene matches Jasper's, he won't be getting out anytime soon."

"Jasper is the man who attacked you in high school."

"You remember . . ."

"Not a lot of men are named Jasper. It's difficult to forget. *You're* not easy to forget, either," he added.

She wasn't sure how to respond to that, so she didn't cut in; she let him continue.

"But this DNA you mentioned — the police have DNA they weren't able to match to a member of the victim's family? Or anyone else? Or what DNA are you talking about?"

"The woman for whom Charlotte was babysitting when she was murdered had only lived in that house for a short time. The person who rented it before her ran a daycare. Some kids she watched regularly, while others were drop-ins."

"That means quite a bit of human DNA

went through that place."

"Exactly. To add to the confusion, her teenage son threw a party whenever she was gone, and so many kids attended his parties, even he couldn't give the police an exhaustive list."

"I see. They've got several unmatched DNA profiles you'd like to have compared to Jasper's."

"Now that we have his DNA, yes. As soon as possible."

"Sorry if you already told me that. Your message cut off in the middle. Did you say the testing's being done?"

"Not yet. I notified Detective Dressler, the detective who investigated his case, that testing is now possible, but he hasn't called me back."

"No detective wants to be bothered with a closed case. He has too many open ones. And putting the wrong guy behind bars isn't only a travesty, it's a publicity nightmare."

She willed Amarok to come walking through the door as she stared down at Makita. "All true, but we have a moral responsibility to check this out. We've got new information that could have a material impact on whether Fitzpatrick belongs in prison."

"This convicted colleague of yours — he

doesn't have an attorney?"

"Not right now. From what he's told me in his many letters, he can't afford to pay one."

"I see."

"I'll completely understand if you'd rather not get involved, Ashton. Working for free isn't an attractive prospect. But you were the only person I could think of who might be willing and able to help. That's why I contacted you."

"I'm intrigued despite the lack of remuneration, but I'll admit my interest has little to do with Dr. Fitzpatrick's guilt or innocence."

She patted Makita, who'd edged closer in hopes that she'd hang up and take him out. "What do you mean?"

"I'd be willing to jump in and do all I can if there's even a remote chance it'll help capture Jasper. I'm not the only one who hasn't forgotten him. The whole nation's been waiting for resolution on your case."

It would boost his career if he solved it, might even result in a movie or TV deal. That was where the remuneration would come in.

"No one's been waiting more than me," she said. "And capturing Jasper *might* be a possibility. We know he was in San Diego only a few days before Charlotte was murdered, and that he was most likely in Arizona, where we think he lives, shortly after. In order to kill Charlotte in between, he must've flown to Boston from San Diego and from Boston to Phoenix in a very short time. We could check the airline manifests to see how many people did that in the days before and after Charlotte's death."

"He can't be using his own name."

"No, he's got to be using an alias, but this could help us figure out what that alias is."

"There must be hundreds of people who fly into Boston from San Diego every day. And he might not have come from San Diego. What if he flew from Los Angeles, where there are three major airports?"

Evelyn could see why Ashton might be skeptical. This was a long shot. But they had to follow every lead. "His mother said he's a family man now. If he has a wife and kids, he probably didn't have a lot of time to fly all over — or drive, for that matter. I think he'd fly to Boston from San Diego and from Boston to Phoenix. And I'll bet not too many of the people who fly to Boston from San Diego turn around and go to Arizona right after."

"True . . ."

"Plus we could automatically rule out all

women, and anyone too old or too young, if birthdates are given, which I think they are. Once we narrow down the list, we should have a manageable number. After that, we simply look at each and every individual we have left and see if we can't get DNA on anyone who seems even slightly suspicious."

"It's worth a try," he said. "Where's Fitzpatrick incarcerated?"

"Souza-Baranowski Correctional Center. It's about an hour's drive from Boston —"

"I'm familiar with it. I'll see when I can visit him."

Having Ashton on board should help with *everything.* Despite her immediate anxiety over Amarok, Evelyn felt a great deal of relief that Ashton was willing to get involved. "Will you contact Detective Dressler with Boston PD and tell him you're taking the case?"

"I will. We should move on the DNA testing right away."

"We won't get anything quickly if we go through whatever lab the police use."

"You're suggesting a private one?"

"Yes. I'll pay for it."

"That could get expensive."

"I don't care. We don't have any time to waste." She should've offered to pay before, when they were trying to test the DNA found under the nails of one of the Peoria victims against the mitochondrial DNA of Jasper's mother, but she'd never guessed it would take eight months.

"You're sure?" he said.

She thought of Sierra Yerbowitz and how slim the chances were that Amarok would find her alive. If they didn't catch Jasper soon, others would be hurt. "Positive."

"Okay, I'm familiar with a lab in Philadelphia that might be able to work us in. I'll see what I can arrange."

"Thank you. And I'll let Tim know you're coming."

Eager to hang up, she almost put down the phone. She wanted to figure out what'd happened to Amarok. But he spoke again.

"It's good to hear from you, Evelyn."

"Good to hear your voice, too. I can't tell you how much I appreciate your help."

"It's time to catch the bastard who nearly killed you. It'll be a win for all of America," he joked.

"I could use the peace of mind." Once again, she thought he'd hang up, but he didn't.

"Are you happy up there in Alaska?" he asked. "I have to admit part of me hopes you're lonely as hell and almost ready to come back to Boston, where there's a certain attorney who never had the chance to take you out."

She laughed. "I'm all for having dinner with you. It'd be great to catch up. But I should warn you that my heart belongs to a lawman up here."

"You're in a relationship?"

"I am."

"That's surprising. You once told me you'd never marry. Do you remember?"

"I remember telling almost everyone that, but Amarok has helped me over certain . . . hurdles, and that makes it more of a possibility."

There was a slight pause; then he said, "As jealous and heartbroken as that leaves me, I'm happy for you."

"I'm flattered by your interest. I really am. And I'm grateful you're taking Tim's case. It might help us find Jasper. We have to find him *soon.*"

"That sounds kind of desperate for it having been twenty-plus years. Is there something else I should know?"

"I'm afraid he might be up here," she told him.

"In Alaska? Why do you say that?" He sounded instantly concerned.

"Finishing what he started with me has always been his end game. And I think he's getting awfully tired of waiting." She told him about Sierra Yerbowitz and the piece of scalp that didn't belong to Sierra.

"You keep your lawman focused on finding her, and I'll do what I can here to make sure Jasper doesn't come back into your life. I like imagining you happy."

"Thank you. Again." The moment she hung up, she put on her coat and boots to take Makita out. She hadn't dressed for the day yet, but she didn't care about that. She had no neighbors to see her, and she was more and more worried about Amarok. Surely he'd call her, even if he *did* stay over somewhere.

She left the front door open, despite the cold air that would let into the house, so she could hear if the phone rang. She couldn't risk missing Phil's call. She was getting so worked up it was beginning to feel as though she had a thousand pounds of sand crushing her chest.

"Come on, come on," she muttered as Makita did his business, but she wasn't talking to the dog. She was exhorting Phil to get back to her.

She hadn't heard the phone while she was out, so she tried calling the trooper post when she went in.

No answer.

tional Airport in a little over an hour. Even if she was late, Brianne could wait. Amarok's well-being came first. Evelyn wouldn't be able to function properly until she was assured of his safety.

"I'm not convinced that's a good idea," he said.

Phil's hesitation only added to her concern. Obviously, he was afraid of what they might find. "I'll drive up there myself, if I have to," she threatened.

"If there's anything wrong, Amarok will have my hide if you're in the middle of it."

"Amarok's lived with me long enough to know I have a mind of my own, Phil."

He still hemmed and hawed, so she put even more force in her voice. "I'm getting my keys. I'll see you there."

"No! No need for us *both* to drive," he said quickly. "I'm leaving now to pick you up."

She swallowed against the fear that seemed to be clawing its way up her throat. After what she'd seen, how Jasper had mutilated her high school girlfriends and posed them like mannequins, she probably understood far better than Phil did what they could be in for. "I'll be waiting."

What was going on?

She was about to jump into her Land Cruiser and drive over when the phone finally rang.

Caller ID indicated Trooper Post #213. She'd seen that pop up a thousand times before.

She prayed it was Amarok and not Phil.

"He's not there?" she said as soon as she heard Phil's hello.

"Take it easy," he said in a soothing voice. "I'm sure Amarok's fine. But no, he's not here, and I've called a few people around town — Leland Yerbowitz, who's staying at The Shady Lady, Shorty over at the Moosehead and old man Boyle at Quigley's. No one's seen him."

"What does that mean?"

"I don't know yet. I'm heading over to the cabin, since that's where he was going when I last talked to him."

"I'm going with you," she said.

"Don't you have to pick up your sister from the airport today? Amarok asked me to go with you if it's storming."

Fortunately, as forbidding as the sky was beginning to look, it wasn't storming yet. "I've got time," she said. Brianne wasn't getting in until three. If the weather held, Evelyn could reach Ted Stevens Interna-

What was going on?

She was about to jump into her Land Cruiser and drive over when the phone finally rang.

Caller ID indicated Trooper Post #213. She'd seen that pop up a thousand times before.

She prayed it was Amarok and not Phil.

"He's not there?" she said as soon as she heard Phil's hello.

"Take it easy," he said in a soothing voice. "I'm sure Amarok's fine. But no, he's not here, and I've called a few people around town — Leland Yerbowitz, who's staying at The Shady Lady, Shorty over at the Moosehead and old man Boyle at Quigley's. No one's seen him."

"What does that mean?"

"I don't know yet. I'm heading over to the cabin, since that's where he was going when I last talked to him."

"I'm going with you," she said.

"Don't you have to pick up your sister from the airport today? Amarok asked me to go with you if it's storming."

Fortunately, as forbidding as the sky was beginning to look, it wasn't storming yet. "I've got time," she said. Brianne wasn't getting in until three. If the weather held, Evelyn could reach Ted Stevens Interna-

16

Before Evelyn could see the cabin itself, she spotted smoke. At first she thought it was just the gray of the low-lying clouds resting on the horizon. The sun didn't come up until nine, so it was just growing light, and they were getting a little snow. "What is *that*?" she asked, pointing.

Phil didn't have a chance to answer before they drove around the final bend in Nektoralik Road — when they could both see the burned-out cabin.

"No!" she cried. "It can't be!"

Phil shot her a nervous glance. She could almost read his mind. *I shouldn't have brought her.* He loved Amarok, too. The way his knuckles whitened as he gripped the steering wheel testified to his fear and panic. The whole community relied on the Alaska State Trooper. Amarok was one of their own, had been born and raised in Hilltop, and he did everything he could to take care of the citizens in his community — which was why he'd originally been opposed to Hanover House. He hadn't wanted an institution that incarcerated so many dangerous men in the area.

"It's Jasper." Any question she'd had about his involvement was now gone. "He's in Hilltop."

"Lightning can start fires, too," Phil said. But he didn't sound committed to his answer. There'd been no lightning last night that she knew of — and what were the chances lightning would strike *that* particular cabin at *this* particular time? The one in which a woman had recently been kidnapped and probably murdered?

Evelyn pressed her fists into her eyes. She wouldn't look anymore, *couldn't* look. "He's killed Amarok, just as I was afraid he would. Amarok's gone." The idea that she could ever leave the man she loved to go back to Boston seemed impossible in that moment. She felt as though Jasper had ripped her heart from her chest, that she could barely breathe for the gaping wound. She couldn't go on — didn't want to go on — without Amarok. Everything that'd had such meaning suddenly had no meaning at all.

"Evelyn, look!" Phil leaned over to pull her hands away from her face.

Tears were welling up. Only after she'd blinked several times did she see Amarok striding out of the woods, coming toward them with his rifle resting on one shoulder.

They parked next to his truck, and Evelyn nearly fell out into the snow, she was in such a hurry to reach him.

Phil came around the front, and Amarok handed off his rifle before pulling her into his arms and kissing her head. "It's okay," he murmured as she buried her face in his chest. "I'm right here."

She struggled to choke back the tears, but her relief was so profound she couldn't manage it. "Jasper's back," she said between gulps for breath. "I know he is."

His hand stroked her head. "Yeah. I'd say he's back. But that isn't entirely a bad thing."

That statement shocked her enough she was able to get hold of her emotions. "Are you kidding? He'll kill you! He'll kill both of us."

"He tried to kill me last night. Fortunately, he's not a very good shot. I hit him, though."

An unexpected surge of hope caused Evelyn to pull away. "You *shot* him?"

Motioning for Phil to join them, he took her through the trees in the direction from which he'd come. After warning them to stay behind him so they wouldn't destroy any evidence, he pointed at footprints, tire tracks and eventually . . . several drops of red. "He was bleeding when he left. I would've caught him if he hadn't slashed my tires."

"So when did he set fire to the cabin?" she asked.

"Before the gunfight, but I didn't notice until after he'd made a run for it."

"How'd you know he was here in the first place?"

"I didn't. He must've come after I did. Once he saw my truck, he slashed my tires and crept up to the cabin. I'm sure he expected me to be inside, but I wasn't. I was at a smaller shack I found up the mountain, looking for places someone could've kept an eye on Sierra Yerbowitz and her party. He must've figured out I wasn't in the cabin, doused the place with gasoline, started the fire and then spotted my flashlight as I came through the trees."

"Which is when he shot at you."

"Yeah."

She looked Amarok over carefully, but he raised one hand. "Don't worry. He missed, and I returned fire. Once he got hit — I'm assuming that's what made him decide to take off — he ran here, where he'd left his car, and got the hell out."

"If the cabin was burning when he left, where'd you spend the night?" Phil asked.

"At that shack I was checking out when he arrived. I could've stayed in my truck, but I felt too vulnerable there. I wanted to be somewhere I could stand or kneel while keeping watch with my rifle at the ready."

"Did you have any dry wood?"

"A little, but I didn't dare start a fire for fear I'd give away my position, or that I wouldn't be able to see as clearly."

Judging by the lines around Amarok's eyes and mouth, he was exhausted. "So you've been up all night, freezing?" Evelyn said.

"I wasn't about to go to sleep knowing he could come back. I was also worried that the cabin fire might somehow spread through the forest. As wet as it's been, that wasn't likely, but it was windy, so I was being cautious."

"It didn't spread, thank God. But it sure got the best of the cabin." Phil wrinkled his nose. "Stinks like crazy out here."

Evelyn wiped away the rest of her tears. "Jasper was trying to destroy any evidence he'd left behind."

"That's my guess, too," Amarok said. "To be honest, I have no idea why he didn't burn it to begin with."

She peered through the trees to see the charred remains of what had been part of someone's livelihood and couldn't help feeling sorry for the Barrymores, two brothers from the Lower 48 who were, according to Amarok, the owners. They'd collect on their fire insurance, but that wasn't always an easy process and often didn't cover everything. "Jasper didn't want us to know he was in Alaska. That's why he left it in the first place. He was hoping whatever he'd done out here would go unnoticed. But it hasn't."

"The news about that piece of scalp might've tipped him off that we know more than he'd like."

With a nod, she turned around, searching for any sign of Jasper . . . or someone else. Fortunately, she didn't see anyone or anything that might make her believe they were in immediate danger. "This is going to turn into all-out war between us."

"I say bring it on." Once again, Amarok gestured at what he'd brought them to see. "He made a mistake coming back here. Now I have his blood."

"You've collected it already?" she asked.

He took a small vial from his pocket. "Yep. Did that last night using my flashlight. I couldn't risk losing it. There was some on this tree, too, before I pulled off the bark."

Evelyn's heart beat faster. "You'll be able to test it to confirm his identity."

"*And* I have his tire tracks. I might even manage to get a few footprints."

Phil checked the sky. "So are you done? We need to gather what evidence we can before the weather gets any worse."

"I'm close. I've photographed the tire tracks and the foot impressions. I didn't have a tripod, which would've helped, but I started as soon as there was enough light. I'm about to get a cast of any tracks or footprints I can."

"You have the materials to do that?" Evelyn asked.

He gave her a wry smile. "Sweetheart, since you came to town, I've had to equip myself in ways I never had to worry about before. With a few squirts of snow impression wax, I'll be good to go."

"Where are you supposed to find that?" Phil asked.

"It's in my truck. I was going to grab it when I heard you pull up."

"Even if we get good impressions, it won't be easy to match them against a perpetrator," Phil said with a scowl. "We're searching for a needle in a haystack."

"You've told me that before, and yet I

keep searching." Amarok winked at Evelyn. "That asshole will never get rid of me, not until I bring him in."

The throbbing in Jasper's shoulder woke him. Amarok's bullet had gone through the fleshy part of his arm. He had both an entrance and an exit wound, so he hadn't taken the risk of going to a hospital. Anyone who'd been shot would be reported to the authorities. Instead, he'd done what he could to doctor himself. He'd stopped by the drugstore to pick up a few supplies; then he'd bathed in Epsom salts, poured hydrogen peroxide down the hole in his arm and bandaged it. Nothing he'd ever experienced hurt quite so badly. And the damn thing wouldn't quit bleeding. He'd been up most of the night trying to get it to stop. Even now, the bandage was soaked and leaking blood onto the sheets.

"Son of a bitch," he growled when he saw it. He needed to do something. But when he sat up, his head began to swim. He had to bend forward to regain his equilibrium.

He'd screwed up last night, and Amarok had taken advantage of his miscalculation. But how could he know the night would end like that? He should've been able to win a battle where *he* had the advantage of surprise. Amarok hadn't even known he was in the area, and Jasper had *still* gotten his ass kicked.

That wouldn't happen again, he vowed. The sergeant would pay for what he'd done, and so would Evelyn.

Once he could stand, he used the walls to help him reach the bathroom. Who would've thought a simple flesh wound could leave him feeling so shitty?

He'd have to take plenty of pain meds to tolerate work today, he decided as he stared at his own ashen face in the mirror. But he didn't have anything strong — only over-the-counter stuff — and he had no idea how he'd handle a full shift. What if he bled through his uniform?

He considered calling in sick. He could say he wasn't well, that he still felt poorly from when he'd left early on Friday night. But Amarok would expect whoever he'd shot to show the effects of it, so Jasper was going to make sure he seemed perfectly fine. He'd change his bandage every hour, if he had to, and flush the used dressings or shove them in his lunch pail.

Fresh blood oozed as he peeled away the gauze. He wasn't supposed to remove it once it was saturated. Every tutorial he'd read online advised him to add more bandages on top of the old one, but he wanted to see if his arm looked as though it was getting infected. He'd also read that infection was his greatest danger. He might need antibiotics.

Considering how much his shoulder hurt, he thought the hole should be bigger. . . .

He turned to look at the back and, once he'd wiped the blood, saw that the exit wound *was* bigger. Where the bullet had gone in was the size of a dime; where the bullet had come out was more the size of a quarter.

Bracing for the pain, he poured on more antiseptic, which burned through his arm like fire. He swore, even kicked the wall. Then he struggled to tie fresh gauze around his biceps using only his right hand. He needed to put some pressure on the wound, but not enough to hinder his circulation — not if he ever wanted to use that arm again.

What would he do if that didn't work? One website had suggested a hemostatic dressing, which contained clotting agents, but he'd been reluctant to go out and buy something like that. He didn't want anyone to see him purchasing it, didn't want to be recorded on some store's video camera. And what he'd read about those dressings indicated they could be difficult to remove once applied.

He didn't need any new problems. He was already worried that the bullet had pushed scraps of clothing inside him. He'd examined his injury carefully and hadn't seen any sign of debris, but with the constant flow of blood he couldn't tell for sure. Hopefully it would flush out whatever debris might be there.

Once he was finished in the bathroom, he dragged his tired and hurting ass out to the kitchen, where he popped some ibuprofen and sat down to have a bowl of cereal. He didn't think he'd ever been in such a black mood. He should take off and disappear; that would be the wisest move. But he wasn't about to give up. He was finished letting Evelyn believe she'd escaped him — and letting Amarok believe he could protect her.

He turned to look at the clock. He didn't have to be at Hanover House until ten tonight.

Hoping to distract himself until the pain eased and he could sleep again, he went into the living room and turned on the TV, watched an episode of *Forensic Files* and managed to doze off.

When he woke up, the news was on. He listened for a while, grew bored with the politics and other bullshit and closed his eyes in an attempt to get some more rest. But then he heard a snippet that made him sit bolt upright.

A newscaster was saying that two bodies had been discovered in the woods northwest of Anchorage. He saw the TV cut to an "on the scene" reporter and watched as the cameraman filming that reporter panned wide.

Shit. Although the reporter said the police hadn't yet identified the bodies, Jasper knew they soon would.

Other than getting a new short and sassy haircut and possibly losing a few pounds — not that she'd ever been heavy — Brianne hadn't changed in the past two years. Her best features were still her flawless skin and her large, dark eyes. Evelyn was relieved when she and Amarok, who'd slept while she drove, arrived at the airport in time to pick up her sister without making her wait.

A wave of homesickness and guilt for not returning to Boston to visit her folks washed over Evelyn as they embraced. "How was your flight?"

"Long." Brianne smiled, but her smile seemed forced. Although Evelyn noticed, she didn't mention it. She and her sister would have several days together, plenty of time to talk once they'd settled into their old relationship. Brianne had spoken to Amarok occasionally on the phone, but this was the first time they'd met in person. Evelyn preferred to focus on that. "This is Amarok," she said. "I'm so excited that I finally have the chance to introduce you."

"This is the wolf, huh?" she said as Amarok offered his hand.

Evelyn was so preoccupied with everything that had been going on, she didn't immediately realize her sister was referring to the meaning of Amarok's nickname. It took a second to make the connection, even though it should've been obvious, so then she laughed. "Yes."

Brianne made a show of looking him over. "Well, I can see why you might not care to return to Boston."

While she said that as a joke, one that would tease her and flatter Amarok, who winked at her, Evelyn detected a note of bitterness in her sister's voice. Brianne didn't think it was fair that Evelyn was here, chasing her dream and living with such an attractive man, while she was at home, the only one close enough to offer any real support to their parents. And Evelyn couldn't entirely blame her.

Although that inference hit a sensitive spot, Evelyn kept her pleasant expression firmly in place. "The weather's getting worse as the day wears on," she said. "We'd better grab your luggage and head back. Otherwise, we could be cut off."

Brianne's eyes widened. "From Hilltop?"

"Of course."

"How often does *that* happen?"

Amarok answered, "Fairly often during the winter. But the closure never lasts long. We're used to a lot of snow here in Alaska."

"Didn't you tell me a large number of your COs live in Anchorage?" she asked. "What happens if they can't get to work?"

"A certain number of COs remain on call during the winter months. If we're expecting bad weather, we'll have a relief crew stay in a dorm-like situation, in case they're needed."

"How often have you had to do that?"

Evelyn slipped her arm through Brianne's and guided her out as Amarok brought the luggage. "Only in rare instances."

They'd reached the parking lot and Amarok was loading Brianne's bags when Brianne's phone went off.

"That's probably Mom, checking to make sure you've arrived safely," Evelyn said as her sister got out her phone, but she could tell by the look on Brianne's face that Brianne didn't recognize the number.

"No, it's a nine-oh-seven area code. . . ."

"That's from here in Alaska," Evelyn said, and Amarok chimed in.

"Answer it!"

She didn't have time to question him without missing the call and he was adamant, so she pressed the Talk button and said hello. A second later, she handed the phone to Amarok. "It's for you."

Evelyn frowned at the man she loved. "You gave someone Brianne's number?"

"Sorry, I should've mentioned it. I didn't want to be out of reach for too long," he explained, and put the phone to his ear. "No kidding? When?" His eyebrows knitted as he spoke to whoever it was, probably Phil. "Okay, we were just about to head back. We'll go to the coroner's instead. Get hold of Leland Yerbowitz and send him to meet us. If it's her, he should be able to make the identification."

Evelyn could hardly wait until he got off the phone. "They've found Sierra?"

"They've found *two* bodies, both of them female. I don't *know* that one is Sierra, but . . ."

Evelyn clutched her purse tightly. "But . . ."

"They're both the right age, both white. And one has a chunk missing from her scalp."

Brianne scowled as she touched Amarok's arm. "Wait, the woman who's gone missing — the one you told me about on the phone — has been murdered? And someone else was killed, as well?"

"Looks that way." He handed the phone back.

Brianne shifted her attention to Evelyn. "Don't you ever get sick of . . . of evil and death?"

"Of course I do," Evelyn replied. "What do you think I'm doing up here?"

"Whatever you're doing doesn't seem to be working," she grumbled.

Before Evelyn could respond, Amarok held up the keys he'd taken from her so he could load Brianne's bags. "I'll drive."

As they climbed in, Evelyn told herself not to respond to Brianne's remark. Her family didn't understand what was at stake — that *someone* had to fight back. Society would never get ahead of the psychopathy problem otherwise.

The radio came on the second Amarok started the engine. Evelyn let music fill the silence for a minute or two. Then she asked, "How're Mom and Dad?"

"Worried about you," Brianne said. "But they've spent most of your life being worried about you, so I guess nothing's really changed."

There was that note of bitterness again. The news they'd just received about those bodies hadn't put Brianne in a better mood — and of course it wouldn't.

Hoping to distract her with a more personal conversation, Evelyn turned so she could see her sister. "And Jeff?"

Brianne shifted her gaze. "I don't want to talk about him right now."

Amarok took Evelyn's hand as they turned out of the airport. She recalled that he'd guessed something was up with Brianne's love life; this seemed to confirm it.

"Is everything okay, Bri?" Evelyn asked.

Brianne stared out the window. "Everything's fine with me. You're the one who has another psycho on the loose."

Evelyn drew a deep breath. She wasn't sure having Brianne in town was going to make her life any easier, but she understood why Amarok had wanted her to come. "It might not be *another* psycho," she admitted. "It might be the one I've been waiting for ever since he kidnapped me the first time."

Brianne returned her full attention to Evelyn. "You think Jasper's *here*?"

"I do. We both do."

"Why?"

"Because two women have been murdered."

"But how could he hide out in such a small place? You'd recognize him right away, wouldn't you?"

"I'd like to think so. But it's been more than twenty years. Who knows how he's changed."

"Do you have any *evidence* that it's Jasper?"

"Nothing solid, but someone tried to kill Amarok last night at the cabin where Sierra Yerbowitz was abducted," Evelyn said, and told her about the incident.

"You shot him?" Brianne asked Amarok when Evelyn was done. "He's wounded?"

"He was bleeding when he left," Amarok replied.

"What are the chances that you hit him in the chest or somewhere that really matters?"

Amarok shook his head. "I have no idea. Neither of us could see much of anything. But almost any injury can be lethal when it involves a bullet."

"Are you checking the hospitals, to see if someone was admitted with a gunshot wound last night?"

"We just came from the cabin, so I haven't had a chance to do much of anything. There's no cell service where we live, remember? But once I get you and Evelyn home, I'll be heading to my trooper post, and I'll start calling the closest hospitals. I've already sent a guy who works with me —"

"His name's Phil," Evelyn broke in. "He was the man on the phone."

"Anyway, Phil's out talking to the locals," Amarok went on. "We do a lot of our policing up here through informants and word of mouth. Between that and checking the businesses in town to see if anyone has called in sick, we should come up with a few leads."

"Does that mean you'll be contacting the prison?" Brianne asked.

"Absolutely," he replied. "Hanover House is our biggest employer."

Evelyn couldn't help feeling slightly defensive. "All the psychopaths at Hanover House are locked up."

"I'm checking *everywhere,*" Amarok reiterated.

17

Jasper couldn't stop sweating. He kept wiping his upper lip and complaining that the heater was on too high, but no one else at Hanover Houser seemed to find it too warm. Was it the difficulty of doing his job with an arm that ached intolerably? The stress of going into the bathroom at every opportunity to make sure the bandage wasn't getting too soaked? The resentment and anger he felt toward Amarok, which burned brighter with every wince?

Or was it something even worse — was his gunshot wound getting infected?

The fear of infection hovered constantly in the back of his mind. He'd read how quickly an open wound could turn septic, especially a gunshot wound, and how quickly sepsis could kill him. He needed rest in order to recover, but — he checked his watch — he had more than four hours to go before the end of his shift.

How on earth would he make it?

He had no idea, but he was determined not to succumb to the pain. He would *not* let Amarok beat him, even if he had to work with a bullet wound in *both* arms.

At least it was almost time for lunch. Although he was tempted to spend that forty-five-minute period sitting in a bathroom stall so he could be alone — having to pretend he felt fine took too much added energy — disappearing would be a change from his normal routine, and he didn't dare do anything different. That was why, when a CO named Sean Derby asked if he'd be playing poker with the other guards who had lunch at the same time, Jasper said yes.

The next ten minutes ticked by so slowly, he ended up going to lunch a little early.

Relieved to be the first to arrive in the break room, he closed his eyes and rested his head against the cool metal of the locker, where he'd put his heavy coat and other belongings before his shift. He couldn't continue to function for much longer. . . .

"Hey, you okay?"

Straightening immediately, Jasper turned toward the voice. He'd expected footsteps to alert him if he had company, but he'd been so caught up in his own misery he hadn't noticed Delbert Perez, who'd been around the prison much longer than Jasper, breeze in. Jasper hated Delbert simply because everyone else liked him. The dude didn't have to try to make friends. He had natural charisma — a quality Jasper had never been able to emulate as effectively as he wanted. Although Jasper knew he had a face and body that women admired, and he used to be popular in high school, over the years he seemed to have lost his appeal to his own gender. He was rarely invited to any of the COs' off-site get-togethers.

But he didn't care. He understood why. He was better than they were, and no man enjoyed being around a constant reminder of his own shortcomings. "I'm fine. Why?"

Delbert opened his own locker and got out his lunch. "You just looked . . . I don't know . . . upset or sick or something when I walked in."

"Went out last night, didn't get enough sleep," Jasper mumbled.

Delbert gave him a libertine's smile. "You see that stripper again?"

Jasper had been bragging about his night with Bambi. He'd said she'd asked to go home with him and hadn't charged him a dime. He hadn't mentioned the enticement he'd used, of course. Why ruin the story? *Any* guy could pay for sex. "No."

"When you gonna call her?"

"Maybe next weekend." He wasn't ever going to speak to her again, but no one would believe his night with her had been as spectacular as he claimed if he admitted that he had no interest in another round.

"Where'd you go last night?"

Why was Delbert being so damn nosey? Jasper felt a scowl yank at his features as hostility welled up. "It was just a regular bar. *Does it matter?*"

Delbert blinked at his churlish response. "No, doesn't matter to me at all," he said, and carried his lunch to one of the three round tables in the break room.

"Delbert! We playing a couple of hands of poker tonight, dude?" Massimo McKim, one of several COs who walked in together, was obviously excited to see Delbert, who somehow managed to turn any downtime into a party.

"So long as you're ready to lose your ass," Delbert joked.

As three other guys — Sean, who'd spoken to Jasper earlier about the poker game, Easy, who'd found that piece of Kat's scalp, and a CO by the name of Skip Pence — retrieved their lunches and sat down, the banter continued. They all spoke to Delbert, but no one bothered to say much to Jasper.

Assholes . . . Kicking himself for letting the pain and anger he felt creep into his voice while he was talking to Delbert, he grabbed his lunch and slammed his locker. When everyone's heads whipped around at the loud *bang,* Jasper chuckled, but no one seemed to think he was very funny. Massimo went so far as to give him a dirty look.

Growing even more morose than he'd been before coming on break, Jasper bought a soda from one of the vending machines that lined the wall and sat down. He had to eat exclusively with his right hand, which wasn't too difficult since that was his dominant hand, but the constant pain radiating down his left made him sick to his stomach.

Once they'd finished eating and Jasper had thrown the rest of his meal away so no one would notice how little he'd been able to choke down, Delbert brought out the cards. They were just picking up the hands he'd dealt when Amarok knocked on the open door and strode into the room.

Although seeing the sergeant at the prison wasn't entirely out of the ordinary, Jasper had never known him to visit the break room. Even Amarok's attitude was different today. Everything about him said he was now acting in an Official Capacity.

"Gentlemen, I'm sorry to interrupt your lunch," he said, "but I've got a few questions I'd like to ask, if you don't mind."

The others admired Amarok even more than they did Delbert. The deference they showed him as they readily agreed annoyed Jasper. They were so obvious in their attempts to please Evelyn's lover. But Jasper could do nothing except play along and hope his wound wouldn't bleed through his uniform right then and there.

"May I?" Amarok gestured at a chair, which he pulled over from a neighboring table, since there wasn't an open seat at theirs.

"Of course," Delbert said, and they all shifted to make room.

Jasper had been hoping the ordeal the sergeant must've endured last night — once he found his tires slashed and the only decent shelter in the area going up in flames — had taken more of a toll on him. The trooper *did* look tired and drawn. But he wasn't cowed. His flinty expression spoke of raw determination — the determination he felt to keep the community, and especially the woman he loved, safe.

Jasper was tempted to check his wound, but he was afraid that would only draw attention to his shoulder. To avoid the possibility of anyone noticing if he was bleeding through his bandage, he shifted that side of his body away from the table.

Rather than flip his chair around, Amarok sat on it backwards. "Some of you might've heard about the two bodies that were discovered earlier today" — he glanced at the clock on the wall, which said it was nearly two thirty, and amended his statement — "or, rather, yesterday."

To Jasper's surprise, only Sean had caught the news. The others expressed shock at the revelation and began asking questions all at once.

Amarok silenced them by lifting a hand so he could speak. "A snowmobiler came across their remains in a wilderness area on the northwest side of Anchorage. I might not have immediately assumed there was a connection between the woman I've been searching for and this grisly discovery, but there was something about one of the bodies that led me to believe it might have some bearing on my case, and that link has now been verified."

Jasper clenched his jaw. He'd known this might happen, but the more pieces of the puzzle Amarok held, the more precarious his own position became.

"So the Yerbowitz woman is dead?" Sean's face twisted into an empathetic grimace. "Does her brother know?"

"He does," Amarok confirmed. "He's the one who made the identification. He and his friends drove to Anchorage as soon as we learned."

"Will he be coming back here?"

"I can't imagine he will. There's no reason for him to return to Hilltop. He'll make the appropriate arrangements for bringing his sister home, once the body's been released. Then he'll head back to his family in Louisiana."

Skip's chair scraped the floor as he shifted. "How was she killed?"

"The autopsy won't take place until tomorrow, but the detective who's been assigned the case told me there was no obvious sign of trauma — no stab wound, gunshot wound or injuries to the head or body."

When Skip cringed as Sean had, Jasper couldn't help studying his expression and body language. He seemed to care about the Yerbowitzes, and yet he didn't even know them. That was something Jasper had never been able to understand.

"So was she strangled?" Skip asked.

Amarok nodded. "That'd be my guess, but

we'll wait and see what the coroner says."

Sean slid the cards he'd been dealt to one side. "And the other woman?"

"We don't know exactly what killed her, either. The autopsy should determine that."

Jasper had tortured the other woman extensively before her death, and that would be obvious. Amarok had to know it by now, but he didn't let on. Jasper could only guess he was playing the usual cop game of keeping certain information to himself so that anyone who appeared to know too much might give himself away.

"Who was the other woman?" Jasper asked this so he'd appear to show the same alarm and concern as the others.

"We don't have any information on her yet," Amarok told him. "Anchorage PD is still working on the identification."

Easy leaned forward. "So now we're looking at *two* homicides?"

He sounded shocked, but if Jasper had his way there'd be a lot more.

"Yes, there's little doubt about that," Amarok said.

Easy cracked his knuckles. "That changes things, doesn't it? Makes it much less likely one was killed by accident or in a fit of rage?"

"That's true," Amarok agreed.

Sean sat up taller. "You're not suggesting we have a serial killer on the loose!"

"It's possible. From what I can tell so far, these women weren't killed at the same time, which means there was a cooling-off period in between. And they weren't related to each other, weren't friends or even acquaintances. They seem to be totally random victims."

"Holy shit," Delbert said.

"Do you have any idea who the killer might be?" Easy asked. "I mean . . . Hilltop is such a small town. You don't suppose it could be someone from *here.*"

"It could be," Amarok replied. "Or it could be someone who only visits here, for work or whatever."

They all looked at one another.

"Are you suggesting it might be an employee and not an inmate?" Skip asked.

"All the inmates have been accounted for, and something was found on the road to the prison that makes me wonder if there might be a connection to a member of the staff. That's why I'm not only talking to you, I'm talking to everyone — as soon as I get the chance."

Massimo toyed uncomfortably with his cards. "What was found on the road?"

Amarok shot Easy and Jasper a quelling

glance. He didn't want them to mention the piece of scalp. Jasper could easily interpret that glance because Evelyn had already asked him to keep quiet about it, and he'd done just that. He didn't want word to get out himself, didn't want someone to come forward who might've seen him, for one. He also didn't want Amarok to think he was out blabbing his mouth, couldn't afford to stand out in any way. "I'd rather not say, not yet," Amarok told them.

That confirmed it. Amarok was playing games, all right.

"*Two* murders," Easy muttered, still sounding shocked.

"What kind of bastard goes around killing random women?" Massimo asked.

Sean gave him a funny look. "The kind of bastards we have in here."

"And the kind of bastard who tortured and attempted to kill Dr. Talbot when she was just a teenager," Amarok said.

"You don't think *he's* up here, do you?" Massimo asked. "I mean, they never caught him, and people have speculated that he might try to kill her again, but . . . shit, that was twenty-something years ago."

Amarok scrubbed a hand over his face. "I'm keeping an open mind. It doesn't *have* to be Jasper. It could be someone who hates

Evelyn and is trying to scare her by making her think Jasper's returned. It could be someone who's getting high committing murders in the shadow of the institution that's been built to investigate that type of behavior. It could even be someone who's recently become unstable. We don't know a great deal at this point, but twenty-four hours ago, I was at the cabin from which Sierra Yerbowitz went missing, looking for evidence, when someone took a shot at me, so I fired back."

Delbert slapped the table. "*What?* You were in a gunfight?"

"Whoever it was obviously missed," Skip pointed out before Amarok could answer.

"He did, but *I* didn't."

Galled by the pleasure the sergeant took in that statement, Jasper balled his good hand into a fist under the table.

"You got him?" Easy asked. "Are you sure?"

"Positive. He was bleeding pretty badly when he took off, left a trail. So I'm asking all of you to keep your eyes open. I just checked with the warden. No one's called in sick since the incident. That means if whoever it was works here, chances are he wasn't scheduled. I'll check again in the morning, but please let me know if you run across someone who's been injured or is acting strange."

Jasper couldn't believe how narrowly he'd missed the net Amarok had cast. He'd *almost* called in sick. He'd thought he might be able to get away with it because he'd been "sick" Friday night and that was on record. But if he'd succumbed to the temptation, the trooper would've come knocking on his door to see what the problem was.

He'd made the right choice.

He would've let his breath go in a long sigh of relief — except it felt as though he had blood running down his arm. It might only be a few minutes before everyone noticed the bright red drops rolling off his fingertips and dripping onto the floor.

He waited until one of the other COs — Sean — caught Amarok's attention. While Sean talked about some guy who'd seemed a little strange, a guy he'd met in the diner earlier, Jasper risked a glance at his left hand.

Nothing. He was imagining the sensation, probably because he was so nervous. His heart was pounding like a hammer — in rhythm with the pulsing ache in his shoulder.

Amarok listened politely before telling Sean he'd see what he could find out about the "weird" dude and got up. "Thanks for your help," he said, but instead of walking out he took the time to shake each person's hand.

Thrilled by this sign of camaraderie and respect, the others eagerly responded while Jasper froze. Was this some sort of test? Could it be that Amarok was trying to gauge each man's sincerity and physical well-being?

As the sergeant went around the circle, Jasper thought that might be the case. Jasper lied so often he wasn't worried about his ability to act sincere. But he was concerned when Delbert gave Amarok a Styrofoam cup filled with coffee, because then the trooper had only his left hand to offer Jasper.

Jasper had come into physical contact with Amarok once before. They'd shaken hands when he went, as Andy Smith, to visit Evelyn in the hospital after "saving" her last winter. Jasper remembered it clearly. He was so fascinated by Evelyn's lover that there was something stimulating, almost sexual, about a second encounter. After all, it was Amarok's hands that touched Evelyn in the most intimate of places.

The excitement Jasper felt disappeared the moment he had to squeeze Amarok's hand, however. He hadn't had time to prepare for or ease into the movement, and it sent a sharp pain through his body.

He was positive Amarok would see the grimness under his plastic smile or the color drain from his face. But Skip happened to speak just then, and Amarok looked away.

"I saw a woman with Dr. Talbot at the Moosehead last night, when I stopped to eat before work," Skip said. "Are we getting a new psychologist or neurologist or something here at Hanover House?"

Amarok released Jasper's hand as he took a sip of coffee. "No, that was Brianne, her sister. She's visiting for a week or so."

"Dr. Talbot has company from back home?" Delbert said. "Heck of a time to come to Alaska, what with two murders and all the storms."

"I'm happy Evelyn won't be home alone this week," Amarok said.

The sergeant was doing everything he could to cockblock Jasper. It wouldn't work, but Jasper couldn't think about how he'd counter that move right now. He had to get out of the room; he felt like he was about to pass out.

"Gotta take a piss," he muttered as he slipped through the others. "But if I see anything, I'll let you know," he added in a louder voice, along with a little salute using his right hand for Amarok.

Amarok nodded to signify that he'd heard, but was too busy to respond in any other way.

Jasper barely made it to the bathroom before his knees buckled. He grabbed the sink with his good arm so he wouldn't fall and managed to summon the strength to make it into a stall, where he threw up what little he'd eaten.

Afterwards, he sat on the toilet and hung his head, waiting for the pain in his arm to subside. He was fairly certain he was bleeding again, but he couldn't change the dressing right now. He had to have a few minutes.

He was still sitting there when Easy poked his head into the bathroom. "Hey, we're all clocking back on. You about done in here?"

He'd been in the bathroom too long if someone had to come after him, but he couldn't help that.

"Yeah, I'm right behind you," he said.

After Easy left, he took a deep breath and surged to his feet. Then he changed the bandage on his arm and flushed down the other one before walking out as if nothing were wrong.

He had a solid three hours before he could

go home.

He hoped to hell he lasted that long.

18

Evelyn felt terrible leaving Brianne when she headed to work first thing the following morning. Last night had been so stilted and awkward. Even though, once they'd finally returned to Hilltop and Amarok had dropped them off, they'd had dinner at the Moosehead before spending several hours alone, it had been nothing like she'd anticipated when she'd agreed to have Brianne come visit. Her sister simply wasn't herself. Evelyn didn't know why, but she couldn't stay at home, trying to figure out what was wrong. Hilltop was in the middle of another murder investigation, one in which she and the institution she'd fought so hard to create would once again come under fire. Her boss at the Federal Bureau of Prisons would feel the pressure, too. She needed to be there if Janice called.

On top of that, Hanover House was getting its first female psychopath today and there was a news crew coming from Anchorage to document the occasion. It was more important than ever that she be present and ready to reassure the country that she knew what she was doing, that having a prison like Hanover House did not constitute more of a threat than not having one and that whatever was happening had nothing to do with a lack of security.

Because she had so much on her mind, she wasn't pleased to see Dr. James Ricardo waiting for her when she walked through the glass double doors that led into the mental health offices. She could guess what her colleague wanted to talk about and would rather not broach that subject again.

"Not today, James," she said when he started to approach her. "I've told you before, we're not ready to publish."

"Of course we are!" he argued. "We've been doing brain scans for eight months. It's time to tell the world what we're finding."

"That would be premature. You can't draw solid conclusions from too small a sample."

"We have the biggest sample of any research team so far!"

Fortunately, they were both early and could argue in private, since none of the support staff had arrived. Judging by the lack of light in the perimeter offices, the rest of the mental health team wasn't in, either. "It's *still* not enough," she said. "The brain has too many variables. You know that. It can be significantly different from one individual to the next, and yet both can be perfectly normal. We need to continue our studies until our findings are unimpeachable."

"If we do that, someone else will publish first."

"They already have! A number of researchers from around the world are looking into the same topics."

"They don't have access to the number of violent psychopaths we do, so they don't have the same amount of data to back up their conclusions."

Evelyn grappled for the patience she needed to deal with her shortsighted colleague. She knew his wife was unhappy in Alaska, that he hoped to take her back to the Lower 48 soon, but Evelyn couldn't let him push her into risking her professional credibility. "That's part of the problem."

"What do you mean?"

She didn't want anything they put out there to be taken as gospel and used in some kind of diagnostic procedure. Their findings weren't conclusive enough yet. "I'm sorry,

James. I know getting this information out there matters a great deal to you —"

"It should matter to you, too!" he broke in as he followed her into her office. "Everyone in the country is waiting for us to reveal what we're learning. They're going to wonder what the hell we're doing up here — using federal dollars to run this place — if we're not passing anything along to the public."

She flipped on the light before putting her briefcase under her desk and her purse in a drawer she kept locked while she was at work. "So we should make generalizations that could have negative implications for people, based on the size of certain structures in their brains? Even though we can't be entirely sure those generalizations will hold true from subject to subject? Come on, James. You're a neurologist! You know there's a great deal of natural variation in brain structure. If what we've done has taught us anything, it's taught us that."

"The corpus callosum is typically bigger in psychopaths! We're seeing as much as a thirty percent difference."

"The corpus callosum can vary from five to nine millimeters in *normal* individuals! I don't want to echo what others have said and come up against the same criticism. I believe the differences between 'psychopath' and 'normal' lie in the *microwiring* of the brain."

"Brain scans don't show us the microwiring!"

"That's true. Which is why we need better procedures before we publish."

"So until we get these 'better procedures,' we're just going to toss aside the fact that we're consistently seeing a larger striatum in psychopaths?"

"A striatum is no simple thing! It's a connected set of structures, each with its own subcomponents, and we don't yet understand all the functions of those structures. Considering that, how can we say what's normal and what isn't?"

"We know the whole complex plays a role in learning, motor control and integrating information —"

"But we don't have enough data to confirm that a larger striatum is positively linked to psychopathy. We can't even say that psychopaths definitely show lower levels of activity in the prefrontal cortex. While we've seen that trend, we've also seen, with our larger sample and our own scans, that activity levels in the PFC can vary in the same individual from one day to the next."

He threw up his hands. "So you won't do it. I came all the way to Alaska just to research indefinitely, with no end goal in sight?"

"We're doing everything we can to reach solid conclusions — and to share them. We're just not there yet, James. I can't change reality, no matter how frustrated you are. Give it a little more time. We'll only lose credibility — and possibly our funding — if we publish too soon. Why not take advantage of the opportunity to research *in depth* before making any kind of blanket statements?"

He scratched his head as he paced in front of her desk. She could tell he was trying to come up with an argument that might sway her, but she'd already made up her mind.

"We have Mary Harpe, our first female psychopath, arriving today," she said, hoping to distract him. "Including her in our studies might tell us something new. And having her here opens up other issues we can examine. You know how a male with psychopathic traits is more likely to be diagnosed as a psychopath, while a female with the same traits is likely to be given the benefit of the doubt. We're just getting started. We still have a lot of work to do."

His expression said he was reluctant to be

mollified but was intrigued in spite of himself. "When will Mary arrive?"

"You didn't get the e-mail?" Evelyn notified all personnel whenever they were expecting a high-security transfer.

"I haven't checked my inbox recently." He gave her a pointed look. "I've been busy writing the paper I was hoping we'd publish."

She ignored that last part. "By the time the plane lands in Anchorage and the marshals bring her over, my guess is it'll be one or so."

"Okay," he relented, and started to leave.

"You're not going to say anything about Sierra Yerbowitz?" she asked before he could clear the door.

"About what? The fact that her body's been discovered?"

"Yes. Along with another body. What do you think happened?"

He rested his hands on his hips. "Well, we know Tim Fitzpatrick isn't to blame *this* time."

She frowned at the sarcasm. "*I* didn't blame Tim for the last murders. He was charged by the police and convicted by a jury of his peers." She almost added that she had someone looking into his case, on the off chance he was innocent, but decided not to go into that.

"It's not like seeing him go to prison broke your heart."

"After what he did to me, do you think it *should* have?"

Finally, he seemed to let go of the resentment that had pervaded the conversation so far. "No, I don't. He was wrong to do what he did. So what do *you* think happened to Sierra Yerbowitz and the other victim?"

She almost admitted that she thought Jasper was back, but refused to make that conclusion public when there were still other possibilities. "We obviously have someone very dangerous in our midst."

"Here in Hilltop?"

"That'd be my guess. Although the bodies were found an hour and a half away, Sierra was taken from a cabin not far from here. And something that ties in to the other murder — I can't say what — was discovered down the road. So even if the culprit doesn't *live* in the area, he could easily work here."

"You're not including Hanover House in that statement . . ."

"It doesn't matter if I include Hanover House or not. Amarok definitely does, and I can't blame him. As he says, we're the biggest employer in the area."

He rolled his eyes as he shook his head. "Great. That's just what my wife needs to hear. She'll insist we leave Alaska right away."

Penny entered the common area outside Evelyn's office, along with several others who provided clerical support for the team. Evelyn could see them through the interior glass of her office and returned the waves she received. "We need to instruct everyone to keep a sharp eye out," she said. "We can't let anyone else get hurt."

"Will you make an official announcement?" he asked.

She remembered how frightened Penny and everyone else had been — including herself — when Lorraine Drummond, her friend and the woman who ran the kitchen at Hanover House, was murdered eighteen months ago. The fact that Hilltop was so remote was supposed to make the institution safer for society in general, but it made the danger of having a psychopath on the loose even worse for the locals. "I am," she said. "Tim created a tip sheet when . . . when we needed it last time. I'll send that out again."

James seemed skeptical. "The question is, will that be enough?"

If they were talking about Jasper, Evelyn

knew it wouldn't be. If he wanted to take another victim, he'd find a way, and James's wife was at home alone all day, which left her vulnerable. But Evelyn didn't have time to reassure her colleague. Penny interrupted them by popping in to tell her that the crew from the *Alaska Dispatch News* was going through the security checkpoint.

She had a difficult day ahead, and it all started with this interview.

Brianne couldn't sleep. It was four hours later in Boston, past noon. She wanted to drive over to Hanover House and see the prison. After all, that damn thing had cost her the company of her sister for the past two years — even more if Brianne counted all the days and nights Evelyn had been completely consumed with lobbying for it in the years before it was built. But Evelyn had told her Hanover House would be getting a new inmate today, so it wasn't the best time. She'd had Amarok drop her off at work, leaving her vehicle for Brianne to use. She'd suggested Brianne explore the town today and wait until tomorrow to see the prison, when Evelyn would be available to give her the grand tour.

Brianne had agreed, but it wasn't going to take long to see the town. If she blinked, she'd miss it. There were only a few blocks lined with rustic buildings and snow piled along both sides of the road. In other words, not much to hold her interest. The beauty of Alaska wasn't in its architecture or its shopping. It was in the raw land — the towering mountains, clear rivers and lakes upon lakes upon lakes. It was also in the wildlife. She'd seen a moose walking down the street, just lumbering along as if it was no big deal, as she was driving away from Amarok's house.

"A moose!" she muttered, and shook her head. She'd never felt so close to nature. And the air here! It smelled crisp and clean. She could see the appeal of such a place — with all the wide-open spaces, the freedom, the simplicity — and feared her sister could, too. Would the last great frontier, and the best-looking man Brianne had ever laid eyes on, tempt her sister into moving here permanently?

The answer to that question terrified Brianne. She'd been as tolerant of Evelyn's passion for knowledge as anyone, had tried to support her and her goals even when their parents were negative about her getting involved in this kind of research. Brianne didn't want to be a selfish jerk, but Evelyn had been gone long enough. She needed her sister. Who else was she going to turn to now that she'd be raising a child alone? She couldn't rely on her parents. With what they'd been through, nearly losing Evelyn and then having to wonder for the past twenty-two years if and when Jasper might strike again, their mother was almost a basket case, and Lara's many episodes of anxiety and depression took a toll on their father.

She passed a small motel, a diner, a guns and ammo store that looked relatively new and the bar where Evelyn had taken her last night. It had a big parking lot to one side — evidence that it was the most popular place in town — and moose antlers over the door. She stopped to take a picture, since it was light enough. She thought Jeff would get a kick out of this quaint place — and then reminded herself that she couldn't send it to him. She'd made him choose, and he'd chosen someone else. He was getting texts and calls from the new woman in his life these days. He didn't even seem to care that she was pregnant, which convinced her he'd never really loved her in the first place.

Besides, there was no cell service here. She couldn't send pictures or texts to anyone, not from her phone, not unless the bar was open and she could go inside to use their Internet.

She frowned as she shoved her phone back in her purse. She hadn't told Evelyn about the baby yet, hadn't been able to bring herself to start the trip that way. But she should have. Last night hadn't gone well. Evelyn had guessed something was wrong but hadn't been willing to push, so they'd talked about everything except the real problem. Or, rather, problems . . .

Since she was at the edge of town, she almost turned back. But then she saw another building a little distance off. Once she realized it was some sort of grocery store, she kept driving.

"Quigley's Quick Stop," she read from a crude hand-lettered sign on top of the building as she pulled in to see what they had. Poor Amarok had been working night and day. And Evelyn was stressed out of her mind. So Brianne decided to make them dinner.

There were two other vehicles in the parking lot. A large, barrel-chested man walked out as she walked in. The driver of the second car had his back to her two aisles away as the clerk, an older gentleman, looked up and nodded in lieu of a greeting.

She selected what she needed to make meatloaf and mashed potatoes and approached the cashier at the same time as the other patron — a prison guard from Hanover House, judging by his uniform.

"You go ahead," he said, even though he was carrying only a bottle of Tylenol.

"Are you sure?"

"I'm in no hurry."

She smiled and thanked him. If she hadn't been so brokenhearted and in such an unenviable situation, she might've found him attractive. Tall, with thick, dark hair, blue eyes and a close-cropped beard, he had a muscular build and a ready smile that revealed a set of perfect teeth.

The cashier, who had to be in his seventies, considering the gray hair, the slope to his shoulders and the fine network of blue veins in his nose, started ringing her up. "You new in town or just visiting?"

"Just visiting," she replied.

He hesitated, one arthritic hand gripping her loaf of bread. "That's a Boston accent I hear, ain't it?"

"It is."

"You come from the doc's neck of the woods, then."

"If you mean Dr. Talbot, yes. I'm here visiting her. I'm her sister, Brianne."

He made a clicking sound with his tongue. "Hell of a time to come to town, Miss

Brianne, with what we got going on."

"You mean the missing woman . . ."

"I mean the *murdered* woman. Two bodies have shown up so far. Who knows what's going on? We could be looking at even more."

"True. But I'm sure you're aware my sister is no stranger to violence."

The scanner beeped as he ran the UPC symbol on the bread. "You're not afraid?"

"Probably more than she is," she admitted.

"How old were you when she was kidnapped?"

"I'm younger by two years, so I was only fourteen. I'll never forget what it was like when she went missing." Or what it'd been like when she was found. Brianne had sat with their mom and dad in Evelyn's hospital room day in and day out, hoping and praying and wondering whether her sister would survive.

"From what I hear, it's a miracle she lived through that first attack," the man behind her chimed in.

She turned to include him in the conversation. "You work at Hanover House?"

"I do. Been there eight months."

"How do you like it?"

"It's a job." He winked at her. "I certainly

don't feel as passionate about it as your sister does."

"I'm afraid her passion for that place is going to get her killed," Brianne grumbled.

"She might already be dead if not for him." The cashier gestured toward the officer behind her.

Brianne lifted her eyebrows. "What do you mean?"

"You don't know who he is?"

She glanced between them in confusion. "No. . . ."

"This is Andy Smith, the man who saved your sister's life when Lyman Bishop came back for revenge."

Smith modestly waved his words away. "My timing was good, that's all. I just happened to show up at a critical moment."

"You're the one who interrupted Lyman Bishop?" Brianne asked. If she'd heard or read his name, she'd forgotten it.

"I was looking for the sergeant — and found Lyman Bishop trying to give your sister a frontal lobotomy. Like I said, it was a lucky interruption."

"It was a very narrow escape for her."

"She didn't tell you about it?" The cashier sounded surprised.

"I saw it on the news. And I have a Google alert on her name, so I read about it online.

But when I asked her about the incident, she said the media made it sound much worse than it was."

"I'm sure she didn't want you to worry," Smith said. "How long will you be staying in Alaska?"

"A week. I have to get back to my job after that."

The cashier finished ringing her up and bagged her groceries. "Have a great stay."

"Thanks." She sent the Hanover House guard who'd saved her sister's life a farewell smile. Almost all the men in Alaska seemed to be good-looking. . . .

She was just starting Evelyn's Land Cruiser when Smith came out and tapped on her window.

She rolled it down so they could hear each other, and he handed her his card.

"My number," he said with a grin. "And don't worry. I'm not hitting on you, only offering friendship. I know your sister's involved in what's going on right now, and I'd hate for you to be left sitting around, bored, while you're on vacation. There's so much to see and do here. Just give me a call if you'd like me to show you around Anchorage. That's where I live."

Impressed that he'd make such a nice offer, she put the card in her purse. "I appreciate that," she said. "I'll keep it in mind."

19

"Look at him. He looks positively haggard," Samantha Boyce confided to her best friend, Hannah Wilson. "What's that crazy woman he's living with doing to him?"

Hannah twisted around to take a peek but had to wait for Cindy Brandt, one of the waitresses at The Dinky Diner, to step out of the way before she could see Amarok sitting at the bar, finishing an open-face turkey sandwich and drinking a cup of coffee. "He still looks pretty darn good to me," she joked.

"Because he can't *not* look good, but" — Samantha slid over in the booth to get a better view — "she doesn't even cook for him! He deserves better."

Facing forward again, Hannah stirred the ice in her soda with her straw. "I'm sure he can make his own meals. He's probably just grabbing a quick bite so he can get back to work, right? He's knee-deep in a murder investigation."

"You mean *another* murder investigation."

"He *is* the only police officer in the area. Who else is going to investigate?"

"No one would need to investigate if Evelyn Talbot hadn't come to town! Because none of this would be happening. This type of thing never occurred here before. It's the psychos she's brought to the area. She's putting us all at risk. Whoever killed Sierra Yerbowitz and that other woman could kill any of us."

"Not *you.*" Hannah stabbed one of the slices of chicken on her salad. "You can use a gun as well as any man. Heaven help the burglar or rapist who tries to break into *your* house."

Having her skills recognized would normally have brought her some pleasure, but Samantha was too morose today. Amarok seemed to be drifting further and further away from her instead of wanting her back, and yet, when she'd returned to Hilltop, she'd been sure they'd find the love they'd lost. "You're not a bad shot yourself," she told Hannah, adding a few more crackers to her clam chowder although she had little interest in eating it. "And you're getting better all the time."

Hannah gave her a salute. "Thanks to you."

The guns and ammo shop Samantha had opened when she returned to town last winter was doing well. She taught others how to shoot as a sideline business but helped Hannah, who was like a sister to her, for free.

"Did he notice you when he came in?" Hannah asked. She'd been in the bathroom when Amarok arrived, so she hadn't seen him wave.

"Yeah."

"And?"

"He acknowledged me." *Barely.* She'd hoped he'd walk over and say a few words, but he didn't. Even Makita, after a quick tail wag to suggest he recognized her, stayed with his master.

She'd never experienced the kind of pain she'd endured since losing the only man she'd ever loved. It felt like he was putting her heart through a meat grinder every time she saw him.

Hannah set her fork down and leaned forward. "Have you told him how you feel, Sam? Maybe you should. Maybe it'll make a difference."

Samantha had *tried,* but he'd shut her down immediately, and she had too much pride to admit it, especially to Hannah, who'd always looked up to her. He was making a mistake, but he didn't realize it. That was all. Samantha didn't only want to be in his bed; she also wanted to be his wife, have his children, spend the rest of her life with him — and she felt she should have that opportunity. After all, she was willing to give him everything Evelyn denied him. Why couldn't he see how much happier he'd be with her? "He'll come back to me eventually."

"I'm sure you're right. You two are perfect for each other."

"I'm better suited to him than Evelyn is."

Hannah lowered her voice. "I know! I can't imagine what he sees in her! I mean, she's pretty, but so are you. And she's seven years older than he is!"

"Not only that, she's completely caught up in her work. When she first got here, he didn't even want Hanover House in the area. If it wasn't for everyone else talking about the jobs and the prosperity it would bring, he would've fought it much harder." Samantha had been living elsewhere during that time, but she'd heard how it had all gone down — from the townspeople who, like her, were unhappy about the fact that they now had hundreds of psychopaths living a stone's throw away. "She needs to go back to Boston."

Hannah popped a crouton into her mouth. "Well, even if she doesn't, you might not have to worry about her for much longer."

Samantha held her spoon suspended in midair. "What are you talking about?"

"Haven't you heard?" Her friend leaned forward so that no one else in the restaurant would be able to eavesdrop. "Everyone's saying the psychopath who slit her throat when she was sixteen has come back to finish her off. That's what these murders are all about. He's leading up to the main event."

Soup splashed as Samantha let her spoon clatter against the edge of her bowl. "Ugh! I wish that was true," she said as she grabbed her napkin to wipe her hands. "I wish he'd kill her and get it over with!"

Hannah looked shocked. "You don't mean that!" she chided, but Samantha wasn't so sure. Evelyn had *her* man. She had to figure out how to get him back.

"Of course I don't," she said to avoid Hannah's disapproval. "But Amarok needs to relax and let her fight her own battles. He's running himself into the ground, even though *she's* the one who's waging a war against the 'conscienceless,' as she puts it.

He never signed on for that."

"With any luck he'll find Jasper Moore or some shred of proof that it's someone else who murdered those women, someone who isn't a specific threat to Evelyn or our community. *Then* he'll be able to relax."

Samantha eyed Amarok again. Maybe Hannah had a point. Maybe the situation would resolve itself and things would return to normal. But she couldn't tolerate "normal" anymore, couldn't tolerate having Evelyn in the area.

What if the snooty psychiatrist stayed indefinitely?

It would ruin the rest of Samantha's life!

"She doesn't belong here," Sam insisted. "Allowing Hanover House to be built, and having her and the other shrinks in Hilltop, it's all a big mistake, and what's happening proves that."

"I agree. It was only last winter that Sandy was murdered, and a year and a half earlier two other people were killed!"

"Exactly! So we should quit complaining and do something about it," Samantha said. "Stop letting *her* call all the shots."

Hannah took a sip of her Coke. "There's nothing *we* can do about it."

"I'm not going to give up that easily," Samantha said, especially because there was *one* way to get rid of her. If only Samantha could figure out how to hand Evelyn over to Jasper, he'd take care of her once and for all.

"Why don't you tell me how you got here," Evelyn suggested.

Mary Harpe, a heavyset middle-aged woman with a narrow, pointy nose, brown frizzy hair and thick glasses — a former pediatric nurse — sat across from her, behind a plate of plexiglass. Their own Nurse Ratched, Evelyn thought. She didn't feel Mary was much of a threat to *her.* From what she'd been able to determine so far, not just from Mary's file but also from speaking to the prosecutors on her case and some of Janice's staff when they were making the decision to have her transferred, she only took advantage of the very young. And she was sneaky about the harm she caused. She could be sullen and uncooperative but rarely confronted her enemies outright, which made Evelyn respect her even less than the men she dealt with who were openly menacing or hostile. Evelyn would've been willing to meet with Mary in a regular room, but, due to the nature of her crimes, Mary was classified as high risk, so Evelyn had decided to adhere to the proper protocol. She figured that was probably best. If she'd learned anything about psychopaths, it was that she couldn't trust a benign appearance.

Ms. Harpe folded her arms and glared through the glass. "You know how I got here. I flew into Anchorage, and the marshals delivered me from there."

Evelyn took her glasses out of her briefcase and slipped them on, simply to look busy while she let the conversation lapse. She'd found that talking less and listening more produced the best results. What was said when someone was trying to fill awkward silences could be revealing.

"Is that what you meant?" Mary asked, wearing a smirk.

Evelyn opened Mary's file, which she'd brought with her, before glancing up. "What do *you* think I meant?"

"I think you know how I got here."

"And you'd be right, of course."

She lifted her chin in defiance. Now that concealing her true nature offered nothing to be gained — she was sentenced to ninety-nine years behind bars, which meant she'd never be getting out — she was more belligerent than Evelyn had heard of her behaving in the past. "You know what I've been convicted of, so it was a stupid question."

m trying to open a dialogue with you. I ed the beginning would be the best to start."

"A 'dialogue.' "

"A conversation, yes."

She narrowed her eyes. "And you hope to establish . . . what?"

Evelyn folded her hands in front of her. She didn't admire any of her subjects. Almost all of them had committed heinous crimes. But she felt the most contempt for those who harmed children. "First and foremost, I'd like to determine if you've assumed personal responsibility for your crimes, and I want to do that because it'll tell me a great deal about you as an individual."

Mary obviously sensed a trap but seemed unsure how to avoid it. "I pleaded not guilty."

"Is that the stance you're taking today? Are you telling me you're innocent?"

She thought for a second, smiled faintly and nodded. "Yes."

"Despite all the evidence to the contrary."

"I don't care about the evidence."

"You can't just wipe it away. The number of babies who fell ill at the hospital in Milwaukee during the night shift when you were working is a staggering five hundred percent greater than at any other time." Evelyn pulled out the chart displaying this information and turned it so that Mary could see it, too. They weren't sure exactly how she was making the babies sick, but once she was caught and they looked back they found some astonishing statistics. "The spike in respiratory failure cases in the neonatal ward correlates *exactly* with when you started at the hospital and ends when you left." Evelyn pointed at the spot where the graph evened out. "This part here shows where the emergencies go down to a normal level. That's when you were fired."

Mary Harpe shrugged, seemingly unconcerned with the lives she'd taken and the heartbreak she'd caused. "I worked at a hospital. Emergencies happen."

"Then maybe we should talk about what went on after you moved to Richmond, Utah, and started working in Dr. Ivy Maxwell's pediatric practice."

"The hospital gave me a good recommendation!"

Or she wouldn't have been able to get on with Dr. Maxwell. But those at the hospital hadn't truly believed she was a good nurse; they'd simply been eager to get rid of her. That was probably one of the saddest aspects to this case. "I feel like whoever gave you that recommendation should be sitting in here beside you, facing several years in prison himself or herself. Because, according to what I've read, the ambulance was called to Dr. Maxwell's practice seven times in the first month."

Mary studied her nails. "Is there a point to all this? Because we're wasting time."

"You don't want to talk about it."

"No."

"Do you feel any remorse at all? Two of the babies to whom you administered the succinylcholine couldn't be resuscitated. They're dead, their families devastated."

Nothing. It was like staring at a blank slate.

"It says here that your own daughter, who's eighteen now, was admitted for respiratory failure on three different occasions when she was an infant." Evelyn held up the file. "And mysteriously — or not so mysteriously now, I guess — her respiratory problems disappeared the minute she went to live with her father."

"I wasn't convicted of that," Mary said with a glower. "I wasn't even charged."

"But how do you explain what happened?"

Another shrug. "The air's better in Arizona."

Despite all the psychopaths she'd met

with, who'd made similar jokes, Evelyn had to marvel at Mary's callous disregard for those she'd harmed. "Do you ever think about *why* you did what you did? Do you ever consider what drove you to harm those innocent babies?"

Again, no response.

"Did Dr. Maxwell mistreat you? Did you dislike her?"

"She thought she knew everything," she grumbled.

Evelyn slid her chair forward. "So you *did* dislike her."

"Not really."

"And yet you destroyed her practice and caused the community where she'd just opened it to revile and distrust her, all of which put such a strain on her marriage that she's now going through a divorce."

"You're worried about *her*? At least she's out there, living her life." She gestured to indicate beyond the walls of the prison. "She can start over, find a new man. Why don't we talk about what happened to *me*?"

Evelyn nearly laughed. This kind of extreme narcissism, paired with a lack of remorse, was so common among psychopaths. She'd never forget reading a statement from Diane Downs, a woman who shot her own children because she believed the married man she was having an affair with didn't want the encumbrance. Instead of feeling *any* empathy for them, any remorse for what she'd done to them, she complained about the pain she'd endured because of her own gunshot wound, which *she'd* inflicted to make the whole thing look as though there'd been an attack.

"Yes, why don't we talk about what's *really* important," Evelyn said, but she had difficulty listening after that. Brianne's statement in the car yesterday kept echoing over and over in her mind. *Whatever you're doing doesn't seem to be working.*

Was she wasting her time here? Letting her family down by stubbornly resisting their entreaties to come home? Putting the people in this small, simple town at risk because of her determination to understand the kind of person who'd victimized her in the past?

Was she really doing good — or was *she* being selfish?

Somehow, Evelyn managed to finish that interview and get through the rest of the day, but it wasn't easy. For every two steps forward, she seemed to take as many back. And that had never been more apparent than when she caught a ride home with a colleague and found another typed note on the windshield of her car, which was parked in the drive.

Can't you see what you're doing? You don't belong in Alaska. Go back to Boston. No one wants you here.

She couldn't help wincing. She'd become friends with so many of the locals, had begun to feel at home here with Amarok. . . .

She glanced around, wondering who might've left it.

She saw nothing. Nobody. Shoving it in her purse, she made her way up the walk. She didn't want Brianne to know about it, didn't want to add any more fuel to her argument that she should return to Boston. But once they started to talk, she realized Brianne didn't need additional fuel for that argument.

She had plenty.

Jasper couldn't believe it. Just when he'd thought everything was ruined, that he'd never get to use the "playground" he'd put in his basement, he'd had the good fortune of stumbling across Evelyn's little sister. And she hadn't recognized him! He hadn't expected her to, of course. Not only did he look entirely different than he had more than two decades ago, he also hadn't spent a lot of time with her back then.

Still, he always experienced a certain amount of anxiety when he came into contact with someone he knew from before. Had he approached Evelyn as anything other than a prison guard at her own facility, she might've taken a closer look at him or felt a vague sense of recognition. Maybe she would have, anyway, except he'd "saved her life." Until that moment, he'd been just another CO. Getting hired at the prison was such a bold move no one would've expected it, including the great psychiatrist herself. And that put her at a real disadvantage. Even if there were odd moments when she *thought* she recognized him from somewhere, she'd never suspect he was Jasper, never realize how dangerous he was. He'd proven that.

And now luck had smiled on him again.

Although his arm still ached like hell, he whistled the song that'd been on his radio as he let himself into his house. He'd run out of painkillers while he was on duty, had to take the risk of buying more at the Quick Stop just so he could manage to drive home. But anyone could have a headache. Miraculously, he'd acted normal throughout his shift; he doubted anyone could say he might've taken a bullet. And now he had all day to recover before reporting back to the prison tonight. As long as his wound didn't get infected, he'd overcome his recent setbacks and that would leave him free to make the next move.

He carried the bottle of Tylenol Extra Strength into the house, removed his uniform and crawled into bed. He wanted Brianne to call, wanted to spend time with her. He thought it would be funny to strike up a romantic relationship with her, if he could. But he was in no shape to take her out right now, even if she did call. He needed sleep.

He'd give her a few days, and if he didn't hear from her he'd hang around town, hoping to run into her again.

20

"You're *pregnant*?" Evelyn wouldn't have been so distraught at this news except that Brianne had just told her Jeff had found someone else. The wedding was off, exactly as Amarok had suspected.

Brianne tucked her feet beneath her on the couch as she cradled a glass of water in her lap. Evelyn had offered her some Salmonberry Wine, had pressed her when she refused — Brianne loved wine. That was when, instead of continuing to turn it down, Brianne had finally said she *couldn't* drink. "Pregnant and on my own," she added wryly.

"But . . . is there any chance you and Jeff will get back together? You — you were so much in love."

Her lips curved into a bitter smile. "I *still* love him. Problem is, he doesn't love me. He's already with someone else, someone he started seeing while we were together."

Evelyn set her glass on the coffee table. "You mean he cheated on you?"

"Claims he didn't. She's a new hire at his firm. A paralegal the partners assigned to him. From what he told me, he felt a spark from the beginning. He broke off our relationship so he could 'pursue' what he was feeling for her."

"But you were planning to get married! You've been planning the wedding for months!"

She laughed without mirth. "Good thing he bailed now. If she'd started at the firm any later, we would've gone through with it all, and then I'd be looking at a divorce."

Evelyn scooted closer. "Brianne, I'm so sorry! Why didn't you tell me this was happening?"

Brianne stared down at her own lap. "Because I haven't been able to talk about it. This was such a sudden reversal and so painful that I closed up and tried to cope the best I could. I didn't feel I could say anything to Mom, and it always seems like you're going through enough out here."

"So Mom and Dad don't know. . . ."

"Not yet."

Every conversation Evelyn had with Lara these days revolved around the wedding. She'd be as devastated as Brianne. "When will you tell them?"

"Haven't decided for sure, probably when I get home. At first I thought Jeff just had the jitters about making a lifelong commitment and that he'd come back to me when he realized how much he missed me." Brianne pulled the tie from her hair, then put it back up. "Most spurned lovers probably tell themselves that kind of nonsense. But when I found out I was pregnant —"

"Exactly when was that?" Evelyn broke in.

"Ten days ago. I'm two months, due in April."

"You've known that long and didn't reach out to me?"

"I was working up to it. But then Amarok called and told me you had a missing person out here, and I decided I should wait until that was resolved."

Evelyn studied her sister, searching for signs to indicate how hard she was taking this turn of events. "Does Jeff know about the baby?"

"I told him as soon as I heard the news."

"And . . ."

Her chest lifted as if the memory stung. "He asked me to get an abortion."

Evelyn's heart sank. "That must've been devastating."

She cleared her throat. "Let's just say that's when I understood he wasn't coming back."

"Ouch."

"No kidding."

"He'll help out financially, though . . ."

"Of course. He'll have no choice."

Still . . . "I feel terrible for you, Bri."

"I'll be fine. Let's not get maudlin about it." She laughed, but trying to deny the pain only made her eyes fill with tears. "Worse things have happened, right?" She wiped her cheeks with irritation. "It's a blessing I'm not marrying someone who wouldn't be satisfied with me. And I'm in my thirties. If I'm ever going to have a child, why not do it now? I just . . . I don't know how I'll handle motherhood while I'm putting in the hours I do at the hospital. Then there's Mom, of course."

Evelyn straightened her spine. "I thought you hadn't told Mom."

Her sister's eyebrows drew together. "I haven't. I'm afraid to. Her anxiety and depression are getting worse, not better, Evelyn."

"Is she taking her meds?"

"Dad says she is, but they don't seem to be helping."

"Then she needs to try something else."

"*What* else? You're the psychiatrist, and yet *I'm* the one who's dealing with her on a day-to-day basis!"

The resentment her sister felt had finally come to the surface. "You're tired of handling Mom and Dad on your own."

"Yes," she admitted. "I've tried to be patient and supportive. For most of my life I've deferred to what would be best for you. What you went through was terrible, unspeakable. It's amazing you recovered and did everything you've done. But I don't know when it's *my* turn for a little help and understanding, Evelyn. Do I even get a turn?"

"Of course you do! I've only committed to five years here in Alaska, have three left, and then —"

"And then what?" she broke in. "You sign on for another five years? What happens if *we* need you? Does it matter? Can you pull away from this place, or are you so fascinated by your work here that you won't give it up, no matter what? And what's the point in what you're doing? Do you ever ask yourself that anymore? Do you *really* feel you've made a difference? That you can figure out a way to rehabilitate psychopaths when no one else has been able to make a dent in the problem? From what I can tell, building Hanover House, especially here, has done more harm than good."

Evelyn felt as if Brianne had slapped her. There was so much she could say, so many arguments she could make. Just because no one had figured out how to solve the problem yet didn't mean she should give up and walk away. If she and the other researchers took such a defeatist attitude, how would society ever minimize the pain and suffering caused by psychopaths?

But she'd said all of that before. And it was the last thing she'd heard that cut the deepest. "I didn't get to choose where they put Hanover House. The site committee did that."

"You wanted it so badly, I don't think you cared where they put it — or whether it would be good for the community that had to accept it. You were willing to travel to the ends of the earth, so long as you could get your precious research facility. You've proven that. Here you are. You have what you wanted, and yet all I ever hear about is crisis after crisis."

"You don't see *any* value in what I'm trying to do?"

"I know you mean well, but I don't understand why it has to be *you.*"

"Jasper kills wherever he goes, Bri! And

he'll keep on killing until someone stops him. His obsession with me might mean he'll kill people in Alaska instead of Arizona, but one way or the other, he causes suffering. That's what he does. That's what he *delights* in doing!"

"Do you really want him killing *here*?"

She didn't want him killing *anywhere.* "That's not the point."

"If that doesn't matter, what does?"

"I've only been in Hilltop for a couple of years. It's too early to know if what I'm doing will achieve the results I hope it will." She wanted to tell Brianne about all the studies they had going, what they might learn from them, and beg for more time. But her sister was no longer in the kind of situation where she could be supportive.

"Look, I don't mean to be a bitch," Brianne said, lowering her voice. "It's just . . . family should mean something. I'm not the only one who has a responsibility to Mom and Dad." Her voice grew plaintive. "They need you. *I* need you. Will you come home, at least for the next year, and help out while I try to get through this pregnancy and the first few months of my child's life?"

A crushing weight settled on Evelyn's shoulders. She wasn't ready to leave what she'd created, wasn't willing to leave the man she loved, either. She'd never forget how devastated she'd been when she thought he might be dead as they approached the smoldering cabin. "What about Amarok?"

"He can come, too."

"He won't leave Hilltop. He's an important member of this community. They rely on him. What would he do in Boston?"

"He's young, smart. He could figure something out. You never planned on staying here indefinitely, did you? If you're going to come back, why not do it now? It's not as though everything you've done here will be for nothing. Hanover House is up and running. It could continue to run without you."

Evelyn thought of the notes she'd found under the windshield wiper of her SUV. She'd put Hilltop on the map, made it a focal point for the wrong kind of people. But if she left, Jasper would have no reason to come to Hilltop, or stay if he was already here, and Amarok and all the others she'd come to know in this place would be safe. Surely Boston, with its large police force and forensic specialists, would be better equipped to handle the kind of murder investigation Amarok was trying to manage on his own. The best alternative would be to draw Jasper away.

Even if Amarok caught Jasper, as the years continued various inmates would be released. What if they became fixated on her, on another member of the mental health team or on one of the COs and came back as Bishop had?

She could never rule that out entirely.

Regardless, how could she leave Hanover House? Leave Amarok?

She had no idea what to do, had never felt so torn. "I'll think about it," she said.

They attempted to talk about other things, but that part of the conversation had cast a pall over the entire evening. Claiming she was tired, Evelyn went to bed not long after, and once Amarok came home and crawled in with her she pretended she was asleep because she didn't want him to ask how things had gone with Brianne.

"I have to figure out some way to get hold of him," Samantha said.

"Of a serial killer?" Hannah had been leaning on the other side of the glass case that displayed the handguns and ammunition Samantha had for sale. The rifles hung on the wall. But at this, she straightened.

Samantha had given the situation a lot of thought, hadn't been able to think of much else. In her mind, as long as everything went as planned, she'd be Jasper's new best friend, not one of his potential victims. "It's not as dangerous as it seems."

"He's just killed two people!"

The fluorescent lights hummed overhead as she shifted on her stool. "But the person he really wants is Evelyn. As long as I give him Evelyn, no one else will be hurt."

"Providing he gets caught immediately after. What if he doesn't?"

"He will! Amarok will see to it."

"You don't know that!"

"Whether he does or he doesn't won't matter. Jasper is only here because of Evelyn. He'll go somewhere else — somewhere warmer — as soon as he has what he wants. We're too small a community to be of any real interest to a serial killer. They need numbers, anonymity, a lot of activity in order to go unnoticed."

Hannah didn't look convinced. "Jasper hasn't done too badly so far. . . ."

"Because he took us all by surprise. Now that we're watching out for unusual activity, he won't be able to get away with much. He'll become conspicuous."

Hannah bit her lip. "You don't care that you'll be leading Evelyn to her death?"

Not at all. That was the thing. Samantha

wanted Evelyn out of the picture so badly, she didn't care how it happened. And if Evelyn was dead, Samantha could rest assured she wouldn't be coming back. "Better her than someone else we know! She had no business bringing so many dangerous men to Hilltop in the first place! She's like a drowning person who capsizes the nearest boat while trying to get in, causing who knows how many others to drown."

"I agree, but —"

Samantha refused to entertain any objections. She saw this as the perfect way to get what she wanted and couldn't wait to figure out how to put her plan in motion. "Bottom line, if Jasper wants to kill Evelyn, he'll do it eventually. I'm just going to speed up the process so that no one else gets hurt in the meantime, especially Amarok."

Hannah gaped at her for several seconds. "You think Amarok will take you back if Evelyn's gone?"

"I do! Why wouldn't he? With time, he'll realize how ill-suited they were and forget about her."

"Don't do it," Hannah said, shaking her head. "You won't be able to live with yourself if you do."

If she had Amarok, she could. It was living without him that was hard.

Hannah bent to look into her face. "Sam, are you listening to me?"

Samantha jerked her eyebrows together. "Oh, stop! You're no fan of Evelyn's."

"Only because I don't like living in the shadow of what she's created! Sandy Ledstetter was my friend. I miss her, and it's because of Hanover House that she's gone. But Evelyn's never done anything to me *personally.* Besides, what if Amarok realizes that it was *you* who caused her death?"

"He won't. Because I won't have caused her death. Jasper will be responsible for that."

"But . . . how will you find Jasper?"

"I won't. He'll find me."

"You're terrifying me, Sam!"

"Will you quit? You know I can handle myself. I'll be fine!"

Hannah blinked several times as if she was struggling to take it all in. "So how will he find you?"

It was a long shot, but it was the only plan Samantha could think of that might work. "Phil told his wife, who happened to mention it to me, that one of the murdered women was a dancer at a strip joint in Anchorage. It won't be hard to go there and ask around, find out where she worked."

"I wouldn't think so. But then what?"

"Then I hang around to see what turns up."

"Sam, no. I'll go to Amarok if I have to. This isn't safe. You're not thinking straight."

Irritated, Samantha started to put away the ammunition. "Oh my God, Hannah! Don't tell me you thought I was serious."

Hannah's face filled with relief. "You're not?"

"Of course not. I'm just messing with you," Samantha laughed, but she was already planning what she'd wear when she visited Anchorage's seedier side.

21

Amarok hadn't had sex with Evelyn since Brianne arrived. He'd been out a great deal, submitting the tire track impression he'd taken at the cabin to an expert who'd identified it as coming from a fairly common truck tire, a Goodyear All-Terrain tire, which didn't tell him a whole lot. Almost everyone drove a truck in Alaska and most people had snow tires this time of year. Until he had tires from a specific vehicle to cast and compare against the impression, that piece of evidence wasn't going to do him much good.

The shoe impression hadn't revealed enough detail to determine the kind of boot with any certainty, so that wasn't helping, either. He was hopeful the blood evidence would at least confirm whether or not Jasper was the man he was looking for. He'd submitted it to the private lab in Philadelphia that Ashton Cooper had recommended to Evelyn, since they were going to be comparing Jasper's DNA against what was found in Boston, at the scene where Charlotte was murdered. Aside from that, he'd been talking to anyone who might've seen a stranger or spotted anything out of the ordinary, checking hospital records all over the area, including Anchorage, and meeting with the warden at Hanover House to see if anyone who worked there had been injured. Occasionally, he swung by the house to grab a bite to eat or crawl into bed, however, and during those times Evelyn acted . . . remote.

She was stressed, too, of course. He didn't expect her to behave as she normally did. They were in the middle of a crisis. But still. Something was seriously wrong. Even Brianne acted as though she didn't have much to say to him. She didn't seem interested in becoming friends, let alone in-laws, and he could sense a strain in the relationship between the two sisters. He'd expected them to be close, to stay up late at night, chatting and laughing — to show some sign of the relationship Evelyn had told him they'd once had.

That wasn't happening. They seemed to be tiptoeing around each other for fear they'd get into an argument. Amarok was under the impression they were merely passing the time until Brianne had to leave.

Bringing Brianne to Alaska might've been a mistake. He liked the peace of mind it gave him to have someone with Evelyn during the hours he had to be away, but he was beginning to feel pretty unsettled, which was why he went to visit Evelyn at the prison on Friday afternoon.

She glanced up as he came into her office. "Amarok! What are you doing here?"

He shut the door and closed the blinds on her interior window before taking a seat in one of the two chairs facing her desk. "Do you have a second?"

"I'll take one." She pushed her laptop to the side. "What's going on?"

"This isn't about the investigation."

She looked more tentative at his pronouncement. "Then what's it about?"

"Me. Us. It feels like I've barely seen you the past week."

"We've both been busy. And while Brianne's staying with us, there's very little privacy."

"All true. But something else is going on. You've withdrawn from me. I can feel it."

He thought she might pretend otherwise, suggest he'd imagined their estrangement. But she didn't. "Brianne's pregnant."

He wanted Evelyn to be the one carrying

a child — *his* child — so he couldn't help feeling a bit of envy along with his surprise. He was ready to settle down, start a family. He'd made no secret of that, and he had no doubt that Evelyn was the woman he wanted. She was approaching forty, though, and because of Jasper and the physical damage he'd caused, she'd probably be facing a complicated pregnancy, even without her age working against her. He was afraid that if they didn't do whatever they could to conceive now, they'd lose the opportunity. "*Brianne's* pregnant?"

"Yes. And you were right — things aren't going well with Jeff."

Amarok had hardly seen Evelyn's sister since she'd arrived, but the few times he had been home she hadn't mentioned her fiancé, confirming his earlier suspicion. "What happened?"

"He's found someone else."

"When?"

"It's been a month or so."

"Before or after she knew she was pregnant?"

"Before."

Forming a steeple with his fingers, he studied the woman he hoped to marry. "So . . . what's she going to do?"

"She's going to have the baby."

"Alone."

"Yes."

"Will she keep her job?"

"She'll have to. She needs to support her child."

Dropping his hands, he sat forward. "I'm sorry things didn't work out with Jeff."

"So am I. She's broken up about it."

When her eyes slipped away instead of holding his gaze, he knew there was something else going on, something more than what was happening with Brianne. "And that means you're having second thoughts about *us* somehow?"

He could see the sadness in her eyes when she looked at him again. "She's asked me to return to Boston, Amarok. My mother isn't doing well. That, in addition to the baby . . . Well, bottom line, Brianne needs me to spend a little time with the family right now."

Amarok caught his breath. "What about your job? Your commitment to stay and run this place for the first five years?"

"I know. I don't want to break that commitment. I don't want to leave you, either. This has been the most difficult decision I've ever had to make."

She was going to return Boston. She didn't need to spell it out; he could tell.

His heart began to pound. *Damn it!* This was the reason he'd been so determined, in the beginning, not to open his heart. His own mother had left him, his father and Alaska, for the Lower 48. His father had warned him that Evelyn would do the same. She wasn't outdoorsy, wasn't anyone who'd naturally be inclined to come to such a remote place. But he'd wanted her from the beginning, and fighting the attraction hadn't saved him. He'd never forget the first time they made love, when she'd joined him in the shower. She'd finally been able to trust him and that had left him feeling helpless against her. "When will you go?"

Tears filled her eyes. "I don't know yet. As soon as I can make the arrangements."

He got up and started for the door.

"Amarok . . ."

He needed to get out of there before she could see how badly she was tearing him apart. The worst aspect of this whole thing was that he couldn't blame her. He was surprised she'd lasted this long. She wasn't safe and wouldn't be safe until he or someone else managed to catch Jasper. If only he'd done that, maybe she and her family would've been able to heal. Evelyn would be looking at an entirely different situation if that were the case, a much more *normal* situation.

He didn't answer. He reached for the door, but she hurried around the desk to stop him.

"*Please* try to understand," she begged. "I don't see how I can stay. What happened to me hurt my whole family. They've been pulling for me, looking out for me, making special allowances for me, ever since — for more than *twenty years.* When do I give back? When do I make sure *I'm* there for *them*? It can't always be about me, about the research I want to do, the resolution I need. It can't even be about getting to stay with the man I love," she added.

He stared down at her hand as it gripped his arm. "Will you come back?"

"Not unless I'm going to stay here for good. I can't put us through this twice."

That was far from a commitment. His throat tightened, and he had difficulty speaking. "What will you tell your boss?"

"I'm going to ask Janice for a leave of absence."

"For how long?"

"A year."

"You'll spend a year in Boston, and then you'll decide whether to return."

"Yes. I'm going to get counseling, try to gain some perspective on the trauma I've been through and do what I can to make my family whole. I was hoping to last through this latest crisis. I know it's a terrible time for me to leave, but with Brianne pregnant and feeling so fragile, it has to be soon."

"But she's months away from having the baby."

"She needs someone now, to help her through the pregnancy, when she's so brokenhearted over Jeff, and to remove the pressure she feels because of my mother's condition. As you know, I've been struggling, anyway. Maybe this is a sign that I need to make a change, that I'm pushing too hard and it's detrimental to me and my family."

Neither one of them said that leaving right now and for so long would likely destroy her chances of ever retaking the helm of Hanover House and might make it impossible to return in the future. She had to be cautious about how others perceived her, especially the Bureau of Prisons and the press. She'd worked so hard to convey that she'd completely recovered from the past and could be trusted to handle anything that was thrown at her.

This would undermine all of that.

"When were you going to tell me?" he asked.

"Not now. Not while you're dealing with so much. To be honest, I just decided this morning. I haven't even told Brianne. That's why you've probably felt some tension between me and my sister." She wiped at an errant tear. "She isn't happy with me, either."

He'd give anything to persuade her to stay. A year would seem like forever without her — especially knowing those twelve months might turn into forever.

But pressuring her would only chase her away. If she stayed, she had to do it because she wanted to, because she could be fulfilled here in Alaska, with him, satisfied in the long term. He had no interest in continuing the relationship if he had to live in constant fear that she'd leave him.

Maybe it was time for them to figure that out. Maybe, if she did come back in a year, she'd be willing to get married and have a child.

And if she didn't? She probably wouldn't have lasted, anyway.

"I want whatever makes you happy," he said, and slipped out of her grasp.

Evelyn hoped to stop Amarok, to talk until

they both felt better. But she wasn't sure they *would* feel better, because she didn't have anything to say that he'd want to hear.

Penny knocked before she could speak, anyway.

Amarok opened the door so fast Penny stumbled back. Fortunately, he caught her before she could fall.

"Whoops!" she said as her other hand gripped the doorframe. "S-sorry to interrupt. I just got a call from Phil, who works with you. Or for you. Or . . . anyway, he needs to talk to you."

Penny had always had a thing for Amarok. Evelyn had noticed the way she flushed whenever he was around. She'd found it slightly amusing in the past. Penny was so obvious about it, it even made Amarok a little uncomfortable. But she didn't find her assistant's reaction to her boyfriend so amusing now that she'd be leaving soon and there was no guarantee she'd be back. That meant Amarok might end up with Penny or someone else in the area, maybe even his ex-girlfriend Samantha, who'd made no secret of the fact that she was waiting for just such an opportunity.

"Thanks." Amarok started to go around Penny.

"You might as well call from my office,"

Evelyn said, but it hadn't been easy to regain his attention. She'd had to say his name three times before he finally looked back at her.

He seemed eager to get away, as if he couldn't tolerate being in the same space with her any longer. That made Evelyn feel even worse. But what was she supposed to do? It wasn't fair that she'd left Brianne to deal with their parents for so many years. And now that Brianne had a baby coming, *she* was going to need Evelyn, too.

Evelyn stepped aside as Amarok came around the desk.

Plainly curious as to what was going on that would send Amarok charging out of Evelyn's office like that and then make him slow to respond when she called him, Penny stood in the doorway, glancing between them until Evelyn walked toward her. At that point she ducked out so Evelyn could close the door.

"What's up?" Evelyn heard Amarok say after he'd dialed. "*Who* said that? . . . It's nothing. . . . Just another excuse to take my time. . . . Right, I know. I have to check it out, anyway. Tell her I'll be right there."

When he hung up, Evelyn raised her eyebrows in expectation.

Amarok gestured toward the phone. "Samantha claims she saw something suspicious in the alley behind her gun shop. I've got to go check it out."

"Samantha." She supposed it was childish, but just hearing that name brought an upwelling of jealousy.

"Yeah."

She blocked his path to the door in an attempt to stall him. "I'm sorry, Amarok."

He gave her the lopsided smile that always made her knees go weak, and she thought her heart might break. She ached to touch him, to reassure herself that everything was going to be okay. But she was afraid that after what she'd told him he'd no longer welcome her touch, so she kept her hands to herself.

"I know that," he said. "I'd better get going."

"Amarok . . ."

"There's nothing you can say, Evelyn, not until you know what you want."

"It's not just what I want!"

He swung around to face her. "Yes, it is. And as much as I'll miss you, hard as it'll be, I'll give you the time you need. Just promise me one thing."

"What's that?"

"If you come back for more than the job — if you come back for me — you'll agree to get married."

She took a deep breath. "You're giving me an ultimatum. All or nothing?"

"All or nothing," he replied, and the conviction in his voice scared her. "I want a commitment. I want to know I can rely on your love the way you can rely on mine. And whatever problems arise, we handle them together. Going back to Boston or anywhere else for more than a visit won't be an option, not unless you've quit loving me, or I've done something to deserve losing you."

That was a reasonable request — that she step up and promise him what he was willing to promise her. She couldn't expect him to remain in a holding pattern forever, never really knowing if she was going to pick up and move back to Boston or if they'd be able to start a family. "Okay," she said.

After a curt nod, he slipped past without touching her, without so much as brushing against her. That was when she knew he was going to stand behind the line he'd just drawn. It was over between them until she could say she was in for good.

Brianne craved a drink. She watched the other people in the rustic Alaskan bar order beer and wine, the occasional mixed drink, and resented the fact that her pregnancy wouldn't allow her to have any alcohol. She felt she deserved a drink after the month she'd had. She'd lost the man she loved, found out after the fact that she was having his baby and learned that her only sibling was once again facing the psychopath who'd nearly killed her twice before. To make it all worse, even though Brianne had come to help, she'd ended up creating tension between her and Evelyn that had never existed before.

She was screwing up everywhere. Evelyn had called shortly before Brianne left the house to say she was going to ask for a leave of absence and return to Boston. But getting her way only made Brianne feel worse. Just because she'd wrecked her own life didn't mean she had the right to wreck her sister's. She'd tried to talk her sister out of returning home, but Evelyn wouldn't listen. Brianne had piled on too much guilt about not being there; she couldn't take it back now.

"Good going," she muttered to herself. It wasn't her sister's fault that she'd been dumped, that she was pregnant or that their mother couldn't handle life. Evelyn hadn't chosen to be tortured and nearly murdered when she was sixteen, either. "God, I'm such a bad person." Instead of coming here and providing the support Amarok had wanted her to give and then going back to take care of her own problems, she was the reason Evelyn was giving up the job — and the man — she loved.

Misery loves company. That old saying came to mind and definitely didn't make her feel any better.

The owner of the bar, a squat, bowlegged man who could've walked out of a John Wayne Western, stopped by to see if she needed a refill. "From the look on your face, you could use something a bit stronger," he joked. "That Shirley Temple isn't going down too fast."

She removed the cherry resting on top of the ice. The drink was too sweet, but she hadn't known it would be because she couldn't remember ever ordering one before. "No, I'm fine," she said. "But thanks."

He refilled the dish of nuts nearby. "You're the doc's sister, right?"

She'd been to the Moosehead three times so far. He'd even served her a burger last night, but the bar had been busy and it was the heavyset woman — his sister — who'd waited on her the other times. "How'd you know?"

"Besides the family resemblance?" He winked at her. "Nothing happens in Hilltop that doesn't get discussed in here. And anything that involves the doc is especially big news."

She looked glumly at the people around her. Business was slow tonight, but it was still early, only six — not that anyone would be able to tell by the darkness outside. In Alaska the sun went down at five in October. She wondered if Amarok might stop in and what he'd say to her if he did. She wouldn't blame him if he pretended not to see her. He had to be disappointed by the way she'd handled her visit. Evelyn hadn't been comforted. Brianne had only caused her more stress.

She was disappointed in herself.

"Hey, why haven't you called me? Big-city girl like you — I figured you'd be bored by now."

She twisted around to see who was speaking to her and recognized Andy Smith, the prison guard she'd met at Quigley's on Monday morning. She'd thought about calling him, considered it several times, actually. Evelyn and Amarok were gone so much, and she knew prison guards didn't necessarily work a nine-to-five schedule. That meant he might be available to distract her from her heartbreak and self-loathing.

But she wasn't going to be here long

enough to strike up a relationship with anyone. Besides, expecting someone else's child wasn't a particularly appealing trait when meeting a new romantic interest.

Being so limited made her angry. Jeff could move on as if nothing had happened, while she was stuck with the aftermath of their relationship — stuck with only three decisions, and she didn't like any of them. She could get an abortion. She could give the baby up for adoption. Or she could become a single parent.

"I'm getting there," she joked, and breathed in the scent of his cologne as he took the seat next to her. He smelled fresh, clean.

"That can't be very appetizing." He eyed her Shirley Temple with disdain. "Let me buy you a real drink."

"I wish you could. Trust me."

"I can. Watch this." He waved down Shorty. "What would you like?" he asked as the bartender approached.

Again, Brianne was tempted to cut loose. What was one drink? Surely a small amount of alcohol couldn't hurt the baby.

But what kind of mother would she be to even take that chance?

A selfish one. And she was feeling selfish enough already, having behaved the way she had since arriving in Alaska. "I'll have a Sprite," she told Shorty, and pushed her current drink, which she wasn't enjoying, away.

Andy scowled at her. "You've got to be kidding me. Sprite? That's the best you can do?"

"I can't have any alcohol."

He hesitated. Then he lowered his voice. "Maybe it's not polite to ask, but now that you've raised my curiosity . . ."

He wanted to know why. Of course he would. She preferred not to explain, but she thought it was only fair, since he was showing interest in her and she was tempted to enjoy the evening with him. Staying at the Moosehead would give her a break from another night spent in her sister's company, another night of pretending everything was okay between them when it wasn't. Evelyn had been coming home later and later as the week wore on, and Brianne believed she was beginning to make up excuses in order to do so. "I'm pregnant."

"Oh." He straightened. "I didn't realize that, didn't know you were with someone. I mean, you *are* seeing someone. . . ."

She ruffled her own hair. "Not anymore. It didn't work out."

His eyes swept over her. "You can't be

very far along."

"I'm not. I found out *after* the relationship ended. Nice, huh?"

"So *that's* why you haven't called."

"I can't imagine you or any other man wanting to spend time with me while I'm in this condition."

"Why not?"

She blinked in surprise. "Because most men would consider me anathema — for the next year, anyway."

"Your condition doesn't bother me. I've never been out with a pregnant woman before, but so far, it doesn't seem very different."

Shorty returned with her Sprite, Andy slipped him a few bills, and she took a sip of it.

"It's not like you're planning to move here, are you?" he asked when the bar owner was gone. "So it doesn't matter if I like children, which I do, whether I'd be a good stepfather, even though I'd be amazing, or anything else."

She laughed. "I guess you've got a point there."

"In Quigley's, you told me you'd be here for a week. I'm guessing you're down to what . . . two days?"

She liked that he'd made a mental note of

when she'd be leaving. It showed that the information mattered to him. "If you don't count today, yes. I leave Sunday."

"Then we don't have much time left. As far as I'm concerned, we might as well have some fun while we can."

"Seriously? Even though I can't drink?"

He leaned in to whisper, "You can do other things, can't you?"

She reared back. Did he expect her to go home with him? They'd just met! *"Like . . ."*

His smile widened at her shocked and chilly response. "Dance," he said with a chuckle at having raised her hackles, and held out his hand.

22

He had Evelyn's younger sister in his arms. Jasper could hardly believe it. Holding her body against his felt almost as good as if it were Evelyn's. Brianne wasn't quite as pretty. She wasn't nearly as smart, either, and it was Evelyn's quick mind that created the challenge he most enjoyed. But since Brianne hadn't called him, he'd hoped to run into her when he showed up at the Moosehead tonight, and that was exactly what had happened. A night spent flirting with her was intriguing enough to siphon off some of the restlessness he'd been feeling — over the murder investigation and his inability to get close to Evelyn since he'd finished the dungeon, where he planned to one day keep her.

"You smell good," Brianne said as they swayed to the music on the dance floor.

Careful not to let her hand come into contact with the bandage on his arm —

which he hoped she wouldn't be able to feel through his jacket, anyway — he bent his head to smell her neck. "So do you."

He thought even that innocent a statement might make her uncomfortable. He'd nearly scared her off at the bar, had to be careful not to do that again. Fortunately, he'd been able to play that comment off as though it were a joke. But he didn't *completely* regret what he'd said. At least now he knew how to handle her. He'd have to put in some time and couldn't be quite so direct. He couldn't have her go back to her sister or Amarok and complain about how forward "Andy Smith" had been at the bar. If he was careful, however, *she'd* eventually make the first move. She was hurting and lonely, and he planned to take advantage of that. It wasn't difficult to manipulate someone who was feeling overlooked and rejected.

Too bad she wouldn't drink, though. Jasper didn't give a shit about the baby. He only cared about the fact that it'd be a whole lot easier for him to get inside her pants if she wasn't paying attention to every little thing he said and did.

"How long have you lived in Alaska?" she asked.

"Only as long as I've worked at the prison."

"Eight months."

"You remember." He'd told her that at Quigley's. . . .

She flushed. "You're sort of hard to forget."

Jasper felt his groin tighten. "So are you. That's why I was disappointed when you didn't call me. I came here tonight, hoping to run into you."

"You're going to admit that — just come right out and say it?" she said with a laugh, but he could tell she was pleased by the compliment, so he gave her his always well-received "games" line.

"Why not? I don't believe in playing games, do you?"

"No." She sounded relieved, and he could understand why. She'd just gone through what had to be a bad breakup, one that left her expecting a baby. "We're too old for that," she added.

He spread his fingers on her back, trying to feel her skin through her blouse. "Exactly. I'm attracted to you. I think you're the most beautiful woman I've ever seen, and I'm not afraid to say it."

She blushed. "Thank you."

"I'm sad you're leaving so soon. Is there

any chance you could stay longer?"

She bit her lip as she considered the question. "I don't think so, but I could come back in a month or two."

"Your job will allow it?"

"I have plenty of vacation days."

"That'd be awesome," he said, and held her tighter to show his enthusiasm.

"What made you decide to become a prison guard?" she asked.

He guessed Brianne had a good job, one with significantly higher pay than his, so he was tempted to create a more impressive work history. Sometimes he told the women he met that he'd once been a real estate mogul, that if his secretary hadn't embezzled thousands and thousands of dollars he'd still have his business. That always seemed to go over well; he'd never had anyone question it. But he had to be extra careful with what he told Brianne. He couldn't make himself out to be such a big deal that if she repeated what he told her to Evelyn it'd create enough curiosity to cause Evelyn to check his story. "I like the benefits," he said. "And I've always wanted to live in Alaska. If you're not involved in the tourist trade, it can be hard to get a start up here. Hanover House provided a way to make the move." He didn't mention that he'd also worked in a prison in Arizona.

"I see. But why are you so interested in Alaska?"

"You're kidding, right? There's so much more space here, and so much less bureaucracy! I find the Lower Forty-eight to be over-crowded and over-legislated."

"You prefer to be left alone to do your own thing."

He hid a smile; truer words had never been spoken. "I do. I guess I'm a breed apart."

"You must be glad you came, then."

"Definitely. I'll never go back." Not unless he had to. Not while he had Evelyn in his sights, at any rate.

The song they'd been dancing to came to an end and another started, but she didn't pull back, so he kept holding her. "You don't see the appeal of Alaska?"

"I like the ruggedness and the physical beauty. But I was born and raised in Boston, love the city. Besides, my folks live there. I doubt I'll ever leave it."

"Not even if you were to meet the right man?" he teased.

"The right man?"

He could see a sparkle in her eye despite the dim lighting. She was flirting, too. "Well, I *am* a hero."

"That's true. You saved my sister's life. . . ."

He puffed out his chest. "Just sayin'," he said, but that wasn't the throwaway joke he'd made it appear. He'd brought it up on purpose — to build his credibility and trustworthiness. Reminding her what her sister would've suffered had he not intervened should make her feel safe around him, even though he was essentially a stranger.

It was such a perfect lie he almost couldn't keep a straight face.

"She must be so grateful to you."

"She was gracious about it," he said, but honestly, he thought Evelyn owed him a bit more time and gratitude than she'd given him. It wasn't as if she'd ever sought him out or invited him over for dinner or anything. He had the feeling she avoided him if she could, which made him resent her even more. When he used to daydream about coming to Hilltop and working at Hanover House, he'd also imagine wooing her back into his bed. There could be no greater victory for him than getting her to fall in love with him again. But now that she had Amarok, she had eyes for no one else. Jasper got the impression she didn't even find him attractive.

Fortunately, there were other ways to get his revenge. And this one was looking pretty damn good. If only Evelyn knew that the man who'd murdered her friends and tortured her for days was now turning his attentions on her younger sister. . . .

"Um, are we dancing a little too close?" Brianne asked, her eyes wide and innocent as she gazed up at him.

Thinking of Evelyn had given him an erection. "Sorry, but I'm not going to apologize for that. I already told you how beautiful you are."

Flattery could cover anything. . . .

"Don't worry. I don't mind." She laughed, too. "After what I've been through, it feels good to be admired and appreciated."

"The father of your baby must've been crazy to let you go."

When she pressed more firmly against him, he nearly climaxed. He had her. Evelyn's sister! He almost couldn't believe it. She was attracted to him, was already lowering her defenses.

After several other songs, during which they talked and laughed and grew more sexually aware of each other, she allowed him to guide her into the dark hallway by the bathrooms. There he pressed her up against the wall so she could *really* feel his erection and kissed her long and deep.

She reminded him so much of Evelyn. He could see the resemblance in their features and the way they talked and laughed. He even imagined he could feel and taste Evelyn through Brianne. He wanted to wrap his hands around her throat and squeeze, watch the recognition dawn as she realized she'd been played. But he couldn't give himself away to anyone except Evelyn — once she was safely his prisoner.

To combat his compulsion to hurt her, he had to flatten his hands against the wall over her head for a few minutes and not touch her at all.

She was touching him, though, far more freely than he'd expected. The father of her baby had damaged her self-esteem, so she was lapping up the attention he gave her like a dog. He wouldn't have expected Evelyn's sister to be quite this gullible.

But why *wouldn't* she trust him? He worked with her sister, circulated in the same small community as her sister and had saved her sister's life. By every indication, he was a stand-up guy.

When he finally pulled away, they were both panting. "Do you have to go home tonight?" he asked, pressing his forehead against hers as though she filled him with such desire he could hardly contain himself.

"Where would *you* like me to go?" she asked, still clinging to his neck, her fingers toying with his hair.

"I live in Anchorage. We could make a night of it, if you want." He couldn't really take her to his place. If all his clothes came off, she'd see — or feel — that he had an injury. He couldn't let that happen, couldn't risk that she might notice the bandage or mention it to Amarok. But he was certainly willing to take off his pants. . . .

"No, my sister wouldn't be happy if I didn't come home."

"Even if you're with me?" he asked, pretending he was somehow safer than other guys. "She knows *I'll* take good care of you."

"There's a murderer on the loose. I can't leave her alone. As a matter of fact, I should go. She's probably off work by now."

A jolt of panic made him stand up straight. Brianne couldn't leave him like this — dying to come inside her and thereby claim a fresh victory over Evelyn. The thought that she might evoked instant rage, but he did everything he could to hide that.

He had to be clever.

"Are you sure?" he murmured, and kissed her again while slipping a hand under her blouse. "You don't have just a few more minutes?"

Her head fell back against the wall as he found and gently stimulated her nipple. "I want to taste this," he whispered. "I want to taste *you.*"

"Maybe I can be a *little* late," she said as though he was tempting her beyond her ability to refuse.

"My truck's outside." He took her hand. "You deserve better than the backseat of a vehicle, but as long as I make you come, what does it matter?"

When she resisted, he was afraid he'd said the wrong thing. He couldn't be too crude, too demanding — not with someone like her.

"We've barely met," she said.

"But we don't have much time." Besides, she liked what she saw. She'd made that clear. And she was down on herself and life in general. He had that working for him.

"Why not feel something good while you've got the chance? How long will it be before this happens for you again?"

"You've got a point," she said, and let him tug her outside.

He almost had her right where he wanted her. If he could only get her into the backseat of his truck, she wouldn't bail on him.

She wasn't that kind of girl.

"I feel like the luckiest man on earth," he told her when she climbed in without balking.

"You're *so* nice," she said as he helped her off with her blouse.

He didn't hear that very often, so he smiled. He knew he should spend some time kissing and caressing her, make sure she was as aroused as he was. But he was out of patience. He was going to get his turn, and he was going to get it *now.* He hoped she didn't suddenly change her mind, because he was at the point where he wouldn't have been able to stop himself from raping her if she did.

Fortunately, she remained pliant, cooperative.

He undid his pants and pushed inside her right away. She seemed slightly put off by how single-minded he was becoming, but he didn't care. The way she was wedged into the backseat of his truck, she could only let him finish.

As he started to move, he moaned with each thrust. He pictured Evelyn crying at the thought of what he was doing to her sister and that made each moment infinitely enjoyable.

As the pleasure built, he thrust harder and

harder. He wanted to hurt her, wanted to clench his hand in her hair and yank her head back while biting her neck until it bled. But he managed to distract himself by thinking about how glad he was that she was already pregnant.

That meant she hadn't demanded he wear a condom.

Evelyn whirled to face her the moment she walked into the house. "You couldn't have left me a message?"

Although Brianne attempted to smooth down her hair, she couldn't get it to cooperate and suspected she looked as guilty as she felt. Andy had been sucking on her neck, even though she'd told him not to, so she was afraid she had a couple of hickeys, too. Just in case, she didn't remove her coat. She hoped Evelyn wouldn't guess what she'd been up to. She couldn't *believe* she'd been so impulsive.

She wouldn't have acted that recklessly if not for Jeff, she told herself. His rejection had cut her so deeply she was looking for anything to deaden the pain and make it possible to forget, even for just a few minutes. The fact that she was marching toward a life-altering event she felt ill equipped to cope with didn't help, either. A child was a huge responsibility, and that responsibility never truly ended. Would she be a good mother? Could she do it on her own? And even if she could, would having a child negatively impact her life in other ways, making it difficult to meet someone or continue pursuing her career?

Those persistent and as yet unanswered questions messed with her normal decision-making ability and had led her to do something she'd never done before.

"I'm sorry," she said. "I didn't expect to be gone so long. I just went over to the Moosehead to get a break from staring at these four walls."

"You didn't think, with what's going on here in town, that I'd be worried?"

She *had* realized that, but by the time she was making out with Andy Smith in the alcove by the bathrooms it'd been difficult to battle the desire to feel something good for a change. After all, she had no doubt Jeff was having sex with his new girlfriend. Why should all pleasure stop for her?

"You often go past the Moosehead on your way home to see if Amarok's there. I figured you'd see your own car and . . . and know where I was, even if you didn't want to stop in yourself."

Evelyn started to stack the files she had

spread out on the table. "I didn't check the parking lot today. I was riding with someone else, which meant I didn't have control. I didn't think it mattered, assumed you were waiting for me."

"I can take care of myself, Evelyn. It's not as though I was hanging out in some dark alleyway or meeting someone who could be dangerous."

"You can take care of yourself? That's what every murdered girl thinks before she meets the man who kills her!" Evelyn cried. "That's what *I* thought when I was dating Jasper!"

Brianne wanted to get into the bathroom so she could see if there were any marks on her neck. She needed to find out if it was safe to remove her coat or if Andy had left the love bites she feared he had. "So why didn't you come over to the Moosehead when you saw that your car wasn't here in the drive?"

Evelyn dropped the files on the counter. "Because you had my car! Besides, I assumed you'd run over to Quigley's to pick up some last-minute ingredients for dinner. It wasn't until I'd been catching up on paperwork for nearly two hours that I realized how long you'd been gone and began to panic."

Brianne had been about to set Evelyn's keys on the counter. At this remark — and the implications that immediately sprang up in her mind — she froze. "What do you mean 'panic'? You didn't send Amarok out looking for me, did you?"

"I did! Of course I did. I got hold of him at his trooper post, and he went out looking right away. Two bodies have been found recently, and one of those victims was killed in a cabin not too far from here. He was as scared as I was! Think about it; if Jasper *is* back, he might like killing you almost as much as me!"

The thought that Evelyn's cop boyfriend might've seen Andy Smith's truck rocking in the parking lot sent a shard of mortification straight through her heart. "He didn't go by the Moosehead. . . ."

"I'm sure he did. That's where people in this town hang out at night. It's the first place to look for anyone."

Dread made her nauseous. *"When?"*

"As soon as I called him!"

"No, I mean . . . when was it that he went to the bar?"

"Does it matter?"

Brianne pulled the lapels of her coat up even higher. It could! "He didn't find me there?" At this point, she hoped not.

"I don't know. I haven't heard back from him yet."

Shit. She hoped she and Andy were done by the time Amarok had arrived. "You'd better call him and let him know you found me. He doesn't need to be wasting his time searching for me when there are so many more important things he needs to do."

Evelyn threw up her hands. "*Now* you think of that?" She turned to close her laptop but pivoted to face Brianne again. "Wait, don't tell me you were drinking. You're pregnant! And you drove home!"

Brianne slid her purse off her shoulder and set it beside the keys. "Relax. I didn't have a drop. I was just . . . I was talking to someone."

"Who?"

"Andy Smith."

Evelyn's tirade came to an abrupt halt. "The CO from Hanover House? *That* Andy Smith?"

Brianne lifted her chin. "Could there be two Andy Smiths in such a small place?"

"Not that I know of, but . . ." She seemed to struggle, trying to decide how to finish her statement.

"But?"

"Nothing. Never mind."

"No, say it. You don't really like him, do you?"

"He saved my life. Of course I like him."

Brianne stepped closer to her sister. "*He* doesn't think so. He said you avoid him. He's afraid he reminds you of that night when Bishop was here."

"He doesn't. I didn't know he was expecting more than the thanks I've given him. I've been so busy, I haven't focused on anyone except Amarok — and my work."

"And that's fine. He doesn't expect anything. But you can at least admit I was in good hands."

The door banged open before Evelyn could respond, and Amarok walked in. The way he looked at her, then glanced away gave Brianne the sickening impression that he knew what had kept her from home. He'd probably gone inside, been told she'd left with Andy Smith, then scoured the lot and —

She refused to entertain the picture her mind conjured up.

Evelyn gestured toward her. "As you can see, you don't need to keep searching. She was at the Moosehead."

He hesitated for a second; then he said, "Yeah. I figured that out."

Brianne saw a muscle move in his cheek

and knew the jig was up. There was no point in continuing to hide the love bites on her neck, because Amarok knew exactly where she'd been. "Oh, just tell her," she said to him. "You're going to as soon as I leave, anyway."

"I have nothing to say about it."

Evelyn's gaze bounced between them. When Amarok refused to speak, Evelyn's focus shifted solidly to her.

"I was having sex with Andy in his truck, okay? That's where I've been — having some fun."

Evelyn stared at her, eyes wide. "You've got to be joking!"

When she took off her coat and slung it over a chair, her sister's jaw dropped.

"Oh my God! You're *not* joking!"

Amarok did an about-face. "I'm out of here. I've got stuff to do at the trooper post," he said, and disappeared as abruptly as he'd arrived.

Brianne had to admit it was pretty cool of Amarok not to judge her or tell her how to run her life, especially when he had every reason to hate her for how she'd behaved since she arrived. She almost wished he'd stay. Maybe then Evelyn would've said they could talk about it later and Brianne would have a chance to regroup before trying to explain what had been going through her mind when she'd agreed to have sex with a man who was almost a total stranger.

"Your behavior doesn't seem a bit . . . juvenile to you?" Evelyn said in the wake of his departure.

It *did* seem juvenile. She felt humiliated standing there with hickeys on her neck and her hair still mussed from her romp in Andy's truck. But she couldn't take back what she'd done. And at least she couldn't get pregnant. She'd already made that mistake. "I like him," she said.

"I'm glad to hear *that.*" Evelyn slumped into a seat. "I'd hate to think you were out screwing some random guy you *didn't* like."

"Stop it! He's not some *random guy.* He's the man who saved your life. And it's nobody's business but mine."

"It's my business, too, if it means you're unraveling." She sounded shell-shocked, which was worse than if she'd been angry.

"Look, I'm going through a difficult time, yes. But I'm not *unraveling.* I'll be fine." She hoped. She felt more certain of it in some moments than others, but she definitely knew she didn't want to feel guilty the whole time Evelyn was in Boston for making *her* unhappy, too. "And as for what I said before . . . You know, about you coming home, I wish I hadn't said it. You're obviously happy here with Amarok. You should stay."

Evelyn shook her head. "No. You were right. I need to come home and take some of the pressure off you. Mom needs me, too."

Brianne took the seat across from her, and they sat in silence — until Brianne broke it. "I'm sorry about the guilt trip. And I'm sorry about tonight. I didn't mean to scare you."

"It's okay. I'm just glad you're safe."

"And so you know, I've never done anything like that before. To be honest, I'm not sure why I did it *this* time."

"You're in an unusual situation."

"But, like I said, I'll recover somehow. You don't have to come to Boston to hold my hand."

Going into therapist mode, Evelyn seemed to calm down as she adopted a professional mask. "Do you plan to see Andy again?"

"I guess. I don't really know him, but I've got another day here, and he's obviously attracted to me. I figure we could become long-distance friends if nothing more."

"There has to be some attraction on your side, too."

Brianne dug at the cuticles of her left

hand. She'd liked him a lot more before they'd made love. He hadn't been a very impressive lover, but they hadn't had the best surroundings and he'd felt under pressure since she'd been acting as if she needed to leave. She was trying to be understanding about all of that and not make a judgment call too soon. "He's flattering. That feels good."

"I can see why."

"Then I hope you won't mind that I invited him for dinner tomorrow night. He asked to see me again, and I thought the four of us could eat together — unless you or Amarok can't take the time, or you'd rather Andy and I ate on our own." She didn't want to be alone with him, didn't want him to think the same thing was going to happen again.

Evelyn's eyebrows slid up, but she said, "No, you're welcome to have him over, and I'll join you if I can."

Brianne studied her carefully. "Are you sure?"

She nodded. "Positive."

"Okay. That way, even if Amarok can't make it and has to stay out late again, at least he won't have to worry about us. Not only will we be together, we'll have an armed correctional officer in the house."

She offered her sister a smile in hopes that Evelyn would forgive her, not just for tonight but for the past several days, and was relieved when she seemed willing to let bygones be bygones.

"That'll be a comfort."

Again, Brianne wanted to ask her why she didn't seem to be impressed with Andy Smith. Aside from Amarok, he was the most attractive man she'd seen in the area. But the phone rang.

Evelyn got up to check caller ID. "It's my attorney friend in Boston." She glanced at her watch. "Wow, he's up late," she added as she answered.

"No, you didn't wake me," Brianne heard her say, but didn't stick around to listen to the conversation. She wanted a shower. She liked Andy — or thought she did — but was annoyed that he'd kept sucking on her neck when she'd asked him not to. And she was more than annoyed — she was downright irritated — once she got in the bathroom, looked in the mirror and realized it was worse than she'd thought.

"Holy shit," she muttered as she fingered three distinct red marks — obvious hickeys. Why hadn't he respected her wishes?

She'd have to wear a turtleneck for the remainder of her trip and even for a few days once she got home.

She hoped Evelyn owned a turtleneck, because she hadn't packed any.

Disgusted with herself for letting the night get so out of control, she turned away from the sight in the mirror and started the shower.

23

Evelyn was still lying awake when Amarok came in. She hadn't been able to sleep. She'd written Janice at the BOP before leaving work, told her boss that she needed to take a year off, despite the earlier commitments she'd made, and return to Boston and had felt sick to her stomach ever since. She'd lost so much in the past ten days — her sense of direction, what little remained of her security, the confidence that Hanover House was finally on an even keel and the illusion that she'd recovered from her past. But the loss she lamented the most was the distance that had come between her and the man she'd felt so close to only a short time before. Amarok had helped her more than anyone else. He'd offered the intimacy — in mind, spirit and body — she'd despaired of ever finding. She'd thought she was too damaged, that she lacked the ability to trust enough to fall in love after her first love had nearly killed her, but he'd refused to give up on her, and his consistency and tenacity had made all the difference. She owed him a lot, and yet she was leaving him as he feared she would, even before he'd originally expected she might do it.

But what else was she supposed to do? What Brianne had done tonight with a man she'd barely met served as proof that Evelyn needed to go home and support her sister and parents. Using Amarok's steady, durable kind of love and what it had done for her as an example, she felt she could help them heal, had to at least try.

She heard Amarok in the living room, speaking to his dog in a low voice, and felt her heart ache. If only they'd been able to catch Jasper. It would've changed everything for almost everyone involved. But Jasper had eluded them, as well as *three* police departments — one in Boston, one in San Diego and one in Phoenix. Now two more women had been murdered, Brianne was in a difficult situation and Evelyn had to give up the job she loved — and a relationship that was more fulfilling to her than anything else.

A cupboard closed. She figured he was getting a bite to eat. She hoped he'd had dinner earlier; he was working too hard and sleeping too little.

After waiting another fifteen or twenty minutes, Evelyn felt her stomach twist into knots and her eyes burn with unshed tears. Where was he? Surely he wasn't planning on sleeping separately!

She was about to get up to see when she heard his tread in the hall. *At last,* she thought. But even after he came in, stripped down to his boxers and climbed into bed, he didn't reach for her as he normally would have.

"What did Samantha have to say?" she asked before he could fall asleep.

Amarok didn't seem surprised that she was wide awake, didn't even comment on it. "She claims to have seen some shadowy figure hanging out in the alley behind her store, was afraid it was Jasper, stalking her."

Evelyn frowned into the darkness. "Do you think it *was* Jasper?"

"Honestly? I don't think it was anyone."

"Samantha was just looking for your attention."

"I wouldn't put it past her."

Neither would Evelyn. Of all the people in Hilltop — granted, that wasn't very many, but still — how was it Samantha who'd spotted the man Amarok was searching for? Evelyn hated how she constantly threw herself across his path, but she didn't say that. "How'd the autopsies go?"

"They were put off until Wednesday, and then it took until this morning to be able to get the notes."

"Why so long?"

"Someone was sick in the office, but that doesn't make my job any easier."

Evelyn pulled the blankets higher. "What about the DNA evidence — the blood you found in the snow and on that tree? Have you heard anything from the lab in Philadelphia?"

"Nothing, but they said it would take a week or so."

"Has Anchorage PD been able to identify the body of the woman found with Sierra Yerbowitz?"

"Yeah. Name's Katherine Sharpe. She was a thirty-two-year-old prostitute."

"So a completely different profile from Sierra Yerbowitz."

"Completely."

"Why do you think the perpetrator chose her?"

"Because she was accessible, her disappearance was unlikely to be noted and . . ."

"And?" she prompted.

"She had your basic coloring."

"Of course." Evelyn had been waiting for that. They'd already established that Jasper's "perfect" kill was any woman who looked like her. This provided even more reason to think it might be him. "Have you talked to Leland about her? Did he or Sierra even know her?"

"They didn't."

"Then how did both women wind up dead and dumped in the same area?"

"They had the same murderer."

She hugged her pillow so she wouldn't succumb to the desire she felt to touch Amarok. "Were they killed in the same manner?"

"No. Sierra was strangled."

"And the other girl?"

"Don't even ask."

Evelyn couldn't help flinching. "She was tortured."

He said nothing, which told her she was right. She closed her eyes in an attempt to stop the images that bombarded her brain — images of the shack where she'd been tortured herself — but it was no use. "Again, that indicates Jasper."

"I think so, too," he said. "I think he's here, and I'm going to catch him."

He sounded more determined than ever, and she was trying to maintain the same confidence. But it was difficult to believe *anyone* could catch Jasper when he'd gotten away with so much for so long. "I appreciate how hard you're trying," she murmured.

He stared up at the ceiling. "I'm going to do it," he said again.

Rather than risk discouraging him by conveying her doubts, she went back to the subject of what he'd found so far. "What do you make of one victim being tortured and the other strangled?"

"He enjoyed killing Katherine. Drew it out as long as possible. But Sierra's death was quick and purposeful. I'd say he killed Sierra because he felt he had to."

"She got in the way, and he had to act quickly because he knew her brother and his friends were coming back."

"I can't say he knew who she was with. I see no evidence that he was watching the cabin. But it would've been an easy bet that she wasn't out there alone, so he figured *someone* would be coming back."

"The luggage would've indicated that."

"Among other things. There was no vehicle at the cabin when she was kidnapped and/or murdered, three beds had been slept in, the amount of garbage, et cetera."

"So she was just in the wrong place at the wrong time."

"That's what the evidence seems to suggest. The wear and tear on the posts of one of the downstairs beds says someone was restrained there. Only Katherine has any ligature marks. Sierra's hyoid bone was broken, which indicates she was strangled."

"So the blood on the mattress we found probably belongs to Katherine."

"The lab that Anchorage PD is using is testing it, so it'll be a while, but I have no doubt that's what they'll find."

"She was tortured and killed at the cabin."

"Yes."

The memory of the vomit in the shed made Evelyn sit up. "And, for some reason, he didn't dispose of the body right away. Maybe he had to be somewhere, or planned to prepare a place for it. So he cleaned up, just in case, and put the corpse in the shed. Then he changed the lock on the shed so no one could get in there before he could get back."

Amarok laced his fingers behind his head as he continued to gaze at the ceiling. "That's what it looks like to me — that he didn't expect the cabin to be rented so late in the year or, even if it was, that the renters would need more firewood than he'd left out."

"But with that storm coming, Sierra *did* need more wood, so she used the ax from the mud room to break in —"

"That's when she found Katherine's corpse."

"And threw up."

"Yes."

"Okay, so if Katherine's from Anchorage, doesn't that suggest her killer is, too? Why would he bring her to a cabin way out here? How would he even know about the Barrymore rental?"

"Our killer is familiar with Hilltop," he said. "That's obvious from the scalp Easy found hanging from his rear axle. One of the victims, maybe both, were temporarily stashed along the road leading to Hanover House."

"You think the perpetrator lives in Anchorage but works here?"

"Or vice versa."

"But I haven't seen anyone who looks like Jasper. Wouldn't we have run into him somewhere?"

"Maybe he doesn't work anywhere. Maybe he's just hiding out."

Evelyn lay back down. She wanted to rest her head on Amarok's shoulder, as she'd done countless times before when she needed comfort, but she wasn't sure he'd want to hold her. He was too consumed with building up his defenses, trying to protect himself against what he was going to feel when she left. "So it was sheer bad luck that the killer returned for Katherine's body while Leland and his friends were out hunting and Sierra was there alone."

He adjusted the blankets. "That scenario seems to fit the facts as we know them so far."

"But if he hid Katherine's body and killed Sierra once he realized she'd discovered his dirty secret, he didn't want his activity in the area to be exposed."

Amarok finally turned to look at her. "Which means what?"

"If it's Jasper, killing those women wasn't part of his plan. He was just trying to relieve the tension that builds up between kills and created a bit of a mess."

"A mess . . ."

"A euphemism, but that's how he would look at it."

"You're smiling," he said in astonishment. No doubt he could hear the pleasure in her voice.

"Damn right I am. For once, maybe he's going to pay for what he's done. I can't tell you how much I hope that he's the one you shot. Even if the bullet didn't kill him, he deserves to feel a little of the pain he enjoys inflicting on others."

"His days of doing whatever he wants — and getting away with it — are numbered. He now has Anchorage PD on his ass. That's four police departments, if you don't include me."

She reached over to smooth the hair off his forehead, but when he didn't react, didn't soften and draw her to him, she knew she hadn't been imagining his withdrawal and pulled her hand back. "I heard from my attorney friend tonight — Ashton Cooper."

"What'd he have to say?"

"He's been in touch with Fitzpatrick, gotten everything signed so he can represent him. And Detective Dressler is sending samples of all the unmatched DNA found at Charlotte's murder site to the lab in Philadelphia where Jasper's DNA is waiting for comparison."

"He moves fast."

"That's what I like about him."

"How long did he say the testing would take?"

"A few days," she said. "We may learn as soon as the first of next week."

"Great. If we get a match, I'll go after the flight manifests."

"We've got to catch a break at some point."

Amarok closed his eyes as though he was drifting off, but Evelyn knew she wouldn't be able to sleep. She felt more unsettled than ever. "You haven't mentioned what Brianne did," she said.

He looked over at her. "Brianne isn't a child. What she does is her own business."

"I wish *I* could see it that way."

"Why can't you?"

"Because I'm her sister, and I'm worried about her. That isn't normal behavior."

He sighed. "Which is why you're going home, right?"

"Part of the reason. You know there are other reasons, too."

He ignored her response, didn't seem willing to engage in a conversation about her leaving, and she knew that was probably for the best. "Does she like him?" he asked. "Is she going to see him again?"

"Sounds like it. She's invited him over for dinner tomorrow night."

"Did you tell her you don't like him?"

"No."

"Why not?"

"Because I don't have a good reason. He's been nothing but nice to me."

"What about that photo incident at the prison?"

"I've decided the warden is right — it

could've been caused by the stress of the job. Prison guards are only human. It's difficult to face aggressive, combative prisoners all day and not react. Perhaps he had some pent-up resentment and he lost control for a few seconds."

"So you've forgiven him."

"To be fair, I feel I have to give him another chance."

Silence fell again, during which he rolled onto his side, facing away from her.

"Will you be here for dinner tomorrow?" she asked.

"Probably not. Tomorrow's Saturday, so a lot of people will be at the Moosehead. I should be there to see who's in town and what they're up to."

"I love you, Amarok. I hope you know that," she said, but he didn't reply.

Ever since Evelyn had told him that she was going to take a leave of absence and return to Boston, Amarok had felt as though he were free-falling through space, as though the ground had suddenly given way beneath him. He knew if she left now she'd probably never get her job back, which meant returning would be unlikely. She had to know that, too.

When he and Samantha had broken up,

he'd felt more relief than anything else. He'd *wanted* to move on. But it was different with Evelyn. She'd become such an integral part of his life; he wasn't sure how he'd go on without her.

Angry at his inability to apprehend Jasper and at Jasper for being such a terrible excuse for a human being in the first place, he clenched his fists. He had to admit he was also angry with Evelyn — for not loving him enough, he supposed. But when he thought of all she'd been through, that hardly seemed fair. She was just trying to find peace, happiness, a respite from the pain of her past. She'd told him that loving her wouldn't be easy, had tried to warn him away. It wasn't as if she'd ever been anything less than honest. He'd been the one who'd pursued her from the beginning.

And now . . . here he was.

His house was going to be so empty without her clothes in the closet, her makeup in the bathroom and her computer and files all over the kitchen and living room.

Hell, he was even going to miss her cat.

Part of him wanted to make love to her while he still could. No one else tasted or felt quite so satisfying to him. But he knew it wouldn't be the same. He'd rather preserve the memory of making love to her when he'd still been optimistic that she'd spend the rest of her life with him.

"I love you, too," he murmured, but he could hear her steady breathing and knew she was already asleep.

24

Jasper's arm didn't hurt much anymore — not unless he bumped into something or put too much pressure on it. He was healing quickly, with no sign of infection. Provided that continued, the wound would soon be nothing more than a small scar, and he didn't mind that. Not many people had taken a bullet and lived to tell about it. He could invent a story about how he'd been shot while interrupting a home invasion or bank robbery, something that would make him look like a hero, and he'd have the proof of where the bullet had gone to help convince everyone. A fellow CO at the prison where he'd worked in Florence, Arizona, had a jagged scar on his torso. He'd loved showing it to the other guards and telling them he'd been bitten by a shark. It was all bullshit, though. That guard had once told Jasper that his father had thrown him through a plate glass window when he was nine, but he'd been drunk when he'd made the admission and denied it afterwards.

Jasper liked the shark story better, anyway. Now he'd have a conversation piece of his own — once he left Alaska. He couldn't let anyone know about the bullet wound while he was here, of course. And it might be a while before he left. Thanks to Brianne, things were looking up. If only he could keep her interest, befriend her through the pregnancy, when she was vulnerable and open to his attention, he'd become so familiar to Evelyn and Amarok that he'd be above suspicion — until it was too late. Even after Evelyn went missing, Amarok would never suspect him. At that point Jasper would be like a member of the family. He might even keep up his association with Brianne while he was raping and torturing Evelyn in his basement. That could add a whole new element.

A knock sounded at his front door while he was unpacking the head harness with a ball gag he'd purchased off the Internet, so he quickly set it on the bondage bed he'd built in the far corner — surrounded by mirrors and video equipment — and took the stairs two at a time to the main floor. Who could be coming by this late?

He locked the basement and shoved the key in his pocket.

A strung-out Bambi stood on his stoop, her mascara smudged from tears. “Hey.”

He eyed her suspiciously. How the hell did she find her way back to his house? She’d been so high when he brought her home. When he’d dropped her off at her place as he drove to work he’d never expected to see her again, not unless he returned to the club. “What are you doing here?”

She hugged herself against the cold. Although she had on a heavy coat, she had bare legs and was wearing strappy heels. “I was wondering if you might have some more — oh!” She nearly toppled over but caught herself on the doorframe.

He was fairly certain she was drunk. “Drugs?” he said, finishing her sentence.

She gave him a sheepish, pleading look. “Just a little something. Like last time.”

“I don’t have anything.”

“Are you sure?” Her voice — a high-pitched whine — got on his nerves. “I could come in, stay the night.”

Except she hadn’t been worth what he’d spent on the coke she’d consumed and she was already messy drunk. He didn’t find that appealing, not after being with Brianne.

"Sorry, not interested."

"Come on." She stopped the door as he tried to close it. "Don't be like that. I'll let you cuff me this time. I trust you more now that I know you better. You can whip me, too." She grimaced. "Just don't do it too hard."

"No." He had the smell of Brianne on him, didn't want to trade that for some lowlife stripper. "You're not worth it."

Fresh tears rolled down her cheeks. "How can you say that?"

"Look at you. You're pathetic!"

Her jaw dropped in outrage. "I just heard that a friend of mine's been murdered! How do you think you'd —"

"Who was your friend?" Jasper broke in, suddenly more alert.

She sniffed. "Katherine Sharpe."

"The girl who was found in the woods."

"Yeah. Did you see it on TV or something?"

"I saw a short clip of it on the news."

"Then you knew before I did. I didn't find out until a police officer showed up at the club tonight, wanting to talk to me and the other girls."

What were the chances that Bambi would know Kat? Jasper asked himself. But when he really thought about it, he decided it wasn't that much of a coincidence. Anchorage didn't have a big red-light district. This wasn't New York or LA. Most of the girls who worked the streets or danced in the clubs had probably met somewhere along the line. "How'd you know her?" Jasper asked.

Bambi's teeth were starting to chatter, but Jasper didn't invite her in. He didn't want her to stay; he just wanted her to tell him what she could about the investigation. "She used to dance at the Foxhole," she said. "We both did, last year. Then she got fired for missing too many shifts and I met the owner of Dick's, who talked me into working for him."

"What'd the police want?"

"They're interviewing everyone who knew her. They asked when I saw her last, if she was dating anyone, if I could name someone who might've wanted to hurt her, that sort of thing."

Now that Jasper's wound was healing, it was beginning to itch. He scratched over the fabric of his shirt, trying to get it to stop — to no avail. "Did they say if they've come across any good leads?"

"They think it might be the serial killer who murdered the friends of that psychiatrist who runs the prison in Hilltop."

"Evelyn Talbot."

"That's her name. Can you believe it? *A serial killer?*"

"Did they say why they think it's the same guy?"

"No, but they warned us not to go home with any strange men — like we'd be able to eat or pay rent if we didn't." She rolled her eyes, but more tears welled up as she continued, "Anyway, I feel *so* bad. Kat was a nice person. She didn't deserve what happened to her. The police officer secretly told me she died an ugly death."

"Oh well. No use crying about it now."

"I can't help it!" She put a hand to her head as if she was suddenly overwhelmed with dizziness. "She was my *friend.*"

"You're drunk. And you look like shit."

"Why are you being so *mean*?" she asked, obviously confused. "I just need a place to sleep. Tonight was a bad night at the club. I spent all the money I earned on a taxi to bring me over here."

"Then you'll have to figure out some other way to get home, because you're not *my* problem."

Her wounded expression grew even more pathetic. "I thought we were friends!"

He couldn't let her in, couldn't have anything to do with her now that the police had her on their radar. He didn't want some little thing like a connection to a stripper to bring him to their notice. "Beat it!" he snapped. "I'm tired and going to bed."

Her eyes widened. With all that makeup around them, she looked like a raccoon. "It's freezing out here! At least give me the money for a cab!"

"Go to hell." He slammed the door but almost instantly realized that if something happened to her tonight — if she didn't make it home — he'd have the police on his doorstep for sure. The cabbie would know where he dropped her off.

Sticking his head outside, he called her back and gave her a twenty.

"Thank you!" she said with a teary sniff.

Her relieved smile made him want to punch her in the face. "Don't come back here again. I won't be so nice the next time."

He spent the next thirty minutes pacing angrily in his living room. Bambi had no business showing up at his house. With all that talk about the investigation, she'd ruined the euphoria and optimism he'd been feeling.

Although . . . maybe she'd done him a favor. He'd been acting as though he had nothing to worry about, daydreaming of when he'd finally have Evelyn all to himself, as if connecting with her sister were going to deliver her to him on a silver platter. But with so many people searching for him, he couldn't get complacent. Amarok, in particular, was no fool. It'd be a mistake to underestimate the forces marshaled against him.

Trying to shake off the dark mood that had taken hold of him, he went online to search for any information he could find on the murders of Katherine Sharpe and Sierra Yerbowitz. He couldn't be so focused on what was in front of him that he forgot to watch his back.

There it was. Janice Holt's response to her request for a leave of absence. Evelyn had hated writing that e-mail, cringed at the thought of what Janice might have to say about her leaving. She felt she was letting down her boss, letting down everyone who'd ever believed in her in a professional capacity, including all the people she worked with at Hanover House.

And Amarok . . . Amarok most of all.

But she wanted to stay, so staying was the option that felt selfish.

Taking a deep breath, she sat at her kitchen table — it was Saturday, so she wasn't going to the prison — while Brianne slept in, and clicked on the e-mail.

Do you have to leave immediately? The institution is in a precarious position, Evelyn. Please reconsider. I've put a lot into Hanover House, too, and I don't want news of your leaving to reach the public right now. With the recent murders up there, everyone needs to believe you're standing firm and not caving under the pressure. At least stay in your current position until this bastard has been caught.

It was a fair request. One she felt obliged to honor. But she knew the next few months would be difficult with Amarok. Now that she was going to leave, she thought doing it quickly would be easier than dragging it out. What if Jasper was *never* caught?

She called Amarok at his trooper post. "Janice wants me to stay until the murders have been solved," she said when he answered.

There was a slight pause. "What did you tell her?"

"I haven't responded. I wanted to see how you felt about my staying."

"I *want* you to stay, Evelyn. I thought that was clear."

With conditions, and she couldn't meet those conditions yet. "I know, but . . . won't it be awkward? It'll be miserable for both of us if you're upset for the next several months. I guess what I'm asking is . . . I feel like I have to honor Janice's request, but would you prefer I moved out?"

"Maybe," he replied.

She winced. There weren't many rentals in the area, but she could find an apartment in Anchorage and make the commute, like so many of the COs and other staff did. "I have to admit that hurts."

"You know my terms."

"You're demanding a commitment."

"I want to be sure, or as sure as possible, that I'm not giving my heart to someone who's only going to break it. We've been together for almost two years. I don't think I'm pushing too soon. At some point, I'm either worth it to you or I'm not."

"You're worth it," she said. "There's no question about that. This has nothing to do with you."

"Then we'll see what you decide," he said, and hung up.

Evelyn sighed as she turned back to her computer to type her reply to Janice.

I'll stay as long as I can.

Samantha checked her lipstick and her hair in the rearview mirror of her Subaru before climbing out and going inside Amarok's trooper post.

He was sitting behind his desk, frowning at his phone, when he heard the door and glanced up.

"Hey." She offered him her sweetest smile. She'd spent *all* of last night going from one strip club to the next on Spenard Road, looking for Jasper but without any luck. Although she'd met plenty of weird guys, none of them were particularly frightening. None of them seemed to know — or care — who Evelyn was, either. She could go back tonight — she had tomorrow off because she didn't open the store on Sundays — but she was exhausted and losing hope that trying to find him in that way was really going to work out.

She needed to think of something else. . . .

"Hey." He seemed distracted, upset. Makita barked and trotted over to lick her hand and she knelt to pet him, but, other than the dog, they were alone. She'd driven past before stopping by, just to make sure Phil, or anyone else, wasn't around.

"Did you find any trace of that guy who was lurking in the alley behind my store?" she asked.

Amarok pinched the bridge of his nose, then lowered his hand. He looked grim, tired. She wished she could circle his desk and massage those big shoulders. He had to be feeling the strain of his job. She doubted he'd ever expected this type of pressure when he became a trooper — not here in Hilltop. He had Evelyn to thank for what he was going through, what the entire area was going through. Samantha was tempted to leave her another note, one more hateful than the last. Maybe she'd finally get the point and get the hell out of town, save Samantha the trouble of trying to come up with another way to get rid of her.

"I'm afraid not," he said.

Makita trailed behind her as she approached his desk. "I'm scared to open up my shop in the mornings — or close up at night. Do you think it's safe?"

"It might not be. You need to be wary at all times. Definitely keep your gun on you."

That was it? Keep her gun on her? She was fairly certain he wasn't treating Evelyn's safety so cavalierly. But then . . . Evelyn couldn't even shoot a gun, which just went to prove she wasn't meant to be living in Alaska. "How long do you think this will go on?"

"Investigations take time. I'm working as hard and as fast as I can."

"I can tell. You look exhausted. I feel so bad for what you're going through."

He raked his fingers through his thick,

dark hair. "I'll be fine, but thanks for your concern."

When she didn't leave, he said, "Is there something else?"

She drew a deep breath. "We're a small community, Amarok. We shouldn't have that kind of crime here. We never had it before."

He raised his eyebrows. "And your point is?"

She knew she was going too far but couldn't help herself. "Why are you supporting an institution you know isn't good for the area just because you're in love with the psychiatrist who runs it? How is that fair to the rest of us, who rely on you to look out for the safety of the community?"

A muscle moved in his cheek. "I was one of the few who spoke out against Hanover House."

"Before it came here!"

"Now it's too late!"

"It's *not* too late. Sandy is dead because of Hanover House! We have two other people murdered. How long will it be before it's another friend? Someonc we grew up with?"

He slammed one of the drawers in his desk, which had been hanging open by a few inches. "Sandy is dead because of a psychopath. *Not* because of Evelyn."

"She brought that psychopath here, and she's bringing others!"

"The research she's doing is important. Someone has to do it somewhere," he said, but he wasn't shouting anymore. She could tell he was feeling beleaguered and disillusioned. The murders, the lack of sleep, and maybe something more personal — trouble between him and Evelyn? — was getting to him.

Samantha lowered her voice beseechingly. "Amarok, listen to me. I know you care for her, but she doesn't belong here. She's not one of us. She doesn't love this place like we do. The only thing that matters to her is what she can achieve with her work. She's *using* you —"

"Stop it," he interrupted with a scowl. "She's not using me."

"Fine, but she's never going to marry you. She's going to leave here, leave *you,* eventually. You realize that, don't you?"

He looked absolutely miserable when he met her gaze. "Yeah, I realize that."

Samantha felt the first surge of hope she'd experienced in a long time when it came to Amarok. He and Evelyn were coming to an end. She could see it in his eyes. "Don't worry," she told him. "Losing her won't be the end of the world."

She'd make sure of it, be there to step in when he needed her most.

"Sam —"

She lifted a hand. "I know you're busy. I'm going," she said, and hurried home to get ready. She wouldn't go back to Anchorage tonight. She'd go to the Moosehead instead. If Amarok ever left his trooper post, he would probably go there. He made it a point to police the bar, especially on weekends.

25

Spending more time with Andy Smith didn't improve Evelyn's opinion of him. He seemed *so* vain. Every story he told featured him as the daring protagonist — and he told story after story. One in which he woke up with his house on fire but managed to pull his ex-wife and her two daughters to safety. "If I hadn't gotten up to go to the bathroom when I did, they would've died of smoke inhalation. That's how bad it was," he said. Some paint rags in the garage had spontaneously combusted, and the fire department didn't arrive in time to save much. He lost all the photographs and mementos of his past. Evelyn had bought into that story, thought it was tragic and felt terrible for him, but as he continued to talk she began to wonder if everything he said could be true. For instance, he also claimed to have spotted a terrorist on a plane and held the guy in the bathroom for the duration of the flight. And that he'd run into Mariah Carey when he was in New York City and she somehow got separated from her security detail, so he threw his coat and his arm around her to protect her from the pressing throng until he could get her safely to her limo.

Although Evelyn was silently shaking her head, Brianne didn't seem to doubt him. She appeared to be enjoying herself, and that was all that mattered. Evelyn just wanted her sister to be happy. She also wanted Amarok to come home. She couldn't help glancing at the door every so often, hoping he'd walk in. She missed him so much, and she hadn't even left Hilltop yet. He'd spoiled her for all other men. As far as she was concerned, no one else could compare. No one else had his well-balanced ego, his sense of fair play, his ability to listen instead of dominating every conversation, his quiet strength.

What he could do in the bedroom was even better. . . .

Warmth traveled through her as she thought of his hands on her body. It seemed like forever since they'd made love. How was she going to survive a whole year in Boston without him?

She wasn't looking forward to that, just as

she wasn't looking forward to moving out of his house.

"So what'd you do next?" Brianne asked Andy.

"I swam out over the reef and dragged him to shore, of course," Andy replied. "I couldn't leave him out there. He would've been shark bait."

Evelyn realized she'd missed a large chunk of the conversation. Andy was now in the middle of relating some ocean experience he claimed to have had. But it was hard not to let her mind wander. She had little interest in Andy or his farfetched stories. And she was getting tired.

Fortunately, the night was almost over. They'd finished eating the delicious salmon and vegetables Brianne had cooked and were sitting around the table. Evelyn had a glass of wine and so did Andy. Brianne had water, but that didn't seem to bother her any more than some of the outlandish things Andy said.

"You could've been killed!" Brianne told him.

"*Someone* had to do it." He went into detail about the different species of sharks that swam around that reef, just to emphasize how dangerous it had been.

Evelyn saw him look at her every few

seconds to make sure she was paying attention and smiled as though she was, but she couldn't wait for him to leave. She was tempted to peek at her watch. She didn't because she was afraid he'd notice. He was Brianne's guest; she needed to be as polite as possible.

"That's not the only incident where I had to save someone on a beach," he said, and told them about a mother who'd lost track of her child and how he'd pulled the little girl out of the surf and performed CPR.

"Did she live?" Brianne gasped.

"She did," he said. "She coughed up water and started to breathe. Her mother was so grateful."

"I bet! That must've been terrifying."

"I almost had a heart attack when I saw her floating in the water. Why her mother wasn't paying more attention I don't know. It only takes —"

"What do you think about the murders we've had here?" Evelyn broke in.

She'd fallen silent for so long, they both seemed startled that she still had a voice. Or maybe it was that she'd cut him off before he could finish his statement. But she had to stop him before he launched into yet another story, and the investigation was all Evelyn could think about these days.

"You mean Sierra Yerbowitz and that other woman?" Andy asked.

Evelyn crossed her legs. "Katherine Sharpe, yes."

"The police have a real problem on their hands."

"You don't believe Amarok will be able to find the killer?"

He finished his wine and held out his glass, since Brianne was offering to refill it. "I'm sure Amarok's an amazing cop, but you and I both work at the prison. We know what those men are like."

"You're assuming we're looking for a serial killer, then."

"Aren't you assuming the same thing? I read in the paper that the victims had no apparent connection to each other, even though they were found together. Two random victims will make the investigation a lot harder."

"Yes, but the killer left evidence."

He leaned back. "What evidence? It's tough to have an informed opinion without knowing all the facts."

"The bodies, for one. Katherine was tortured. Sierra wasn't. Why the difference?"

"The question is . . . *why are we talking about murder*?" Brianne said. "Don't you both get enough of that at Hanover House?" She stood and started gathering the dishes. "I've made a lemon chiffon cake. Let's have dessert and change the subject. I, for one, am sick of dark topics. I wish I never had to hear about another psychopath."

Evelyn thought the conversation was just getting interesting. Since Andy pretended to know so much about everything, she was curious to hear his opinion, wanted to see if he had anything insightful to add. He seemed flattered that she'd asked and keen on answering. But he was Brianne's date, and Brianne wasn't going to let their current crisis ruin what would be her last night in Alaska.

"Of course." Evelyn cast them both an apologetic smile. "I'm preoccupied with the situation, but I don't mean to spoil your evening. I've had enough to eat. No dessert for me." Intent on going to her room so they could have some privacy, she pushed away from the table. "Time for me to find my bed."

"You don't have to leave," Brianne said. "I wasn't suggesting that."

"She's right. Stay," Andy chimed in. "I'm enjoying your company. We both are."

Evelyn picked up her plate. "Thank you, but I'm exhausted. I'll stack the dishes for now. We can do them in the morning, Bri, so don't worry about them tonight."

With the help of Brianne and Andy, she'd just about cleared the table when the phone rang.

Brianne was closest to it. "Looks like it's that attorney friend of yours again," she said. "He sure stays up late, doesn't he?"

"I suspect he's a workaholic, like me." Evelyn's hands were wet from rinsing plates; she quickly dried them. "Plus he knows it's four hours earlier here, so it's okay to call."

"Burning the midnight oil again?" she asked Ashton once they'd both said hello.

"I finally had a chance to go through my voicemail today," he told her.

"And? Have you heard from the lab?" She'd been on pins and needles, waiting to hear back, but she hadn't expected word so soon. To keep from feeling *too* anxious, she'd told herself Monday would be the earliest.

At the energy and enthusiasm in her voice, Brianne and Andy turned to watch her.

"I have," Ashton said. "They left me a message several hours ago. They've matched the DNA."

"To *Jasper's*?"

"Yes. He was in the house where Charlotte was killed, no question."

"What about the blood from the cabin here in Alaska?"

"Everything has to be double-checked by a supervisor, so they won't release the results of that test quite yet. We probably won't hear on that one until Monday, but I wanted to give you what news I had."

"Okay, so . . . if Jasper's DNA was in Charlotte's house, he killed her, as I've always suspected. He'd have no other reason to be there. Tim is innocent."

"That's what it means to me, too. I'll do everything I can to get Dr. Fitzpatrick released. But his DNA was also at the scene. We'll have to see where that goes."

"What is it?" Brianne asked.

Evelyn couldn't choke back the tears. "We have a chance," she said. "We have a chance to catch him."

Her sister grabbed her arm. *"Jasper?"*

"Yes, Jasper!" Evelyn thanked Ashton and told him good-bye. She was so excited she couldn't remain on the phone. Grabbing her purse, she hurried for the door, but Brianne stopped her before she could leave. "Where are you going?"

"To the Moosehead to tell Amarok. They've found Jasper's DNA at the scene where Charlotte was murdered! Tim Fitzpatrick is innocent. It was Jasper who killed

Charlotte, and if he killed Charlotte, he killed Mandy, too."

"Wait! You've always believed that, haven't you?"

"Yes, but now we have proof."

"Jasper's DNA was found beneath the fingernails of one of the women who were murdered in Peoria, and that hasn't come to anything," Brianne said. "Why is this so monumental?"

"Because now Amarok can get a warrant for the flight manifests! We know Jasper was living in the Phoenix area with a wife and kids when he murdered his parents. In order to kill them in San Diego, he would've had to fly there, then go on to Boston that night or the next morning to kill Charlotte. Since he'd have no reason to stay after murdering her, and it would be best to get out of town, he most likely flew right back to Phoenix. So all we have to do is study the manifests to see who traveled from Phoenix to San Diego to Boston and back to Phoenix that week. There can't be a lot of people who did that. Then we eliminate the names one by one until —"

"Until you zero in on the alias he's been using!" Brianne cried.

Evelyn smiled through her tears. "Amarok was right. We're going to get him."

■ ■ ■ ■

Amarok was sending the many pictures of tires he'd taken at the Moosehead last night to the expert, hoping for a cold hit, when the door to his trooper post flew open and slammed against the wall. Makita jumped to his feet and barked before recognizing Evelyn.

"There you are!" She seemed to blow in, courtesy of the strong wind behind her. "I've been looking all over for you. I thought you were going to the Moosehead tonight."

He still planned to go to the bar at some point. He just hadn't been able to summon the energy. But he hadn't wanted to go home, either. He was finding it more and more difficult to be around her. She was breaking his heart. "I had some work to do."

He stood as she wrestled the door closed and crossed the floor. He was going to ask why she wasn't at the house, having dinner with Brianne and Brianne's new love interest, but he didn't get the chance. She circumvented his dog and walked straight into his arms, caught his face between her hands and brought her mouth to his.

Amarok told himself to set her away from him. He was determined to hold fast to his ultimatum. The relationship *had* to progress or they should break up and move on. But she was kissing him as if she was starved for the taste of him and, truth be told, he was starved for the taste of her, too. He'd never loved anyone so much. He kept telling himself he'd step away, but one moment passed on to the next and the passion only intensified.

She was already unbuttoning his uniform when he realized he should lock the door. Although he didn't get many visitors, he had to protect against the possibility that someone might barge in. But Amarok couldn't make himself let go of Evelyn for even that long. He was afraid his resolve would return if he did. So he pulled her with him.

Once no one could walk in on them, the clothes came off in earnest. Her coat and hat. His shirt. Her blouse. One shoe here and another there. She was unbuttoning his pants and unzipping his fly when he nudged her away to be able to move the stapler and a few other things off Phil's desk so they could use it — he had too much paper on his own. Then he shoved up her skirt to remove her panties.

"I hope this means what I think it means," he said as his mouth slid down her neck to her breasts.

She didn't answer. She moaned and dropped her head back as he took her nipple in his mouth.

God, this was good, Amarok thought. They belonged together. Couldn't she see that? It didn't matter that they were from different worlds, that she was seven years older, that her emotional scars sometimes created problems. She was the one for him, the one he couldn't live without. Some things were just meant to be.

"I need you." She stared up at him as if those words held every bit as much meaning as he hoped. "Now. I can't wait."

He kicked her panties aside. He was ready. Just the thought of her could get him hard. Even if she wasn't making a commitment, he wasn't going to miss out on this opportunity. For all he knew, it could be the last time he'd ever be able to make love to her.

Her legs locked around him as he pushed inside her. "Yes!" she gasped. "There you are."

He was too caught up in what they were doing to talk. From that moment on, his world shrank to sensation. The feel of Evelyn. The scent of her. The sounds she made as he drove into her. He gave everything he had to this one act as if it might make a difference, might make her stay.

When she cried out and he felt the spasm of her climax, he wished he could last longer, make her come again. But it was no use. He was barely hanging on. Closing his eyes, he stopped fighting the building tension.

As the pleasure of his own orgasm started to ripple through him, so powerfully it spread goose bumps over his whole body, he wondered if she'd try to slide away at the last second or tell him to pull out, but she didn't. She kept her legs locked around his hips as he came inside her.

Hardly able to breathe for the frenzy that'd swept them both away, they struggled to recover as they stared at each other. "What just happened?" he asked.

Her eyes never left his. "I think I just realized that I can't live without you."

He smoothed the hair off her face. "You're not leaving?"

"I'm hoping I won't have to, not for longer than a month or two, and that wouldn't be until April, when the baby comes."

Already he wished he could make love to her again. He could never get enough of her. "What's changed?"

"We have a match on Jasper's DNA."

■ ■ ■ ■

Amarok didn't have time to react to Evelyn's announcement. Someone was at the door. Makita barked as the handle rattled, then a knock sounded, sending them both scrambling to get dressed.

Amarok finished first. He yelled out that he'd just be a minute while quickly replacing the items he'd knocked off Phil's desk.

"You ready?" he murmured as Evelyn grabbed her coat from the floor.

She shot him a smile to signal that she was, and he turned the lock.

As Amarok swung the door open, his body blocked Evelyn's view for a moment. *"You're back?"*

"I have to tell you something."

Evelyn recognized that voice. *Samantha . . .*

Since Makita was familiar with their visitor, he calmed down.

"What is it?" Amarok stepped back so they could all see one another. Evelyn got the impression he wanted to be sure Samantha knew he wasn't alone, as if that might have some impact on what she said.

Her eyes wandered over the little things they hadn't yet straightened — like a pencil holder Amarok had missed picking up from the floor. Not to mention Evelyn's mussed hair and slightly disheveled clothes.

A hard glitter entered her eyes. She understood the kind of encounter she'd just interrupted. Maybe that was why she'd stopped by in the first place, because she'd seen Evelyn's SUV parked next to Amarok's truck out front and was hoping to insert herself in some way. "I just saw that weird guy again, the one who was lurking in the alley behind my shop."

"Where?" Amarok asked.

She seemed sort of undecided for a second, but then she said, "He was hanging out in the parking lot of the Moosehead."

Was? She was already preparing Amarok for the fact that he wouldn't be there when her report was checked.

"You're sure?" Amarok sounded skeptical. "Because no one else has seen anyone acting strange or suspicious. Only you."

Like Evelyn, Amarok obviously had the impression that she was lying.

Samantha raised her chin to show that she was offended he'd doubt her word. "Why would I make that up?"

They all knew why, but Amarok didn't answer that question. "I'll check it out."

He held the door as though he expected

her to leave, but she lingered in spite of that. "You might want to go now," she told him. "I doubt the guy will be there if you wait."

She wanted to split them up. Evelyn could easily tell.

"You've made the report," he said. "I'll take it from here."

"But thanks for stopping by," Evelyn added. She knew she shouldn't get involved, but she couldn't help herself. Samantha was *so* transparent.

"Hello, Evelyn," Samantha said, her expression hardening. "I hear you're planning to move back to Boston soon."

The wind coming in through the open doorway prompted Evelyn to yank on her coat. "I'm not sure what my plans are quite yet."

"That's too bad, because you can't leave soon enough for me. After all, *you're* the reason for the terrible trouble we've had."

Samantha had never liked her, and she'd made no secret of the fact. Still, Evelyn was surprised by her venom. She opened her mouth to respond, but Amarok jumped in.

"That isn't true." Although he tried to step between them, Evelyn pulled him back.

"Is that why you keep leaving such hateful notes on my car?" She never would've come right out and accused Sam if Sam hadn't started this, but she wasn't going to hold back now.

"I have no idea what you're talking about," Samantha replied. "I wouldn't waste my precious time on that. Or on *you*. But if you're getting hateful notes, it just goes to prove I'm not the only one who thinks you don't belong here."

"Fortunately, it's a free country," Evelyn said. "You're not some Alaskan gatekeeper; you don't get to decide who lives here and who doesn't."

At that, Samantha gave her the most maleficent glare Evelyn had ever received, except from some of the psychopaths who'd wanted to kill her over the years. "Oh, come on. You're going to leave eventually. What would a woman like you do out here for the rest of her life? Why don't you quit screwing around? Especially with Amarok? You're just leading him on. I know that even if he doesn't!"

Forever defensive of his master and whatever or whomever his master was defending, Makita growled soft and low. Amarok had just tensed and thrown his arm around Evelyn. To such a smart dog, that was all it took to signal there was a problem, and he was willing to help out with it.

"If you can't be decent, you need to go,"

Amarok said.

"Decent?" Sam cried. "I'm only saying what everyone else is thinking."

"Stop it! Evelyn is well liked here. Don't try to make her feel that isn't the case."

"How would *you* know? You can't even see the real her!"

"That's it. Good-bye." He was closing the door when she screamed, "I can't wait until he finally kills her!" and stomped off.

Evelyn found a chair and sank into it. "*He* being Jasper, I assume."

Amarok brought her a glass of water. "I'm sorry. That was rough, but don't listen to her. She's just . . ."

"Jealous?"

He scrubbed a hand over his face. "Yeah, I guess."

Makita came over and rested his muzzle on her lap as if he was sorry about how Samantha had acted, too.

"Tell me something . . . ," Evelyn said while scratching behind the dog's ears.

"What's that?"

"Would you go back to Samantha if I wasn't here?"

"No, and I've never led her to believe I would. She may see you as her rival, but I wouldn't be interested, regardless." He sat in his own chair and nudged Makita out of the way so he could roll it close to her. "Forget Sam, okay? She doesn't mean anything to me." He took both her hands. "Tell me what Ashton Cooper said."

Evelyn was still a little rattled, but she'd known all along that Amarok's ex-girlfriend had no love for her. She attempted to shake off her distress as she regained her excitement over the DNA evidence and explained her conversation with Ashton. Thank goodness they'd been able to cull a profile from the material under the fingernails of that victim in Peoria and confirm that it was Jasper's by matching it to his parents. Had they not done that, they couldn't have linked Charlotte's murder to Jasper and couldn't push the investigation forward from there.

"So we don't know if it was Jasper who shot at me?" he said when she was done.

"Not yet."

"Still, this is almost too good to be true. I'll get moving on those manifests."

"How long do you think that'll take?"

He rolled back to his desk. "I might be able to get them by Monday. I'll start with Southwest. Phoenix is their hub, so it makes sense that they'd have a lot of flights going out of there."

As she considered the logistics, Evelyn felt a little overwhelmed. "Sifting through all those records . . . We're looking at a lot of work."

"Not necessarily. If I can get the manifests in Excel — or convert whatever kind of file they send me to an Excel file — I can add a field for the airline and flight number on each document. Then I can merge all of the records and alphabetize them to find the duplicates, so it might not take as many hours as we initially thought."

Makita nudged her hand with his cold, wet nose. "That's hopeful," she said as she scratched the dog.

"Provided Jasper behaved the way we think he did, we might have what we need to arrest the son of a bitch by next Wednesday or Thursday."

Too overcome to speak, Evelyn got up and slid her arms around Amarok from behind.

His hands came up to grip her arms. "If I can catch him, you'll stay, right?"

Even if they were finally able to apprehend Jasper, her family would have plenty of difficulties ahead of them. Especially Brianne with a new baby. But if Evelyn went back for a shorter time — a month or two — after the baby was born, that might be enough if only her family could put the past behind them. With Jasper in jail, looking at a life sentence, they'd have justice, resolution, a brighter hope for the future.

Those were no small improvements. . . .

"Yeah," she said. "That might relieve my worry for them just enough to make it possible for me to stay."

26

All the lights were off when Evelyn pulled into the driveway. Brianne must've gone to bed. Evelyn was tired, too. Fortunately, Andy was gone. Evelyn had stayed with Amarok and Makita at his trooper post for nearly two hours to give her sister plenty of privacy. She couldn't understand why Brianne would have *any* interest in Andy Smith, but her sister was in a stressful situation. Maybe she saw something in Andy that Evelyn didn't.

Grateful that she wouldn't have to face him again, Evelyn braced against the wind as she got out of her SUV and fought her way to the front door. When the wind blew this strong, it could bite through almost anything. Her coat felt more like a mesh screen as she fumbled with her keys so she could let herself in.

The scent of the fire, which still burned in the hearth, couldn't entirely overcome that of the salmon they'd had for dinner. She considered doing the dishes, knew that would help get rid of the residual odor, but she didn't want to wake Brianne by clanging about in the kitchen. They could finish cleaning up in the morning, as she'd initially suggested. Brianne's flight was a red-eye, so she didn't have to be at the airport until evening. They'd have plenty of time.

Evelyn would've gone straight to bed without turning on the lights, but she was worried that Sigmund might not have enough water. Although Amarok had said he'd be home soon, she doubted he'd remember to check. She didn't want him to worry about it, anyway.

After retracing her steps to the light switch near the front door, she set her purse and keys on the counter and was crossing the kitchen to Sigmund's bowls when she saw several drops of red on the floor.

"What's that?" she murmured, but as soon as she bent down she knew it was blood.

"Brianne?" Evelyn dashed down the hallway to the spare bedroom where her sister had been staying. Was she not asleep as Evelyn had originally thought?

Sheer terror gripped her as she turned on the light.

Brianne shoved herself up on one elbow

and squinted at her. "What's going on?"

Weak with relief, Evelyn sagged against the doorframe.

"Evelyn? Are you okay?"

"Yeah, I'm okay." She came into the room and sat on the foot of the bed. "I thought . . ."

"*What?* You scared the hell out of me rushing in here and flipping on the light like that!"

"I thought something might've happened to you."

Brianne blinked at her. "Why?"

"Do I really need to explain? You're aware of what's happened here. We have a killer on the loose. Amarok and I are both afraid it's Jasper, and he'd love nothing more than to hurt me in any way he can."

"You mean by killing me." She dropped back on her pillow. "Stop spooking us both. I'm fine. I had Andy with me for most of the night, so I wasn't even alone."

"Well, Andy isn't here now."

"No, he's probably halfway home."

Evelyn gestured toward the rest of the house. "What's all the blood in the kitchen?"

"The *blood*?" Brianne scowled in confusion. Then her face cleared. "Oh! I cut myself on a knife while I was unloading the dishwasher." She lifted her hand to reveal a finger with a bandage on it. "I thought I'd cleaned up all the blood. Where'd you see it?"

"On the floor."

"Was it a lot?"

"Only a few drops, but —"

"I must've missed them, that's all. I'm sorry."

"No problem." Evelyn pressed a hand to her chest to slow the beating of her heart. "So how'd it go with Andy?"

"He wants me to stay another week."

"Are you going to do it?"

"No."

"Why not? Amarok and I would love to have you here a little longer."

She rolled her eyes. "I can't imagine *Amarok* would love that."

Evelyn remembered the promise she'd given Amarok at the trooper post but didn't mention it. Hoping to catch Jasper and finally doing it were two entirely different things. Nothing had changed quite yet. "He wouldn't mind."

"It would cost too much to change my plane ticket on such late notice. And I'm not that into Andy. I mean . . . it's flattering that he's so interested in me. It was a nice distraction from what I'm going through, but —"

Evelyn gave her a wry smile. "He talks too much about himself?"

Brianne smiled reluctantly in return. "That, and he doesn't like taking no for an answer."

"When did you have to tell him no?"

She pulled the blankets up higher. "He tried to get me to have sex with him again once you left. After what I did last night, I can see why he'd feel safe to make a move. But I told him how embarrassed I was that Amarok caught us in the truck, so he should've been able to understand why I wouldn't want to risk that again, especially right here in Amarok's house."

Since Evelyn didn't care for Andy, she breathed a little sigh of relief that her sister wasn't planning to continue the relationship. At least she wouldn't have to suffer through having him at the dinner table on future holidays. "It's his last chance to be with you, so maybe that's understandable," she said, trying to be generous.

"I guess, but he seemed angry when I said no, and that bothers me."

"Angry?"

"He'd hardly speak to me! He just got up and left."

"I'm sorry, Bri."

Her sister shrugged. "Like I said, I'm not

that interested in him. If it wasn't for how bad I was feeling about Jeff, nothing would ever have happened between us."

"Andy's a handsome guy. I can see why he might've turned your head — until you had a chance to know him better."

"Yeah, I'm glad I had that chance, because now that we've spent more than an hour together, I can tell there's something strange about him," she added with a laugh, and Evelyn chuckled, too.

"Someday you'll meet the right person."

Brianne looked wistful. "I want someone who loves me the way Amarok loves you."

"Any man would be lucky to have you." She got up to go to bed herself, but Brianne called her back.

"Forget everything I said before, okay? You'd be crazy to leave here, leave Amarok."

Evelyn hoped she wouldn't have to. For the first time in a long while, she felt she and Amarok might actually win the war they'd been waging against Jasper, which would do so much for her family, too. "We'll see what happens." She turned off the light. "Get some rest."

Letting Brianne live was the most difficult thing Jasper had ever done, especially because, now that Amarok knew his DNA was at the scene of Charlotte's murder, he'd have to flee the area, anyway. Gone were his dreams of capturing Evelyn and continuing to work at the prison, rubbing elbows with her boyfriend, while keeping her locked in the basement as his sex slave. Those plane manifests she'd mentioned to Brianne would show an Andy Smith flying from Phoenix to San Diego, from San Diego to Boston and from Boston back to Phoenix, just as Evelyn had guessed. Although he'd purposely chosen a common name, seeing it on those flights would be all Amarok and Evelyn needed to realize he'd been right under their noses for the past eight months.

But he'd guessed Amarok would return to the house with Evelyn, and if he did that and found Brianne lying in a pool of blood the jig would be up even sooner. Jasper would already have played all his cards. He'd no longer have any chance of hanging around long enough to get to Evelyn before he had to disappear.

He turned his headlights to bright so he could better navigate the narrow mountain passes on his drive home. Brianne should've lost her life for refusing to have sex with him. The bitch had led him on, only to reject him in the end. She deserved to pay for that, and he'd make sure she did — later.

In order to seize the victory he craved, he had to handle first things first. For now, he needed to stay focused and put all his energy and ingenuity into creating a moment when he could get Evelyn alone, during which he'd have sufficient time to kill her and then slip away. Obtaining those flight manifests would take at least a week. Before Amarok could request them, he'd have to come up with a warrant, and even after he got a warrant, he'd have to wait for the files. After that, he'd have to analyze the data, and there'd be *a lot* of it, which meant Jasper still had a chance. If he remained calm, if he carefully planned out and executed his next move, he'd be able to accomplish some of what he'd hoped to before he had to flee. After having him over for dinner and the way he'd connected to her younger sister, whom he hadn't harmed even though he'd had the chance, he'd be one of the last people Evelyn would suspect.

All wasn't lost yet.

He just had to act fast — in the next few days.

Sunday was Evelyn's best day yet with her sister. They had bagels and hot chocolate for breakfast, cleaned up the rest of the dinner dishes from the night before and watched *Jane Eyre* and *Wuthering Heights,* movies based on books they'd both loved while growing up. Since Amarok had done all he could with the investigation of Sierra's and Katherine's murders and was now waiting on lab results — including the analysis of the pictures he'd submitted of all the tires at the Moosehead on Friday night and the airline manifests that could possibly tie Jasper to Charlotte's murder — he was able to join them.

The three of them laughed and talked until it was time to leave for the airport. Then Amarok loaded Brianne's luggage into Evelyn's Land Cruiser and drove while they continued to chat.

Once they reached Anchorage and her sister had cell service again, Evelyn used Brianne's phone to call their parents.

"When are you coming home?" her mother asked almost immediately.

She heard this every call, hated the pressure she felt as a result, which was what made checking in so difficult. "I'm not sure."

"Can you come for Thanksgiving?"

They'd know by then if the flight manifests were going to reveal what they needed them to reveal. "I'll try. That sounds fun."

"And will you bring Amarok?"

Evelyn glanced over to see him laughing at something Brianne had said about Andy. Evelyn was pretty sure her sister was mocking one of Andy's more outrageous stories and was glad she wasn't the only one who'd been put off by his grandstanding. "Amarok usually spends Thanksgiving with his father and his father's wife in Anchorage, but I'll ask him."

"It would be nice to meet him. You've been together for so long. I'd say it's time, wouldn't you?"

Evelyn ignored the bitter note in her mother's voice. "I'll ask him, like I said. Anyway, it was great to see Brianne. I'm so happy she came. You and Dad should visit Alaska sometime. It's beautiful here."

"Maybe in the spring."

Not *this* spring. Brianne would be having her baby, but Lara didn't know that and Evelyn wasn't about to give anything away. "We can talk about that when it's closer."

"Is Brianne still getting in at six tomorrow?"

Lara and Grant were picking Brianne up at the airport. "Yes. Far as we know, her flight's on time."

"Call us if that changes."

"She will." Evelyn hesitated. She wanted

to ask how her mother was doing, beyond the perfunctory, *Hi, Mom. How are you?* that was part of her initial greeting. But now wasn't the time. She'd wait until Brianne had revealed her broken engagement and the pregnancy; then she'd call and try to offer what support she could.

Lara asked about her work and what Amarok had found so far regarding the murders. After Evelyn had given an update on her research and shared what she could about the investigation, she considered mentioning that they'd found Jasper's DNA at the house where Charlotte was killed and might be able to place him here in Alaska but decided against it. She didn't want to set her parents up for more disappointment if those manifests didn't reveal the information they thought should be there. So she kept her mouth shut and listened as her mother complained about a disagreement they were having with a new neighbor over a fence between their two properties that needed mending, plus the fact that her father was spending *far* too much time on the golf course (translation — her mother was lonely, which didn't make Evelyn feel any better about her desire to stay in Alaska), and raved about how much she loved the new cheesecake-filled banana bread recipe she'd found on Facebook.

They were at the departure curb and Amarok was getting out to retrieve Brianne's luggage by the time Evelyn ended the call.

"How'd it go?" Brianne asked as Evelyn returned her phone.

"You're right. She's struggling. And I feel bad about that."

Her sister drew an audible breath. "I'll do what I can."

"I know you will. And I know you have. Thank you for carrying the heavy end."

She nodded and started to pull up the handle on her suitcase so she could wheel it inside when Evelyn stopped her. "Bri?"

Her sister waited to hear what she had to say. Brianne had been happier this morning than any other day since she'd arrived, but Evelyn could see that the pressure of returning home was beginning to weigh on her. "When will you tell Mom and Dad about Jeff and the baby?"

"I don't know. When I can face it, I guess."

"Sooner might be better than later. You won't be able to pretend he's part of your life for long, not if he isn't coming around anymore."

She blew out a sigh. "True."

"It might be easier to get it over with.

Then you won't have to dread it anymore. Or are you holding out hope that you and Jeff will get back together?" Evelyn could see not saying anything about the breakup if Brianne thought there was a chance they might reconcile. Their mother would probably take longer to forgive him than Brianne would.

Brianne called up her last text exchange with Jeff and turned her phone so Evelyn could see it. "I haven't heard from him the entire time I've been here. I think it's safe to say it's over."

Evelyn embraced her. "His loss. There'll be other men."

"That's the kind of stuff Mom's going to say once I tell her," she grumbled. "I feel so pathetic."

Evelyn looked into her face. "Heartbreak happens to the best of us. So keep your chin up."

Brianne hugged Amarok. "Sorry about what you had to see at the Moosehead. I'm beyond embarrassed."

"Like I said, none of my business." He grinned at her as if he'd already banished any negative opinions.

"I can see why she loves you," she said.

Amarok slung his arm around Evelyn as Brianne took her luggage, but before she could disappear into the building he stopped her. "Actually, you're a little early. Would you mind if I used your phone to check my voicemail before you go? I'm going over to rent a satellite phone after this, but —"

"You are?" Evelyn asked. "You've mentioned wanting one before, but I thought they were outrageously expensive."

"They are. At this point, however, I don't care what it costs. Your life could be at stake. I need to be accessible at all times."

"Where do you even get one?"

"There's a place here in Anchorage. A lot of hunters and fishermen use them."

Evelyn thought of Sierra and the terror she'd likely faced in the Barrymore cabin. "I wish Leland had had one."

"Me, too," he said. "But at two dollars a minute, it'd be better for me to use Brianne's phone while I can. I'd like to see if there's been a change in the investigation. And I should find out if anyone's trying to reach me sooner rather than later."

"I agree."

"I don't mind." Brianne pulled her cell back out of her purse.

"It's Sunday, so it might be too soon to hope for that warrant, but you never know," Amarok said.

She and Brianne talked while he dialed

his voicemail and went through his messages. Evelyn was just suggesting that Brianne buy a sandwich to put in her purse for the long plane ride when she saw Brianne give Amarok a funny look and turned to look at him, too.

"What is it?" she asked when she saw the grimace on his face.

"Nothing," he replied, but when she pressed him he punched a couple of buttons and handed her the phone.

The message wasn't about the warrant for the flight manifests or the investigation of the murders in Alaska, as Evelyn had expected. What she heard was Samantha's voice. "Amarok, *please.* I've grown up a lot since we were together. I know I was immature before, but now . . . things are different. We'd be perfect for each other. Give me the chance to prove it, okay? I don't understand why you're wasting your time with Evelyn. She's only going to break your heart. Come over tonight or *any* night. Let me show you what you're missing. And if you need a little time to compare what you get from both of us? I won't say a word to anyone."

Evelyn shook her head in disbelief. "Wow, she doesn't give up, does she? How are you going to respond?"

"I'm not." He took the phone back and deleted the message before returning it to Brianne.

Where the heck was Jasper Moore? Samantha wondered. If he was so dangerous, why was Evelyn still alive and breathing? Surely if he was as smart a psychopath as he was supposed to be — as Evelyn said he was — he would've been able to figure out some way to kill her by now.

"Must be a freaking idiot," she muttered as she drove past Amarok's house; she was so obsessed with Amarok, she couldn't make herself stay away.

Evelyn's SUV wasn't there, but Amarok's truck was. Was he home alone? Had he gotten her message?

If so, how would he respond?

The thought that he might appear on her doorstep one night — if not tonight, then when he came to realize that his relationship with Evelyn wouldn't last — made it difficult to breathe. It'd been ages since she'd been with a man, and after the many months she'd longed for Amarok she could hardly wait. She dreamed constantly of his mouth on hers, of lying beneath him. . . . Because she'd been with him before, she knew what she'd been missing, understood that not every man could make love the way he did.

She'd probably climax the second he touched her, she thought with a laugh. But that was okay. She'd take as many orgasms as he'd give her — and she'd give him as many as he wanted in return.

Tempted to drive by his place one more time, just in case he might be home alone, she slowed at the corner. But his house looked dark. It was possible that he and Evelyn were both gone. . . .

She forced herself to head back home. She didn't want anyone to see her hanging around his place. She'd finally worked up the nerve to extend the invitation she'd wanted to extend. Now it was time to wait and hope he took her up on it.

27

Jasper had his flight all arranged. He'd be flying to Mexico City first thing Thursday morning. The various police departments that were looking for him would soon have his picture, and they'd publicize it, which would remove the benefit of the cosmetic surgery that'd served him so well for the past two decades. He had to get out of the States, but that wasn't an entirely bad thing. After the cold of Alaska, he was looking forward to spending the next five or ten years in a warm, relaxed climate with plenty of sun, sand and *cerveza.* He could get a girlfriend who'd take care of him in Mexico as easily as anywhere else. He could also kill there as easily as anywhere else. And he'd have the memory of Evelyn to sustain him, since by the time he left she'd no longer be breathing. He had it all planned out. Everything would happen Wednesday night, and he'd disappear the next morning.

Finished packing the only suitcase he was going to take, he left it open on one side of the bed so he could add a few things he wasn't ready to put in yet and went to take a shower. He had to be at the prison in two hours. It was unfortunate that he was scheduled to work each of his final days in Alaska. He still had so much to do in order to be ready for Wednesday night. But if his plan was going to work, he had to keep up appearances.

Just before he went into the bathroom, he walked out to take a final look at the furniture and other possessions he'd accumulated over the past eight months. Too bad he'd have to leave it all behind, especially his dungeon downstairs. That'd taken *so* much work and expense, and he'd never even had the chance to use it.

Sacrifices had to be made, however. It was important he travel light and disappear the second he hit Mexico. Maybe he'd even work his way down to Central America, to some place like Costa Rica or Nicaragua. He'd heard they were both beautiful countries.

Once he came up with a new alias and the documentation to go with it, which could all be had for a price, he could go anywhere.

■ ■ ■ ■

Waiting for those manifests wasn't easy. Evelyn had expected there to be a holdup over the weekend, since everything moved more slowly then. But both Monday and Tuesday passed with nothing — no news on the DNA culled from the blood on the tree or in the snow the night Amarok was shot. Nothing from the airlines, either.

Despite the pressures of her own job, she'd checked in with Ashton twice, since they were still waiting for a supervisor at the lab to verify the DNA results that were supposed to have come in on Monday, and she seemed to be calling Amarok every few hours. He assured her again and again that he was hounding every airline employee he could contact who might have some say in the matter. They all told him they'd received a copy of the warrant and were doing their best to expedite the process, but none of the information arrived until Wednesday.

She was having lunch when Amarok called her at Hanover House to say he'd finally received the manifests from Southwest and two other large carriers. "I've got a few of the files," he said.

The hesitancy in his voice made her

uneasy. "That's *good* news, isn't it?"

"It is, except there's a lot more to go through than I was expecting — and I don't have everything yet. There are nearly fifty airlines at Sky Harbor alone."

"Chances are, he would've taken one of the major airlines for the sake of convenience," Evelyn pointed out.

"Yeah, but the logistics are crazy. And I'm missing the manifests from Delta altogether." He sighed. "This sounded easier than it's turning out to be."

"What are you saying?"

"I'm saying it's more of a long shot than I wanted to believe, and I'm afraid I might've gotten your hopes up too high. I can do what I initially planned but not as thoroughly and not as quickly."

"Wherever Jasper is, we have to catch him before he strikes again, Amarok. I have no idea what his cooling-off period is like. It's different for every serial killer, but without something to interrupt them — a new girlfriend or wife, a stint in jail, an illness, *something* — the kills usually accelerate. And he's been out there doing whatever he wants for more than twenty years, so I'd imagine his bloodlust is pretty intense. If he hasn't taken a victim since Sierra, he'll be getting the urge to kill again soon." For all they knew, he'd already killed another victim. There could be another body somewhere, maybe more than one.

"Considering how much the person who shot at me was bleeding that night, I can't believe he didn't go to a hospital," Amarok said.

"If it *was* Jasper, he'd only go if he absolutely had to. That tells us whoever it was must not have been hurt badly enough that he had no other choice."

"I've checked with every business in the area. No one's even called in sick."

"Maybe the person who killed Sierra and Katherine doesn't have a job. Maybe he has the money he needs, so he doesn't have to work. We've talked about that. He could be hiding out, waiting for the chance to make his next move."

"That means he could be almost any stranger who stops to get gas or have a drink at the Moosehead."

"Those tire impressions haven't turned up anything?"

"Not yet. Dunnigan, the expert, is still working through them. If I'd sent him a set of photos from the primary suspect's car, he would've jumped all over it. He's a nice guy, but he's busy working on other cases, too, and the photos I sent were so random that he has to do them in his spare time."

"Well, don't get discouraged. We should hear from Ashton soon. And I'll help you with the manifests this evening."

"That's okay. Phil's willing to help. You have plenty of other stuff to work on. Call me as soon as you hear from Ashton," he said.

Just then Penny poked her head into Evelyn's office to say the attorney was on line two.

"He's calling me now," she told Amarok. "I'll get back to you in a few."

After he hung up, she switched over. "Ashton?"

"I'm afraid I have some unpleasant news," the attorney said.

She tightened her grip on the phone. "What kind of unpleasant news?"

"He's there. Jasper's in Alaska. The DNA tests prove it."

So she and Amarok had been right. Jasper had followed her to Hilltop, and he could have only one reason for doing that. He was planning to kill her. Otherwise, why wouldn't he stay in the Lower 48 and continue to satisfy himself by murdering women who looked like her?

"Evelyn?"

She blinked and her office came back into

view. "Yes, I'm here."

"I'm sorry," he said. "I hate that you have to deal with this — with *him* — again."

"Don't be sorry. I'm *glad* he's here."

"Because . . ."

She could hear the surprise in his voice. "I want to get him as badly as he wants to get me."

"But are you prepared? How will you see him coming? How will you defend yourself?"

She thought of the manifests. Would they be able to use those to identify him?

If not, they wouldn't have a lot to go on besides the tire evidence, which wasn't particularly effective without a suspect who had a vehicle to compare against the impression Amarok had taken at the cabin. "I'll just have to be careful."

"This is crazy. As long as I've dealt with the criminal justice system, I've never come up against a situation quite like this."

"Have you told Tim about the DNA evidence found in the house where Charlotte was killed?"

"I have."

"He must be relieved."

"He is. He's also grateful to you."

"If he's innocent, he doesn't belong in jail." She paused. "I'd better go. I need to let Amarok know that we're facing exactly what we thought we were."

"Okay. Be safe, and please stay in touch."

"I will." She hung up and called Amarok. "Jasper's here," she said as soon as he answered.

He muttered a curse. "Then I shot the bastard."

"You did."

"If only I'd seen him better!"

"He could be seriously injured. Maybe that injury's the reason *I'm* still breathing."

Amarok didn't respond.

"What are you thinking?" she asked.

"I'm thinking we could be running out of time. Don't go anywhere alone."

"I won't," she promised.

It was four o'clock in the afternoon, and Jasper had just finished the last shift he would ever work at Hanover House. He'd loved being so close to Evelyn for the past eight months, had taken great pleasure in creating his torture chamber while waving and smiling at her as they both entered or exited the prison. Imagining and anticipating the day she'd learn that the man who'd saved her from Lyman Bishop was the same man who'd nearly killed her before — and would kill her in the end — had been beyond titillating. But he'd hated everything else about having a real job, although he had to admit he'd miss the freedom that came with supporting himself.

Still, he was more than ready to go back to the good old days when he let someone else pay the bills. He'd been through two marriages so far and neither wife had any inkling of who he was deep inside or what he'd done.

And yet . . . his first wife must have realized she was dealing with someone dangerous. The day she left him, she abandoned everything she'd owned before they met. The only reason she'd make such a sacrifice was because she understood things would not end well for her if she upset him too much. So he guessed she understood what he was capable of, if not what he'd actually done. He hadn't heard from her since, so it wasn't as though she'd ever caused him any trouble. He had no idea where she'd gone. As soon as she had the chance, she moved out of the area where they'd been living at the time, without leaving a forwarding address. She'd run instead of standing up and fighting — unlike Evelyn, who'd been so visible in her crusade against him. Maybe that was why Evelyn mattered infinitely more than anyone else. She was the only one who'd ever really dared to defy him. Even his parents had played along.

He stopped to get a bite to eat at The Dinky Diner. Then he went over to the gas station, where he filled his tank before driving partway down Nektoralik Road. He figured it wouldn't hurt to go through what he was about to tell Amarok. He just hoped Amarok wouldn't leave the trooper post while he was driving around, frittering away thirty or so minutes. Jasper had rolled by and seen Amarok's truck in the lot. He'd been tempted to stop while he had the chance to catch him there. But he'd known he couldn't deviate from his plan, couldn't send Amarok out of town too early. Tonight timing would be everything. He'd visited Spenard Road again last night and left Amarok a little present at the shack near the cabin he'd burned down, one that would keep the trooper busy for a couple of hours, at least. But Jasper would still need to make the most of every second Amarok was away, couldn't waste that time waiting for Evelyn to leave work.

Everything had to come together at once.

After three miles, Jasper turned around. It was starting to get dark. It would be five o'clock when he reached the trooper post, which would be just about perfect. Although

Evelyn often stayed late at the prison, he'd walked up to see her before leaving Hanover House himself, told her he'd been talking to Brianne, who was worried about her safety, and that he'd be happy to act as an escort to be sure she got home and remained safe until Amarok could join her. And she'd said that wouldn't be necessary today, that Amarok would be meeting her at their house as soon as she left at five thirty.

That was valuable information to have. But Amarok could always head home a little early, which was why Jasper wanted to get to the trooper post barely after five. Hopefully Amarok wouldn't leave *that* early. And if he did? Jasper would have to catch him at his house.

Either way, everything was going to be fine, he told himself — and he knew that was true when he rounded the corner to see Amarok's truck still in the lot.

It hadn't moved.

Amarok was so deeply immersed in cross-referencing the flight manifests that he didn't want to be interrupted. That was part of the reason he'd sent Phil, who had a tendency to talk too much, to get himself some dinner. Amarok would soon be eating with Evelyn, who'd said she'd cook, but he was craving a bit of solitude so he could make some good progress before he had to pack up and move everything to the house.

When the door opened and Makita barked, he assumed it was Phil returning, so he was surprised to hear Andy Smith's voice.

"Sergeant?"

Amarok pulled himself away from the computer work he'd been doing, trying to get the manifest files ready for cross-referencing, and silenced his dog with a quick, "Makita!" Then he looked at the CO. "What can I do for you?"

"I think I might've seen the man responsible for the murders we've had here recently."

Forgetting about the manifests, Amarok got to his feet. This was the first time he'd had anyone — other than Sam, whose reports had been dubious, at best — come forward with possible information. "What do you mean? *Where* did you see him? What made you think it might be the man I'm looking for?"

Smith appeared to be a little rattled by what he'd just seen. "I was buying some gas and this guy — about my age, I guess — climbs out from behind the wheel of a Ford Excursion at the other pump."

There was only one gas station in town,

and it had exactly two pumps. Amarok could see why Andy might notice the other driver. "Go on. . . ."

"He accidentally dropped the gas nozzle, and when he bent over, I saw that he had a bandage around his middle. You'd told us to look out for anyone who'd been hurt, remember?"

"Of course I remember."

"So that caught my attention right away. He stood up and pulled his shirt down really fast, but still . . . I thought it didn't mean anything. Finding the guy who killed those girls, seeing him at a gas station, just seemed too easy, you know? I didn't think I could be that lucky, but I kept watching him, in case."

"And?" Amarok was eager to get to the bottom line.

"By the time he finished pumping the gas and got back in, I'd convinced myself that I was being a paranoid idiot, so I turned away to take the nozzle out of my own tank. But when I glanced over as he was leaving, I noticed something in the back of his truck."

Amarok felt his pulse kick up. "What'd you see?"

"I can't be positive. The windows in an Excursion are tinted, and it was already almost dark out, but I thought I saw someone in there."

"Someone?"

"A woman. With long, blond hair. She appeared out of nowhere, as if she'd somehow just managed to sit up, and she pressed her hands against the window like . . . like they were tied and she was pleading with me to save her. I tried to get a clearer look, to be sure my mind wasn't playing tricks on me after seeing that bandage, but the vehicle was already in the street. I couldn't make out anything behind the dark glass. So I got in my own truck and followed him."

"Where'd he go?" Amarok asked.

"Down Nektoralik Road. He was driving pretty fast, too. It freaked me out, knowing the cabin where Sierra Yerbowitz went missing is down that way. I kept asking myself if I should continue to follow him and try to help, if there *was* a woman bound in the back of his SUV, or if I should come back to get you."

Amarok tensed. "You should've come here immediately! Maybe I could've caught him before he got too far out of town."

"I know, but no one wants to be the asshole who raised a false alarm. I just wasn't sure. I'm still not, to be honest."

"Did he see you?"

"I think he did. That's why I turned

around. The way he kept looking back at me in his side mirror made me suspect him even more."

Amarok would give anything for another chance at Jasper. He hoped he wasn't getting this information too late. He hated to contemplate the disappointment he'd feel if Jasper slipped through his fingers. "I'm glad you came back. At least I know which direction he was heading."

"So you think it might be him?"

"I do."

"The bastard who tried to kill Evelyn?"

"Yes. He's here in Alaska. He's the one who murdered those women."

"I'd heard that, but I wasn't aware you knew for sure."

"DNA confirmed it today. Did you happen to get the guy's license plate?"

"Only the first three digits. There was so much mud on the rest of the plate I couldn't make out any more. The whole truck was filthy, as though he'd been four-wheeling."

Amarok grabbed his coat and hat and scooped his keys off his desk. "Write down every detail you remember about the man you saw, his truck, the woman in the back — all of it. Put it on that pad right there." He gestured to indicate Phil's desk. "I'll call Phil once he's back from dinner and have him read it to me while I take Nektoralik to the cabins that are out that way. If I hope to catch him, I can't waste any more time."

"You're going after him, then?"

"I don't have any choice. I have to try and save that woman." Amarok was about to walk out. He'd never been in more of a hurry. But, at the last second, he remembered that he'd left his new satellite phone, which he was now glad he'd rented despite the expense, in the drawer of his desk. He returned to get it as Phil came in, holding a soda.

Phil didn't have a chance to say anything; Amarok spoke first. "Phil, can you take over with the manifests? Keep working until you're done. I don't care how late it is. No one'll be safe until we learn Jasper's alias and track him down. I'll call you in a few minutes to get the information Andy here is about to give you."

Phil set his drink on the filing cabinet near the water cooler. "Whoa! What's happening? Where are you going?"

"I believe Andy just saw Jasper. The guy had an injury and everything."

"Where's he at?"

"With any luck, he's still driving toward the Barrymore cabin."

"But why would he go there? It's so

burned-out, it's not safe to go inside."

"There's also the woodshed, or that smaller, shack-like cabin behind it. He might even be going to a cabin past those two, which is why I have to get on the road. I can't let him get too far ahead of me." He might already be too late, but he had to try.

"Shouldn't I go with you?" Phil asked. "I don't think it's safe to go alone. We know what this guy is capable of."

Amarok shook his head. "Makita will go with me, right, boy?"

His dog had jumped to attention the second he'd started to put on his coat.

"Besides, I'm not some defenseless woman who's been bound and gagged," Amarok added. "I have no doubt I can take him one-on-one, and you need to keep working on the manifests, just in case I can't find him." He started for the door again, but this time it was the memory of Sandy Ledstetter swinging from a tree in the middle of town while Bishop went after Evelyn that made him pause. He couldn't leave Evelyn alone, wouldn't take that risk, regardless of what he had to do for his job. "Actually, I've changed my mind, Phil." He glanced at his watch. "Don't worry about the manifests right now. Evelyn's heading home to make dinner. Can you go over and stay with her until I get back?"

"Why don't *I* do that?" Andy piped up. "I don't know anything about these manifests you're talking about, so I can't help there, but I could certainly keep Evelyn company for a few hours."

Amarok felt a wave of relief. He knew Evelyn didn't care for Andy Smith, but Smith was one of her COs — he was still in uniform — so at least she'd feel safe with him. Besides, she'd had dinner with Andy and Brianne last Saturday. Surely she could bear a few more hours of his company. "That'd be great," he said. "I'll check in when I can."

28

Evelyn was eager to get home. She wanted to help Amarok with those manifests, wanted to be sure the night ended with an answer one way or another. Either they established that there was at least one person who'd made all three flights — to San Diego, Boston and Phoenix — or they established that they'd have to try something else.

She had her mind on that, so when James came into her office while she was packing up to leave and asked when they could schedule Mary Harpe for some of their studies she tried to put him off until she was prepared to deal with that.

"Let's give her a chance to settle in first," she told the neurologist as she slid files into her briefcase. She probably wouldn't have time to update them — due to what she hoped to accomplish with those manifests — but she was taking them home, anyway.

"Why?"

She heard the slight whine in his voice and couldn't help being irritated. "Because I haven't even gotten a feel for her yet. There's no rush."

"For crying out loud, Evelyn! What difference does getting 'a feel for her' make?"

"I don't know. I guess . . ." She shook her head. "I'm sorry. I'm too distracted right now, not ready to make a decision."

"You've been distracted a lot lately."

She closed her briefcase. "What's that supposed to mean?"

"Rumor has it you're thinking of leaving Hanover House."

With a sigh, she rested her hands on top of her briefcase. She hadn't made that announcement to the mental health team because she wasn't sure what she was going to do. Nothing had been finalized. "I have some personal issues that I might have to attend to. But nothing's been decided quite yet."

"If you do leave, who'll take the lead here at Hanover House?"

She lifted her eyebrows. "Are you hoping to replace me?"

"Someone will have to do it. Why not me? I feel I'm the most qualified."

"Except that you're always talking about

leaving yourself. What about your wife? I thought she hated Alaska."

"She can hold out."

Suddenly Annie could be tough? He'd acted as though he was on the verge of quitting so many times. "Provided you have sufficient power here?"

"If I have power over my own career and can actually publish my findings, it'd be worth it."

Evelyn checked the clock. It was five fifteen. She'd told Amarok she'd make dinner and didn't want to be late in case he was hungry. "James, I can't deal with this right now. I promise, when things calm down, we'll have a meeting, and we'll discuss everyone's goals and desires, as well as their limitations."

"And when do you think that'll happen?"

"James, I —" She caught herself before she snapped at him. "Look, I found out today, only a few hours ago, that Jasper is indeed in the area."

He seemed taken aback. "You did?"

"Yes. So forgive me if I'm a bit scattered or abrupt. You'd be a little rattled, too, if the person who'd slit your throat and left you for dead twenty-two years ago — and tried to kill you again far more recently — had come back to finish the job."

"I'm sorry. But you haven't even mentioned that, so how was I to know?"

"I'm coping as best I can. I need you to do the job you were hired to do and be patient a little while longer."

"Okay. But if you *do* decide to leave, will you put my name forward with Janice?"

Evelyn couldn't believe his self-interest but managed to refrain from firing him on the spot. "I'll think about it," she said, and slipped past him on her way out. She knew she should also alert the rest of the team to Jasper's presence and probably should've done that first thing. But she could feel the clock ticking. If they couldn't come up with some way to identify who Jasper was so they could catch him, nothing else — at least for her — would ever matter again.

Bambi had kicked off her high heels and left them in the car, so her feet were freezing. "Hurry up. I can't even feel my toes!"

Mason Anderson, one of the bartenders who worked with her at Dick's, was hunched over the lock on Andy Smith's back door while she stood behind him, keeping an eye out to make sure they weren't going to get caught. "I'm working as fast as I can. Would *you* like to try it?"

"If I could do it myself, I wouldn't need

you," she muttered, but she'd never have come back here alone. There was something about Andy Smith that'd frightened her the last time she'd seen him, some . . . evil in his eyes he'd managed to hide before. Remembering how he'd looked at her — with such loathing and disgust — right before he slammed the door in her face still gave her goose bumps. She wasn't sure why he'd relented and thrown that twenty at her, but she could tell it had nothing to do with compassion.

"If you don't get us in soon, we'll have to give up." She was too nervous, felt as though she was about to have a heart attack.

"Shut up!" he snapped. "I'm almost there."

She'd told Mason that Andy Smith had some crystal meth in his house. She wasn't positive, but she'd been so angry when Andy turned her away empty-handed that she'd complained about him to Mason the next day — and that was when they'd hatched this plan. She couldn't recant, but she wouldn't need to. She and Mason would take other things if they didn't find the drugs they wanted. Once they sold that stuff, they could buy their own meth. As far as she was concerned, Andy deserved what they were doing to him.

"Here we go." Mason put his shoulder to the door as he turned the handle.

They both rushed inside. He went straight for Andy's big-screen TV, since that was the most obvious item of value, while she hurried down the hall to the bedroom and dug through the dresser drawers and an open suitcase she found on one side of the bed.

She could hear Mason coming toward her even before he appeared in the doorway. "Anything?"

"No. Nothing."

He propped his meaty fists on his hips. He had dark hair, almost black eyes and a pockmarked face. Bambi thought he tried to compensate for that in the weight room. She suspected he also took steroids, because he was almost *too* muscle-bound. "Where could he keep his shit? Did you check that suitcase?"

"Of course."

"Looks like he's going somewhere," he mused.

"Good riddance. That's all I can say."

"He'd take his dope."

"I'm telling you, there's nothing in there. What he gave me when I was here before he got out of his top drawer, but I've already looked there, too."

"Damn it." Mason went into the kitchen, where, from the sound of it, he was slamming cupboards and emptying out drawers, and she moved on to Andy's bathroom.

There was nothing particularly interesting in the medicine cabinet — just a box of rubbers, nail clippers, Q-tips and antiseptic. Under the sink he had the usual — plus a box of hair bleach, which was odd given that Andy had dark hair.

"Damn it! I'm not finding anything!" Mason yelled out to her.

"You got his TV. That's something!" she called back.

"I'm taking his laptop, too."

"Where'd you find that?"

"Right here on the kitchen table."

She didn't care what he took. She grabbed the shampoo out of the shower and squeezed it all over Andy's bed, carpet and the clothes she'd dumped out of his drawers. "Take *that,* you pompous asshole."

Mason stood in the doorway. "What are you doing?"

She tossed the bottle on the bed. "Having a little fun."

"Let's get out of here. There's nothing else worth staying for."

She handed him a watch and a ring she'd taken from the counter in the bathroom.

"There's this."

"I don't want this shit. It's too easy to identify." He gave it back, so she kept it herself. She wouldn't pawn it. The cops would be able to trace it that way. She'd give it to her younger brother.

"Come on," Mason said, an impatient edge to his tone.

As she followed him to the living room, she noticed a door that hadn't been opened. "Where does this go?"

"I have no idea. I didn't even see it until now."

She turned the knob only to find it locked. "This could be where he keeps his meth."

"In a linen closet?"

"Why not? Besides, maybe it's not a closet. Can you open it?"

Mason peered out the front windows.

"Anyone coming?"

"No."

"So? Should we see what's in here or not?"

"We've come this far. . . ." He pulled the tools he'd used to pick the lock on the back door from his coat pocket.

Bambi could feel her heartbeat vibrating through her whole body. She wanted to flee before they could get caught, but she was intrigued by what might be behind this door. "I don't think it's a closet. I think it's a basement or something."

"Probably. But why the lock?"

"Maybe he cooks his own meth."

It took Mason only a few moments to get the door open. His hands weren't shaking quite as badly as when they'd been standing outside in the cold and could easily have been spotted by a neighbor.

"You're amazing!" she exclaimed. "And I was right. This is a basement."

She hurried down. Mason turned on the light before she could descend into utter darkness and quickly followed.

Instead of the damp, musty odor one might expect, she smelled fresh-cut wood. Someone had been building down here. She could see only a cement floor until she went low enough, but then a room came into view. That wasn't so unusual for a basement, she supposed, but everything else she saw certainly was.

She came to an abrupt stop. "Holy shit! What is this?"

Mason was a step behind her. Because he was taller, it took longer for him to be able to see the room, but he ducked down when she spoke — and froze, too. "It looks like a fucking torture chamber!"

"It *is* a torture chamber. What else could it be?" Bambi gazed in shock at the whips on the wall, the chains coming out of the floor, the bondage bed, the many different kinds of restraints — and the knives. There were all kinds of implements designed to inflict pain and suffering. "I knew he was into S and M, but this is way over-the-top."

"He didn't bring *you* down here, did he?"

"Of course not. I would've known about it then, wouldn't I? What's this?" She picked up a metal hook-like object dangling from a chain.

"It's a pussy hook," he said. "A friend of mine showed me one once." He started to retrace his steps. "I'm getting out before he comes back and locks us in."

"Wait! What's *this*?"

As she crossed over to what she'd found, he turned. "What's *what*?"

"It's a *shrine* or something."

Although he hesitated, he eventually approached the far corner area where she was standing and gaping at the pictures and newspaper articles affixed to the wall.

"There have to be fifty photographs here," he said, marveling at the display.

Some candles and flowers, even jewelry, were stacked on a small stand beneath the photos, but it was the photos that drew Bambi's attention. "They're all of the same woman."

Mason smoothed out a newspaper article that still had the headline attached. "Evelyn Talbot."

"*Dr.* Evelyn Talbot," she corrected, reading from a different newspaper clipping. "She's the psychiatrist who started the prison where Andy works."

"Hanover House. In Hilltop."

"Yeah, the one with all the psychopaths and serial killers."

"That gives me chills." He took her arm, but she pulled away so she could smooth out the other clippings that were beginning to curl at the edges. Someone — presumably Andy — had circled certain phrases. "Renowned psychiatrist," "determined to unlock the secrets of the psychopathic mind," "these men feel no conscience, no need to restrain their baser desires." He'd also scribbled out one particular name wherever it appeared — Sergeant Benjamin Murphy.

Some articles hadn't come from a regular newspaper. They'd been taken from the Internet. A lot of the pictures had, too. There was even a Wikipedia entry giving information on Evelyn Talbot, where she was born, what she'd experienced and the path of her career. "Why would Andy have collected all of these?" she asked. "And why would he care enough to display them — as if . . . as if she's all he can think about?"

"You said he works at the prison, so he knows her," Mason responded. "He's obviously obsessed with her."

"Look. Here's a clipping about Kat's body being found."

Mason hadn't worked with Kat. He didn't know her like Bambi did, but he knew of her, since the police had questioned all the bartenders, too. "Why would he keep that?"

"Maybe he's the one who killed her —"

"That's it." He started to drag her away. "We're out of here."

"Oh my God! Did I sleep with a *murderer*? *Kat's* murderer?" she cried, sickened by the thought that the hands that had touched her had also taken a life.

"I don't care."

"How can you not care?" she asked as he yanked her across the floor. "He's got a lot of weapons. He's dangerous. Someone should know."

"Yeah, someone should know, but we're not going to be the ones to say anything. Do you want to get busted for breaking and entering?"

"No . . ."

He gestured with his free hand. "Then you'll forget all of this."

Once he got her as far as the stairs, he didn't need to prod her anymore. What she'd seen terrified her. Sweat rolled down her back even though the place wasn't even close to being warm. "He's a serial killer!

"Mason?" she said when he didn't respond. But he continued to ignore her. He was too intent on making sure they got out of there to bother with anything else.

Jasper pulled right into Evelyn's drive and got out. After all, he'd been invited to the house by none other than Amarok. Amarok had even taken Makita with him. That left only Evelyn's cat to defend her, and the cat wasn't going to do anything.

Everything was proceeding according to plan, except that Amarok already had the damn airline manifests. Jasper had thought it would take longer to get hold of those and to go through the information they contained. But what Amarok had said to Phil — that Phil should stay until he was finished — indicated that they were closing in on what they were looking for.

Jasper had to act fast, he decided, much faster than he'd planned, which made him angry. *Damn it!* Amarok was a constant thorn in his side, making *everything* more difficult.

While he waited on the front porch, he recalled his visit to the trooper post and all the crap he'd handed Phil after Amarok had left — the fake description of the man pumping the gas, the fake description of the supposed "victim" and the vehicle itself. Phil had, no doubt, fed the same pile of horseshit to Amarok. That should've been funny. Amarok was so set on capturing *him* he'd raced off after the mysterious man driving the Ford Excursion. He'd fallen for it all, but Jasper wasn't laughing.

This contest between them . . . Jasper was no longer so convinced he'd win. He wouldn't have nearly as much lead time as he'd imagined when he left his suitcase and computer at home. He should've brought them to work, so he wouldn't need to go back to Anchorage. He'd thought of that, of course, had wanted to bring them so he'd have more time if he *did* get into trouble. But because of the murders, everyone was looking at everyone else so closely in Hilltop, he'd decided, at the last minute, that it wouldn't be wise. If he had a suitcase in his truck, people would start asking if he was about to leave town. His vehicle was inspected whenever he went in and out of the prison.

In hindsight, that would've been better

than having to take off without his shit, but what was done was done, he told himself as he stepped out to peer down the road. He needed to get into a more positive mood. Needed to shake off his anger. Amarok had already cost him the months and months he'd planned to enjoy torturing Evelyn in his basement. Amarok would *not* cost him the pleasure of killing her tonight.

Closing his eyes, he imagined how it would all go. Once Evelyn arrived, he'd smile and joke with her as he followed her up the walkway. She'd welcome him; they were friends, after all. Getting in the house wouldn't be hard. Then he'd come up behind her as she set her keys on the counter or turned away to get him a drink, and that was when she'd learn how very close he'd been for almost a year.

He imagined her crying and whimpering for Amarok to save her, imagined telling her that Amarok would never be able to make it back in time, since that was true. And finally, after years of craving the taste of her, he'd grab her by the hair and force her to kiss him, a deep, openmouthed, messy kiss in which he bit her and licked her to his heart's content. He'd force her to do a lot of other things, too — things she'd consider much more degrading than that. He'd fulfill all his greatest fantasies. But he'd do it in less than an hour. At the end, he'd kill her and be done with it, move on to a new life in Mexico. *To hell with those manifests!* He'd be gone before Phil could figure out that Andy Smith was Jasper Moore and sound the alarm.

From force of habit, he looked at his wrist to check the time, but he'd forgotten his watch at home when he thought he was going to be late for work. He'd realized it while he was at the prison earlier — another annoyance. Fortunately, since he'd left work, he'd been able to rely on the digital clock in this truck, so it didn't matter.

He walked back to his vehicle and turned the key so he could see what time it was. Five thirty. Evelyn should be here any minute.

Closing his door, he looked up and down the street again. Then he smiled.

There she was, he thought as her headlights appeared at the corner.

He was too late. Jasper wasn't anywhere along Nektoralik Road. Amarok wasn't sure what Andy Smith had seen, but the woman Amarok found in the shack behind the Barrymore cabin wasn't a fresh kill. She couldn't have been the person who sat up and pressed her hands against the window of the Excursion Andy had spotted at the gas station. There was no rigor mortis. Even with the cold slowing decomposition, rigor typically eased after twenty-four hours. And something else was strange. What rigor mortis Amarok could see indicated the woman had been in an entirely different position at the time of death. According to the blood patterns on her naked body, she'd been lying on her side, not her back. That told him she'd been killed elsewhere and dumped here.

It was also interesting that Jasper hadn't bothered to torture this victim. He'd slit her throat and possibly raped her, either pre- or postmortem, but that was it. And unlike most of his other victims, she didn't look like Evelyn. She had bleached-blond hair and was significantly overweight.

Jasper had seen her as merely a means to an end, he decided. That was the feeling he got. But *what* end? What was Jasper up to now?

Amarok had ordered Makita to stay outside so the dog wouldn't muck up the scene. He squatted in the small room and stared at the body. Did Jasper have another victim in his truck? Someone he hadn't yet killed? If so, there was nothing Amarok could do about it. He'd driven to a handful of other cabins, farther up the road, but he could tell no one had been up that way, not since the last snow. There were no tracks, and these roads weren't plowed.

So he'd come back here to see if he could find *something* that would give him more information about who Jasper was and where he might be.

He was just trudging out to his vehicle to get the rest of his forensic equipment when the satellite phone he'd carried in with him went off. Because it had to have a direct line of sight to the sky, it didn't work that well inside or where there were a lot of trees. Phil hadn't even been able to give him all the information Andy had provided. Amarok still needed a good description of the vehicle, the driver and the woman. But none of that mattered right now. It was waiting for him; he could read it himself later.

He strode out into the open in order to get a clear signal. "Hello?"

"Amarok?"

Transmission still wasn't the best, so Amarok moved farther into the road. He thought it was Phil, but he couldn't be sure. "Yes?"

"You're not . . . believe . . . Andy Smith."

It *was* Phil. He could determine that much. Everything else was too garbled. With a frown, he plugged his free ear. "What'd you say? Something about Andy Smith?"

"I've been . . . on the manifests."

"You've been through the manifests?"

"Yes. Once I . . . Andy Smith . . . I searched . . . on all flights."

With a curse, Amarok moved to yet another spot. "Say that one more time."

"I've found something I think you should know about on the manifests!"

At last, Amarok could hear what Phil was saying. "Calm down. I finally have decent reception."

"There're two people who appear to have flown from Phoenix to San Diego to Boston and back to Phoenix on these manifests."

"Then we'll have to take a look at both of them."

"We might not have time to approach this too carefully."

"Because . . ."

"The name of one of them is Andy Smith."

Terror blew up inside Amarok with the force of a hand grenade, and his knees went so weak he nearly crumpled to the ground.

"You don't think it could be *our* Andy Smith, do you?" Phil said. "I mean, that's a common name, but it's also quite a coincidence."

Fighting through the sudden weakness, the dread and the fear, Amarok whistled for Makita and started running for his truck. He was leaving part of his forensic kit and that poor dead woman behind, but that didn't stop him. *Nothing* could stop him. He'd sent Andy to look after Evelyn. Andy was with Evelyn *at their own house.*

And Andy was Jasper.

Bits of memory flashed through his mind. Andy carrying Evelyn when Amarok came to the house last year. Evelyn telling him about Andy callously tearing up the photograph of that inmate's dead grandmother. Andy's complete self-absorption and the fact that no one really knew anything about him until he showed up in Alaska eight months ago.

Amarok was willing to bet that, if they had time to check, they'd find out he'd come from Arizona.

"That's no coincidence," he managed to say as he wrenched his door open and waited for Makita to jump in. "Get over to my house. *Now!*"

29

Phil was standing in the yard looking dumbstruck when Amarok turned down the street. He glanced toward Amarok's headlights as he pulled up but didn't approach. He returned to staring at the house, hands shoved in the pockets of his coat, shoulders hunched against the cold.

The panic Amarok had been feeling during the entire trip had his stomach tied in knots. Evelyn's SUV wasn't in the drive, but Andy Smith's F-250 was. Where was her vehicle? Had he taken it? Was it already too late?

If Andy — or, rather, Jasper — was gone, it had to be too late. Amarok knew it was when, after ordering Makita to stay in the truck, he jumped out and saw the expression of defeat on Phil's face and the tears streaking down his cheeks.

Amarok grabbed him by his coat. "Evelyn?" he asked, her name a question pregnant with all the hope that'd fueled his race back to Hilltop.

Phil shook his head, couldn't even meet his eyes. "I'm sorry, Amarok. She's gone."

Amarok clutched his own chest as he stumbled back. "No!"

"No one could've survived what he did to her. There's blood everywhere. And the cruelty!" Phil tilted his head back and squeezed his eyes shut as though he couldn't bear the mental image of what he'd witnessed. "I've never seen anything like it. I felt for a pulse, just in case. I wanted to . . . to do what I could if she was still alive. For you. For her. But it was too late."

"You didn't see him."

"No, he was gone."

Just that fast. A murderous rage rose up inside Amarok. He would find Jasper. He would hunt him to the ends of the earth if he had to, no matter what the cost, no matter how long it took, and he would annihilate that monster.

As he started toward the house, Phil, suddenly galvanized into action, came after him. "No, Amarok! Don't go in there. You don't want to see what I saw. You'll never" — his voice wobbled — "you'll never forget it. It's better to remember her as the beautiful, intelligent, vibrant woman she was."

Phil was right. Amarok didn't want to see the woman he loved mutilated like some of Jasper's other victims, especially since *he'd* failed to recognize Andy Smith as the threat he'd been.

But he couldn't remain where he was, couldn't leave Evelyn alone in the house simply because he was too much of a coward to face what had happened. He was drawn to her side by something far more powerful than reason. He had to touch her in order to believe she was really gone, had to gather up what was left of her and hold her in his arms one last time.

He managed to shake Phil off as he continued to the porch. He could hear Phil calling his name and, more dimly, Makita barking in his truck. But he ignored them, left them both where they were. He had to do this.

He could see footprints in blood before he even crossed the threshold. He didn't know if those footprints belonged to Jasper or to Phil, but it made him light-headed, nauseous, to know that it was Evelyn's blood.

And yet he went in, compelled beyond his ability to resist.

The house was eerily quiet. Why had he taken Makita with him? If only he'd dropped the dog off here at the house, maybe Evelyn would've had *some* protection. Instead, he'd left her completely vulnerable. . . .

That thought, more than any other, tore him up inside. Tears began to cascade down his cheeks as he followed those bloody footprints down the hall to their bedroom. Jasper had killed Evelyn in Amarok's own bed, where she'd learned to make love again after what Jasper had done to her so many years ago.

Hand shaking, he pushed the door, which had swung partway closed, open enough to be able to catch a glimpse of the naked and bloody corpse lying across the bed. "Oh God."

Amarok had never seen so much blood. Spatter covered the walls, even the ceiling, bathed Evelyn's body red and soaked the blankets and mattress. Jasper had beaten Evelyn so badly he'd completely obliterated her face, and her hair was so matted it didn't look the same color anymore.

As a cop, he knew better than to touch the body. He needed to detach himself emotionally, photograph the scene, start gathering evidence, go after her killer. But he wasn't a robot; he couldn't think like that right now. He'd been reduced to nothing more than a brokenhearted man who'd loved the woman lying dead in front of him.

He knelt beside the bed and took her hand. The defensive wounds on her arms made his gut hurt so badly he felt as if someone were stabbing *him.* She was still warm but not alive, and that made everything worse. He'd tried to do all he could to stop Jasper, but he'd let Jasper outsmart him in the end. He'd never dreamed Jasper, or *anyone,* could be quite *that* diabolical or quite that bold. Andy Smith had pretended to be a hero last year when he saved her life. That must've been his way of covering up when Amarok arrived to find him carrying Evelyn out of the house, but it'd seemed so believable at the time. He'd been wearing a Hanover House CO's uniform, and he'd told such a convincing story!

"I'm sorry," Amarok whispered. "I'm *so* sorry."

Jasper had played his part well. Amarok wished he could go back and redo the past eight months, wished he could've spotted *something* that would've given the son of a bitch away. But the small things that seemed to reveal Andy Smith's lack of character had seemed too insignificant. He and Evelyn had both rationalized —

Suddenly Amarok pulled back. The ring

on the hand he'd kissed wasn't Evelyn's ring. Where did she get that? Had Jasper put it on her finger? Was it some sort of final "gift"?

No. Amarok stiffened as he stared down at it. Although it was difficult to judge with all the blood, when he looked more closely, he could tell that the hand he held wasn't Evelyn's, either.

As grotesque as the sight was, he studied what used to be the woman's face, searching for other signs. A little lower down he saw a mole on her shoulder.

Evelyn didn't have a mole there. He'd touched her shoulders enough to know how smooth they were. But, like the ring, he'd seen that mole before, recognized it . . .

Her feet were tangled in the bedding. He yanked the comforter away so he could see the rest of her. Her toes, the color of the polish on her toenails, the shape of her legs, the size of her body. None of it was right.

This wasn't Evelyn.

It was Samantha.

The door to the house stood open, Makita was barking like crazy in Amarok's truck, which was parked next to Andy Smith's F-250, and Phil stood beside his own vehicle, hanging his head, when Evelyn pulled up.

"What's going on?" she asked as she got out.

Phil gaped at her. "*Evelyn?* But I thought —"

"What? You thought what? Where's Amarok? And why do you have blood on your coat? *Is he okay?*"

"He —"

Phil didn't have time to explain before Amarok came charging out of the house. He had even more blood on his coat than Phil did, but he seemed to be moving normally, as though he was unharmed.

"Amarok —" she started, but he didn't give her a chance to speak. He pulled her into his arms and held her tight.

"Where have you been?" he asked, his voice thick with emotion.

"At the prison," she said into his shoulder. "I'm sorry I didn't call, but I never expected to be this late. I was getting in my car when one of the COs came running out to stop me. Brianne was on the phone, and she was in tears. She'd just told Mom and Dad about her broken engagement and the baby. I couldn't leave her like that. So I've spent the past hour and a half trying to help her and my parents."

"You were there the whole time?"

She looked up at him. "Yes. My sister was having a complete meltdown, so I didn't feel comfortable asking her to hang on. I knew you'd assume I got involved at work again, that you'd call if you were getting anxious and someone at Hanover House would tell you. I tried calling the trooper post as soon as we hung up, but I was over an hour late by then, and no one answered. So I called here. No answer, either. I even tried your satellite phone."

"It's in the truck with Makita. The reception isn't good unless I'm in the open. Or maybe you tried to reach me after I got here and went into the house."

She glanced between him and Phil. "Where's all this blood coming from? Has someone else been hurt?"

"Samantha's dead," Amarok told her.

"Dead?" she echoed. "How do you know? Where'd you find her?"

"Right here, in our house."

"How can that be?"

"I have no idea, but it was Jasper. There's no question this time."

Evelyn had difficulty absorbing the fact that Amarok's ex-girlfriend had been murdered. And by Jasper! "He killed Samantha. . . ."

"Yes. I feel terrible that she's dead, but

I'm so glad it wasn't you."

"Poor Sam," Phil said.

Evelyn shook her head. "I don't understand!"

"Andy Smith is Jasper Moore," Amarok explained.

"No." She stumbled back. "It can't be! Andy saved my life last year —"

"Or did he just save you from Bishop?" Amarok broke in. "Was he trying to carry you off himself when I stopped him? What would he have done if I hadn't come home when I did?"

She couldn't answer that. She'd been unconscious at the time, had no recollection of when Andy had interrupted Bishop. "We've been grateful to him ever since!"

"And what a fine joke he must've thought that was. But what I can't figure out is . . . why didn't he try again? Why would he allow us to live in relative peace and happiness for so long?"

"He had to be planning something." Evelyn covered her mouth. "I know this is minor considering what happened to Samantha, but poor Brianne. She *slept* with him!"

"That isn't the worst of it. He could've killed her so easily, and he knew how badly that would hurt you."

"But if he'd hurt her, we would've known he was dangerous and he would've had much less chance of getting *me.*"

"He was waiting for the perfect opportunity, the perfect set of circumstances."

"And he had plenty of time. We had no clue who he was. He could've stayed in the area indefinitely."

"If not for those murders."

Evelyn's mind raced as the pieces came together. "He thought he could get away with what he did to Katherine. Then he thought he could hide it by killing Sierra. When it didn't go that way? I'm sure he felt some anxiety."

"We were closing in on him with those manifests," Amarok said. "We would've gotten him."

"That's why he had to make his move. Still, he's exhibited far more patience than I ever would've thought possible for someone like him. Where is he now?"

Amarok spread his hands. "He could be anywhere. He was gone when Phil arrived. I got here after Phil did."

"We can't let Jasper get away again!" she cried. "I can't keep going through this. I need to know he's no longer a threat. My family needs that. Have you called Anchorage PD?"

"Not yet," Amarok said. "I just barely realized the woman I was holding wasn't you."

"Her face . . . it's destroyed," Phil explained. "And there was so much blood."

She started for the house. "We have to call them now!"

"Don't go in there." Amarok let Makita out and grabbed his satellite phone from the truck. "Call the prison and get Andy Smith's home address from his personnel file. I'll give it to Anchorage PD. They could have someone at his place in minutes."

She frowned. "If he's stupid enough to go back there."

Shit! Shit, shit, shit! Jasper smacked the steering wheel so hard he broke a blood vessel as he drove Samantha Boyce's Subaru through the mountains to the small town of Butte. After all the hard work he'd put in! After the perfect résumé he'd crafted in Arizona! After moving here and going to all the work and expense of building his torture chamber! After getting on at Hanover House and working for Lieutenant Dickey (who was so aptly named everyone referred to him as Lieutenant Dick)!

How could his time in Alaska end like this?

Everything had gone wrong, beginning with Kat's unsatisfying death. She'd died far too easily, on a day he wasn't prepared for it and had to be at work — the bitch. Because of that, he hadn't had time to dispose of her body, so he'd decided to go back to the cabin where he'd hidden her. By then someone had already discovered her remains, which had forced him to kill again, and on and on. He couldn't catch a break. Even when he should've been able to shoot Amarok, he'd missed!

If he believed in divine intervention, he'd assume a higher power was working against him. Tonight had been nothing but a huge clusterfuck. Those headlights hadn't belonged to Evelyn; they'd belonged to Samantha Boyce. Why she kept driving by, hovering around Evelyn's and Amarok's house, Jasper couldn't say, but it pissed him off to think she was watching him. He probably wouldn't have noticed if he hadn't been so intent on keeping an eye out for whatever might be coming his way, but when he'd caught her sneaking around the back to peer in the window he'd made her sorry.

After he'd grabbed her and dragged her in the house, she'd told him she loved Amarok, that she'd deliver Evelyn to him if only he'd let her live. She'd claimed that she wanted what *he* wanted — Evelyn dead — and she'd been quite passionate and convincing. But by then he'd known it was too late; he had to run. Evelyn hadn't arrived home as expected, and he was out of time. The whole structure he'd so carefully and painstakingly built here in Alaska was crashing down on him. Better to get out while he could and live to fight another day.

At least he'd stripped Amarok of one of his female admirers and left him another dead body to deal with. The count was rising, which had to be making him crazy. Imagining his anger was Jasper's only solace.

He slowed at the next road to see if that was his turn. He'd charted his course before leaving for work and printed it out, since he didn't have a cell phone he could use to navigate. He'd stuffed the map into his coat pocket in case he couldn't get back home, and now he was damn glad. He was going to stay as far away from that side of town as possible — circle wide and go an hour north, where there was a municipal airport. He'd chartered a small plane there to take him to Vancouver. He'd fly to Mexico from Canada. He'd also booked a flight from Anchorage, however, just to throw off Amarok and anyone else who might come looking for him, since they'd probably expect him to fly out of Ted Stevens International. As much as he'd hated to waste the money, it never hurt to add a little subterfuge. Hopefully the cops would be so intent on catching him at the airport, they wouldn't even look at his laptop, which was now going to fall into their hands, until after he reached Mexico.

He fiddled with the radio, trying to get something to come on. The Subaru was relatively new — maybe three years old. It had navigation, he belatedly realized, but he didn't know how to use it and he wasn't about to take the time to figure it out. He wanted to get to Butte as soon as possible. He had to find a place to ditch the Subaru where it wouldn't be found for several days. He'd only taken it because he'd wanted to erase any immediate sign that the body in Amarok's bed wasn't Evelyn in hopes that it would cause him a scare. He'd wanted to make what he'd done in Amarok's house as traumatic as he could, a reminder to Evelyn of what he'd eventually do to *her* — once he had a chance to recover and regroup.

Finally, he found some music he liked and settled back for the drive. He'd arrive in Butte soon. He'd be early, but he wanted to get off the road. He was assuming Amarok had sent out a BOLO, or Be On the Look Out, for Samantha's car and didn't want to pass a police officer.

Once he got to the airport, he could just lie low and wait for his flight.

Soon he'd be gone — well out of Amarok's and Evelyn's reach.

30

"He hasn't shown up yet," Amarok said.

Evelyn drew a deep breath. Amarok had left Phil at their house to await the coroner, who was coming out from Anchorage, and had driven her, Makita and Sigmund to his trooper post. Amarok needed to return and take charge of the scene, but catching Jasper before he could leave the state or the country came before everything else. If they didn't catch him, there'd just be more dead bodies.

"He's not going back to wherever he was staying," she said dully. It was too much to hope that he'd fall right into their hands.

"The detective at the house he's been renting told me there's a suitcase filled with clothes in his bedroom, so they think he was planning on returning. But the place has been burglarized — I know, terrible timing — so it's a mess. They've been searching for a computer or something else that might give some indication of where he might be, or where he might be going, but so far, they have no clue." He pulled over a chair and sat down next to her. "And there's something else. . . ."

She rubbed her arms as she braced for more bad news. She could tell by his tone and his manner that she wasn't going to like what he had to say. "Tell me. . . ."

"He's tricked out his basement."

"In what way?"

"Turned it into a torture chamber."

"If he had a torture chamber, why did he kill Katherine at the Barrymore cabin?"

"It appears to be brand-new. And your pictures are all over one wall."

"He was saving it for me," she said as the realization dawned. "That's what he's been doing with his time — besides building our trust and the trust of everyone else who lives in Hilltop." She let her breath seep out. "From a clinical perspective, that doesn't surprise me."

"And from a personal one?"

"It's terrifying. If we don't catch him, he'll come back for me."

Amarok stretched his neck. It was getting late and the strain of what had started with Sierra Yerbowitz going missing was beginning to wear him down. It'd been a rough two weeks, with a lot of stress and very little sleep. Evelyn felt bad for him, but she was too anxious, too worried, to offer him any comfort.

"I'm sure you're right," he said. "He heard me talking to Phil about the manifests earlier. He knows we have them. I'm assuming that's why he killed Samantha. He no longer had to worry that we'd figure out who he was. He knew we were about to do that. So when you didn't come home as expected — thank God for Brianne's call — he got angry, killed her instead of you and is now on the run."

"What was she doing at our house, Amarok?"

He didn't look particularly comfortable with the question. "I can only imagine. You heard her voicemail the other day."

"She was almost as obsessed with you as Jasper is with me."

"I guess."

As much as she'd disliked Sam, as much as it'd bothered her that Sam was always coming on to Amarok, Jasper had no right to take her life. "Has Anchorage PD alerted airport security?"

"They have. He'll be arrested as soon as he tries to board a plane. They're waiting for him at Ted Stevens. So there's still hope."

She nibbled nervously on her bottom lip. This thing between her and Jasper had to come to an end. He couldn't continue to terrorize her forever.

Except he *could* — there was nothing to ensure against that — and chances were better that he'd escape than that he'd be caught. He knew how to avoid capture. He'd done it for twenty-two years.

"What if he isn't going to Ted Stevens International?" she asked. "What if he's going into hiding? He could reappear at the earliest opportunity. And maybe he'll settle for a quick kill instead of some elaborate scheme to build another torture chamber. No matter how careful I am, I could never be careful enough to avoid a hit that comes out of nowhere."

Amarok took her hands. "We know what he looks like these days."

"He changed his appearance once before. He could do it again. I didn't even recognize him. He's had plastic surgery, looks nothing like the boy I knew."

"Quit beating yourself up for not seeing this coming. It's been more than twenty years. And that kind of surgery isn't cheap. He no longer has his rich parents to pay for stuff like that, remember?"

"Because he killed them."

"Yes, but think about what that means. He's slowly cutting off one avenue after another, which limits his ability to do certain things. It's only a matter of time before the odds swing in our favor."

The phone rang. He got up and crossed to his desk. "It's Anchorage PD," he said as he picked up the handset.

She listened to his side of the conversation, but when he hung up he repeated most of what she'd already heard. "They've found a record for him. He's flying out of Anchorage."

Amarok sounded cautiously optimistic, more optimistic than she could be. "I gathered that," she said. "But . . . going where?"

"Chicago."

She shook her head. "No. That's too easy. He knew we'd check Anchorage right away."

"Maybe he's hoping to get out of the state before we can arrest him."

"Even if he flew off before we could catch him, we'd have the police waiting for him in Chicago. That flight's a trick, a decoy. We can't fall for it. We have to look at other possibilities."

Amarok frowned. "There are too many possibilities to predict them all. He could be on his way to some small Arctic community where no one even has a TV. How would we find him then?"

"I don't think he'd do that."

"Why not?"

"Because murder is what makes him happy, and he couldn't function in that kind of environment. He needs people, a lot of people, in order to hide who he is and what he does."

"Canada?"

"Or Mexico. It's warmer, more relaxed there and has loads of tourists."

"Okay, Mexico gets my vote, too. But he'd need a passport."

"He has other ID. Why not assume he has a passport?"

"True." Amarok motioned her over to his desk, where he got on his computer and called up a list of airports in Alaska. "Everyone knows about Juneau, Fairbanks and Ketchikan, of course. Those are international, so we'll start there. But look. There are smaller airports everywhere. There's nothing to say he won't use one of them."

Evelyn's heart sank. She'd seen Alaska as so sparsely populated that this would be an easy job, but she couldn't have been more mistaken. There were far too many options to cover them all in the short time available. "He's going to get away again. . . ." Tears sprang up. She was so distraught that she wasn't paying much attention when the phone rang — until she heard the confusion in Amarok's voice. That was when she tuned in.

"Did she say who she was? . . . Okay, just a minute." He scribbled down a phone number before hanging up.

"What is it?"

"A woman's been calling the prison. She won't give her name, but she's adamant about talking to you, refuses to speak to anyone else. And she says it can't wait until morning. Claims it's urgent."

"That's her number?" She gestured toward what he'd written on the pad.

"Yeah."

"What could this mean?" she muttered as she came around the desk to dial.

Someone, a woman, picked up immediately.

"This is Dr. Evelyn Talbot from Hanover House. Someone from this number has been asking to speak to me."

"Yes, um, that's me."

"What's your name?"

There was muffled talking, which indicted the woman wasn't alone. Then she said, "I'd rather not tell you that."

"What is it you want?"

"To warn you."

"Against . . ."

"There's this guy named Andy Smith. He has all kinds of knives and torture devices in his basement."

Evelyn's heart began to beat faster. "You've seen it."

"Yes. And there are pictures of you and newspaper articles all over the wall. He's been collecting articles about the murders of those two women whose bodies were recently found, too."

"He took you there?"

"No, but I saw it."

"When?"

"Today."

Andy was in Hilltop all day. They knew that much. So how was this woman at his place? "Are you the one who broke into his house?" she asked as the answer to that question occurred to her.

When the woman hung up, Evelyn groaned in despair and called her again.

The phone rang several times with no answer, so she kept trying.

Finally, the same woman picked up. "I just wanted to warn you," she said. "I don't want any trouble. Please, don't go to the police."

"There won't be any trouble, but I have to know one thing."

"What's that?"

"Do you have his computer?"

There was a second long pause. "What if I do?" she asked at length.

"He's killed another woman. We don't even know who she is yet. And he'll come after me again if we don't do something. I've run from him for most of my life. I want that to be over. I'm sure you can understand."

"That's why I called."

"I appreciate it." Evelyn's mind quickly sifted through the possibilities. She'd much rather the Anchorage police handled this, but there was no time for that. Jasper would likely be gone before they could find this woman, take possession of the computer and search for the information Evelyn thought it might contain. "I'll take your help, no questions asked. But I need more than you've told me so far. Are you able to access his e-mail account, or is it password protected?"

"It's not password protected. It was open when we . . . when I took it."

"Then search through his inbox. Look for anything that gives travel information. An airline reservation. A bus ticket. Anything. Check his browser to see what pages he might've visited on the Web. If we don't get this information immediately, he'll escape."

"One minute." Evelyn could hear more muffled talking while she waited. She was going crazy, wondering if this woman would ever get back on the phone. Finally she heard the same voice.

"There's a flight booked out of Ted Stevens International going to Chicago. It leaves first thing in the morning."

"I don't believe he's really taking that flight. Is there anything else? Anything at all?"

This time the wait was even more excruciating. Evelyn had just about given up hope that they'd get what they needed in time when the woman returned. "It looks like he's chartered a flight going to Vancouver."

Evelyn grabbed the pen and paper Amarok had used. "Does it say where he's leaving from? I need the name of the airport."

"Butte Municipal."

"Is there a company name associated with that flight?"

"Looks like he booked it through a site where you can pay people who have their own small planes — kind of like Turo does with expensive cars."

Evelyn wrote down everything she'd learned; then she asked to have the documents forwarded to Amarok's e-mail address, so they'd have the originals. "Will you answer the phone if I call again?"

"Are you going to tell the police how you got this information?"

"No," Evelyn replied. "And I'll give you a computer in trade for the one you have, so don't destroy any of the information. As far as I'm concerned, you can keep everything else you took — I just want to catch him."

Jasper had little to say to the pilot who'd be flying him out of Alaska. He'd paid the guy online. Now it was just a matter of taking the flight.

"No luggage?" the pilot asked when they walked out to the tarmac.

"No luggage." Because he'd been an idiot. He'd been so concerned about dumping the body of the prostitute he'd killed last night at that shack behind the cabin before he went to work, he'd made the wrong decision about his luggage and computer.

The dude — Jasper didn't remember his name and didn't care shrugged as if it made no difference to him whether he had luggage or not and waved him toward a four-seater Cessna.

"Nice plane," Jasper said. "How much does something like this cost?"

"New? Half a million or more."

Jasper whistled. "That's steep."

"Yeah, but I'm a mechanic as well as a pilot, so I was able to get something a little older and put her back together."

If he'd had a choice, Jasper might've hesitated to board. "She's airworthy, though, right?"

"Of course. I fly her all the time."

"And the weather's okay today? To go to Canada, I mean?"

"It might be a bit bumpy here and there, but we'll manage."

"You checked?"

"Of course I checked. Are you a nervous flyer?"

"Not on commercial flights, but this is a bit different."

"You're right about that." The guy gave him a maniacal grin. "It's a lot more fun."

"So we're taking off soon? You've done whatever checks and other stuff you have to do?"

"Yes, sir."

Wonderful. They were exactly on time. In another ten minutes, he'd be on his way to Vancouver. And there were so many cities where he could be going, there wouldn't be much chance of having law enforcement waiting for him on the other end. He'd spend four hours on a layover, which would seem like an eternity, but then he'd be back on a plane, this time on a flight to Mexico. Once he reached Mexico City, he'd be safe as long as he kept moving and didn't cause a stir.

After helping him get strapped in, the pilot patted his own pockets, mumbled that he'd forgotten something and walked back toward the airport.

While he waited, Jasper leaned back and stared up at the sky. It wouldn't get light until ten. It'd be nice to go someplace that saw more of the sun. He'd thought he liked Alaska, but the damn darkness got old.

It wasn't until the pilot had been gone for more than ten minutes that Jasper began to fidget. Where the hell was he? The guy had been paid; he needed to do his job.

Jasper was just about to undo his seat belt so he could go find the bastard when he heard a familiar voice.

"Jasper Moore? Get out of the plane and put your hands up. And if you're *very* lucky, I won't shoot you."

Amarok! Jasper's heart leapt into his throat as he looked out the window and saw the Alaska State Trooper standing on the tarmac with a rifle aimed at him. With the lights on the building and the ones that illuminated the runway, he had no doubt Amarok could see well enough to put a bullet in his brain despite the darkness.

How did the sergeant find him?

It had to be because he'd left his laptop behind. That was a catastrophic error.

Could he get out on the other side and make a run for it? There were some trees along the runway, set off a bit. If he could reach them, he'd have cover. But the pilot held a firearm, too, and he'd gone around to block that option.

"Give me the slightest provocation," Amarok yelled, "I'll shoot you and consider it a public service!"

Jasper glared down at him, but he could tell by the trooper's stance that he wasn't bluffing.

There was nothing he could do. It was over.

For now, he told himself.

Amarok took Jasper to the Anchorage jail, since they were better equipped to handle an inmate like him. Everyone who had a criminal complaint against him — in Boston, in San Diego, in Arizona — would be able to prosecute eventually. Amarok wasn't worried about that. He was just glad he'd been the one to bring him in. There was something extremely satisfying, even cathartic, about snapping on those cuffs. He'd been waiting to do that for so long. . . .

"This isn't the end," Jasper hissed, twisting around to get a final glimpse of Amarok as they booked him.

"Yeah, I think it is." Amarok grinned at him. "Have fun making new friends."

The baleful glare he received could've cut through stone, but that didn't bother Amarok. A huge weight had been lifted off his shoulders. Now, finally, maybe Evelyn and her family could get past what Jasper had done, since he could no longer terrorize them.

Amarok had the satellite phone in his truck, but he saw no point in paying two bucks a minute if he could use the pay phone at the jail for so much less.

He put in his credit card and dialed the number for Phil's house. Phil had gone over to Amarok's earlier to take a video and photos before the coroner removed Samantha's body, but Amarok still had a lot of work to do at the scene. He wanted to make sure Jasper was convicted for Sam's murder in addition to all the others. So he'd insisted that Evelyn go home with Phil and spend the night.

The phone barely rang before Phil answered. "Did you get him?" he asked without preamble.

The exhaustion of being up all night and of having so much adrenaline pumping through him hit Amarok hard. He leaned against the wall to help him remain on his feet. "I did."

"It's done," Amarok heard Phil say, and rested his head against the wall, too, as the phone was transferred to Evelyn.

"He's in custody?" she asked.

"They're booking him now."

"Was he surprised to see you?"

"Absolutely. But Fitz, the pilot, played it perfectly."

"What'd Jasper say when you appeared?"

"Not a lot. He thinks he's going to kill me one day, of course. Swears it's not over between us. But he'll spend the rest of his life behind bars."

"You did it," she said. "Thank you, Amarok. There were times, plenty of them, when I was afraid I'd never see this day. I can't thank you enough."

He grinned at her words. "I know of one way. . . ."

She laughed softly. "You don't have anything to worry about. I'll have to help my family from a distance, because I could never leave a man like you."

Epilogue

Six months later . . .

Evelyn sat behind the plexiglass and studied her newest inmate. Jasper didn't look particularly dangerous and never really had. He looked like a rather handsome but regular guy, one who was probably even a little frightened of what lay ahead but was trying hard not to show it. Prison wasn't an easy place, even for a serial killer. Maybe he'd experience what it felt like to be raped — or worse. After all, the other men in Hanover House were just as bad as he was, and as much as prisons tried to protect their inmates, there was no question that some of that kind of thing went on.

"Welcome to your future home, Jasper," she said once the CO who'd dragged him to the interview left. "I hope you'll be comfortable."

"I suppose you think it's funny that I'm here, under your control, some kind of poetic justice," he said.

She tucked the strands of hair that'd fallen from her messy bun behind her ears. "I suppose I do."

So many friends and family members had expressed shock when they'd learned that he was coming to Hanover House. They couldn't understand why she'd petitioned to have him transferred there and expressed concern that she might not be able to tolerate the daily reminder of what he'd done to her and those she cared about. But those people didn't understand. What Jasper had done wasn't something she could forget, regardless of where he was. And it was *his* brain she most wanted to study. Who knew more about him than she did? She could examine him in a way she wouldn't be able to examine any other psychopath — because she'd been one of his victims. He'd revealed his true nature to her, and she was one of the few to live through the experience.

Besides, there was nothing he'd hate more than having her in a position of power over him. She finally had justice, closure, all the things she'd needed so badly but had been denied for so long. Not only that, she was as safe as she could ever be. At least she could keep an eye on him herself, because it didn't matter what prison they locked him up in; if he ever got out, he'd come after her again. So what good would it do to incarcerate him somewhere else? She'd just have to wonder, *constantly,* how things were going.

She made a show of straightening the papers in his file. "My, how things have changed since you were Andy Smith. I hear your trial in Boston progressed nicely."

He said nothing, just glared at her.

"Tim was sure grateful to be set free. I know that. And, if it's any consolation to you, we won't be seeing much of each other this coming year. Maybe longer. You've got quite a bit of travel on your calendar, what with all the trials that remain." She ticked them off on her fingers. "Let's see . . . you've been charged with killing those five women in Peoria. That trial will be next. Then you'll be taken to San Diego to answer for murdering your parents. And, last but not least, you'll stand trial here, for Katherine, Sierra and that poor prostitute you murdered last. Ruth was her name, wasn't it? The one you dumped at the shack near the Barrymore cabin for Amarok to find? Oh, and Samantha, of course. The woman you murdered in my own bed."

This elicited a small smile.

"I doubt you'd be feeling that smug if you

knew there wasn't another person on earth I liked less. I would never have wished her dead, because I'm not like you. I don't wish terrible things, even on my enemies. But let's just say . . . I feel worse about the others." She clasped her hands on the desk. "So . . . will there be any surprises? Any other charges?"

"Fuck you," he said.

"I'm guessing yes," she went on, ignoring his vulgar language. "Police departments wherever you've lived are digging through their unsolved cases, trying to determine what other missing persons or murders you might be responsible for. I predict you'll set a murder record at Hanover House — and considering the men we have here, that's really saying something."

Nothing. No response.

"You know . . . I realize I shouldn't, but I actually feel bad for your parents. They loved you so much. What happened? They just became too much of a liability or what?"

"Go to hell," he growled.

"You don't have a pithy or clever quip now that the tables have turned?" She wagged a finger at him. "Don't be a sore loser. You'll have plenty of time to get used to your new position in the world. I predict you'll become more tractable eventually."

He jumped to his feet. "I won't become more tractable! I won't ever be one of your guinea pigs! The research you do here is ridiculous! A waste of time!"

"Perhaps, but we have to make the effort. Anyway, you will volunteer soon enough."

"You can't say that, you don't know anything about me."

"That's where you're wrong. I know more about you than anyone else, which is why I can also predict that boredom will soon replace me as your greatest enemy."

"Forget it," he insisted. "You're delusional."

"We'll see." She started for the door but turned back at the last moment. "Oh, and in case you'd like to congratulate me" — she smoothed a hand over her belly — "I just learned that I'm expecting Amarok's baby. I plan to tell him tonight."

She'd managed to surprise him. She could tell by the expression on his face. "You can still have a child? After everything I did to you?"

"Apparently so," she said with a smile.

ABOUT THE AUTHOR

Brenda Novak and her husband, Ted, live in Sacramento and are the proud parents of five children — three girls and two boys. When she's not spending time with her family or writing, Brenda is usually working on her annual fund-raiser for diabetes research. Brenda's novels have made *The New York Times* and *USA Today* bestseller lists and won many awards, including three Rita nominations, the Book Buyer's Best, the Book Seller's Best and the National Reader's Choice Award.

Brenda is the author of the Dr. Evelyn Talbot Novels, including *Hello Again* and *Her Darkest Nightmare.*

The employees of Thorndike Press hope you have enjoyed this Large Print book. All our Thorndike, Wheeler, and Kennebec Large Print titles are designed for easy reading, and all our books are made to last. Other Thorndike Press Large Print books are available at your library, through selected bookstores, or directly from us.

For information about titles, please call:
(800) 223-1244

or visit our website at:
gale.com/thorndike

To share your comments, please write:
Publisher
Thorndike Press
10 Water St., Suite 310
Waterville, ME 04901